RAGGED

ISLANDS

RAGGED

ISLANDS

DON HANNAH

ALFRED A. KNOPF CANADA

PUBLISHED BY ALFRED A. KNOPF CANADA

www.randomhouse.ca

Every effort has been made to contact the copyright holders of material reprinted here. Grateful acknowledgment is made to Alfred A. Knopf, a division of Random House, Inc., New York, for permission to reprint a portion of W. S. Merwin's translation of Dante's *Purgatorio*. A portion of the lyrics to "The Happy Wanderer" by Friedrich W. Moller and Antonia Ridge, copyright Alfred Publishing Co., Inc., is reprinted on pages 159 and 160.

LIBRARY AND ARCHIVES CANADA CATALOGUING IN PUBLICATION

Hannah, Don
      Ragged islands / Don Hannah.

ISBN: 978-0-676-97791-2

I. Title.

PS8565.A583R35 2007   C813'.54   C2006-905395-2

Text design: Leah Springate

First Edition

Printed and bound in the United States of America

10 9 8 7 6 5 4 3 2 1

For Doug

For my brothers, John and Scott

And in memory of Dianne Lee Martin

Poi quando fuor da noi tanto devise
quell' ombre, che veder più non potiersi,
novo pensiero dentro a me si mise,

del qual più altri nacquero e diversi;
e tanto d'uno in altro vaneggiai,
che lim occhi per vaghezza ricopersi,

e 'l pensamento in sogno trasmutai.

Dante Alighieri
Purgatorio, Canto XVIII

Then when those shades had gone so far away
from us that we could not see them any more,
a new thought took up its place in me

from which others of several kinds were born
and I wandered so from one to another of them
that my eyes hazed over and I closed them

and transformed what I was thinking into a dream.

W. S. Merwin, translation

The life of a wild animal *always has a tragic end.*

—ERNEST THOMPSON SETON
Wild Animals I Have Known

The MacDonalds

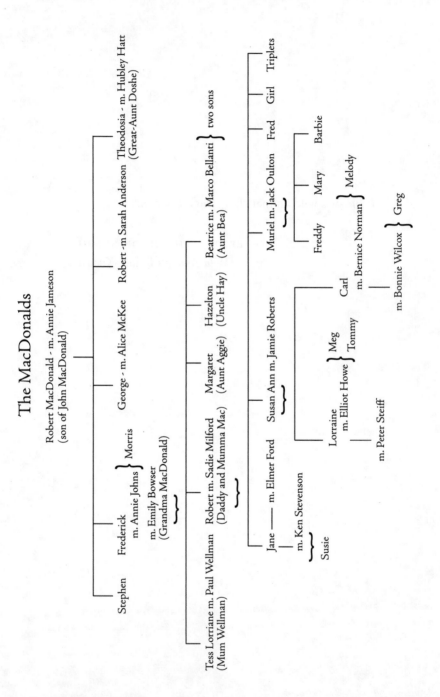

The Wellmans

The Roberts

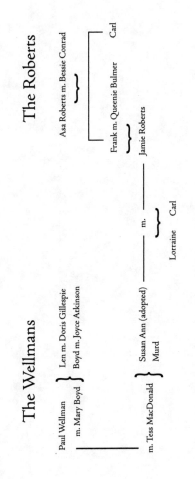

Paul Wellman
m. Mary Boyd

Len m. Doris Gillespie
Boyd m. Joyce Atkinson

m. Tess MacDonald

Susan Ann (adopted)
Murd

Asa Roberts m. Bessie Conrad

Frank m. Queenie Bulmer

Carl

Jamie Roberts

m.

Lorraine   Carl

CARL FOUND THE PACKAGE *when he stripped the bed. A huge padded envelope, dog-eared, wrinkled with time and use, and worn so soft— somehow it had worked its way down between the sheets and come to rest at the bottom, where it lay lodged between the mattress and the footboard like some forgotten nighttime comfort, a hot water bottle or a doll.*

The envelope had originally been sent to his mother in Ragged Islands. In the upper left-hand corner, where the return address label had been torn away, there was a square of exposed bubble lining, a small translucent window through which he could almost see the inside.

When he turned it over, he saw the words she had printed across the back in a wide black marker: TO BE SAVED

1 —

SHE WAS IN THE DARK darkness.

Where's this? she said. *Where am I?*

Dark, nothing but darkness, thick and deep, and it wasn't home, she could sense that, it was somewhere else. Susan Ann was trying to think, trying to remember the last thing she remembered—what day was this?

Monday Tuesday Wednesday Thursday Friday Saturday Sunday Monday Tues—

She didn't have a clue. Had she wandered off into a strange room? She'd better take a look-go-see and—

My feet!

There was nothing down below—she couldn't feel the far end of her at all!

Where're my feet?

It was empty-feeling down there. Up above, the darkness was pressing against her all around—heavy upon her chest, her head, holding her fast.

Calm down, calm now, think.

She must've had another episode, yes, and somehow she'd managed to lose her feet this time.

But where was this dark place? Had she gone somewhere to visit? Where was this, where?

Lorraine, dammit!

Yes, that damn Lorraine!

Susan Ann had been stupid enough to listen to her kids—that was what this was, that was why this was happening. She should never've listened, never've let them talk her into coming here.

Lorraine thought she was so smart—and Carl, on the phone, "Mum, you know it's for the best." What could he possibly know from out there? He hadn't seen Ragged Islands since his father's funeral, he stayed out there in the West and let his sister run things. Her own son had no idea of what was really going on, no idea at all.

Lorraine, the last summer back home, out in the yard—"The apartments in that building are nice and big, Mum." Susan Ann would find out all too soon that the only big things there were the fibs her daughter told.

That bedroom's so small if you want to make the bed properly you need to be able to fly!

"Mum, you know it's for the best. We worry about you all alone in the house. And you've made it very clear that you won't go to Surf Side Manor."

Yes, because then no one would ever come see her, she'd never see her own grandchildren again—there'd be nowhere for them to visit and stay. She'd be stuck in the TV room all day long, stuck in there with a bunch of nosy old people she'd never cared for all yak-yak-yakking, and there was nothing but crap on the old box nowadays anyway—young people parading their private lives about like fools—

You should never've left Ragged Islands, should never've let that house be sold—Jamie's house, Jamie's house, Jamie's—

Don't, now don't go and get all upset, it won't get you anywhere so just calm down.

But Jamie's house, I let them talk me into selling Jamie's house.

That's a while ago, that's ancient history, just—

But it was Jamie's house!

And that apartment Lorraine shoved her in—

Kitchen cupboards were so narrow that she couldn't put a plate in them—there wasn't enough counter space to chop an onion, and no window at all—at Ragged Islands there were the beautiful new cupboards Jamie had put in, and while she washed the dishes she could look out and see the islands themselves, just offshore, and the back harbour and the edge of town—almost an island itself—in the distance. But no window in that damn apartment kitchen *or* the bathroom—and even an outhouse has a window. Up at the farm the outhouse had *two* windows—*two!* But oh no, not that "nice big apartment." Not a foot of decent woodwork anywhere, the doors all thin as cardboard, and that *miserable* wall-to-wall rug. There was no satisfaction in cleaning a place like that, none at all. At nighttime, the street outside was so bright and noisy that she had to keep the windows closed and the drapes shut or she'd never sleep a wink. The full moon could come and go time and again, but she'd never know, oh no, not in there. And stars, she could just forget about wanting to see any of them ever again!

It's no fair!

"—restless?"

What?

Who's that? Is someone there?

Hello?

She thought she heard someone say something. She was still as could be, listening. . . .

Not moving a muscle, quiet as a mouse. . . .

Listening. . . .

Hssssssssss. . . .

What was that? What was that sound? Take a look-go-see and—

How in the name of God could a person lose her own feet?

They must be down there somewhere, but she couldn't feel a thing, nothing seemed to be going on down there at all. And in this light, without her glasses, she couldn't see worth a damn.

If she tried to take a step, what would happen?

My feet, my poor old feet.

Were they ashamed of themselves and hiding? Who could blame them? But where?

Jamie would be shocked to see those old feet of hers now. When was the last time she'd touched them?

Putting on my slippers.

No, touched them closer than that, took a real good look at them. How long had it been since she'd trimmed her own toenails? Months and months, oh, ages and ages ago. Her granddaughter did that these days, cut her toenails when she came to visit. It was an awful thing to ask a young person to do. Susan Ann couldn't watch; she hated the sight of those tough old things, all ancient and gnarled, and an awful dirty yellow colour, like claws. Poor Jamie would be shocked to see them. She used to have such nice feet.

And his were *so beautiful*. He had the loveliest, longest toes. She teased him that he could tie and untie knots with those toes.

"They're my monkey fingers."

Don't say that, no.

They were so long, and white, and beautiful.

On Sunday mornings after they first married, he'd stretch out upside down on the bed, those beautiful pale feet beside her face, and she'd kiss them while he giggled and whispered and licked the soles of her feet. His mother was down in her room off the parlour; she wouldn't hear if they were careful. And Queenie Roberts hadn't walked up those stairs since the day after Jamie's father fell down them—she refused to go up to the second floor—so Susan Ann and Jamie had taken to lying around in bed bare naked. "We're nudelyweds," she said, and they both got giddy and couldn't stop laughing. They were like kids playing, and she'd been so worried that this part of marriage, the sexy part, would be the worst because no one had ever talked to her about it. But to her surprise and delight, it wasn't.

> *This little piggy went to market*
> *This little piggy stayed home. . . .*

His feet were lost now, lost and gone forever.

And where were her own? That end of her was miles away. Miles and miles.

How long had it been since she was able to bite her toes? She couldn't remember. She used to be able to do that too, easy as pie. He teased her about being double-jointed. How easy everything was back then, when they were nudelyweds, prancing about the bedroom. The two of them laughing and laughing until they heard something slam from downstairs—

We better calm down before we drive your poor mother crazy.

Queenie Roberts downstairs slamming things around because she hated it when they were off by themselves upstairs, having fun. They were acting crazy, like foolish little—

Well, they were, they were still kids. Thought they were all grown up, but they were silly kids still in their twenties.

After Susan Ann's own kids were born, Jamie's mother softened her resentment, just the slightest; her daughter-in-law had finally proved herself capable of doing something useful. Queenie was still jealous, still upset that someone had come between her and her son, but she adored her grandchildren so much that

Susan Ann had to be careful or Queenie would've spoiled them rotten. Candies, cookies, little secret treats. She was always trying to wedge herself in there, trying to make sure those kids loved her the best.

"I'll do bath time tonight and you and Jamie can wash the dishes."

Next thing she knew, Lorraine or Carl would be hooting and screaming from the bathroom while Queenie went, "Tickle, tickle, tickle!" Their grandmother would get them higher than kites, then leave them bouncing off the walls just before bed. Susan Ann would have to go in and play the villain to calm them down; she started to make up bedtime stories so they would lie still and go to sleep.

Once upon a time there was a little girl named Lorraine who lived with a blue jay on top of the clothespole in the backyard where they could see everything and everyone for miles around.

Once upon a time there was a little boy named Carl, who lived beside the ocean inside a big rock with his name carved on the side of it.

Then they were too big for made-up stories with their own names in them; they wanted real ones, from books, *Sleeping Beauty*, *The Little Red Hen*. They snuggled against her happily, repeating their favourite lines along with her—"Very well then," said the Little Red Hen, "I will do it myself"—until they were too old for stories altogether and bath time was an ordeal.

"I'm not dirty, I don't have to, you can't make me."

Like brushing their teeth: a battle, a war at bedtime.

"But I brushed them already."

No, you didn't, Carl, I can tell. Do you want to end up with store teeth like mine?

She would reach up and take hold of her upper plate—

"Don't! Don't do that, Mum! Don't take them out!" He'd be jumping up and down, waving his hands and making faces, terrified that she might yank out her denture.

Is thith what you want, mithter? A thet of teeth like thith?

"Don't! Don't do that, Mum! Don't take them out!"

Then go brush, and toot sweet!

It worked every time.

Oh, but he was a dear wee thing back then. Why did he never call her now? Why had he let his sister lock her away in that miserable apartment?

Where *were* her store teeth? The pink plastic cup she soaked them in? Where had everything gone?

She couldn't even begin to look, because she *had no feet.*

At this rate, there'd be nothing left to bury, not a thing. A morning would come when she wouldn't wake up, and they'd just shake what was left of her out of the bedclothes. Dust to dust.

Where in hell's everything gone?

"What is it?"

What? Someone there? Who's that?

"What is it, dear?"

I lost my stupid old feet.

"I'll get someone."

What? What? Who's that?

"I'll be right back."

Wait, wait—don't go! I've lost my feet!

"Mrs. Roberts, I'll be right back."

Wait, wait—who're you?

Whoever it was was moving away, away and—

Where is this?

The dark was so thick, she still couldn't see. It was indoors, inside, all quiet and—

Hssssssssss. . . .

That sound—was it an animal of some kind? Some wild thing inside the room? That poor snake Queenie had killed in the kitchen that time? Slipping along the floor, trying to get to the back door when she went at it—

"Just lie still now."

Lie still? Oh no! Did I fall? When? How long ago?

She'd been so careful, holding onto the railings up and down the stairs, making sure there were no little mats to trip her up, never ever wearing those Phentex slippers because they were too slippy, because if you started to fall it was the beginning of the end.

How did I fall? Where? Why can't I remember?

She tried to sit up, to see if she could get a better look, but there was something pulling across her chest, there was some—

Damn dammit!

Something tight, holding her, she couldn't breathe—

Not that snake!

No, no snake, but a rope, a leash—

Like a dog! They've got me tied up like some poor old dog!

She was in bed somewhere and tied to—*Don't panic, don't*—a rope, a leash, she was tied to—

No oh no—

And then she was feeling that terrible panic she hadn't felt since she was a sick little girl—her lungs all heavy and wet, hard to breathe, so hard, impossible, drowning—and something, someone, somehow pinning her, squashing her, pushing her down and down into the darkness and deep.

HIS MOTHER'S APARTMENT *was jam-packed to the rafters with things he hadn't seen in years: the scuffed coffee table, the wine-coloured daybed sofa, the blue china dog sitting on the stairs of the crescent-moon-shaped knick-knack shelf. The past surrounding him was his own as well as hers: the piano with its mismatched bench—as a small boy, he'd sat beside her while she played hymns and old songs, "When He Cometh," "Roll Out the Barrel," "The Maple Leaf Forever."*

His parents' mahogany bedroom set was crammed so tightly into the tiny bedroom that he could pull the bottom dresser drawers only partway out. Everything looked out of place and sad, and it was eerie to be here for the first time and be by himself. Carl knew he should call his wife again, but she'd probably say that she didn't want him to be alone tonight, and he didn't want to see or listen to a soul. He'd considered unplugging the phone, but if anything else happened and his sister tried to call and couldn't reach him, he'd never hear the end of it.

At least he wasn't condemned to another night on that scrawny old roll-away mattress back at Lorraine and Peter's—so hard and thin, that thing, it made him think of the lead apron he wore at the dentist when they x-rayed his teeth. As if the day hadn't been miserable and upsetting enough, his sore back had made him short-tempered and unreasonable.

He'd spread the contents of the TO BE SAVED *package out over the top of his mother's bed: smaller envelopes, some of them labelled, letters bundled in elastics, photographs, loose papers and cards—all manner of things that she had saved over the years. A lot of it looked like junk—the sort of stuff his parents used to refer to as* culch.

He picked up a postcard of a little girl holding an orange-coloured puppy, a spaniel. The girl had blonde curls, like Shirley Temple, and was wearing a bright blue cowgirl outfit—the colours were cheery in a forced, gaudy way. The handwriting on the back was shaky and uncertain.

Hello Susan Ann
This made me think of poor little Sally may she rest in
peace. All those long years ago. I am with Muriel and her family
and she has asked me to stay on at Railway Avenue for awhile.
I am so very sorry for <u>everything</u>. Please forgive me. Belated
Birthday wishes.
Love, Aunt Aggie.

Below the address, there were three words in his mother's clear handwriting.

Died in summer

Aunt Aggie, Carl's great-aunt—her photograph was still on his mother's dresser, just as it had always been back in the bedroom in Nova Scotia: a stout woman with a face like a potato sitting on a kitchen chair in a farmyard. She'd come to Ragged Islands to visit one winter—Lorraine probably remembered the details of those months, but he'd been too young.

Please forgive me
so very sorry for <u>everything</u>

There'd been some kind of awful row, that he knew; Aunt Aggie had been mean to his Grammy Queenie and left a lot of bad feelings behind her.

He did remember that summer when she died in Moncton, because his parents and Lorraine drove off to New Brunswick for the funeral, and he and Grammy Queenie had the house to themselves for the better part of a week. They drew pictures and made fudge. On Saturday night they'd stayed up past midnight playing cards: Rummy and Go Fish and Strip Jack Naked. His grandmother had not been a particularly religious woman, but at the very moment that she realized it had become Sunday morning, she'd yanked the cards from his hand and put them back in their box.

"Time to hit the hay, buster."

The postmark date was 1955—the summer before he started school.

I am with Muriel and her family

Muriel was his mother's youngest sister, and the bane of her childhood. Whenever their teasing and tormenting had escalated into door-slamming and tears, Carl and Lorraine had been told that they were "mean as your Aunt Muriel." Carl had discovered early on that a sure way to send his sister into orbit was to call her Muriel. "Murielmurielmuriel." It worked every time.

When he grew older, he'd wondered if she was really as bad as their mother let on; the enormous resentment that his mother harboured against her sister and her MacDonald parents seemed to increase with time. Stories that might have interested him when he was a boy became whiny and tedious. Besides, on those few times that he'd been around his Aunt Muriel, she'd seemed like a lot of fun.

poor little Sally may she rest in peace. All those long years ago.

But Sally—who the hell was she?

The cowgirl was blandly cute, an image from an old primary school reader, cheesy and false.

"Giddy-up, pardner."

Flicking his wrist, he sent Aunt Aggie's card sailing through the air, over the bed and towards the wastepaper basket beside the bathroom door. It flew straight into the far edge of the rim and dropped inside.

Ancient history now, of no importance to anyone.

UPCOUNTRY

When Susan Ann reached the foot of the lane, she stopped to catch her breath. It was so early that the morning star still gleamed sharp and bright above the trees beyond the fields. Not a cloud could be seen; all about the countryside, the birds were singing fiercely. She stood and took deep breaths of the sweet air, her heart racing.

She had done it, and all by herself: she'd outfoxed the lot of them. They thought she was going to just give up and die, but she'd tricked them. "Ha!" she exclaimed. "'Very well then,' said the Little Red Hen, 'I will do it myself.'" Her voice was loud and clear. "And she *did*."

The lane ahead of her was overgrown—Queen Anne's lace and goldenrod so high, higher even than the alder bushes; she could see potholes and stones that would trip her if she wasn't careful. Wild raspberries were crowding in from the edges, their thorns trying to scratch her legs. "Better walk close to the middle," she thought, even though the middle of the lane was a long ribbon of high grass.

Everything was covered with dew; she could smell clover.

She knew she might not have all that much time before people realized that she'd disappeared. She'd better be quick: go straight to the front parlour, see if she could find anything in the old high-back desk where all the MacDonalds had kept their papers. Then upstairs: Aunt Aggie's top dresser drawer. The sort of things she was looking for were tucked away in shoeboxes, in envelopes at the back of closet shelves, in Bibles. Although a great deal of time had passed, she was sure there would still be something. Those things were saved; they were kept. God was not cruel; he would not let her get this far and then keep her from knowing.

From a clump of trees, she heard a blue jay call *Queedle queedle!*, a sound so much like a squeaky clothesline that her kids used to call jays the clothespole birds.

Jeeah! Jeeah! came a response from another.

Queedle queedle!

Then, suddenly, as if this were a signal, it seemed that jays were calling to each other from all directions, and she could see two of them flying about in the air above her, then three, then a half-dozen. Flying from the trees to perch on top of the poles running up the lane, then darting down to the bushes, then back up—calling and flying about as if they were all getting ready for some important thing.

When she was a little girl, eighty or more years ago, she had run up and down this lane in her bare feet, the soft dust so warm between her toes. "Naked feet are common, they're *sinful*," said Great-Aunt Doshe, so Mum Wellman and Aunt Aggie made her wear shoes when Aunt Doshe came for her visit every August, whispering, "We won't give her the satisfaction of complaining."

To Susan Ann growing up, when Mum and Aunt Aggie were together they were like people in a story: they knew the names of all the birds in the sky, and at nighttime they pointed out the constellations that circled overhead: the Dippers, Queen Cassiopeia's Chair and, in late summer, early, early in the morning, Orion and his dog Sirius, who chased the Seven Pleiades sisters across the heavens.

Once upon a time, when Mum and Aunt Aggie were little girls, they played with the Leaman children, who had a tame crow; it could jump through a hoop and Randall Leaman had taught it to say, "Bye-bye."

"It didn't matter that it was smart," her Mum told her, "I never liked the dirty thing."

"Did it burn in the fire?"

"I can't remember. Maybe it flew away."

"Did it have a name?"

"No. We just called it Crow."

"Can all birds learn to talk?"

"No, they can't, and why should they bother with such foolish nonsense?" said Aunt Aggie. "They can sing." And she sang their favourite bird songs, "Chick-a-dee-dee-dee! Chick-a-dee-dee-dee! Chick-a-dee-dee-dee!" and "Poor Tom Peabody-Peabody-Peabody!"

The farm was where Mum Wellman and Aunt Aggie had been born; they were sisters and their brother Robert was Susan Ann's real father, Daddy Mac. There had been six MacDonald children and Mum Wellman was the eldest—except for old Uncle Morris, their half-brother, whose mother had died in childbirth way, long before. When Grampy MacDonald remarried, years and years later, his second wife was a whole year younger than Morris.

"My father was twenty-four years older than my mother," Mum Wellman told her. But if that was the case, what young Susan Ann couldn't understand was why old Grampy MacDonald was still living. "How old is he now?"

"He's not quite Methuselah yet."

But all her grandfather seemed to do was sit in his rocker and drool, while her Grandma MacDonald, who Mum Wellman and Aunt Aggie had adored, was buried in the cemetery next to Grampy's first wife.

"I had two Grandma MacDonalds?"

"Well, yes, I suppose so."

"And I have two mothers."

"That's right," said Mum. "You've got me and you've got your Mumma Mac. Aren't you the lucky duck!"

Only she didn't feel lucky, most of the time. Her Mumma Mac confused her terribly.

As she walked up the lane, she concentrated on the ground, paying nervous attention to the ruts baked into the hard, reddish dirt; the last thing she needed was to fall and break something. If that were to happen, she'd never hear the end of it; her family would drive her foolish. She held tight to the smart little bag that her granddaughter had given her, clutching it as if it might save her if she did start to fall, and she kept her eyes glued to the surface of the lane.

The bushes were so high, and the wildflowers, too; she walked by a Scotch thistle as tall as she was. The house would be visible soon. "It probably won't be as big as you remember," she told herself. "It'll be smaller." She knew that the big barn had been gone for quite a few years. Would the house be very rundown? Muriel's family had left it empty for a while now. The farm had never mattered to her sister as much as to Susan Ann; she had loved spending her summers here, while Muriel was always going on about how much better things were at home. "If she likes it so much there," Susan Ann used to say to herself, "why doesn't she just stay in the fabulous city of Moncton and leave the farm to me?" Moncton was where both sisters had been born, in the house on Railway Avenue, but for reasons she has never understood, Susan Ann was given away to Mum and Dad Wellman. Muriel was born a year later, and Daddy and Mumma Mac kept her; they kept her brother and other sister as well.

Where was the roof of the house? She was certain that she should be seeing it by now. The dark shingles, the high peak with the lightning rods—one of them had been struck during a thunderstorm while she was here visiting. One sultry July afternoon—she was with Mum and Aunt Aggie in the kitchen when the storm hit: thunder so loud that they had measured all storms against it for years to come. Uncle Hay had come running into the house from the barn and stood there trembling beside the stove, trying to roll a cigarette, while his sisters went right into action, fussing about him, trying to soothe his nerves and calm him down. Whenever the thunder boomed, he'd jumped and made whimpering sounds, high and odd, like a little dog. After he came back from the Great War any kind of loud noise or commotion upset him terribly. Whenever Susan Ann heard sirens screeching by, or listened to the racket they played on the radio nowadays, she thought of her poor Uncle Hay and how it would have driven him foolish. He couldn't even tolerate the small congregation at Five Points Baptist. "The organ spooks him," said Aunt Aggie.

"Not to mention the minister," said Mum. "But that Reverend Trites is a spooky fellow."

Aunt Aggie would give her big sister a gentle backhand. "Tessie, now you mind."

When Susan Ann was alone with Mum and Aunt Aggie, she felt that she was quite special, included and wanted: sometimes she felt a connection to their childhood years that was so close it seemed possible for her to slip back into that time, for the three of them to be girls growing up together. She loved sitting between them on Sundays, when they went to Five Points Baptist. Whenever Reverend Trites got carried away in his sermon and started waving his hands about, the spittle flying from his mouth, Mum and Aunt Aggie would lower their heads and try not to laugh. The hymns there were faster than they were at the Methodist church at home in Shediac, and when folks were baptized, they went down to John MacDonald's River by the covered bridge. Aunt Aggie showed her how to sew little lead weights into the hem of a dress so it wouldn't float up and be indecent.

Sweet hour of prayer! sweet hour of prayer!
That calls me from a world of care,
And bids me at my Father's throne
Make all my wants and wishes known—

Mum Wellman had a cameo on a silver chain—it made her different from all the other ladies at church, it made her special. It was a beautiful thing; the cameo woman had a lovely neck, the setting was pure silver, and Mum had promised it to her, but after the funeral Muriel and her bunch had taken everything. It wasn't fair that they had ended up with the farm, as well. Muriel had never enjoyed coming here, she did nothing but complain, every single summer, complain complain, and then for her to end up with the deed to this place, "Not fair, it was no fair!"

She was almost at the end of the lane now, and she should be able to see something above the alders, she *should* be able to see the roof—

Unless that Muriel had gone and done something stupid—

She picked up the pace, walking faster and faster, and then the lane opened up into the old farmyard and she walked into—

"Glory be to God!"

She stood stock-still, her mouth open in shock, for it was in ruins, everything was in ruins, there was nothing left standing, not a *thing!*

The whole farm was gone; the house had been pulled apart, torn down and scattered all about. Everything—barn, sheds, chicken coop—every single thing had been ripped to pieces. The destruction was so great that her first thought was that something violent must have come by in the night: a hurricane or one of those twister things like they had out west. She could scarcely believe her eyes. She was standing right close to where Aunt Aggie's day lilies had once been, standing and staring at a crushed heap of plaster and wood. Then she realized that the ground all around was a mess of great ugly tire ruts and huge tracks; machines of some kind must have torn the place apart. She couldn't believe it: that lovely old house had been smashed to bits and flattened. Laths were scattered about in the wreckage like splintered bones.

The oldest parts of that house had been built by her great-great-grandfather; he had come here when there was nothing, not a blessed thing, and built this farm. And now it was gone, the whole enterprise. It was a crime.

Muriel must have lost her mind for good. How could she go and do something so stupid?

"The miserable stupid thing!"

She had moved a few steps closer in; "*Miserable*," she said, again. As she looked, she realized that she could identify nearly everything that lay before her: a piece of the sloped ceiling from the upper room where she used to sleep; a bit of baseboard from the upstairs hall near the stovepipe, the varnish on it bubbled from the heat. And sticking out from under a sheet of roof shingles was a big chunk of the front stairs.

Then Susan Ann was seeing things down there in the rubble that should have been kept, that should have been taken out of that house and saved—lovely things that Aunt Aggie had so patiently cleaned and tended over the years. The cabinet from the parlour, the picture of Wellington at Waterloo—all broken up and torn. Things hadn't even been moved out of the house—had people even gone inside to look? No, they'd just smashed it all to pieces!

Uncle Hay's cane chair!

And what of the things she had come here to find? The papers and letters tucked away, the information she had a right to know because it was her own—what of all that? She wouldn't be able to wade into this mess and sort through things. Was that knowledge lost forever now?

She felt sick.

She looked down at what remained of the staircase poking up out of the rubble. She'd sat on that, years and years ago, crept down and sat there in the evenings and listened, trying to overhear conversations from the kitchen, trying to find out what was going on with her real Daddy and Mumma Mac back on Railway Avenue in Moncton.

The delicate colours in the eastern sky were fading, and all around the huge heaven was turning blue; it would be a fine, sunny day. By now, her family probably knew that she had flown the coop and they would be on her tail.

"Well, you stupid ass, what's your next bright idea?" She was looking beyond the yard, towards the fields and the woods—everything was starting to look a little lonely.

Caw! Caw!

There was a crow in the spruce across the pasture; she could see it perched up on the very top of the tallest tree.

"Damned crow," she said. When she was ten years old, she'd made an enemy of an old crow up here, she had chased him away from a baby robin in the grass by the side of the house. The robin had fallen from its nest under the eaves.

"Hear that?" Aunt Aggie would tease. "That old crow knows you're back. He's the one that doesn't like you 'cause you robbed him of his supper that time."

Caw caw caw!

As she watched the line of spruce, the crow extended his wings, stretched them out and up and began to flap them slowly, once, twice. He leaned forwards, then lifted himself up from the branch.

What had happened to the baby robin that Susan Ann had saved all those years ago? Her Daddy Mac had been up at the farm that week; she remembered this because he'd made her cry. "Might as well feed it to the cat," he said. "The other birds won't have anything to do with it after you've gone and touched it. Give it to the cat and put the poor thing out of its misery."

Did it get better and fly away? Did it grow up?

"I put it on some straw in a box," she said, but that was all she remembered.

The crow was screeching at her again.

"Yes, yes, it's me. And you're still here? Filthy thing."

The crow was rising, high above the tree now, climbing up and up, and then, as she watched, he turned and, swooping down, began gliding across the field in her direction.

"What's he up to?"

As he advanced, he seemed to be picking up speed—it was almost as if he was aiming himself in her direction. His feathers were shining in the sunlight; he was travelling at quite a clip, getting closer and closer—he was cawing like crazy and flying straight at her!

She stuck out her arm, holding up her little bag like a shield. She wanted to shut her eyes but she knew that was cowardly, so she didn't; she held her ground. If need be, she would try to swat the thing.

At the very last moment he lifted up, screeching *Awk awk awk*, and sailed just over her head—she could feel the air from his wings, bare inches away; she heard them go *swoosh swoosh swoosh*.

"Get away!" she called out. She spun around and saw him turning back towards her, to come at her again.

She didn't duck, just lowered her head a bit when he came roaring back.

"Leave me be!"

He didn't seem to be more than a foot from her face when he swerved away. Then he turned once more and began flying in wide arcs around her—cawing and circling once, twice, three times.

"Get away from me, you!" She was frightened, but she was not about to be intimidated by some old crow.

Awk! Awk!

He was slowing down, and flying just above the heap of rubble where the house had stood. His wings were the size of a hawk's, the feathers on the tips like outstretched fingers.

"You're a big ugly thing." She and her Mum Wellman had never cared for crows, ever, even though they knew that they were smart. They didn't like them because they killed little birds and ate dead things by the side of the road. Their voices were so raw and scratchy—just the opposite of bird songs.

Awk! He flapped down and settled on the bit of broken staircase.

They watched each other. Susan Ann's heart was racing; she was still a little frightened, and mad as could be.

"You think you're some smart, now, doncha?"

He was looking at her, listening, eyeing her carefully.

"Pah!" she said.

Ignoring her now, he turned his head this way and that, and began his inspection of the ruined house; he hopped out of sight behind the staircase. She could hear him scratching around.

All around her, creatures were starting to move about. The blue jays were calling from the trees, and the mourning doves from down in the lane; a butterfly went flitting past, some sparrows and goldfinches darted about. Bugs were buzzing in the air:

a devil's darning needle, a couple of pesky mosquitoes. She thought that if she stood very still and watched the woods, she might even see deer—it was still early enough. Or maybe a fox running home across the pasture, on its way home from a night of hunting.

"What in the name of God are you going to do now?"

There was nowhere here for her to stay, nowhere to spend the night, nowhere, it seemed, to even sit down and wait for her family to come find her—although that was the last thing she wanted; she had no interest whatsoever in having them drag her back. To hell with them and that miserable place they'd stuck her in; there was nothing to do back there but lie down and give up the ghost, and to hell with that for an idea.

She had no desire to even *see* her family right now. And this was not only because she had broken her promise to Lorraine.

"I'm sorry," she'd said. "I'm sorry and I promise I won't go off again without telling you."

"Mum, we were worried sick!"

A month after they'd made her move into that hateful apartment, Susan Ann had started going off on her own. Lorraine had shown her how to get to the bank on St. Clair Avenue, and to the grocery store, but one fine morning she decided to go farther afield. She took the subway down to Union Station and sat there for a while, thinking of the time she and her brother Murd had passed through Toronto with Mum and Dad Wellman on their trip to Winnipeg. The men who worked on the train were kind to them because Dad had a long-service pass. She and Jamie had taken the train to Toronto once, too, but most times they had come by car: a drive that the both of them hated because of the freeways around Montreal, and that awful 401. Sitting in the train station had been a way to try to connect Toronto to her own life.

She enjoyed her little trip so much that she went back the next week, and the one after. It thrilled her that Lorraine knew nothing of these jaunts, that they belonged to her alone. Once, she timed things poorly and ended up in the station during rush hour—the crowds scared her to death, and she was sure, after that, to watch the clock.

A few weeks later, she decided to see if she could find the island ferry. On those trips with Jamie years ago, they had always taken their grandkids to Centre Island; Meg and Tommy had loved to ride on the swans. The traffic outside Union was confusing, she got herself turned in the wrong direction a few times, but eventually she found her way down to the docks and bought her ticket. The ferry ride was lovely, even though the air was nothing like the good salt air back home; she felt pleased with herself for being able to get around so well.

But after she stepped off the boat and walked for a few minutes, she realized that nothing was familiar, that this was not the way to the swans but somewhere else, and she didn't know quite what to do. When a young woman asked her if she was all right, Susan Ann said that she was fine, thank you.

"I live right in there," the woman said, pointing to a cottage on a corner. "If you need anything, just knock on my door."

She thanked her and decided that she would wander around for a bit, then go back and wait for another ferry. The little cottages were so close together that it made her think of the cottages on the shore back in Shediac; she followed a path through some trees and found a beach, where she decided to have a rest. By that time, it was the afternoon.

It was the young woman who found her. There was nothing really wrong, "I must have fallen asleep," she said, but it was embarrassing. She went back to the little cottage on the corner and had tea and agreed that perhaps she should phone Lorraine, just to say she was fine.

"You're *where?*" her daughter had said.

Susan Ann had not been ready for the reception she got when the ferry returned her to the city. Lorraine had decided to drop in on her mother that morning, and had been frantically looking for her ever since. She had even called the police.

"Don't you *dare* do that again! We were worried sick!"

"I won't, Lorraine. I give you my word."

Yet she had broken her word, and gone much farther afield than the island ferry this time. When her daughter caught up to her, she would be furious. But what else could Susan Ann have done? She could scarcely believe that Lorraine could be so uncaring, or Carl so thoughtless. And even those grandchildren of hers were no help right now, either. They had all abandoned her.

But where was she to go from here?

"I need somewheres I can go sit down to collect my thoughts."

It was then she noticed that what remained of the old outhouse was still standing, hiding there beyond the apple tree, beside the clump of lilacs, so she made her way gingerly across the wreckage of the yard towards it. The door was gone, and the glass in both windows was cracked and smashed. The lids for both holes were missing, but the wood on the seats still looked smooth and comfortable.

"I'll try and have a BM," she said, stepping inside. It was so long since she had had any real success in that department—maybe the outhouse was just the ticket. The ugly room her kids had foisted on her had the worst toilet in the world: windowless and with a fan that sounded like an airplane taking off. It roared every time she turned on the light, driving her so crazy that she had taken to using that toilet in the dark with the door open.

She hoisted her skirt, pulled down her pantyhose, and sat herself down. The morning air felt good on her old bum. She was glad the outhouse was still standing, although it was a mess; but it probably wouldn't be around much longer. In the old days, Aunt Aggie had kept it so clean; every other year she gave it a fresh coat of whitewash. Great-Aunt Doshe was the only one who had ever found fault with the way this outhouse was looked after, she who found fault with everything.

"If she doesn't like it, then why does she park herself out there half the morning?"

Great-Aunt Doshe was Grampy MacDonald's sister. She had massive bosoms and she had married a Presbyterian who hardly ever came to the farm, "Because he thinks his arse is too fine an instrument for my outhouse," said Aunt Aggie.

The bad feelings between Aggie and Doshe went way back to the time that Grandma MacDonald caught a chill at choir practice and Aunt Doshe was still saying she was perfectly fine and didn't need a doctor at all on the very morning that Grandma had dropped dead. Then things got worse after Uncle Hay came home from France. That year—the Great War was over, it must have been, what, 1919? It would have been around the same time that the lightning hit the roof, that same summer.

She remembers the famous Sunday dinner when Aunt Aggie flew at Great-Aunt Doshe. When the family told that story through the years, they talked and laughed as if it were funny, but it hadn't been funny at the time, not one little bit.

Susan Ann could remember that moment in the kitchen as clear as yesterday. Dinner was over, they had finished the berries that she and Aunt Aggie had picked for dessert, and Uncle Hay had gone out into the yard to smoke. It was one of those rare times when Susan Ann's real father and mother were there, Daddy and Mumma Mac both, with her real brother and sisters. Susan Ann remembered this precisely because Mumma Mac hardly ever came upcountry, and Daddy Mac was making a big fuss over Muriel, who was just learning to walk. Mum and Dad Wellman were back home in Shediac; they had left her up at the farm on her own for a week.

Aunt Aggie had cleared all the dishes and was getting ready to wash them when Aunt Doshe arose from the table and walked over to spy out the window; she pulled back the curtain and started watching Uncle Hay like a hawk.

"What did I tell you? Smoking. Shameful, that's what it is, and on Sunday. A dirty, filthy sin."

And that's when Aunt Aggie had flown right at her, spun around from the sink pump, her face red and terrifying, and shouted, "Why don't you keep your big Presbyterian trap *shut!*"

Everything stopped.

Susan Ann had been playing on the cot with Sally, and the room became so distant around her that she suddenly felt she was in the wrong place; she felt that she didn't belong in the old farm kitchen any more, had never belonged there, she was a foreigner, a cut-out little girl pasted on the wrong family picture. No one at the farm really wanted her, they were just pretending. No one really wanted her anywhere, not even Mum and Dad Wellman— that's why they left her at the farm. She was very small and alone. It was so horrible, that moment of unbelonging, that she burst into tears.

"What's wrong with her now?" said Mumma Mac, the voice of exasperation. She turned and scowled at the cot. "You want me to give you something to *really* cry about?"

Her tears had made everything worse. Great-Aunt Doshe glared at Aunt Aggie and said, "Satisfied now?" and so Aggie grabbed Susan Ann and took her out into the garden to pick beans.

"That miserable old Doshe! She thinks she's too good, that one, that's why she sees dirt in everyone else. Thinks her *shit* doesn't stink. Old Tidy Bowels!" Aunt Aggie and Mum Wellman called her that because Doshe was obsessed with regularity, and went on and on about the virtues of bran.

"A good dose of Doshe's bran wouldn't hurt me right now," thought Susan Ann. She was having no luck in the bowel-movement department at all. And just as well—she realized there was not a scrap of paper in the old outhouse to wipe herself with. "I'm in enough mess as it is. I don't need to go traipsing about with a dirty bum."

And with that she stood up, adjusted her clothing and went back out into the yard.

It was turning into a real fine day; there was that to be thankful for, she supposed. "But I can't stay here," she said, looking at the wreck around her. "And I'm *not* going back. That family of mine is more interested in watching those fool Americans on the old box. I'm not going back to where no one has any time for me."

The crow was still poking about in the ruins of the house; suddenly he was flapping his wings, agitated and excited.

"What's he up to?" she thought, and so she went over to see.

Looking down from the edge of the destruction, all those bits and pieces of things below made her think of her granddaughter, who went off to weird places to dig around and look for old bones and pots. Meg had told her that you could sift through rubble and figure out who had lived in a place and how long ago they had lived there. She dug up seeds and teeth and Lord knows what else, and could tell what cavemen had for dinner way back before God made Adam.

The crow was rummaging around a pile of plaster, moving bits of rubble aside with his beak; he was tugging at something shiny, like a little silver ribbon or a bright piece of string. "What is it? What have you got there?" She knew that crows were thieves and packrats.

He was working away, scratching with one foot, pushing aside broken pieces of plaster, nudging a bit of lath, tugging and pulling.

"That's mine," she wanted to say. "Give that to me, whatever it is. It's mine."

The crow gave a good yank, and the shiny thing came free.

"What's that? Show me."

He opened his mouth and dropped it and screeched at her once again. He sounded mean this time.

RAAWK! RAAWK!

He snapped down his beak and picked the object up, lifted it to where Susan Ann could clearly see it—

"You give that here!"

Then he opened his great black wings and flapped up into the air.

"*Stop!* Come back!" she shouted. "You come back with that!"

But the crow paid her no mind, and flew up and up, high, high above her, with Mum Wellman's beautiful cameo necklace dangling from his beak.

"Wait! Wait!"

He was soaring away, off over the fields and the woods, towards the cemetery at Five Points, the silver necklace glinting in the sunlight, and she was all by herself, standing beside a pile of rubble, not sure what she should do or where she should go to now.

THE ENVELOPE *was labelled* MUM WELLMAN / MURD, *and when Carl pulled out the letter, an old newspaper clipping dropped onto the bed.*

LT. MURDOCH WELLMAN

A graduate with distinction from Shediac High School and Oulton's Business College, a former leading hockey player in Shediac, and one of the most highly esteemed young businessmen in New Brunswick, Lt. Wellman gave his life for his country. News that he had been killed in action reached his family shortly after New Year's Day. He had been at the front since early in the autumn.

The obituary seemed barely adequate, given the circumstances.

"You're just like Murd," his mother had told him when he was a boy, "How well you and your uncle would've gotten along." He'd felt guilty, as if he had let her down somehow by being born too late, by not being able to be her young brother's childhood friend.

Whenever his father had been angry and annoyed with him, he had shouted Carl's name in full—"Carl Murdoch Roberts!"—an admonition. Carl and his father had gotten on each other's nerves from the very beginning; they had rarely seen eye to eye on anything. Nearly every day, his father would come home from the fish plant, the family would sit down for supper and within five minutes the two of them would be caught up in a bitter argument. No matter what the subject, his father would end up saying, "You don't have a clue what you're talking about."

The letter from Mum Wellman had been written four years before Carl was born. Both of his parents had always referred to this woman as some kind of saint.

MacDonald's Sett.
West. Co., N.B.
March 1945

Daughter Dear,

Hello Susan Ann. I thought it was high time I wrote you. I apologize for the paper, it's not too "classy."

Your father left on the train the day before yesterday. He will be in Montreal till the end of May. I'm praying this visit with Boyd's family does him good. I think that we will never recover from the loss of our Murd, it hurts us all so deeply, but he is beside himself. I think we gals are made of tougher stuff than men.

I hope and pray that this miserable old war will come to an end soon. Your Daddy and Mumma Mac are worried sick about Fred and nearly everyone I know has lost someone or is worried about losing someone. I try not to cry when I think about Murd. I try and think about our Maker and to take comfort in knowing that we will all meet by and by, but comfort is hard most days I can tell you.

I am up at the farm helping Aggie out. She is having a hard
time of it with Hay this winter. The war news upsets him so
and he is not sleeping through most nights. It's hard to remember how happy he was when we were all kiddies growing up. He
was full of the devil back then. Right now they are both out
visiting poor Mrs. Leaman. I should be there myself, but I
wanted to write you a nice letter, and send on these few things
of Murd's, so I told a little white lie and said I had a headache.
I don't think the Lord will mind a wee fib like that, and I'll have
supper ready when they get back. I put a bird in the oven for
them. I felt that I just couldn't face Mrs. Leaman right now,
she still talks about that fire like it was yesterday.

Things have changed up here. There are no young fellows
around these days of course. Your Daddy MacDonald was
here last Sunday and we talked about old times and had a
laugh or two. We can still try to have our fun. I was hoping that
Mumma Mac would come, but she leaves the house on Railway
Ave. less and less.

Early this morning, I went out for a nice long walk. It has been
grey and cold, but spring is on its way this week. I saw my first
robin sitting out on the old snake fence. I was thinking of the
walk that you and I had when we were up here together last. I
am glad that this old farm means so much to you. We never had
much growing up here, but we were happy none the less.
I never wanted to leave here, but if I hadn't gone to work at
Eaton's, I would never have met Paul Wellman living at Mrs.
Colpitts' rooming house. When I met him that first time, I
thought, "Poor unhappy fellow, a widower with two young boys,"
but then those boys became my own, then you came along as well,
and then our own wee Murd. We all were happy, were we not?

I'm going to tell you something and I want you to keep it
to yourself. I was worried sick when Paul Wellman asked me to

marry him. I knew that my brothers would be dead against it. Just look at how miserable they have been to your Aunt Bea. But sometimes you have to pay no attention to your own people! You know how fond your father and I are of Jamie. Don't pay any mind to what anybody else says or thinks. Pay that foolish Muriel no mind, she just likes to hear herself talk. And be patient with Jamie's mother. Remember she was living in that house long before you. It will take some getting used to for her. Give her my regards and tell her I hope to meet her one of these days. Ragged Islands is such a wild sounding place name!

It does feel strange to have to write to you but we'll talk in the flesh soon God willing. We'll have to wait awhile, but then I must try to come see the wee treasure after the stork arrives. If it's a boy I do hope he enjoys these old "woodsy" books that Murd loved so.

I had better stop this now and get the rest of supper on. I know that Murd is in heaven with our Maker and that he is blessing you both.

Your loving,
Mum

Carl found himself caught up in the feeling of particular Saturday mornings back in his bedroom in Ragged Islands—he couldn't have been any older than twelve—when, for a time, all he wanted was to live by himself in a camp up the river where he could track and trap animals and be a taxidermist. This was because he had been given two books that had once belonged to his Uncle Murd, Two Little Savages and Wild Animals I Have Known. He was thrilled by the idea of foxes standing in glass cases, of owls displayed in bell jars. He imagined learning to cut gently open the bellies of songbirds and pull the skin, thin as tissue paper, back from the muscles and bones; how wonderful it would be to stuff them and mount them on branches.

Where had those books gone, he wondered. They didn't seem the sort of things that Lorraine's kids would be interested in reading.

He wished that he could call his son, but Greg would still be at work—the restaurant would be open for awhile yet. With the time difference, it would probably be the middle of the night before he could phone. And how to tell him what he was feeling? He'd probably end up sounding no different from Lorraine. "Everything's changed now," she'd been saying all day long, "Nothing'll ever be the same again." Over and over. "The world's all different now." He could imagine his son on the other end, exhausted from bartending and rolling his eyes.

Greg had never really known his grandmother—just that one awkward vacation when he was still a kid and they'd driven through the Rockies. Even though she had been game for nearly everything—she'd walked up Tunnel Mountain with them, and she was in her seventies by then—she'd been tentative, somehow, so unlike herself. At the top, when they looked out and over the Bow River Valley, she said, "It's beautiful, I suppose, but there's too much to look at and my old eyes can't take it in. It's not for me." And she'd turned away and sat down on a rock.

Greg was living there now, in Banff; he'd just turned twenty-three.

Carl's mother had told him repeatedly that he was just like his uncle, who had died young and tragically in wartime, and this had made him feel special—until he realized that his uncle and his father had been best friends in the army. Then, somehow, it all felt like a ploy, another one of her old tricks to convince him that he should think kindly of his father, that he should always be patient with a man who had never had an ounce of patience for him.

FIVE POINTS

Susan Ann had left the ruined farmyard and started back down the lane; she was not even halfway to the end of it when she stopped and stood there, wanting to turn around and look back. "Like Lot's wife," she thought, "way back in Bible times."

When that poor soul had turned around to see Sodom go up in flames, God had turned her into a pillar of salt; Susan Ann had never understood why. It seemed like such a natural thing to do, and a harmless one, turning around to look at fire and brimstone raining down on the place you used to live. Was it because Lot's wife was nosy, or still worried about her old neighbours, who were evil, or was it because she disobeyed and didn't listen to God? God had always seemed mean in that story, petty, no better than the evil people he was bent on destroying. She and Lorraine had talked about it when Lorraine had told her about her boy, Tommy; they had talked about everything the Bible had to say about being like that, "gay" they called it now. Because that's why God destroyed Sodom—the men there were like that.

"Why do you think God turned her into a pillar of salt?"

"I just think it's a load of crap," Lorraine answered. "They didn't even give the poor woman a name. *Lot's wife.* Not even her own name. Or her daughters either. *The Daughters of Lot.* Just a load of idiotic patriarchal crap. Why do you even pay attention to it?"

Tommy's friend, that crazy boy with the crazy hair, had been so young, not even twenty. She knew there were people who said that God had punished him, and she had been scared to death that He would punish her grandson as well. Wasn't it like Sodom, the way they carried on, all that wild dancing and things those young fellows got into?

And then Meg had told her that the story was confusing because it was made up of bits and pieces of other stories, older ones, and that some of them went back before Bible times, way back before Israel even *was*, back to those places her granddaughter had been to, to look for ancient treasure. "Don't take it literally, Gramma," Meg said; but it was hard not to, because that was the way it had always been.

Lot's wife had done what most people would do, she had turned around to look at something terrible happening to a place where she had lived, she had looked back out of worry and concern, and for that she had been destroyed.

Maybe, in turning back to look, she had hoped that bad things weren't really happening. Maybe, by turning around, Lot's wife was simply hoping to see Sodom sitting there safe in the sunshine. So what? Why was that such a bad thing to do?

Because that was the reason why Susan Ann had stopped halfway down the lane and was turning to look back—in the faint hope that there had been a terrible mistake, that she was just old and confused and the MacDonald farmhouse was still there after all. Safe and sound.

But it wasn't. There was nothing beyond the alders and wild-flowers but a pile of rubble.

"Damn her," she said. "Damn that Muriel." And with that, she turned around and started off again, feeling angry and sad.

And Lot's wife, she wondered, what had happened to her? Had God let her into heaven or just kept her there, a stupid pillar of salt? What a mean story that was. When it came to Lot's wife, it was hard to be on God's side—even more so because Susan Ann and her grandson had gotten along so well. Tommy was a fine young fellow, and she had decided that everything she had been taught about people like him while she was growing up was wrong.

What would her mum and Aunt Aggie have thought of all that? Would they have been ahead of their time? She had always believed that there was no one as generous or open-minded as Mum Wellman.

No doubt it was folly to try to rescue Mum's cameo necklace from a thieving crow, but she had to try. He had flown off towards Five Points, and she was hoping to find him there. She loved that necklace, had thought about it so much over all these years, and she was determined to get it back.

When Aunt Aggie came down to Ragged Islands to stay with Susan Ann and Jamie, that time when things went so badly, she said that the necklace had disappeared up at the farm the week after Mum Wellman died. "I knew how much you loved that old cameo," she said. "Muriel and I tore the house apart and we couldn't find hide nor hair of it." Her poor aunt had passed away at Muriel's place not too long after that visit, and Muriel, who had never even cared for the farm, had inherited it. Or rather, she and Jack had convinced Aunt Aggie to sign the deed over to them.

And the *very next* Christmas—the Christmas of 1955—Muriel and Jack sent out that card! On the front there was a family portrait they had taken with their three kids. "Jamie, oh my God, come take a look at this!" For Muriel was parked smack dab in the middle of the snapshot, a big smirk on her face, and stretched around her big pink neck was the cameo necklace. When had she gotten her old paws on it? Had she found it up at the farm, or had she pocketed it when she and Mumma Mac went to help Aunt Aggie the week that Mum Wellman died?

"It's rightfully mine!" Susan Ann said aloud as she marched down the lane. "If she wanted it so badly, why didn't she look after it! Careless, she was always careless. And lazy, lazy as—"

She stumbled on a rock, lurched sideways and fell into the alders.

"Shit!"

She was stuck half inside the bushes, at a forty-five degree angle to the ground, the dark green surrounding her. There were bitter leaves in her mouth—she spat them out and clamped her lips shut. The branches were holding her, for the time being, but she couldn't push herself back and stand upright. She would have to try to work her way downwards.

Slowly, slowly, she lifted her bag, sliding it up her chest until it was pressing against her face; she held it there so her eyes wouldn't get scratched. Then slowly, slowly, she wiggled her body, lowering herself down, the branches scraping and flipping along her side, slapping against her bag, until she was finally on her knees at the edge of the lane. She crawled backwards into the middle, and then, somehow, she got to her feet.

For five full minutes afterwards, she stood very still, holding her hands to her chest, terrified, her heart racing. "Pay attention," she whispered. "Pay attention, *pay attention!*"

What if she had fallen and broken something? Maybe no one would find her here. She was terrified of falling; look at poor Ellen Firth. After Susan Ann's friend fell down and broke her hip, she was never the same again. Her family had put her in Surf Side Manor, she got all confused, forgot who she was and died. And if Susan Ann fell and broke something out here, what would happen to her? Would she just lie there until she starved to death? It was probably going to be a hot day and she would fry in the heat.

She should have brought that stupid cotton hat that Lorraine had given her, even though she hated the thing, she should have brought it and she should be wearing it. She didn't want the crows to find her lying here dead and pick the meat off her bones. Then she'd never be buried with Jamie.

"Watch where you're going," she said. "Just watch and be careful."

Apart from a small red scratch on the back of her hand, she seemed to be fine.

So she started off again.

Despite everything going wrong, it was good to breathe the country air and to see all the familiar surroundings.

A few minutes later, she realized that she had somehow missed the Leaman homestead where she used to go visit with Mum and Aunt Aggie. Where could that old house have gone? Had they torn it down, too? Did people nowadays have no use whatsoever for anything that was old?

Poor Mrs. Leaman had lived there for years and years with her sister-in-law. She had lost all her children in a fire, and lost her husband too, that same year; he died of a broken heart. Martha Leaman, the oldest daughter, had been Mum's childhood friend. Susan Ann had made up a rhyme with the Leaman children's names in it; she used to recite it when she hopped on their stones in the graveyard:

> *Randall, Rebecca,*
> *Martha too,*
> *Ewan, Charlotte,*
> *Harvey and Hugh*

She began chanting it to herself as she walked along.

In a little while, she took a shortcut that she remembered, down through the pasture. At the far end, she followed a narrow path through a thicket and came to a clear patch where the path ended at a deep ditch. It was dry and filled with lupins, purple and pink, taller than she was. On the other side of it was the road. It was not all that hard to walk down into the ditch—she took her time—and then to get herself up the other side; she grabbed onto the stalks and they helped her. "Late in the year for lupins," she thought. "Damn lucky for me."

When she got herself up onto the road, she could see Five Points Baptist just up ahead, and perched way up on the steeple, on the tip of the weathervane rooster's high-flying tail, was a crow. And he was holding something shiny in his beak.

She walked smartly down the road and stood in front of the church.

The crow sat up there staring off into the distance, in first one direction and then another, as if she didn't exist. He lifted his shoulders in a shrug and, turning his head away, gazed off into the east. She moved back a few steps so that she was again standing in the middle of the road; there was nothing coming, not a car or anyone walking—not a sign of human life, it seemed, for miles around. The countryside was so quiet; the only sound was a chickadee behind her in the graveyard.

She watched that crow for what felt like ten minutes; occasionally he would move his head, and she could see the silver of the necklace shine in the morning sun. After a while, she was starting to get a crick in her neck.

Finally, he shifted around and looked down at her. He shook his head vigorously, rattling the necklace. Then he jumped from the rooster's tail down to the arrow of the weathervane, hopped from that to the top of the letter N, and jumped back up and perched on the rooster's head.

"Don't tease me, you."

But it seemed as if he wanted to do nothing else. He flapped down to the church roof and puffed himself up, then he began strutting along the ridgepole, from one end of the church to the other, back and forth, the necklace dangling smartly from his beak.

"Vain thing. Isn't he some pleased with himself," she thought. "Well, pride goeth before a fall, mister," and she watched intently, walking backwards to the other side of the road so she could be sure to keep her eyes on that cameo, hoping he would get careless and let it drop. If it slid down the shingles, she would be able to dash over and get under it, so that it could fall straight into her hands where it rightfully belonged. But the crow was smart, and the grip of his beak was sure.

"Selfish old bugger," she whispered. "It's of no use to you whatsoever."

He kept strutting along the top of the roof, swaggering, preening and showing off his shiny black feathers.

Then Susan Ann thought maybe she could trick him into cawing at her and dropping the necklace.

"Caw!" she called out. "Caw caw to you, Old Crow!"

He stopped his strutting and turned to her.

"CAW!" she hollered. "Big mean crow!" She pointed her finger at him and shook it. "Caw-caw!"

He opened his wings and flapped them.

"Cat got your tongue?" she said.

He was glaring at her, but he didn't answer, he didn't open his beak.

"Come on, you bugger! CAW CAW CAW!"

Then that old crow flew straight up and over to the weathervane and draped the necklace over the arrowhead. Susan Ann could see the little cameo lady swinging and spinning high in the air as the crow began screeching at her and jumping all over the place. From the arrow to the rooster's tail, then down to the four compass points, north east south west, up and down, round and round, again and again, all the while mocking her, till his *caws* sounded like *aws* and then his *aws* were like *haws*, and he was going *haw-haw-haw*.

"Dirty sacrilegious creature," she thought. "I'm not going to give you any more satisfaction." So she turned her back to him and walked into the graveyard. She could feel his eyes on her, so she walked slowly and deliberately towards the MacDonald graves.

Haw-haw-haw-haw!

It was so hard to keep from turning around and answering. "Miserable bird," she thought. "He's not going to get my goat." And she made her way deeper into the cemetery.

The path was overgrown and the grass on either side badly needed mowing. She walked past the Lutzes, the MacPhersons, the Blakes—and there, suddenly, was Mr. and Mrs. Leaman's grave. Susan Ann couldn't see the line of stones; they were hidden in the high grass. She left the path and walked over to look. Aunt Aggie would be horrified to see the state of things: her bleeding hearts were long gone, there was nothing in their place but grass and weeds, dandelions everywhere. Susan Ann stood and stared and finally caught a glimpse of one of the stones. She got down on her knees and pulled out the grass in handfuls. At first, only two letters could be seen:

R T

She tugged away at the grass, tore out dandelion leaves and smoothed away the dirt.

A R T H

91—19

The stone was at a terrible tilt—one end of it had sunk a good five inches into the earth—but she managed to clear away the surface.

MARTHA

1891—1908

"There, that's better."

From across the road, the crow called to her once again.

"Don't you even turn to look at him," she said to herself. "Ignore him and just take your time. *Everything comes to He who Waits!*"

She sat back on her heels and looked for the other Leaman stones, Martha's brothers and sisters. Even if her feet were still young and nimble, they would no longer be able to hop on those little stones the way they had all those years ago; the stones had fallen into the ground so, and were very crooked. When she was a girl, she had come to Five Points with Mum and Aunt Aggie to tend the graves. She had hopped from *Randall* to *Rebecca* to *Martha* to *Ewan* to *Charlotte* to *Harvey and Hugh*—the twins, just babies, they were buried together—then turned and hopped back on her other foot. If she never wavered, never lost her balance, she made a wish, because the Leaman children lived in heaven, where they could grant wishes. Sometimes she pretended they were stars in the sky over the barn—they were the names of the stars in the Big Dipper: *Randall, Rebecca, Martha too, Ewan, Charlotte, Harvey and Hugh* pointed to the North Star.

Aunt Aggie and Mum Wellman had known them all; they had seen the terrible fire. Martha Leaman had been their best friend. "Oh, Susan Ann, she had the loveliest hair you ever saw."

Back then, she was jealous sometimes of their friendship with Martha Leaman. If only she could've had a friend as true as that. When Muriel was mean-acting and turned their older sister, Jane, against her, she used to sneak off, sometimes, to where the burnt house had been, to play by herself. There was not a trace left—nothing charred, not even a scrap of soot—but she found a piece of broken saucer in the foundation, white china with a tiny embossed leaf, and kept it, hid it: just a slice of china, like a hop-scotch glass, a lucky one.

Poor Mrs. Leaman never set foot in the cemetery after her husband died—"She can't bear to see those wee stones," said Mum Wellman—so Aunt Aggie tended those graves. She planted a line of bleeding hearts, six of them, one for each—except for the twins, who shared because they were buried together.

Seven children were buried right under her feet, seven children who had died on the coldest night of the year. The stovepipe had caught fire in the closet upstairs.

"Sad wee things," said Susan Ann. "I hope you are happy with God in heaven."

When she stood up, she slyly stole a glance across the road. There he was still, perched up on the steeple, watching her every move.

"Ha," she thought, making her way back to the path and on towards the MacDonalds. "Now he'll wonder what *I'm* up to." She had a small package of soda crackers with her, and she fished around inside her bag until she found it, then opened it, took one out and began nibbling at it.

Something moved.

She saw it out of the corner of her eye, on the little hill over by the oldest graves. It startled her, so she stared to see what it was. A movement—something running from the bushes to hide behind a gravestone? "Probably a squirrel," she thought, although it had looked larger than that. She watched the spot for a few moments longer, but saw nothing.

"My old eyes must be playing tricks on me." But then, as she was turning away, there it was again! She was sure of it: something was up there, moving about in the bushes. It made her feel uneasy.

"A squirrel," she told herself, "or a chipmunk."

The very oldest, oldest grave was up in there, her great-great-grandfather, John MacDonald, who had come to this place from Cape Breton, the first settler. She could see it clearly on the rise, see the rounded top that she knew was a crudely carved death's head with scraggly-looking wings on either side; she had avoided it when she was a child and she would do so today, especially if there was an animal of some kind up there in the bushes. The skeletons on those old gravestones gave her nightmares.

Late in the night, Aunt Aggie sat on her bedside, quieting her fears, and told her that the dead were all together in heaven, where they sang hymns and prayed, and watched over her.

"Will Sally be there?"

"Of course," her aunt answered.

As Susan Ann started to make her way towards the grave-stones of those she was closest to, her nearest and dearest, she was overcome by the saddest feeling of yearning; it took her by such surprise that she stopped in her tracks right in front of Grampy MacDonald and his two wives. "Oh," she said, "oh," because she knew that they were all just ahead of her: her real father and mother, Daddy and Mumma Mac, and Aunt Aggie, Uncle Hay, and her Mum Wellman. She had thought about them so much, nearly every day of her life, she imagined, every single day for all these years, but the prospect of seeing their names in stone, and being here, walking on the earth above their very bones, this near-ness to them seemed like no nearness at all. She felt apart from them in a new and terrible way, felt farther from them than she had ever felt before.

The world had gone all still and quiet. The birds were silent now: the sparrow and the jay, the chickadee, the mourning dove—even the crow. There was not a breath of air, no sound of the wind in the trees, not the whisper of a leaf. Susan Ann looked all about her. It was as if the whole of the world were frozen, motionless; it seemed to her that she was all alone in this hushed-up world, that there could not be a soul around, not a living soul. So many of the things that she wanted to know about her own life were known by the people lying buried beneath her.

At that moment her eyes caught sight of something, a shape on the ground—a great huge anthill was growing square in the middle of Mum Wellman's plot. It stuck up above the grass, and was the size and shape of an ottoman. Something like that would take years and years to develop, she thought—it wouldn't just spring up overnight like a mushroom. And right overtop of poor Mum. The sight of it made Susan Ann feel sick.

The surface of the hill was bald and flat and brown; as she watched, dozens of ants were scurrying over it, running off on errands, carrying things. Dozens and dozens—there were probably hundreds of them living there. No, thousands. How far down into the earth would their tunnels go? Were there millions of ants deep down, running around on her poor mum's bones? Living their lives, laying their eggs? There would be a big fat queen in there somewhere—and that queen of the ants, would she have set up shop inside the earth, down in the coffin with Mum Wellman? Maybe even built her nest inside Mum's ribs? The thought of it made her shiver.

She walked around the anthill and went to kneel down beside the headstone. It was a smart-looking small rectangle of black, polished granite; Dad Wellman and Aunt Aggie had picked it out when he came back from Montreal. For more than fifty years, Susan Ann had felt terrible that she had not been able to attend Mum Wellman's funeral. She crouched down and began to trace the letters of Mum's name with her finger:

T E S S

She had seen the stone only a handful of times before, on those rare occasions when she and Jamie came up to New Brunswick

for a visit. The last time she was here had been with her friend
Ellen Firth, on their last jaunt together; they'd spent a week driving about the countryside, visiting each other's old haunts.

TESS LORRAINE MACDONALD

1887—1945

LOVING WIFE OF PAUL WELLMAN

PARTED BELOW

UNITED ABOVE

When the telegram came about Mum, Susan Ann had been
upstairs in the bedroom. She had just reread a letter that Mum
had sent her from the farm. It was the first warm day of spring,
and she had the window open. Jamie was at work at the plant, and
his mother was downstairs getting lunch. The baby was due in
two weeks and Susan Ann was the size of a house. She heard the
truck and went to the window and saw Ellen's husband walking
towards the front door. A few minutes later Hiram Firth was
driving back up the muddy lane, and Queenie called up to her,
"There's something down here for you. A telegram."

Her first thought had been of her brother Fred MacDonald,
who was overseas; poor Murd hadn't been gone all that long, not
Fred too! Would this war never end?

She was annoyed at Queenie for not coming up the stairs—
that whole thing was crazy, her never going upstairs again after
the night Jamie's father died.

"Please, God, not Fred, may it not be Fred," she prayed.

Coming down the stairs, she could feel it—like a stone slipping inside her. The baby wasn't due until the fifteenth of April.

And Queenie said, "I know it's your mother," because Hiram
had told her what was in the envelope. "I told Hiram to go to the
plant and get Jamie."

What an awful time that had been.

"Parted below, united above," she read, running her finger along the letters. Then she sighed. "But what if we aren't?"

Aunt Aggie had a little Bible with a soft black cover and gold letters. When she came to Ragged Islands, she kept it on the night table beside her bed. Inside the front cover it said:

> *To Margaret MacDonald*
> *from her Dearest Friend*
> *Martha Leaman*
> *Christmas 1907*
> *"May the Giver and Receiver Meet in Heaven"*

Susan Ann was thinking of this as she stood up and gently rubbed the top of Mum's stone. "Parted below, united above," she said again. It was as near to a prayer as she could muster. The years had worn away her old beliefs; even though her daughter thought she was silly and old-fashioned, she had become quite modern and ecumenical. She no longer believed in the heaven that her Aunt Aggie had believed in. She did not expect pearly gates and streets of gold, but as she stood there surrounded by the names and dates of her family, she realized that she did wish she could believe in those old-fashioned stories still. She wanted their certainty, for without it, where was comfort? "Parted below," she repeated, then went to pay her respects to her aunt and uncle.

HAZELTON JOHN MACDONALD
1895—1953

She remembered her Uncle Hay out in the farmyard, sitting there for hours, looking nervously towards the pasture and smoking. Aunt Aggie would go and kneel beside him, her hand on the chair back, and they would look out at the pasture together and talk so quietly, almost whispering.

"Don't bother your uncle, dear," her aunt would say. "You just run along and play." Because Susan Ann had wanted to ask him questions about France, about the King, about the shot that was fired in Sarajevo and heard around the world.

The first time she and Jamie had come up to the farm after Mum died, Uncle Hay held little Lorraine as if he were terrified of breaking her. "Wouldn't this one've made Tessie happy?" he said, in that strange, high voice of his.

"God's wee messenger," Aunt Aggie had said pointedly, and Hay had awkwardly handed the baby back to Jamie and left the room.

It was later, during the unhappy winter that she spent with Susan Ann down in Ragged Islands, that Aunt Aggie told her how Uncle Hay had talked about being in a trench in someone's field when he was in France, how he had been stuck in there for months on end. "It was just a little farm," she said, "no bigger than ours." In the field between him and the German line there were bodies, boys just left there to rot because no one could get to them. "In a place no different than our own back pasture."

She knew that her Uncle Hay had stopped believing in God altogether; he had seen such terrible things in the war, things he could hardly speak of, even to Aunt Aggie, and those things had taken away his faith. He stopped going to church because he wanted to be all alone on Sunday mornings, all alone to think about God, he told his sister; and then came that awful Sunday, while Aunt Aggie was singing in the choir as if it were any ordinary Sunday morning, that awful day when she had come home and found him in the shed.

MARGARET THEODOSIA MACDONALD

1892—1955

Their graves were so close together, and Susan Ann imagined them beneath her, imagined Aunt Aggie's bony hand reaching across, beneath the earth, to comfort her brother.

Would God forgive him and let him into heaven? Wouldn't it be only fair for Uncle Hay to be in heaven and happy again, just as he was before the war, when all his life stretched out before him, young and carefree?

Between her aunt and uncle and her grandfather with his two wives lay her MacDonald parents.

ROBERT FREDERICK MACDONALD

1890—1960

HIS WIFE

SARAH MILFORD

1889—1949

There had been no place for her in their house on Railway Avenue, not even, it seemed, when she only went for a weekend visit or a holiday. Why had they not raised her? It would have been more understandable if she had been the last, if there had been no one born and kept after her, but that wasn't the case. Why her and not Muriel, not Fred?

Daddy Mac worked at the CNR shops in Moncton with her Dad Wellman, but the most either one had ever said about the other was "He's a good worker." Considering that Dad Wellman had been a Catholic until he married Mum and that Daddy Mac had been as Mum said pointedly, "a real *good* Orangeman," Susan Ann had never expected more. Daddy Mac had always been a figure in the distance; he seemed, at times, so apart from his brothers and sisters on the farm that he could not have grown up with them. Had he always been that way, or had his marriage made him like that?

On those few times when she had screwed up the courage to try to talk to Mumma Mac, Mumma had become even more sarcastic than usual and Susan Ann had retreated, never daring to have any of the conversations she so badly wanted to have. Even the most inconsequential comments could lead to unhappiness. One Christmas when she was staying at Railway Avenue she said, "I've always wanted a red scarf," and Mumma said, "You don't know what you want, you never did," in such a definitive and nasty way that it implied that all red scarves were idiotic and that Susan Ann had been stupid since the day of her birth.

There was a cranky neighbour in Shediac named Elsie Steeves; she was as mean as could be to Susan Ann, and to Mum and Dad Wellman, too. Everyone in the whole family said so, but not Mumma Mac! "I think Elsie Steeves has had to put up with a lot," she said.

"But she hits Sally," Susan Ann started to explain.

"Where there's smoke there's fire," Mumma interrupted.

"But you don't understand!"

"That's enough out of you!" Mumma shot back. "No more backtalk!" and the subject was closed.

When Mumma Mac died, Susan Ann thought there might be a keepsake, some token that would be part of an explanation, but there was none. In later years Susan Ann tried to draw close to Muriel, but to no avail. When their father died, she hoped for some small thing—even a scrap of his handwriting—but the day before the funeral, when she and Jamie pulled into the driveway on Railway Avenue, Muriel's kids were screeching around a bonfire in the snow: the contents of Daddy Mac's bedroom. "He had more crap stowed away in there than you can imagine," said Muriel.

"Didn't you sort through anything?"

"For what? Nothin' in there worth keepin'!"

If there ever had been anything for Susan Ann in that house, it vanished on that day.

Her parents had been a mystery; even their stone revealed nothing. *His Wife*, it said, without an ounce of affection. "Well, I suppose she fared better than Lot's wife," she thought. "At least they carved out her name."

In her memories of Five Points she had thought of the dead sleeping, lying peacefully asleep, getting ready to awaken. She had thought of the Judgment as a kind of special Sunday morning, a day of happy resurrection and glorious reunion, as if the earth and grass were blankets and sheets, the headstones rows of bedsteads. But that was a Sunday school story; in truth, the earth below her was filled with worms and ants. Beneath her, the wood of their caskets was rotten and crumbling, the flesh was gone and their bones were being picked clean.

"They're lost," she thought. "Lost and gone forever."

And her own bones, too, beneath her skin. Soon they would be lying beneath the earth.

And then she was thinking of Jamie, and how she had loved to feel his shoulder bones, how she had loved his hip bones. When they were first married, when they were in bed and he was hovering above her, she had lifted up her hands and cupped those hip bones; his skin wonderfully warm and smooth. She had seized his hips, squeezed them tightly—thrilled that she had discovered something so exciting that there were no words to describe it, just the intensity of feeling. Those bones beneath his skin were part of a secret they shared. In middle age, when they were both packing on the pounds, those bones were cushioned in lovely softness. And before he died, those last months when the bones were horribly pronounced, as if they might push out, break right through the skin of his hips, she had caressed them so gently then.

In the hospital room in Bridgewater, after he died, after they left her there so that she could be alone with him for a few minutes, so that she could say goodbye, she just stood and stared at him, relieved that the ordeal was over, feeling so worn out and exhausted. She stared and stared and wished that he were living still, that he had never been sick, that things could be the way they had been years before—even one year before. He looked terrible, because he had been through hell. She thought she should kiss him but she didn't want to, and so she just stared. It didn't occur to her until later that she could have said a prayer.

When she was ready to leave, she turned away and then turned right back to him. She couldn't imagine that this was the last time she would be near his body. He would be taken away, and that would be that. Nearly forty years they had been together. She reached out and touched his face—it was warm and frozen—and then she ran her hands over him, his shoulder, his arm, his hip. He was so thin; those bones were never so close to her fingers. She thought of those terrible old pictures of the crucifixion, those old Catholic paintings where Jesus was so broken and dead that his bones were poking through his skin.

How strange that his body was still there but he was gone.

Her friends and family had been no comfort, the minister's eulogy had been no comfort: "And I John saw the holy city, new Jerusalem, coming down from God out of heaven, prepared as a bride adorned for her husband."

When she was a little girl, she had imagined Jerusalem floating down from the sky on a plate: a toy city with golden steeples and rows of marble buildings. But at Jamie's funeral, when the minister was reading, she sat there thinking of the pretty nightgown he had given her when they were unpacking on their wedding night. She had been a bride adorned by her husband, and she sat in that front pew regretting every single time they had not made love because she was too tired, or because he was, or because the kids or Queenie would hear them. She had sat through Jamie's funeral thinking that she was the most selfish person on the face of the earth, because all she could think about was sex and how it was finished for her. She had known how lucky she was to have him, but why had she not realized that *he* was the new Jerusalem? Now that he was gone, the holy city was gone. Would God punish her for the rest of her life for thinking something so sinful? She couldn't bear the thought that she would never again see his face coming out from under the covers, the grin on him as he lifted himself up and over her and rubbed his nose against hers like an Eskimo. The memory of the look on his face had filled her with such despair. What did she care about seeing the world any more, or watching her grandchildren grow up? She would never hold Jamie again, and anything else was worthless.

Caw-caw-caw!

Suddenly she was overwhelmed because everything was lost and gone. Jamie was gone, his house was sold, her family was mean, the farm was no longer standing, the necklace was stolen, the crow was mocking her—when she had set out this morning, she had done so with a certain amount of hope; she felt now that it was gone too.

"I might as well die right now," she said, "with no answers and no reward."

What kind of reward did she expect?

"What do you want?" she asked herself.

Mumma Mac's headstone taunted her: *You don't know what you want, you never did.*

There was a flurry of movement off to her side, less than twenty feet away, and she jumped. Was it that animal she thought she'd seen up on the crest by the old graves?

Caw!

It was that miserable crow, sitting on top of the anthill. At first she thought he was preening himself, but he was hunkering down into the hill as if it were a nest. He stretched his wings wide open and spread them out, then he was shimmying his body down, rubbing against the hill. The ants appeared to be crawling up and over him. He quivered and ruffled his feathers. Then his head lunged forwards, and he was picking up ants in his beak—dozens of them. Susan Ann couldn't understand it—if he wanted to eat them, why didn't he just stand there and peck at them? Why rub himself all over the top of the hill?

But he didn't seem to be eating them at all. He took the ants he had snatched up in his beak and, bending forwards, began rubbing them into his breast.

"That bird's gone crazy," she thought.

It was then she realized that the cameo necklace was lying on the grass beside the anthill, a little over a foot away from the crow.

Could she get over to it and grab it without the crow stopping her? If she tried, would he bite her?

He jabbed his beak at the hill again and grabbed more ants. Then, turning his head around, he began rubbing them over his wings and body. It looked as if he was tucking them in between his feathers, mashing them against him.

She set her bag down on top of Daddy and Mumma Mac's stone and began inching her way towards the necklace, making as few movements as possible.

The crow was shivering now, he seemed to be trembling. Susan Ann couldn't understand for the life of her what he was doing. He seemed to be oblivious of her as she moved slowly across the graves of Daddy and Mumma Mac, of Aunt Aggie, and Uncle Hay—

AWK!

He screeched so loudly that it startled her. She froze in her place, watching him nervously.

Awk!

He wasn't acknowledging her existence at all; he went on rubbing his feathers and hunkering down into the anthill. If he was aware of her, he wasn't showing it.

The necklace was only a few feet away. When she was younger, she would have been able to jump from where she stood and grab it in her hand. She took one step, then another, and then, a few feet from the anthill, she crouched down slowly and carefully and began crawling on all fours. She could see the cameo lady's head on a cushion of dandelion leaves.

Shifting her weight to her left hand, she raised her right one from the grass and began to lean forwards—

The necklace, so close, the necklace—her fingers were open, it was inches away—

Then the crow spun his head, finally noticing her there, glaring at her. Even though she thought he might fly right at her, she lunged forwards, grabbing—

She lost her balance, fell on her face, but the necklace was in her hand; she held it tight.

When she looked up at the crow, so close to her now, she thought he would squawk at her, but he didn't. They watched each other for a long moment. There were ants streaming up from the hill and onto his wings; the feathers of his breast seemed alive with them. She could not understand why this made him seem quite grand to her, but it did, grand and glorious.

"Mister Crow," she said finally. "This necklace belonged to my mum. She is buried right beneath us." The crow stretched his wings out, the tips of them scraping the hill. "I know that you found it, but I'm going to keep it."

He cocked his head slightly, eyed her. She could see bits of ant stuck to the side of his bill.

She watched to see if there was any reaction, but there was

none. He kept staring at her, then his body twitched and he shoved his beak into his breast feathers and pecked at an ant.

Susan Ann backed away on her knees, just a couple of feet, and she wondered if her behaviour was as mysterious to him as his was to her.

"Thank you," she said, and she stood up.

The crow said nothing; he shivered again, ignored her and began a fresh attack on the ants that were running all over him.

At Mum's grave, she opened her hand and studied the cameo. She traced the familiar profile with her finger. "Hello," she said, "hello pretty lady." She realized that the picture she had carried in her head of Martha Leaman contained these same delicately carved features.

"She had the loveliest hair you ever saw," her aunt had told her. The cameo seemed to contain all of the longing Susan Ann felt for that lost time when she was a girl.

Once it was fastened around her neck, she felt her spirits lift. "I want to go home," she said aloud, knowing, as soon as she said it, that this wasn't possible; Ragged Islands was a few hundred miles away, and she had no way to get there. Besides, Jamie's house had been sold.

"But you got this far," she told herself. And hadn't her great-great-grandfather walked here from Cape Breton, back before there were any roads, back when it was all woods? Hundreds of miles he'd travelled on shank's mare.

"You could do it in stages," she said. "If you went to Shediac first, that's fairly close by and on the way...."

And maybe there would be something for her there, in the old house on Inglis Street, the house that Dad Wellman built.

Her eyes were closed, her finger tracing the journey in the air. She might be able to get to Shediac by late today or early tomorrow. Maybe she would find someone there who could give her a drive. Or maybe someone from the Settlement would offer her a lift for part of the way, someone she had known, or their children or grandchildren. She thought of Ellen Firth's son and daughter, how they had always seemed to arrive at her house just when she needed them most:

"Would you like a ride on town, Susan Ann?"

"Yes, thank you kindly-kindly."

She walked out of the graveyard and set off down the road towards the river. It wasn't mid-morning yet, the weather was perfect, and it felt so good to be back here, to be walking along this road on such a fine, fine day. She was imagining the journey that lay ahead, all those familiar roads she had travelled. Possessing the necklace made her feel adventuresome.

Fairly soon, she came to a break in the woods, and was walking past fields of potatoes. Then a field of corn. She came upon a grassy meadow, and in it was a huge flock of blackbirds—so many that she stopped to look. Each bird was perched on a tall stem of grass; they were bobbing up and down like strange, dark flowers. They were startled suddenly by something she couldn't see. Leaping up into the air as one, they flew away.

"What could have made them do that?" she wondered.

A little ways afterwards, as she walked through another stretch of woods, she realized that she was not alone, she was being followed; she knew it because she could feel eyes watching her. Then she heard a noise, beside her, quite close by.

When she saw the flash of movement through the trees beside the ditch, she knew it was the thing that had been watching her in the cemetery. It was much bigger than a squirrel; it looked to be the size of a fox.

"Hello? *Stop!*"

When she heard a woman's voice behind her, she thought for a moment that someone might be offering her a ride. She turned to look.

There was someone back there walking quickly along the road towards her. She squinted her eyes, and even though she wasn't able to see clearly, her heart sank.

"Lorraine," she muttered. "It's that Lorraine. I know it. She's figured out where I am, and she's come to drag me back to that damn place to die."

"MUM, MUM?"

What?

"Mum? Are you awake?"

Lorraine? How could Lorraine be back already? What time was it?

"You're having a bad dream."

What was she talking about? What was she doing home?

Susan Ann had been up since the crack of dawn with the washing and dusting, then cleaning the floors all morning—she had just sat down on the chesterfield after lunch—had she slept away the whole afternoon?

Were the sheets still on the line? Had she done the breakfast dishes? Was supper started? Jamie'd be home from the plant before she knew it.

Oh no, did I take the hamburg out of the freezer?

"It's okay, Mum, it's okay. We're here, we're right here."

Dishes! There were still dishes in the sink!

"Should I get a nurse?"

"No, not yet. Mum? It's okay."

A nurse? Who was that there with Lorraine?

She was aware that fingers were stroking her hair, smoothing it back from her forehead, the hand was warm and gentle, yes, and the room, now she could see the room opening out—

But it wasn't the chesterfield, it wasn't the living room—

"Hi there." Lorraine was close by and looking down. "You awake now?"

Behind her, an awful wall—

Hospital!

"It's okay. Just relax."

No no, this was where Jamie died!

"Mum—"

The hospital—in Bridgewater?

"Just—"

Where's Jamie?

Lorraine's hands were on her forehead—

Bridgewater, Jamie, hospital—

Oh, wait, she was remembering now, wait, that was a while ago, wasn't it? She wasn't even in Nova Scotia any more.

Where?

"It's the hospital, Mum. You were having a bad dream, I think."

Now she remembered. They'd tied her up and they'd taken away her feet! They'd left her alone for hours on end, all night long, tied up with a rotten old leash.

"What was that?"

Tied me up like a dog.

"I'm sorry?"

Tied like a dog.

"You'd like a dog?"

"That can't be what she said."

"Oh, you don't know her and her dogs. Does he, Mum?"

Tied. Tied.

"You loved your old dogs."

With a leash of some kind. The nurses, they did it, they tied her up in the night.

"Remember Scamp? We were talking about her just the other day."

No not Scamp, no.

"The one you had when you were a kid? The one they were so mean about? A cocker spaniel, wasn't it?"

"Hello, Susan Ann."

Who's that? Peter. Peter and Lorraine. They must have called the ambulance. Susan Ann had been feeling a little woozy, and had gone to lay down on the chesterfield after supper. That glass of wine had been too much. But Lorraine must have gone and called the ambulance.

"How you feeling?"

She was just woozy, that's all. There had been no need. That awful racket, that siren going outside, and then men clomping snow all through the house and carrying her out of the door like a piece of furniture. That orange stretcher. There had been no need for all this fuss, she'd just gone to lay down.

"You want to go back to sleep? Sorry to disturb you, but you were really restless. Like you were having a nightmare."

I was on the chesterfield.

"You were calling out. We couldn't tell what you were saying."

She was tired, unable to catch her breath—

Hsssssssss

What in the?—

"That's just the oxygen, Mum. You've knocked it—Here—"

And Lorraine was fiddling with her nose. Oxygen again. Or was this the same time? The hospitals were confusing. Itchy thing, they stuck it right up her nose. That tube like a hard little long, long worm. Stupid itchy thing, how could she get rid of it?

Her hands weren't working, for some reason she could barely feel them. What'd they done to them?

"There. That's better."

Time to go home now. *Get me out.*

"Mum—"

Right now! I have to get cracking.

Because there was such a lot to do. Dishes, supper, the dusting—

"Just relax, Mum, try and relax."

But they were taking away her hands in here, she couldn't use them! And her feet—where were they?

"Calm down, just calm down. Ssh, ssh."

Wait, wait, what was?—

They'd stuck something in her arm too—a needle, a darn old needle stuck in there! Her nose, her arm—if they wanted to stick something in her why didn't they stick it up her ass? She hadn't had a decent BM in days. It was packed in there like cement.

Let me up, send me home—

"Mum, stop now."

No, you listen, I have to get to work!

"Tommy sends his love."

Tommy? Where's he?

"He phoned. He sends his love. And Meg will be by tomorrow."

Meg?

"Yes, Meg."

Oh—

"She said to tell you she's sorry. She told you *yesterday* that she would be in *tonight*, but she won't be able to come and visit you *until tomorrow.*"

Yesterday, did she see Meg yesterday? That didn't sound right. Maybe they'd talked on the phone?

But wait, didn't they have ice tea outdoors somewhere not too long ago? In a park of some kind?

"Here Gramma, let's sit over here."

Yes, they did; they drank sweet ice tea in a can, and they sat on a bench, and there were birdies and squirrels, and they sat on a bench and watched people walking their doggies. A warm day, not too muggy. Meg was going to visit that French fellow she met overseas, her boyfriend in Quebec. *What's his name?*

"Who?"

He had two names. Jean Claude. That was it, yes. Nice enough fellow. She only met him the once. But she and Meg sat on a bench and had their tea and that red bird, the Catholic one, it sat right above them. What's its name, that *red bird?*

"Did she say something about a bird?"

The red bird. *Cardinal!* That was it. Wait a minute, then. Just wait—

So this couldn't be the time that those ambulance men tracked all that snow through the house. She was sorry, she had things mixed up before. This wasn't wintertime, this was the *summer.*

"Summer, Mum?"

Wasn't it summer?

"It's September now, Mum. It's Sunday."

Sunday.

"Yes, you were admitted on Thursday. Can you remember?"

Thursday. Thursday. That was laundry day, Thursday morning, because there was hardly ever anyone else there. Thursday. She couldn't hang the clothes on a line any more and had to pay to use someone else's dirty old dryer. Thursday . . .

Wait, yes! Now I know!

She remembered how she had got there. She was too tired to get up because it was so hot, that was it, yes. She was lying there looking at the apartment and thinking there was little point in getting out of bed in all that heat, so she just hadn't bothered—

That's when you did it.

"Did what?"

Made that phone call.

"The telephone."

Yes. Lorraine came over to the apartment because she hadn't gotten out of bed to answer the phone. She had just let it ring and ring. She knew that if she didn't get out of bed, Lorraine would get worried and come over, but that was no reason to phone the ambulance. There was no need to get back at her for that. There were people who could really use this bed. Sick people.

No need for this.

"Now, don't start, please."

No need at all!

"You need to stay put for a while."

Why now, why was that?

"Because you need to stay here until you're strong enough to go home. You need to be where the doctor can keep an eye on you."

The doctor? What did she know? When they operated on her lungs, they did it on the kitchen table. People didn't run off to the hospital for every little thing in those days. That was a real emergency. *On the kitchen table.*

"The table?"

Yes. That old pine table Dad Wellman had made. Dr. Foster came to the house after supper and did the surgery right then and there.

Mum Wellman held onto my hand.

"Is this Shediac you're talking about now?"

Yes. Mum and Dad Wellman's house on Inglis Street. Right on that old kitchen table. She would have died if they hadn't. For years afterwards, Mum said, "We were worried sick we'd lose you."

It had hurt, too! They took out part of a rib to get at the lung to drain it. *Empyema*, they called it, *pleurisy*.

"Mum?"

Pleurisy. No one even got that any more.

"I'm sorry but . . ."

What?

"I'm sorry, dear, but it's so hard to hear you."

Was she mumbling?

"You mean a time when you were living with the Wellmans?"

Yes, yes, yes, and they had done it all on the kitchen table. There was no need to be here in this old hospital. No need at all. *I want to go home.*

"You have to stay here till you're well enough."

I was home with pleurisy!

"Now Mum, now—"

"Maybe she'd like some jelly salad?"

"Yes. Peter, go wash this spoon off for me, will you, and I'll get some ready."

She didn't need any old salad, she didn't feel like it. Back then she was much sicker than this. Dr. Foster cut her wide open and hacked at that rib.

"Are you comfortable?"

It hurt like hell.

"Hurts? Where?"

On the kitchen table!

"Okay, okay, shh now."

People went to the hospital now for the least little thing. If a kid fell down and scraped his knee, his parents dragged him off to Outpatients. *No need for this, no need at all.* She wasn't sick, she was old and tired, period. *This is nothing.*

She'd never felt so awful as she did that spring and summer, her lung filled up, her chest so heavy, lying there in the bed, drowning.

Mum and Dad Wellman said, "Be brave! Be brave!" And she was, because she knew that God had sent the pleurisy, it was His plan, a test to show them that even though she was sickly, she was worthy.

All those nights back then she couldn't sleep, and she was frightened because there were bull faces like devils in the flowered curtains. They watched and snorted in the moonlight, their horrible eyes glaring at her. Other people thought they were roses, but their ugly faces jumped right out of the pattern the first moment she saw them in the dark. As she lay there at night, they laughed at her, made fun of her. They moved in the breeze from the open window, drifting across the room towards the bed, all the while whispering, "Nobody loves you, nobody," and "Stupid stupid stupid."

Len and Boyd would come to her bedside when she called them—her stepbrothers were so kind—but she couldn't call in the middle of the night, and she didn't want to wake up little Murd, and nighttime was when the devil faces snickered and sneered. She was too old for Dolly, but Susan Ann hugged her anyway. Sally wasn't allowed upstairs to visit because she was sick. And it was at the worst of all that mess with poor Sally and Elsie Steeves.

Mean old thing!

"What's that?"

Elsie Steeves.

She was a rotten, miserable woman to be mean to Sally, and mean to Mum Wellman. She came into the yard, the rotten old thing, she came right into the yard, right up onto the steps, swinging that damn cane of hers.

"Don't stick out your tongue at her! You're no better than she is when you do that!"

The one and only time Mum Wellman lost her temper with her, she slapped Susan Ann and sent her to her room. "Don't make me ashamed of you ever again!"

She made Mum lose her temper. She disappointed Mum Wellman, who really loved her, who really wanted her.

"You're no better than she is when you do that!"

But Elsie, but—*she came into the yard!*

"—tired?"

What?

"I said, 'Are you tired?'"

Am I tired? Yes.

"Go back to sleep."

She was trying to sleep, she wanted to sleep. It was so hard with those things watching her. "*Nobody loves you, nobody.*"

Make them stop.

"Who? Make who stop?"

Curtains.

"The curtains?"

Yes. No one could see the devil faces but Susan Ann. Those nights were the longest nights of her life.

Dr. Foster told Mum, "She's such a brave little soldier." He was a famous doctor, too, Mum said. She was teasing, because he was in a book of nursery rhymes:

> *Dr. Foster went to Gloucester*
> *In a shower of rain.*
> *He stepped in a puddle*
> *Right up to his middle—*

There was no need for the hospital, no need at all. There was a scar on her back to prove it.

Not quite a scar, a soft dent halfway down her back. Jamie used to kiss it.

"I'm going to fix your pillow, get you feeling more comfortable. Straighten out these sheets."

She wanted Jamie to rub her neck. He used to kiss her neck, all up and down her back; he would lick that scar, flick it with his tongue. "No, it's not ugly. Is it ticklish?"

Jamie's fingers, his mouth, how much she trusted him.

Her sister Muriel would tease her about that scar and say miserable things. She waited until Aunt Aggie and the others were busy and then she would trick Susan Ann into the barn and tickle and torment her. When both her MacDonald sisters came up to the farm, sometimes Muriel would get Jane to gang up with her and they would hold Susan Ann down inside the barn and tickle her, Muriel bouncing up and down on her stomach while Jane laughed and laughed. She never gave them the satisfaction of knowing how much she hated it, how upset she really was.

My own sisters.

And she knew that she had to keep that panic well hidden so no one would see it, because if they did, then things would be worse. She would lie on the barn floor like a stick, Muriel bouncing up and down on top of her. "Don't touch the hole in her back! She'll give you pleurisy!"

And that one time, Muriel bouncing up and down, her big fat carcass, when Daddy MacDonald came into the barn. "Get up, Susan Ann, get up from there!" as if it were all her fault, as if she could even think of moving with that great big lug on her.

"Get up!"

I can't!

"Get up! Do as you're told!"

Why doesn't he help me? Why, why? Isn't he my father?

And panic, that awful panic pressing down—

Get off me you great fat thing!

"Calm down, shh, calm down."

There's something—something—

"Calm down."

Something was pulling her down—what?

"Calm now, shh. . . ."

She was in bed and awake and her eyes were shut tight because she didn't want to see the devil faces in the curtains.

"Mum?"

What was—Who was touching her head?

Lorraine?

Oh. The hospital.

"I'm sorry, Mum, but you seem so upset. Do you know who I am?"

What? Don't be crazy!

"You were talking about Aunt Jane."

She didn't think she'd been talking.

"Tell her about Carl."

Carl? What about Carl?

"That'll do it, look."

Where's Carl?

"The mere mention of the Prodigal Son makes you perk right up, doesn't it?"

Don't make fun of me, where's your brother?

"We talked to them late last night."

Where?

"Vancouver. He called to see how you're doing."

Carl called? He called to see how his mother was doing? Thank you God.

"Just after we got home from seeing you."

When was this?

"Last night. Carl called us *last night* to see how you were."

Why couldn't he call his mother himself if he wanted to know so badly?

"They send their love."

They?

"Carl and Bonnie."

Bonnie? That sounded familiar.

"You know Bonnie."

Yes, yes, his wife, Bonnie. She was stupid to forget Bonnie. Stupid stupid stupid—

Oh, but that poor little Bernice, she was the one. *Poor Bernice.*

"Bernice? That was ages ago. She was his first wife."

She was fully aware of that. She knew perfectly well who Bernice was. Bernice ended up down near Cape Sable Island with all those wild Baptist relations of hers.

"Bonnie sends her love. I talked to her last night, too. And Carl and I had a long chat."

Were her kids talking to each other now? They used to fight all the time. When they were growing up, they could never agree on anything. They teased each other from the time they could talk.

"Greg's doing well, they said."

Greg.

"Yes, Greg."

Greg, the grandson who had never sent a thank-you card in his life. But blame what's-her-name Bonnie for that—thank-you cards, they were a mother's territory.

"He's in Banff."

Banff? That miserable place. They dragged her up the side of some fool mountain. He was still there? Some trip that was. All that dry heat—her skin went all cracked and funny. Greg sulking in the back seat beside her, reading comic books. She'd given up wondering about him a long time ago, the little boy in the school photographs that used to arrive in the mail, one every two or three years. Carl stopped sending them before the kid was even in high school. Terrible, the way your own grandson could be a stranger. Never a word of thanks, not one birthday, not one Christmas. Why even bother sending him any more cards and money?

Oh well, but at least he didn't send them back. Poor Bernice. And little Melody, a wild Baptist now too, probably. Jamie and Susan Ann's first grandchild. Then who could blame her? She didn't have an easy time of it, not with that crazy old mother of hers. *Poor Bernice.*

"What's with you and Bernice this morning?"

What do you mean?

"Did you hear me tell you that he'll be here tomorrow?"

What?

"Mum? Carl. He'll be here tomorrow."

Carl? He's coming here? Then I need to get back home right away!

"Now, just—"

She couldn't have company come when she was stuck in a place like this!

"Mum—"

She wanted a real visit with Carl, not some half-assed thing with him sitting there not knowing what to say. Men hated going to the hospital to see anyone; Lorraine knew that. It would be uncomfortable as hell.

"He's arriving in the afternoon."

There wasn't much time then. If she got home today, what could she give him for a treat? Those Chinese chews he loved so much! Oh, but were there any raisins in the pantry? Was there any icing sugar? Glory be to God, was she all out of dates? *Where are the dates?*

"The date? This is the ninth—"

No, no, dates like date squares!

"He got a flight yesterday and he'll arrive tomorrow and come straight here. On the tenth."

But I want him to visit me at home.

Carl could sleep on her daybed. No, he could have her bed and she would sleep there. And it wouldn't hurt him to look after her a little if she was feeling under the weather, God knows she sat up with him enough times.

"You need to stay put for a while. Until you're strong enough to go home."

I'm ready *right now*.

"Mum—"

It wasn't fair, Carl finally coming to see her while Lorraine had her stuck away and tied up like some old dog.

"Look, Mum—"

But she wasn't listening. She didn't care what Lorraine had to say—all that *yak-yak-yak*—

Susan Ann had shut her eyes. Her son was coming to see her and so she started making plans.

HE'D TURNED ON *the television a few times, but always found himself zipping through channels, relentlessly punching the remote, with no desire or ability to actually light anywhere. It all felt unreal—the nightmare images from that morning playing over and over again, like movie previews.*

He should've stayed at home until everything was over with, finished and done. Besides, God only knew how long he'd be stuck in Toronto now. "Here for the duration," he said aloud, mimicking his mother's old-fashioned country lingo.

At ten o'clock, he was back on the floor beside his mother's bed. The wastepaper basket was filling up; she'd saved so many useless, stupid things: thank-you cards, church service programs, phone bills from Ragged Islands, scraps of nothing. A piece of scribbler paper with a definition carefully printed on one side:

ZUGENRUHE *pron* ZOO GEN ROO HA
THE RESTLESSNESS OF CAGED BIRDS IN
MIGRATORY SEASON

And on the other side, an old grocery list:

dates	gold raisins	gr clove
br sug	ice sug	cinnamon
lard	butter	nutmeg

Carl found a Christmas card from Uncle Boyd; his mother's stepbrother was a relative that Carl had always liked.

Happy holidays and all the best for 1962
Love Joyce and Boyd

1962. Boyd's father had died in 1961; Carl remembered this because his mother always said that she lost her Dad Wellman in a year that read the same way when you turned it upside down.

Inside the card was a letter.

Boyd wrote about the difficulties of the old man's last months: of how he would get lost on his morning walks, of how, near the end, he would confuse his daughter-in-law with his dead wives. Boyd also wrote about his own childhood, of the two years following his young mother's death when he and his brother, Len, were sent to live in the orphanage in Saint John. They were only allowed to see their father at Christmastime, in the convent parlour, while grumpy-looking nuns knit mittens and glared at them.

As he read, Carl began to realize that the letter was responding to something that his mother had written:

I wish I knew the answer to your question, dear, but I do not. It is not something that Dad ever talked about. He and Mum used to roll their eyes when they talked about your father because he was such a "good Orangeman." Your Daddy Mac gave Mum a book one time that I remember because it had pictures that showed tunnels between convents and monasteries. I was too young to understand what it was getting at and Mum was upset at me for looking at it.

Sad to say, I have very few memories of your "real" mother. Mumma Mac stayed pretty close to home, it seemed. Your father usually came to visit on his own. I do remember her coming to the house when you were so sick that time. I remember looking through the door and seeing them all kneeling by your bed.

I do not think I ever really thought too much about why you came to live with us. It seemed right at the time, that we were all living in the same house. Len and I were just so happy to be back home and away from those rotten sisters of charity and having a little sister arrive felt like a bonus. You were like a toy to us. Len always kept things to himself, he didn't have a big mouth like yours truly (haha) but he worshipped you. I still remember the day you learned to walk. He was so proud of you. Little Murd, too. He was a fine fellow, our Murd. Dad and I went to the ceremony at the cenotaph up here every November 11 to remember him. At the end of the ceremony, he would cross himself. Old habits die hard.

Most of my memories of when you were little are about how much Mum Wellman doted on you. Remember when she flew at old Elsie Steeves after little Sally was taken away? She was as mad as an old bear that time. She was quite the gal! Len and I both knew how lucky we were from the word Go.

Carl glanced through the letter again, but there was no other mention of Sally, no real clue to her identity.

When he was a kid, Boyd and Joyce would come for visits to Ragged Islands; despite his mother's insistence otherwise, they always slept in their camper trailer beside the house, saying, "No, Sis, there'll be no arguments. We're not going to put you out." Boyd seemed happy-go-lucky, always calm and reasonable about the sort of things that would send Carl's father through the roof, inconsequential things: the cup that slipped from Carl's hands and broke, the hat forgotten outside in the rain, the lost toy.

After his marriage to Bernice had ended—a bad, stupid marriage that his father had convinced him was the right thing to do—Carl had left Nova Scotia. On his way west, he had spent two days with his aunt and uncle in Montreal. He remembered the square house on Fortieth Avenue in Lachine—the small bedroom where his Grandfather Wellman had slept, the walls in the dining room covered with Aunt Joyce's teaspoon collection in mahogany frames that Boyd had made for her in his basement workshop. After the supper dishes were cleared, his uncle put a photo album on the table, and they looked at pictures of Shediac: the house on Inglis Street that Grandfather Wellman had built, the boat that was named the Susan Ann. There were pages of photographs of the famous day when Italian airships landed in Shediac Bay on their way to the 1933 Chicago World's Fair. In one of them his mother and his Uncle Murd, a gawky teenage girl and her adolescent brother, were standing on the beach in a great crowd of people, all of them pointing at a line of big black dots in the sky. Boyd stood apart from them, young and handsome, with his arm around Joyce.

His uncle showed him another picture of his mother and Murd, when they were both young adults. They were beside each other in the back of a rowboat with the Pan Am Clipper floating in the water of Shediac Bay, a short distance behind them. The first time he watched Raiders of the Lost Ark with his son, Carl froze the video frame when the seaplane appeared and said, "A plane like that used to land in your grandmother's hometown back in New Brunswick. It stopped there on the way from New York to London."

The next time they watched the movie, when Carl said, "Here comes that scene with the Pan Am Clipper," Greg had moaned and said, "We know, Dad, we know," as if Carl had been boring everyone with that story for years.

Before he left Lachine, Uncle Boyd had driven him to the cemetery where Grandfather Wellman was buried. While they stood by the grave-

stone, his uncle told him that his own mother was buried in Shediac, in the Catholic graveyard, and his stepmother, Mum Wellman, was buried near the farm at MacDonald Settlement, "and Dad's up here," Boyd said sadly. "All alone, all three of them."

THE BROKEN BOWL

What had Lorraine gone and done to herself? Was she dyeing her hair again? She hadn't worn it down long like that since her kids were little, and she was way too old for some hippie hairdo.

But she'd been wearing her hair really short these days, Susan Ann was certain. Yes, cut real short. So was that a wig she had on, or one of those things, what were they called? A fall. Had she dug out that old fall she used to wear in university? What in the name of God was she thinking?

Then Susan Ann realized that the person walking towards her was moving along far too smartly to ever be Lorraine, who had always dragged her feet; this could not possibly be her daughter. She squinted her eyes to try and see better. Whoever was approaching her was far younger, and her hair was dark and wild-looking. She was carrying something white in each of her hands. When she came closer, Susan Ann could see that they were two halves of a large china bowl.

"Have you seen anyone on the road?" she called out. There was an edge of desperation in her voice.

"Only you," replied Susan Ann.

The girl was much more slender than Lorraine had ever been, and her clothes were black and dirty. "I'm looking for my family," she said. "You haven't seen anybody?"

"Not a soul."

Susan Ann looked closely at the young woman. She had a pretty face, quite delicate and pale, although she seemed unwashed and fairly filthy: one of her cheeks had a dark smudge that ran from the corner of her mouth up to her temple. Her eyes were too dark to be blue, they were midnight, and Susan Ann couldn't help but look into them. It was the oddest feeling—she wasn't aware of being stared back at; she felt as if she were looking into the deepest thing imaginable, a well that went down so far there was little chance of seeing anything reflected in it, not even the sky.

"How long ago did they go missing?"

The girl looked uncertain, and then she lifted her hands to stare at the two pieces of broken china. They looked as though they would fit together perfectly; the break was even and clean, it could be glued. The curious thing was that the broken bowl looked familiar to Susan Ann; she knew that she had seen it before somewhere. Long ago, on a shelf perhaps, or a side table. Which house had that been in? There was an embossed pattern around the sides, tiny leaves and vines tangled in a ring of garlands. It was a bowl that no one ever used, and it always had the same thing in it, something peculiar, like homemade wax fruit. She couldn't quite place it yet.

The girl looked strangely at what she was holding, as if the two halves of the bowl had appeared suddenly and she was wondering how she had acquired them. "I've lost them," she said. "They're nowhere to be found."

"Did your family go off without you?"

"What will my mother do to me now? She'll say it's all my fault. I'm always the one."

For some reason Susan Ann had thought the girl was searching for her parents. "Who did you lose?" she asked.

"My brothers and sisters."

"You were left in charge?"

"I am *always* left in charge!" This was said with a great deal of bitterness.

"But they haven't been out all night?"

The girl didn't answer her; she stood in the middle of the road and called out, "Randall!" She waited for a moment, then she shouted, "Randall? Rebecca!"

A shiver went through Susan Ann.

"Ewan? Charlotte?"

A shiver went through Susan Ann because she knew right away where she had seen that bowl before. It had been on the shelf in the kitchen of Mrs. Leaman's sister-in-law's house at MacDonald's Settlement. There had been wooden apples and pears inside it, and they were frightening because they were such crude, ugly things—they had been carved by Mr. Leaman after the fire, before he died of a broken heart. The bowl was famous because it was all that was left—everything else had been lost in the blaze. It had been spared because Mrs. Leaman had forgotten it at her sister-in-law's after a church group meeting. No one was allowed to take it off the shelf, ever.

"Randall? Rebecca? Ewan? Charlotte?" She was looking up and down the road and off into the fields.

Susan Ann wasn't sure what to do or say, so for a long moment she stood and did nothing. She heard a crow call from far away, his call fading as he flew away farther. The girl was looking at the two pieces of bowl again, as if a meaning and purpose might be gleaned from staring at them, twisting and turning her hands slowly to examine each piece separately, all the while never attempting to try to fit the two back together. To Susan Ann it was like watching a fly crawl back and forth over the same inescapable patch of window screen, and it seemed to her that her own presence on the road had barely been noticed; the girl was behaving as if she were all alone.

This moment went on for a long time, and then, without lifting her face to look at Susan Ann, the young woman began to speak.

"I was asleep and dreaming about my birthday," she said, "when Charlotte woke me up. *'Something's burning,'* she whispered. Rebecca was coughing in her sleep. When I opened the bedroom door, the upstairs hall was filled with smoke. I started calling out the boys' names. I couldn't get to their room. Rebecca was awake and crying, and I told her that she would have to be brave. I told her that I had to go and get the twins and that she and Charlotte were going to break the window and jump out into the snow. Charlotte picked up the washstand and was smashing the glass."

Susan Ann didn't know what to say.

"The snow was deep and soft. I know they got away."

Susan Ann could not take her eyes from the girl's face. Beneath all that dirt, she was so very beautiful.

"I took the washcloth from the dresser and covered my nose and mouth, then I went into the hall. Flames were everywhere. I kept calling the boys' names over and over. The stairs were on fire and I knew that Randall and Ewan would have to jump out their window above the front door. So I started shouting that, too. *'Jump out the window! Randall! Ewan! Jump out the window!'* The fire was so *loud*. I couldn't tell if I could hear the babies crying or not. I hoped the fire was only at the front of the house. If it was, I could grab the babies and go through the far door and wake Mother and Papa. But as soon as I stepped into the babies' room, everything there—"

She stopped speaking, and was staring so intently across the road that Susan Ann squinted to see what she could be looking at. Was something over there in the fields, watching them? She couldn't see anything but long grass and spruce. When she looked back, the young woman was staring at the broken bowl again.

"Everything. Everything everything," she repeated. "The curtains on the window, the hooked rug on the floor. The needlepoint alphabet I worked on for so long. My mother's Bible in the table beside the bed. She would read it while the twins were sleeping. She was so fussy about that thing—we weren't allowed to put anything on top of it, not even a flower. She told me that it was called The Holy Bible because it was so sacred and special. But it was burning too, same as everything else."

Susan Ann had a sudden urge to hold her, to move close beside her, to put her arms around her and hold and comfort her the way she had been able to with her own children when they were young.

"Everything, the whole thing."

"But the twins?" asked Susan Ann.

"The bed was a bonfire. I reached into it and grabbed Harvey and Hugh and held them close." She was standing so still, and hugging the two broken pieces of china tight to her chest.

Susan Ann shuddered, and was about to take a step towards her when she turned suddenly and moved away, crossing to the other side of the road and calling, "Randall! Rebecca!"

It broke Susan Ann's heart.

"Ewan! Charlotte! Randall?" She waited but there was nothing, not even an echo. And then, unexpectedly, she angrily hurled one half of the bowl into the ditch. What a frail thing she was, and so pale! Her skin was like milk. And her hair! The luxuriant thick darkness of it! Susan Ann couldn't remember the last time she had felt close to someone in this way—how she wanted to move closer and reach out and comfort her, to kiss her. The girl's sighs were so soft and tender; she was rubbing away the first wet on her cheek with the palm of her empty hand. Was she going to cry?

Her sadness was so large and important that everything else seemed small beside it.

When she was a little girl, how Susan Ann had yearned for Martha Leaman! She had played alone on the foundation stones of the burnt house and imagined Martha playing beside her. She had pretended to talk to her so many times, telling her stories about Mum and Aunt Aggie. Susan Ann had been the thread secretly running between those friends, secretly joining the living and the dead. She had stood out in the yard at night, imagining that the seven Leaman children were the stars in the Big Dipper over the roof of the barn. She remembered the sadness and longing in Aunt Aggie's voice when she said, "Oh Susan Ann, she had the loveliest hair you ever saw."

And it was.

But was it lovely despite its unkempt wildness or because of it? Did she seem even more beautiful because her face and clothes were smudged with dirt and soot? Susan Ann could not take her eyes from Martha Leaman; in all her beauty and her sadness, she seemed to shimmer.

Susan Ann's own sadness seemed unworthy, all of a sudden, and small. It had no true beginnings, but was a makeshift thing, all patched together. She'd gathered bits and pieces of it from overheard whispers on the stairs at the farm and at Railway Avenue; from conversations that ended when she came into rooms; from an ache that sometimes turned to unreasonable jealousy as she watched baby Murd sleeping under his wee quilt; from Mumma Mac's terrifying scowl; from her own children's recent neglect. Her own sadness was so unsatisfying because no one had had any patience for it since Jamie died; no one else ever wanted to understand it or care about it, not even her friend Ellen Firth, who used to get impatient and say, "Why do you allow yourself to get so stewed up over the past?" Her children had always wished it would just go away because it embarrassed them. Her own mother cared so little, and she had cared so deeply, and what difference had that made? Her children had abandoned her at the end just as surely as Mumma Mac did at the beginning.

Martha was standing by the roadside staring helplessly into the ditch. After a moment, Susan Ann went and stood beside her. She watched a tear streak through the smudge of soot on that beautiful young cheek. How she wanted to touch that cheek with her finger, to taste the sadness of each tear. She wanted that sadness, wanted to know it, to wrap herself up inside it. For Martha Leaman's sadness was boundless. And because she was so young and lovely, and because her sadness had descended upon her with such a terrible fury, people would always be forgiving, would always give in and indulge her, in the same way that everyone had always been kind and generous to poor Mrs. Leaman sitting in the rocking chair in her sister-in-law's kitchen, sitting there staring at that bowl of ugly carved fruit.

Susan Ann was thinking, "If that sadness were mine, I could be so happy."

Martha was scratching at the broken edge of the remaining half of the bowl with her dirty thumbnail. Susan Ann shifted her body towards her and said, "I remember your mother."

Martha looked over at her as if she were seeing her for the first time, sizing her up, and then she seemed to shrug her shoulders ever so slightly, and her eyes went back to the ditch. Susan Ann had thought it was dry, but she could see now that there was a trickle of water running through it, washing over the white shard.

"She always sat with her head down in church, and sometimes we would go visit afterwards at her sister-in-law's. There was a bowl just like that one, on the shelf beside her."

Martha's nail was flicking back and forth against the broken edge.

"I remember coming away this one afternoon, and hearing my aunt say that she wasn't so much living as putting in her time."

Flick flick flick—making a dull plucking sound.

"She was just so sad and lonesome."

Martha's shoulders lifted again in a mean little shrug. Susan Ann hesitated, uncertain how to continue.

Then, without lifting her head to look at her, Martha began to speak. "Mother sits around all day in her dark little corner feeling sorry for herself while I'm the one out roaming the countryside looking for them! I'm still the one doing all the work!"

"There, there." When Susan Ann moved a little closer, Martha did not turn away from her. Softly she leaned forwards, and gently kissed Martha's cheek. The skin was surprisingly cold.

Martha did not move; she did not acknowledge the comforting gesture at all. "Sometimes," she said, "I think Randall and Ewan took my sisters and the babies, and they're all off somewhere having a fine time without me."

"No, I don't think they would do that to you."

"What do you know?" Martha said, impatience and irritation in her voice.

Susan Ann thought she saw a movement in the field beyond the ditch. "I know what it's like to feel unwanted and left out," she said.

"*Ha!*"

Why did she sound so exasperated and spiteful? "My mother didn't want me," Susan Ann continued, "so she gave me away."

"Who to?" Was there a trace of interest hiding behind the sarcasm in her voice?

"To my father's sister."

"To an old maid?"

"No, she was married, she'd just gotten married to a man named Paul Wellman. A widower with two sons."

Martha looked at her curiously. "And they were mean to you?"

"Oh no, Mum and Dad Wellman loved me very much. They adopted me."

"You were well treated?"

"Yes."

"Then don't start talkin' to me about being *unwanted*."

Martha was glaring at her now, in a manner both condescending and disdainful. When had someone last looked at her that way? Not her children, they wouldn't dare. Not even Jamie's mother had been so cold. Queenie had hardly looked at her at all, in fact; when she spoke to Susan Ann, her eyes were usually fixed on Jamie. Not since she'd been with Mumma Mac in the house on Railway Avenue had anyone been so directly scornful. Susan Ann couldn't bear it; she turned and looked down at the ditch. The water was two or three inches deep, covering the bottom half of the broken bowl.

"Don't *you* talk to *me*," Martha said, with such contempt that Susan Ann wanted to disappear. She looked off into the fields. She saw something skitter in the tall grass—a rabbit?—then something else moving behind it. Two rabbits?

No, something was after the rabbit; something was chasing it.

"What's that you've got around your neck?" Martha asked suddenly.

Susan Ann's hands jumped up to protect the necklace. "Why?"

"Because I'm pretty sure I know what it is. Show it to me."

But for some reason, Susan Ann was determined to keep the cameo lady hidden. "It's a necklace that my mum gave to me," she said, as calmly as possible. Then she said, "Look, there's something out there."

"Don't change the subject!"

"But there is—an animal of some kind!"

"Where'd you get that necklace from!" It wasn't so much a question as a command.

"It was my Mum Wellman's! Now stop, you're frightening me!"

"She's not your mother she's your aunt, you just told me that, and you're a liar! I know that necklace. It's a cameo and Tessie MacDonald borrowed it from me and never gave it back. Give it to me!"

"No!"

"It's rightfully mine. She was jealous because her sister gave it to me."

This couldn't be true; Susan Ann had never heard of this at all.

"That Tessie was jealous and sneaky because Aggie was my true friend. Hand it over. *Right now!*"

Martha took a step towards her, and Susan Ann pushed at her, terrified that there would be a struggle and she would lose the necklace.

"Aggie gave that necklace to me on my very last birthday." Martha was lowering her head, as if she were about to come at Susan Ann and butt her. "Give it here!"

"*No!*" she shouted. "It belonged to my mum!" And she slipped the handbag off her shoulders and held the straps tight in her fist; she would swing it and hit out if necessary.

Martha glared at her. "You're a *snake*, just like she was."

"She was not!"

"A *snake* and a *liar* and a *thief*," said Martha, flinging down the remaining half of the bowl to smash on the road at Susan Ann's feet. "You deserve to be alone and miserable!" She stuck out her tongue, making a horrible face; then, spinning on her heel, she turned and crossed to the other side of the road.

"Mum Wellman was no snake!"

But Martha didn't even turn her head. She jumped onto the bank on the far side of the road and scrambled up through the grass and weeds. She lost her footing, slipped, nearly falling, then righted herself and stomped out into the field. As she went storming towards the woods on the far side, she started calling out, her voice angry and crazy-sounding, "*Randall! Rebecca!*" She seemed small all of a sudden, a tiny figure struggling through waist-high grasses, her voice growing fainter as she moved farther away. "*Ewan! Charlotte! Randall! Rebecca! Ewan! Charlotte!*" She shouted the names over and over until she could barely be heard.

Susan Ann wiped her face with the back of her hand, then clutched her fingers around Mum's necklace. Was there any truth to what Martha had said? Was the cameo lady a token of her friendship with Aunt Aggie, a friendship that had made Mum jealous? But Aggie and Mum had both been close to Martha—at least, that was what Susan Ann had been told, and what she had always believed.

Where, exactly, had Mum gotten the necklace? Hadn't it been in Mum's possession from way, way back, from long before she married Dad Wellman? Or was it a gift from him? Somehow, Susan Ann had never associated it with Dad. So where had she imagined it coming from? A childhood beau? Some long-lost boy? Or was it something Mum had purchased for herself? When she left the farm and went to Moncton to work at Eaton's, was it something that she had bought for her own self?

No, it had always seemed to Susan Ann that it was far older than that.

What was that word her granddaughter had used when they'd talked about old things and where they came from? It started with a P. Like *province* but a little longer, with an extra syllable. *Providence*. No.

Provenance. Yes, that was it. What was the cameo lady's *provenance*?

Fragments of the bowl were lying on the pavement all about her feet, gleaming in the sunlight, completely shattered—it would be a hopeless task to try to glue them together. She bent down and picked up a tiny piece. One side was smooth, with a leaf embossed on it. It made her think of a hopscotch glass, of scratching out squares in the dusty farmyard and playing with her sisters.

Water was running in the ditch now, like a brook. The other piece of broken bowl was gone—it had been covered by the water or swept away.

Martha was gone now too, she had disappeared into the woods and could no longer be heard. How long had she been looking for her brothers and sisters? Would she just go on looking until the end of time?

Susan Ann tossed the china leaf into the ditch and watched the water carry it away.

"Am I like her?" she thought. "A poor dead soul roaming the countryside?"

But that couldn't be. She couldn't be dead. That couldn't have happened. How could she have died and not remember? She was standing quite still, wondering what she should do next and where she should go, when she was aware of a sound, something breathing on the side of the road. She peered into the field, unable to see a thing. But then a movement, something darting through the bushes across the ditch. It was a good size, too.

A large branch snapped so loudly that she practically jumped out of her skin. She turned back quickly to the road and began walking.

She was all confused now and didn't know what she should do. "You stupid ass," she muttered. "You stupid stupid ass!" There was nothing to do but keep going towards Shediac, that was all she could do. "I can't be dead," she thought. "If I died, I'd remember. I *know* I would."

While she walked, she was aware of the animal thing, whatever it was, moving beside her in the bushes, running through the weeds in the deep ditch. She could hear it panting, she could hear its body tearing through the high grass. When she glanced to the side, she could see nothing. She stopped to take a really good look.

That was when she heard something growl, and quite close nearby. "Oh God," she thought, because the growl was deep and menacing, like the warning a wild animal would make before it attacked. Her hand lifted to touch her neck, to feel for Mum's cameo necklace, tucked inside her blouse like a good luck charm. "The Lord is my shepherd," she began, "I shall not want."

She crossed a bridge over a stream, and walked past a hayfield; all the while, that animal never moved ahead of her, but kept veering off to the side or running behind. "Yea though I walk through the valley of the shadow of death," she said as she entered a stand of hardwoods. She heard crashing through the underbrush. Beyond the wood, she walked along a pasture where a dozen or more cows were gathered around a blue salt lick. They lifted their heads in her direction, staring, then turned and bolted to the far side of the field.

WHEN HE SAW THE HOMEMADE *Christmas card, Carl gave out a tiny cry of "Oh!" Made from a sheet of 8 ¹/₂ by 11 construction paper that had been folded in half and then in half again, the card had a drawing of a candy-cane, the red stripes carefully outlined and coloured in, the white ones painted with glue and then sprinkled with salt. He felt a sudden rush of feelings for his Grammy Queenie—when he was a small boy she had shown him how to make this exact same thing. For a moment he thought this was the one he'd made; then he realized that it was too neat, too tidy.*

But perhaps his own was here too, on top of the bed somewhere? The candy-cane card he had made for his parents forty-some years ago? His yearning to see it surprised him; it was almost embarrassing.

He was vividly aware of the sweet smell of the oilcloth on the kitchen table back in Ragged Islands, of its pattern of diamonds and tiny flowers.

The letter on the inside was neatly written, in a delicate hand, with a very sharp red pencil point. He had not seen his grandmother's handwriting in years.

Dear Jamie

I hope you are good. I have a real bad cold but don't worry about me. Your father is the same, no better no worse. I am glad you are with the Wellman chappie. He always sounded very nice. You are fortunate to have a friend to keep you company. It is not going to seem like Christmas here without you this year. Are you sure you can't get away on leave and come home?

I have no news. Write back soon. I am lonesome.

Please be careful.

Forever, Mother

There was a handwritten letter on a 5 by 7 sheet of white paper folded inside the card.

Shediac, December 1942

Dear Jamie

Thank you so much for the chestnuts. I have always wondered what "real" ones were like. We roasted them just like your letter said, and we all enjoyed them immensely! Now we feel just as "sophisticated" as you and Murd.

It was so good to have you boys at the house. Let's hope this war business is finished soon and you both can come home where you belong. There's a little something for you in Murd's Christmas box. Don't let him try and "cheat" you of it!

Mr. Wellman and Susan Ann join me in wishing you a very Happy Christmas.

Yours truly,
Tessie Wellman

The war had always seemed a remote thing, far away from the time in which he lived; "wartime," his parents would say, and it seemed a

*hundred years before, even though he'd been born only four years after it
ended.*

The envelope had been labelled JAMIE / QUEENIE. *It also contained a newspaper clipping, an old sepia photograph, and a sheet of thick,
stiff paper, folded very neatly—an official document of some sort.*

*The photo was of a young man in uniform, sitting in a wicker chair in
front of a bare canvas drop. His legs were crossed, his right hand rested on
his knee, and his left was rigidly posed on the arm on the chair. He was as
much boy as man, and had a slight grin on his face despite the formality of
his posture—he was looking just to the right of the camera, as if amused
by someone standing next to the photographer. A note was written on the
back:*

Be a good girl Queenie and I'll see you when I'm back.
Say hello to Frank and kiss the little fellow for me
Love Gordie

*Gordon Bulmer; Grammy Queenie's brother Gordie, who had died at
Vimy Ridge.*

The clipping was the colour of a nicotine stain, and extremely brittle.

RAGGED ISLANDS MAN LOST
Schr. *Eliza and Mary*, Captain Ephraim Smith,
arrived at Yarmouth Saturday with her colours
at half-mast, bringing sad news of the drowning
of Carl Alfred Roberts, who was lost this week
while the vessel was homeward bound from the
fishing grounds at Emerald Bank.

On Thursday last, when the *Eliza and Mary*
was in a heavy wind, the main sail was lowered
and a sudden slat of the boom carried the
young fisherman overboard. Jacob Whynott

and Alexander Pierce jumped into a dory to rescue young Roberts. It was evening, and although they could hear him calling out for assistance, they were unable to find him in the growing dark.

Captain Smith brought his craft about and searched in vain for several hours. It is believed that the lad drowned shortly after falling into the sea.

The unfortunate young man was 16 years of age and well thought of by his companions. In consequence, the news of his death will be deeply regretted by many people who will extend their deepest sympathies to the family so suddenly bereaved. The deceased was a native of Ragged Islands, where his mother and brother still reside, and came from a line of seafaring people. His father, Asa Roberts, was lost in the tragic wreck of the *Schr. Pleiades* on April 18, 1899.

Someone had written "1899–1914" on the edge of the clipping. Carl had never seen this before, had not known a thing about his Uncle Carl, had not realized until this moment that both of the men he was named for had died so young.

When he'd first seen the names carved on the flat stretch of rock by the back shore, Carl had been excited to discover another, mysterious Carl Roberts who had lived before him, who had chiselled his name there in 1912. "He was your father's uncle," his mother told him, when he asked. "A sailor of some sort." And Carl had connected this great-uncle with the whale's tooth that sat on top of the piano, an exotic and glamorous object that thrilled his boyhood. Even though he knew that the tooth came from his great-grandfather Asa, that it probably had nothing to do with his sailor uncle, he felt as if he had been named for an adventurer.

Until he found out that he shared the name with his father as well, as unadventurous a man as ever lived.

When he unfolded the heavy paper document, beneath the heading, N.R.M.A. SOLDIER, he saw:

Name (in full) <u>James Carl Roberts</u>

It took him a moment to realize that he was holding his father's discharge certificate, the information neatly typed onto the dotted lines of the form.

THE DESCRIPTION OF THIS SOLDIER ON THE DATE BELOW IS AS FOLLOWS:—
Age <u>26</u>
Height <u>5'8"</u>
Complexion <u>Medium</u>
Eyes <u>Blue</u>
Hair <u>Brown</u>
Marks or scars <u>Nil</u>

The date was 29 April 1943. Wartime. "Half as old as I am now," he thought.

Could the description have been any more innocuous?

Medium Brown Nil

His father could have been anybody. His signature at the bottom was bland as well, the indistinguishable good penmanship of grade school and business college.

Some boys at school had tormented Carl about his father's discharge. Georgie Ringer told him that his own father considered Jamie Roberts to be "a chicken and a no-good traitor." When he asked about it, his mother *told him to "pay those boys no mind. Your father is twice the man that Georgie's father will ever be. Lloyd Ringer watched the whole war through the bottom of a bottle!"*

He read the body of the certificate through three times:

> This is to certify that <u>No. G 600108</u> (Rank) Private
> Name (in full) <u>James Carl Roberts</u> was enrolled under the <u>National Resources Mobilization Act—1940</u> at <u>Fredertiction, N.B.</u> on the <u>27</u> day of <u>March 1941</u>
> He served in <u>Canada</u> and is now discharged under the Routine Order <u>1029(12)</u> by reason of <u>His services being no longer required (on compassionate grounds)</u>

Discharged in the middle of a war, while his friend Murdoch went overseas and was killed. Here, with no real details whatsoever, is the evidence of his father's disgrace, and Carl's earliest humiliation as well.

INGLIS STREET

The last few hours had been horrible; the creature had teased her so, toying with her like a cat with a mouse. It would go tearing off into the woods, snapping and crashing through the underbrush, the sounds growing fainter and fainter behind her, making her think it had left, gone away for good, but as soon as she breathed a sigh of relief and slowed her pace a bit, she would hear it approaching her from another direction. She might hear nothing for ten minutes or so, and she would stop walking to listen and catch her breath, but then she would hear a low growl from the bushes only a few feet away, and she would hurry on.

Now it had been over half an hour since she had last heard anything, or been aware of its presence; just before she reached the bridge into Shediac, she had begun to feel that maybe, finally, she was safe. She had just turned quickly in the middle of the Foch Bridge, spinning around to look, and the road behind her was bare: nothing approaching, nothing moving in the ditches, not a trace of anything at all as far back as Chapman's Corner. Could whatever it was have left her and returned to the woods?

After a moment she dared to whisper to herself, "Good riddance."

The bay was so smooth and calm and blue. There were sailboats way out on the water, and gulls gliding and calling in the air above her, but there was no other sign of life: not a soul on the sidewalk, and no cars on the road. The tide was coming in; below her, the current was moving from the bay up into the mouth of the Scoudouc River. At high tide, her brothers had jumped from this very spot; they had climbed over the railing and leapt from the side of the bridge into the channel. Murd was so brave and reckless that he had climbed way up onto the top of the span and jumped from there. It made her dizzy to even think about it. Susan Ann had been afraid of deep water back then, and had only gone swimming at the beach, wading out slowly, shivering and nervous, before finally dunking herself under. All the while, her brothers encouraged her—"Come on, Sis! You can do it!"— jumping and swimming in happy circles round and round her. There had been summers when she could not go swimming at all, because she was sick or because Mum was worried that she would get sick again; consequently, she had grown up quite timid of water, and had stayed that way until Jamie came along, until the two of them went swimming near Ragged Islands. Everything had changed then, everything, and she was thrilled to find herself beside him, wet and happy as a seal; she had never been so happy as when the two of them taught Lorraine and Carl to swim in the river, up at the camp.

She looked nervously back across the bridge again. Nothing.

When she looked across the bay, every landmark on the far shore was familiar still: steeples, cottage roofs, lines of trees. The shore wasn't wild like the one at Ragged Islands, it wasn't dangerous and exciting the way Jamie's shore could be. This was a pretty place, while his was rough and beautiful. That was why the flying boats had come here: because the bay was so protected, smooth and clear; there was hardly ever a trace of fog.

At the centre of the bay were two islands: Skull Island, the little island where the arrowheads were, and Shediac Island, where Dad Wellman went on Sunday afternoons to visit the lighthouse keeper, rowing over after church with the week's newspapers, or skating there in winter once the ice was safe enough. One time he got caught, stranded there in a snowstorm, and Mum confessed later that she'd been scared to death he'd fallen through and drowned.

In the spring, the whole family would sail over to pick mayflowers on the *Susan Ann*, Dad's boat that had been named for her.

Dad Wellman had built his house here because he loved to be on the water; he could hop on the train every morning to go to work in Moncton. But as soon as that house was finished, in 1909, his first wife had died of pneumonia: Mary Boyd, who had come over from PEI to visit her sister and had fallen so in love with Paul Wellman that she had only gone back home once more, and that was to pack her things and tell her family that she was engaged. Young and in love and the mother of two young boys when she died, and Len and Boyd were sent off to the orphanage, where the nuns were so mean to them, and Dad was forced to rent out the new house and move to Moncton, where he boarded with Mrs. Colpitts, where he met Susan Ann's Aunt Tessie, who adopted her and became her mother, and they all—

What was that? Over there, something moving—

Dammit. There was something back there in the tall grass, halfway between the last house and the bridge, watching her. That animal, that thing, whatever it was that was following her, she could see it out of the corner of her eye, and she could hear it panting.

"Just get going," she told herself. "Just start walking and pay it no mind. Maybe it won't follow you into town." So she set off across the bridge and up Main Street, past the fishermen's houses on the shore, past the grand houses of the high and mighties, and on towards the little hill.

She couldn't imagine what it was. But it was trailing her, she could sense that. She stopped walking, and whirled around on her heel to look; the street was empty, the sidewalk too, and she could see nothing in the yards. But she knew that it had crossed the bridge and was in the town with her. What was it, what did it want? If it wanted to attack her, why hadn't it done so out on the highway? It must want her for something else, but what could that possibly be?

She hurried on up the hill, past the grand houses with their grand-sounding names—Elmbank, Brookside—past wicked Banker Chipman's and Knox Presbyterian Church—no, that church was gone, she was upset and getting confused—and just beyond the Mercantile Store, Kitty White's house on the corner of Inglis Street, where she used to play on the wide veranda.

Why was the town so empty? Where had everyone gone? If that thing caught up with her, was there anyone around to come and help? If she cried out, would anyone even hear her?

She turned right, and up Inglis Street she went, past the Whites' big yard, past the Legers,' the LeBlancs'—and then there it was, the house that Dad Wellman had built—a big square clapboard house with dormer windows and green trim—but there was no time to stand in front of it and gawk, no, not with that creature following her, so she marched herself up the walk and across the veranda, opened the front door and let herself in.

The front hallway was so dark that she couldn't see clearly at first; it was often gloomy because of the shadow from the veranda roof outside. She shut the door quickly and stood there, catching her breath. When she looked out the window in the door, she could see nothing in the yard, but there were lots of places for that thing to hide: behind the maples at the foot of the walk, or in the lilacs across the street, or the mock-orange bush. It could go up the street to old Elsie Steeves' place and hide behind the stone wall.

"What in the name of God are you?" she whispered. "If what you wanted was to eat me, you've had plenty of chances." She watched and waited, but could still see nothing moving in the yard or out on the street. She remembered a moment—she hadn't thought of it in years and years—when she was up at the farm and heard an uproar in the middle of the night. She jumped out of her bed in the upper room and ran to the window just in time to see a fox sail out of the henhouse with a chicken in its mouth; a silver fox that had escaped from a fox farm on the other side of Five Points and was raiding every farm in the county.

After making sure that the door was securely closed, she turned and looked about her.

She had not been inside this house in over fifty years.

Nothing seemed to have changed. At the far end of the dark hall, the sun was shining through the dining-room windows, reflecting brightly off the polished top of the round oak table. To her right, the living room looked as cozy as ever; just inside the archway, the big, wine-coloured chesterfield that Mum had bought at Eaton's. There was some knitting left on one arm: a half-finished grey sock; the ball of yarn was tucked down between the arm and a cushion. On the fireplace mantel, next to the clock in its bell jar and the Toby mug sitting on the starched white doily, there was a pair of bronzed baby shoes, Murd's little shoes, in the spot where Mum had first placed them.

"Hello?" she called out, but there was no answer.

She walked down the hall into the dining room. The chairs were all pulled back from the table; the fruit bowl had been pushed to one side of the tabletop, which was pulled slightly apart. Standing on the floor, leaning against the table's edge, were two of its leaves. The silver bowl on top of the oak sideboard was freshly polished and gleaming in the light from the window. The cake dish had been taken out of the cupboard and was sitting beside it. Mum only ever put cakes on the pedestal dish if it was a special occasion: company for dinner, or a birthday.

In the kitchen, there were potatoes and carrots on the counter beside the sink. Someone had started to peel them and stopped midway through. She spied the paring knife on the floor and bent down to pick it up, setting it back beside the vegetables. The roasting pan had been taken down from the shelf. There was a pot in the sink, the one that Mum used to boil her vegetables; it was clean and empty and sitting beneath the tap. The stove was warm; the woodbox beside it, half-empty. Mum's green teapot was sitting on the top, on the side farthest from the fire. Her favourite cup, the cream-coloured one with the yellow band, was beside it, and when Susan Ann went over to the stove, she could see that it was half-full. The cup was warm.

"Mum?" she called out.

There was no reply.

The clock on the clock shelf seemed to have stopped, its hands frozen at ten after three. When she stood next to it, she couldn't hear the trace of a tick; it had wound down—something that, to her recollection, had never happened before.

The pine table looked so small; it didn't seem possible that Dad and Dr. Foster had once placed her on top of it; that Mum had watched from the dining-room door while they cut out part of her rib. It was bare except for an old worn pillow sitting on one corner, the scrub pillow that Mum would put under her knees when she washed the floors. Who could have left it there? It was always in the wooden box beside the scrub bucket, at the top of the cellar stairs.

Where could everyone be? It seemed as if everything had just been left suddenly, as if things had just been dropped and everyone had run off.

She walked back through the dining room and the hall, towards the front of the house. When she got to the foot of the stairs, she called up, "Is anybody home?"

She started up, walking past Queen Victoria and her Diamond Jubilee; past the photo of Len and Boyd at the orphanage, standing at attention with all the sad orphans and those mean-looking nuns; past the baby pictures: Len, Boyd, Susan Ann and Murd, who had looked so handsome even when he was no more than an infant. On the landing, in a dark oval frame, there was Murd in his uniform, so good-looking and smart; Mum had hung that picture not too long after he went overseas—

No, wait—when had she hung that picture up? Was it then or was it—

Susan Ann was getting a bit confused.

She stopped and looked at him in his uniform. Lieutenant Murdoch Wellman. What a lovely smile he had! She had always called him Burdock, a silly nickname, and when Jamie started calling him that he blushed and grinned so. What fun they had all had teasing each other.

Then she remembered that Mum had hung the picture up before Murd went overseas, and had taken it down after the telegram came and hung it by her bedside. And his baby shoes, too—the last time Susan Ann had been in Mum and Dad Wellman's bedroom, the bronze shoes had been taken upstairs and were sitting on the little table in the window.

The four wedding pictures were next: Mum seated beside Dad at Crandall's Studio in Moncton; Len and Doris in a studio in Winnipeg, looking so starched and formal; Boyd and Joyce posing beside her father's house near Ring's Corner, the both of them with big wide grins! In the corner of the picture was the new Ford V-8 they were so crazy over. That had been such a grand day all around, even though everyone knew that Boyd and Joyce would soon be leaving them behind and moving to Montreal.

The last wedding picture was her own: Susan Ann and Jamie standing in the backyard in front of Mum and Dad's garden. She stood on the step beside it and looked at it for quite some time. In all the years, their wedding had been the only one to have ever taken place in this house; the service had been in the United Church on Main Street, and afterwards Mum and Dad had had the reception right here, in the backyard. If things had worked out the way they'd planned when Jamie first proposed, they would have lived here with Mum and Dad. In the picture, she was holding her bouquet of roses, her arm linked through Jamie's, and the yard about them was so lush—even in an old black-and-white photo, that was the first word that came to mind, *lush*—with flowers of all sorts everywhere, and the vegetables in back so plentiful and healthy, the raspberry patch, the berry bushes, the snowball tree, the lilacs, the chestnuts and maples. "Eden was no better," Dad used to say; he was so proud of that yard. He and Mum would be out there working for hours.

It was no wonder Susan Ann was shocked when she got down to Ragged Islands and saw Jamie's house for the first time. That yard! Nothing but old spruce trees, some scrappy grass and rocks; her mother-in-law's idea of gardening was the patch of rhubarb that Jamie's grandmother had planted beside an outcrop that looked like the top of a buried moon.

How smart Jamie had looked in his dark suit. That smile on his face, a young fellow on his wedding day, you'd never know how awful the last couple of years had been. "You'd look a darn sight better in *uniform*," Muriel had said to him outside the church, and Mumma Mac, who was standing beside her, had smiled for the first time all afternoon.

No, not a smile, more of a smirk. They had both been so mean. Neither of them had wanted or even tried to understand how much it had cost Jamie to go along with that discharge from the army. What had happened to Muriel's boyfriend was a tragedy— Alex McCallum had died in a road accident in England before he ever saw the war—but that had nothing to do with Jamie's situation. And besides, Muriel had up and married Jack Oulton less than a month after poor Alex perished.

It was a small picture, in a little golden frame. She lifted it off the hook and turned it over. There was a small clasp; she opened it, lifted the back, took out the picture and hung the empty frame on the wall. She slid the photo into her bag.

The hallway upstairs was dim and gloomy because all six doors were closed, the four bedroom doors, and the ones to the bathroom and the attic, all shut tight. "That's strange," she thought; she could not remember if she had ever seen all of them closed at the same time. "The doors in this house were always open."

The first door, the one at the front of the house, was her own dear bedroom. It had been her nursery and, when she was so sick with pleurisy that time, it had been the room where she nearly died. Both her mothers had knelt down by her bedside and prayed. She had been a foolish teenager in there, reading her magazines about movie stars, dreaming of the likes of Ronald Colman, the Man of Mystery, and wondering what it would be like to be a glamourpuss like Greta Garbo or Marlene Dietrich. And in that room, she had put on her wedding dress one Saturday morning, and taken it off five hours later, her life completely changed; she had packed up all her belongings and gone off forever to Ragged Islands with Jamie.

She reached for the worn, black doorknob and started to turn it, but it stuck. She jiggled it and tried to pull the door open, but it wouldn't budge. The door couldn't be locked, because there was no way to lock it—what could be making it stick? She rattled the doorknob, then tugged at it, but something had caught inside the latch and was holding it tight. She leaned against the door, pushing her weight against it, and felt it give a little while she twisted the doorknob, trying to hear it catch, but by this time it was spinning uselessly in her fingers.

She had stopped for a second, to try to figure out what she should do next, when she heard a sound from behind her, a sound like someone clearing his throat.

"Oh!" turning around quickly—

Her head cocked, as she listened—

"Hello?"

She waited but, again, there was no answer. She was sure she had heard something, as sure as she could be.

"Who's there?"

Could the creature that had been following her have gotten into the house somehow? Was that why everything had stopped and been abandoned?

Would it attack her now that she was inside?

She listened and listened, but there was only quiet.

She crept a ways into the hall, listened at the top of the stairs, looked at all those shut doors. Could someone be behind one of them?

Then she heard a rustling sound—bedsprings, maybe—and something like breathing. She was not alone. She was sure the sounds hadn't come from the room next to hers, Mum and Dad's bedroom, or from the older boys' room beside that. And they were too close by to have come from the attic. Was it the back bedroom?

Maybe she wasn't supposed to be here. Maybe she was in trouble and someone was angry at her. Should she hide?

Or maybe someone was trying to play a trick on her?

"Who's there?" Her voice sounded weak and fearful.

Another rustling—like the sound of a hand or foot sliding over the top of a bedspread.

"I can hear you."

A breath, almost a sigh. She knew that sigh, she did!

"Murd?"

She walked towards the door at the end of the hall. "I know it's you."

And then, so faintly, a sound like a little *ha!*, like someone trying not to laugh, and another creaking of bedsprings.

Quickening with excitement—it had been such a long, long time!—she didn't knock, she grabbed the knob, pushed open the door and stepped into the back bedroom.

The air smelled like apple blossoms.

He was sitting up on his bed, his legs stretched out on top of the bedspread and a book in his hands, sitting there under the picture postcard of *The Spirit of St. Louis*, pretending not to see her. Teasing her. He had such lovely hands, such long fingers. He wasn't wearing his uniform, no, not that rotten thing, no, even though he was so handsome in it. He was in a white shirt, a Sunday shirt, with his sleeves rolled up.

"Murd!"

He was trying not to smile, she could tell that; he was trying to ignore her and pretending to be interested in the foolish book he was holding. What was it? Oh, it didn't matter, she didn't care. If only he were a wee thing still, and she could run to him, pick him up in her arms and twirl him in the air above her, the way she had when they were kids out in the yard. It was stupid the way boys shunned all manner of affection as they grew up.

"Burdock!"

But he wouldn't look up. He continued to look at the book, to pretend.

And then she realized that he was asleep. He had been reading his book and had fallen sound asleep with his eyes open.

She tiptoed over beside his bed and looked down at him: so quiet and still, he seemed lost in a deep, deep sleep. She reached out her finger and touched his cheek, so warm and soft. He had never had much of a beard, just a bit of soft down for sideburns, a few delicate hairs along his upper lip. What a shame he had never had children, because he was so good-looking, the best-looking one of the lot: Mum and Dad Wellman's only true child. When she looked into his face, she could see them both.

But asleep like that, with his eyes wide open—that was disconcerting, so she turned and looked about.

His room looked just as it had before he went away.

Beside the open window was the wooden chair that Mum Wellman had covered with some blue fabric from the farm; it had a nice soft cushion, and Susan Ann went over to it and sat down. The smell of apple blossoms was coming in from the yard, as strong and fragrant as mayflowers in the spring woods. Placing the smart little bag that Meg had given her on the floor beside her feet, she leaned back in the chair and took a deep breath.

"I'm home," she said quietly, and then, "I walked here, all the way from the farm. It's gone, Burdock, all gone! Everything up there, all torn down. Only thing left is the outhouse."

He was so calm and still she could barely see him breathe; his chest was moving ever so slightly.

"Something was following behind me, watching me, all the way along the Shediac Road. An animal of some kind."

Were his eyes moving a bit? Just a tiny bit?

"I'm not fibbing."

If you were asleep with your eyes open, she wondered, wouldn't you blink?

She relaxed into the chair; it felt good to rest her weary bones.

"Murd? I found Mum's cameo lady. Look." She pulled the necklace up and held it out for him to see. He didn't look.

Sitting there watching him made her think of a Sunday afternoon in spring, after church and after lunch—rolls and cheese and Mum's pickles. Old-fashioned cheese from up around Five Points. Murd loved rolls; in the letter that had arrived after the telegram came, he said he missed good home cooking, and was having dreams about finding a pan of Mum Wellman's rolls. That was their little treat coming home after church, pickles and cheese and rolls.

On a Sunday like that, he had been home on leave with Jamie.

Across the room from her, between the closet and the door, was the tall white dresser, with most of its drawers half-open, clothes hanging out as usual. Mum had always had to hound him about putting things away properly, about tidying up. She could see socks on the floor beneath the dresser and, just inside the closet door, a dirty shirt and some pants in a pile.

"Clean up that culch!" That's what Mum would have said.

His desktop was cluttered too: pencils, geometry set, scrapbooks, scribblers, Ernest Thompson Seton's *Wild Animals I Have Known*, a half-dozen volumes from The Book of Knowledge, Charles Lindbergh's *We* and pinned to the wall behind them all were two pictures. One was the Pan Am Clipper out in the bay— Murd had taken that picture himself, from the wharf. The other was of Balbo's armada. It had been taken from high in the air; all of the flying boats were anchored in a long chevron across the bay, a wide V like geese flying. There had been a series of pictures of the armada in the Moncton papers, and this one had been their favourite because at the very edge of the right-hand side they could see Inglis Street. That had excited them so much, being able to see the place where they lived the way that only God and the birds had seen it before.

"You loved your old planes," she said softly. "You had such a big crush on them all."

There was a secret about his airplanes, though, a big secret—what was it?

Or was it something Lorraine had been talking about with Meg? Had a plane crashed somewhere? That sounded familiar.

The Spirit of St. Louis was in a frame on the wall behind him. Lucky Lindbergh—

That was the secret, that was it! Aunt Bea had sent that picture to Murd from Boston, and they couldn't tell anyone who it came from because Daddy Mac would have had a fit. He was furious with his little sister for marrying a Catholic and turning, and that was that. No one was supposed to communicate with her or her husband in any way, shape or form.

"I lost touch with her too," Susan Ann thinks. "After Mum died. We sent the odd Christmas card for a while, though. I was the only one in the family who even did *that*." That was a big regret; it would have disappointed Mum.

The Spirit of St. Louis. That was the secret about the airplanes—

But wasn't there still another one? Hadn't Carl and Lorraine said something about airplanes? A crash somewhere?

She couldn't keep their secrets straight any more. All that whispering!

She looked at the picture of the armada, remembering the time when the Italians had stayed at the house, those two fellows. Boyd had talked to them in French, translated back and forth for everyone at the table. One of them went up to bed straightaway, he was so tired, but the other was all wired up and talked for quite a while. His skin was so dark, his hair was so black and thick, his French sounded so different from the Acadians who lived in town. There was something exciting about his foreignness, his uniform.

Mum said to tell him that her sister was married to an Italian fellow. She told Boyd, "Tell him that my sister Beatrice is married to Mr. Bellanti and they are living in Boston." She said to tell him how proud and happy they all were to have him stay in their home.

He had given Mum and Dad a souvenir picture of Balbo and Mussolini; it was propped up on the mantel for a long time, beside the clock. Dad never got around to having it framed, which was a good thing because then they were at war with the Italians, with those same boys. Mum put the picture away in the attic. After Murd went overseas, Dad tore it to pieces and burned it. He said, "Those damn Italians were just here to map our coast, that's all that was about."

Susan Ann was thinking that those Italians had been right here—on that night, those two boys had stayed in this very room while Murd slept out in the tent in the backyard—and no one had dreamed that there would be a war, or that they would be the enemy.

But there was still something in this story that she could not quite grasp, something about the airplanes. Had one of them crashed somewhere along the way?

After supper, the Italian had sat on the back step drinking Mum's coffee and smoking a cigar, Murd sitting beside him holding the encyclopedia. The aviator had traced his journey for them with his finger—from Rome to Holland, Ireland, then out over the Atlantic, Iceland, then Labrador, then right here.

One of the flying boats had crashed, yes, in Holland, she remembered now, and one of his comrades had died.

And just before he went upstairs, the three of them all stood at the foot of the back steps and Susan Ann and Murd gave him the Fascist salute. "Good night," they said.

"Buona notte," he answered, and smiled at them both.

"That day," she whispered to Murd, asleep, "was your birthday. 'Lucky unlucky thirteen,' you said, because you were thirteen and it was the thirteenth and the armada came to town. Hundreds and hundreds of people came to see."

Nearly seventy years ago.

Murd seemed to be stirring a little, was he waking up? While she watched him, she spoke very softly. "We were all down on the shore," she said. "You and me, and Mum and Dad. Boyd and Joyce. Daddy Mac wouldn't let anyone in my family come out from Moncton because the papers said that the armada had been blessed by the Pope."

Her brother sighed suddenly, a long sad sigh that seemed to be filled with longing. He could hear her, she knew that; he was awake.

He was stretched out on the bed, his feet crossed at the ankles, holding the book propped up on his tummy.

"Murd?"

When he turned his head, his eyes went right through her to stare at the window. They looked so cold. Could he even see her? Was he under some kind of spell? Was it possible that they could both be back here in this room, that she might have this one chance to be with him again, but that he would not be able to see her?

"Murd?"

His eyes went back to his book.

"Murd? Can you hear me?"

She wanted to hear his voice so badly!

"*Please!*" she said. "*Please* talk to me! I've waited for so long!" Why was he teasing her in this way? "Burdock, please, don't be an old meanie."

Then suddenly he was sitting bolt upright—

"Shut *up!*" he shouted, slamming the book against the side of the bed—

"Shut up!" Slamming the book over and over—

"Shut up, just shut up, just *shut up!* Prattle prattle prattle yak-yak-yak!"

She cowered back in the chair.

Murd's face was turned from hers and red as a beet; he kept whacking the book against the bed and shouting, "I want you to leave me alone! I want you to leave me alone! Just *leave leave leave leave leave me alone!*"

"But Murd—" she started.

He threw the book on the floor and turned quickly. "Jesus H. Christ!"

He was sitting on the side of the bed, and glaring past her. "I hate the way you sneak in here and watch me," he said. "I know you do it. You drive me foolish! You think I'm asleep and then you come in and stand beside the bed, just stand there and look at me."

What was he talking about?

"You watch me, you touch my face, you kiss me when you think I'm asleep—"

"No, I don't, I do not."

"Bending over to kiss me all the time."

"When you were a baby," she said, "I kissed you and watched you sleep, when you were a baby."

"Watching me, staring at me—"

"Because you were such a lovely baby!"

"The way you sneak in and stand there beside the bed and stare at me, like I'm a little doll! I hate it!"

He was talking about another time, wasn't he? He was talking about when she was six or seven or eight years old, so long ago, when he was just a little baby all wrapped up in swaddling clothes, and she would sneak in to watch him in his crib. She couldn't stop herself from watching him because he was so perfect, he was like Baby Jesus asleep on the hay. Baby Murd was so perfect that she couldn't stop herself from kissing his fat, rosy cheeks.

"You're always patting me and mauling me, like I was a pet, like I'm your stupid dog."

"No!" she said. "No, I—"

But he interrupted her, he started calling out in a sarcastic voice that was so cruel, "Here Burdock! Here Burdock! Burdie Burdie Burdie!" As he spat out the words, he bent down and grabbed up the book. Then he quickly turned from her and jerked his feet back up onto the bed. He was all stretched out again, with the book propped open on his chest, looking just the way he had when she first came into the room.

For a moment she just sat there, staring at him in disbelief; but then she thought of how he had said that he hated her looking at him, so she lowered her head. Her eyes were darting about the floor, unable to focus on anything. She was too upset to cry, too taken aback; although she tried to focus, her mind was in such a jumble. She was trying to think of a time she had crept into the room to look at Baby Murd sleeping but she couldn't think straight, she couldn't remember.

She was trying to concentrate on anything, on a mark on the floor, but she couldn't even decide what the floor looked like. Was it wooden? Linoleum? Was there a rug? What was she looking at? It just seemed to be murky and confusing. *What was she looking at?* All she knew was that she was not looking at Murd, because he didn't want her looking at him any more.

She closed her eyes. She couldn't see anything, not a blessed thing, just black nothing.

"Is that *it?*" she thought. "Is *this it?*"

She took a deep breath, and the air was so stale-tasting that she realized she could no longer smell the apple blossoms.

She reached down both her hands; one of them grabbed the edge of the chair that Mum Wellman had covered with blue fabric from the farm, and the other grabbed the straps of her bag.

She clutched them both for dear life. "Our Father which art in heaven," she prayed, "help me to think."

When she opened her eyes, he was still lying there looking at that book. She didn't know what to say next. She hoped that he might say something else, something nice, that he might turn and look at her and apologize; but he didn't speak, he didn't move—he just lay there. When they were young, he had never been mean or sullen like this, never; he had always been a good boy, kind and full of beans.

She lifted up her bag and reached inside for a Kleenex. She blew her nose. After a moment's thought, she asked him, very quietly, "Are you mad because I married Jamie? Because he got out of the service during the war and didn't go overseas?"

"What do you think?"

"I don't know, that's why I asked."

He muttered something under his breath.

"He was so upset when you died," she said. "It was one of the few times he lost patience with his mother. He—"

"I don't care," Murd interrupted. "I don't care about either one of you and what you did."

"Oh." A long moment passed, and then she asked, "What does it feel like to die?"

Murd let out a sigh of exasperation and went on staring at the book.

"No, tell me, *please*."

She didn't dare glance away; she felt that if she let go of him with her eyes, he might disappear forever.

"Murd?"

He sighed deeply, but he closed the book and put it beside him on the bed.

"Oh, *please* talk to me," she said. "I know it was a long time ago. We were just kids, really."

"I was twenty-four!" He said this as if he were telling her that he had been fifty. But he said nothing else.

She wished now that she had not said anything, that she had stood up and walked out of the room while he was being mean to her, that she had never come into his bedroom to begin with. But she couldn't stop what she had started.

"Tell me, tell me how it happened."

"It wouldn't change a thing."

"Yes it would. I would *know*." For she had imagined her brother's death a thousand times, but she did not truly know what had happened. Had there been a bomb? A gunshot? Had he died in a hospital? In a field? She didn't know. And if Mum and Dad Wellman knew, they never told her, they never spoke about it.

"You were buried in Holland."

"Oh Sue, it was so long ago."

She was willing him to turn his head, to look her square in the face. But he wouldn't.

"My daughter went to that place in Holland, to Groesbeek. She saw your grave, and brought me a picture of it."

"Why do you want to talk about this?"

"So I'll know."

"You'll know soon enough."

"But that's why I want to talk to you!"

He turned his head again, but his eyes moved past her to the window. Was he looking at it, or just *not* looking at her? She could see his hands clearly, but his face was becoming fuzzy, as if she were looking at parts of him through water. How much time had passed since she had sat down?

He sighed again and started to reach for the book, but stopped and folded his hands over his stomach.

She was thinking that all she had from Murd was a postcard he had sent to Jamie and a flower, a flower she had pressed into the pages of *The Good Earth*. She had forgotten all about until it fell out when she was packing, the day that Lorraine and Peter went over to town to get more cardboard boxes. It was in an envelope that she had made of wax paper, and it was flat and brittle and as fine as lace, and she was surprised that she had forgotten all about it hidden away. How could she have not remembered a souvenir from that afternoon so long ago? It was the weekend that Jamie Roberts proposed to her. The three of them played cribbage late at night and the next day was Sunday and Muriel arrived with Alex McCallum and they all went for a long walk in the after-noon. Muriel and the McCallum boy were engaged too, oh the poor fellow, Susan Ann would never see him again. But that Sunday was springtime, and the woods up the street were thick with the smell of mayflowers, that smell so powerful it could be surrounding her now. Muriel and Alex kept laughing and kissing and Jamie kept blushing, and Murd picked that flower and gave it to Susan Ann and she put it in *The Good Earth*, where it was lost in a space between a time long ago and that packing day. The pressed flower fell out and—

Murd, poor Murd, poor lost Murd.

Time stretched out unbearably; he looked uncomfortably at the door, she stared and stared at him until she couldn't bear it any more, and she turned quickly and looked out the window.

It was so late in the day, growing dusk, but she could still see outside fairly clearly. Dad Wellman's backyard seemed to be all flat lawn now, right up to the property lines. The gardens were gone, the bushes, the fruit trees; there was nothing out there but dull flatness. The sky was grey and overcast; there would be rain in the night. It had been such a long day and she was so weary.

"Dad came up to the farm one time to bring me back here for something special," she said. "It was a hot, hot, hot July day, and he came up to the farm to fetch me.

"'There's a big surprise waiting for you at home,' he says.

"'What?' I asked him.

"'A new baby brother,' he says.

"And the first thing I said was 'Oh, can we keep him?' And oh how they laughed at that!

"And you were so lovely in your little basket, all of us just stood around and looked at you. Mum and Dad, Len and Boyd and me. We were just crazy over you. You were the most unusual baby anyone had ever seen—you were *handsome*.

"And Mum and Dad always laughed and told that story, about how the reason they kept you was because I asked them to. But it wasn't just some silly thing a kid says. A part of me really worried that they might give you away. I thought that's what parents did sometimes. You see—"

And she turned around to face him, but he was gone. The bed was empty. He had left her, and she knew somehow that she would never see him again, in this life or the next.

She was so very tired. She wanted to go to her own room, to have a sleep in her old bed, but she didn't have the energy to walk down the hall and struggle with the door. Her whole body was exhausted; her old feet were so sore from all that walking. She stood up and moved to Murd's bed. Pulling back the bedspread, she lay down and tucked herself under it. She curled up clutching her little bag to her chest, hugging it tight like a comfortable old doll.

Just before she fell asleep, she was thinking of Murd's gravestone, then of all the other pictures that Lorraine and Peter had brought to her from that trip, and she wondered if maybe she should have told her brother that Peter had come from over there, that her son-in-law had been born in Germany.

But something like that would have been so hard to explain. Could someone from the past understand how so many things could change in such a short time? Both times Lorraine had married, she hadn't even changed her name, because women didn't need to do that any more.

But that didn't mean that she wasn't really Mrs. Peter Stieff.

And would knowing that have made Murd feel that he had gone to war for nothing?

"I'm glad I didn't tell him," she thought, and then she was asleep.

After a while she was aware that she was no longer alone, that someone was watching over her. She thought of her mum, of the night long ago when she had been so sick that both her mothers had prayed at her bedside, but when she opened her eyes she could see that, in her dream, Jamie had come into Murd's room and was standing by her bedside. He was looking down on her very tenderly, and she knew that he was waiting for her inside the house where he had lived all his life, he was waiting in Ragged Islands. He said, "I miss you terribly and I am counting the days."

He reached down to touch her gently.

"Murd was mean to me," she told him.

His warm hand, the hand she loved so.

"I miss you terribly and I am counting the days."

It was a dream, she knew that, but she didn't want it to end because there he was . . .

So close by . . .

His hand touching her . . .

He was . . .

A barking dog woke her up.

It was morning already, just before sunrise, when the sky was starting to glow in the east.

She lay for a minute, caught between Jamie and the morning.

Jamie was waiting for her, he was . . .

"You can't walk to Ragged Islands," she thought, "it's too far."

She was groggy from sleep still, and she lay watching the ceiling grow lighter as dawn approached.

And what about her family? They must be looking for her by now. Would they be angry at her, the way that Murd had been last night? Would they be worse?

But then, she thought, what if it was prophetic, the dream? What if it was a dream like Joseph and old Pharaoh?—

It was at that moment that she heard a great loud commotion from down in the yard.

"What in the name of God?—"

Banging and barking and all manner of noise—

"Susan Ann!"

Whose voice was that? Was that Mum's voice? *Mum?*

She jumped out of bed and flew over to the window.

In the first light of the sun, the lawn was impossibly green, as bright as emeralds, and dew sparkled on the grass. Down there, running round and round in the centre of the yard, chasing her tail and barking like crazy, was the nicest, nicest doggie in all the world! Susan Ann pulled open the window and stuck out her head.

"Sally!" she shouted. "Sally!"

And her Sally stopped running, and sat at attention, and looked up at her.

HIS PARENTS WERE SO YOUNG *in their wedding picture, and their smiles seemed tentative and slightly goofy. They were standing on a narrow path with a vegetable garden on one side and flowers on the other— the backyard of the house in Shediac, Carl realized, a house that, for a time, he had longed to live in, even though he had never, ever once set foot inside it. Whenever she talked about it—which was often—his mother went on and on about how beautifully Dad Wellman had built it. "Such gorgeous woodwork," she used to say, shaking her head sadly.*

His mother was slender then, and his father was small, a shy-looking man. Her arm was linked through his and she was holding the bridal bouquet so naturally, as if holding bouquets of flowers were something she did every day, like the Queen. When he'd first seen a photo of her in the wedding dress, Carl had imagined that before she moved to Ragged Islands, before he was ever born, she'd led a life of glamour.

August 1943, wartime—and his father in a suit, not a uniform.

It was difficult to reconcile these two with the parents that he remembered—they'd grown so plump in middle age.

And now, his mother's body now—it had become so terrifying: bruised and scrawny.

This particular photograph wasn't familiar to him. The wedding pic-

ture that he remembered—it sat on top of the piano beside the scrimshaw whale's tooth—had three couples: the bride and groom with both sets of her parents, the MacDonalds on one side, the Wellmans on the other. It confused him when he was young—they both looked so much alike: a pair of matrons uncomfortable in their dresses, each with her own tall, stocky, moustached man who looked uncomfortable in his suit.

"They loved your father like he was one of their own," his mother would say, in reference to his Wellman grandparents.

He asked why his father's parents were not at the wedding.

"His father had just passed away, not too long before, and your Grammy Queenie couldn't come to the wedding."

"Why not?"

"She was indisposed."

He knew this was a criticism of some sort, but wasn't clear how.

One summer afternoon he'd run inside the house to get his grammy to quick come and see something in the yard—there were three pretty green garden snakes sunning themselves on the big rock beside her rhubarb. When she said she didn't have the time, he said, "Why not, are you indisposed?"

She looked at him as if he were crazy. "Who's teaching you the ten-dollar words, buster?"

It wasn't the first time he wandered into the minefield surrounding Grammy Queenie's relationship with his mother. Or the last.

The only other instance when his mother used the word was when his father was in the bathroom and she wanted to get inside; "Are you indisposed?" was code for "Are you sitting on the john?"

He had sensed that there was a private, untold story in his parents' wedding; when he grew old enough to understand dirty jokes, he assumed that this concealed thing must have involved sex. One night at dinner, his father had made a remark about a shotgun wedding and his mother had said, "I hate that expression," in such a strident way that Carl wondered if, perhaps, she might have been pregnant on her wedding day. Even though the idea was shocking, it appealed to him because it gave her a reason to leave behind the *gorgeous woodwork of the Wellman house and come to live with a man who was a wartime disgrace; she had made a terrible mistake and was paying the price. It also gave Carl a certain amount of satisfaction to think that—if not for his mother's sacrifice—Lorraine would have been illegitimate.*

But then he realized that well over a year had passed from the wedding day to his sister's birth, and he felt guilty for thinking such a dirty thing about his mother.

The brown envelope he had opened was labelled LOOSE SNAPS. After he put down the wedding picture, he looked at two snapshots of headstones. The first was in a military graveyard:

LIEUTENANT

MURDOCH EWAN WELLMAN

NORTH SHORE (NEW BRUNSWICK) REGIMENT

JANUARY 4 1945 AGE 24

THERE IS A LINK DEATH CANNOT SEVER

LOVE AND REMEMBRANCE LAST FOREVER

Written on the back, in pencil:

Groesbeek

Next was a snapshot of two headstones surrounded by a lush green hedge. Standing beside them were his sister and her husband, Peter. The wording on the brown headstone to the right was indecipherable. The black headstone on the left read:

HIER STEH ICH

AN DEN MARKEN

MEINER TAGE

MARLENE

1901—1992

Written in pencil on the back:

"Here I stand on the marker of my days"
Berlin—Friedenau

Leave it to Lorraine to have her picture taken in a goddamn graveyard—she was as bad as their mother. Phone calls from those two had turned into obituaries:

"You know that Whynott fellow you used to play with? Teddy? I wanted to let you know that he just died. Cancer."

"Do you remember Cy Hemeon, used to live out at the Point? He's dead."

"I thought you should know that Ellen Firth died up at Surf Side Manor."

People he didn't know or couldn't remember, and had never cared about one way or the other.

When he was putting the pictures away, Carl first noticed a fat little envelope with his name on it. He dumped out the contents, and there, on top of the pile, was a picture of his own young self, with his arm around Bernice.

"Oh Jesus," he said, because of course it was a photo of his very own shotgun wedding.

They were standing in front of the weathered white clapboards of her mother's church. Bernice looked so happy, with her head leaning sideways against his—he remembered suddenly the loveliness of her body, her large breasts, the curve of her tummy, her long, plump arms. The first time they made love was on a mattress in an old abandoned camp up the Sable River that had belonged to friends of his parents. He had taken her there on the pretext that they would see flying squirrels. "What a kidder you are." She said that all the time, "What a kidder you are," poking him gently in the ribs. The first year they went together, they had fun. She was so desperate to get away from her mother, an angry, religious widow who, because her maiden name was Verna Dumphee, had had to contend with being called V.D. since she was a child.

He still felt wretched when he thought of that Saturday afternoon when V.D. showed up at his parents' house to inform them of the "situation with my Bernice," and to say that she expected the right thing to be done. After she left, during their whole awful conversation, neither Carl nor his father could look each other in the eye.

It was strange to see a picture of Bernice when she was so healthy-looking and happy. When he thought about her over the years, he always remembered her sitting at a kitchen table, downcast and smoking, her hair in pink rollers. Even her big bouffant wedding hairdo looked pretty. "Nearly a hundred GD hairpins!" she'd said, triumphant and laughing, when she finally came out of the motel bathroom that night. She was holding out a pile of them in both hands for him to see.

He could not believe how idiotic his shirt looked: it was a fruity purple thing, the collar had points like long floppy daggers that drooped down over his chest. His tie was rolled up and shoved in his shirt pocket. This must have been after the reception in the church hall, after a few drinks outside with the boys. His father had even come out and had a drink with them. "She's a darn sweet girl," he told Carl. "You're darn lucky."

He'd been astounded at how well Bernice had gotten along with his father; they'd been so relaxed together, teasing each other, laughing at silly things, private jokes. Because they both did the daily crossword in The Chronicle Herald, they'd often phone each other in the evening after supper. "Could you figure out 17 across? Has me stumped!" For a while, during the first few months of the marriage, Carl had thought that he and his father would not be so distant any more; that Bernice was bringing them together.

It had been a fools' paradise, all around.

There was another photograph in the envelope—a baby in a pink, knitted sleeper. His mother had written on the back:

Melody Verna Roberts
6 lb 3 oz
First Grandchild

He took the elastic from a thin stack of papers that accompanied the two pictures. On top was a small envelope postmarked Barrington, Nova Scotia, March 1974. The letter inside was written on the same cream-coloured stationery.

Dear Mr and Mrs Roberts,

This is a hard letter to write and I'm sorry. Please don't send any more cards or presents to Melody. Her father hasn't helped out for three years and its too hard to explain to her why. I know that this has nothing to do with you two and I'm sorry. It's easier if she has nothing to do with Carl in any way and his family too. She started in the church kindigarden this year and is doing real well.

You always tried to be real nice to me and Melody and I'm sorry but thats the way it is.

Yours truly,
Bernice
P.S. I wish things could be different.

He wondered what sort of thing Bernice and V.D. had told Melody about the disappearance of her Roberts grandparents.

He sifted through the little pile. His mother appeared to have saved every scrap of paper that Bernice had ever scribbled upon. There were thank-you cards with messages like:

Carl and I will treasure your wonderful present for the rest of our lives!

and a sympathy card when Grammy Queenie died that said:

She was a remarkable woman

and was signed:

Mrs. V. Norman, Bernice and Melody

Grammy Queenie had been friendly to Bernice but she couldn't stand her mother; in fact, one of the few things that his mother and grandmother had agreed upon was that V.D. Norman was a hypocrite, and nasty.

"Poor old V.D. had a hard life," his father used to say to them.

"Who hasn't!" Grammy Queenie would shoot back.

By the time his father died, Bernice hadn't spoken to his parents for more than half a dozen years; even so, she'd sent a sympathy card. He had seen this before; his mother had shown it to him the night before the funeral.

I was so sorry to hear about Mr. Roberts passing away. May the Lord God bring you comfort and blessings in your time of sorrow.

Sincerely, Bernice Nickerson

She'd married a man from her church, had four or five more kids and become a devout Baptist. When Melody graduated from high school, Bernice had wanted to send her to a Christian college in the States.

Carl was annoyed at his mother for saving all of these things; he felt that, somehow, they were nobody's business but his own.

When he saw the postcard of the cross on Mount Royal, he thought for a moment that it must be in the wrong place. It was postmarked Lachine, Quebec, 1971, and was addressed to "Mrs. J. Roberts" in Ragged Islands:

Sat. Night.

Dear Mrs R. Your brother and his wife are being very kind. Everything went very smooth. They were all very nice. The plane trip had me more ascared! I will talk to you when I get back. Give the little baby doll a kiss from me.

Love.

Unsigned, but Bernice's handwriting, he was certain: a memento of the secret trip to Montreal that had taken place behind his back.

He tore it in two. Then tore each piece again.

3—

WHEN JAMIE CRAWLED BACK into bed with her, she had no idea what time it was. Late, she knew that, but he hadn't tried not to wake her. Half-asleep, she turned towards him; his feet were like ice.

Where've you been?

"I was out for a walk."

At this hour? Where'd you go?

"The shore."

Had she been lying awake and waiting for a while? Or had he just woken her up? She couldn't tell. It was so good to hear his voice, to feel the weight of him there beside her.

Down to the beach?

"No. We headed down through the marsh. Tide was out, so we could walk on the edge of the creek. Saw a fox. Couple actually— mother and a young one. The sea's like glass, not a wave. We walked along the rocks as far as the Point."

Who's we?

"Carl came along."

And how is he?

"Good. He's good."

Lying on their sides, facing each other, his hand on her hip bone.

You two getting along now?

"Getting to know each other, yes."

That's good, that's nice. And she was thinking how great it would be if Carl and his father could start to get along finally.

Jamie's hand was so tender.

What time is it?

"Can't say. Sun won't be up for hours."

She snuggled up close to him, lifted her hands to touch his chest; she whispered into his mouth, *You two were out for a walk in the middle of the night?*

"Not exactly."

How's Carl?

"You'll have to ask him yourself."

Where is he now?

"In Mother's room."

Carl in the little bedroom downstairs off the living room—what would he be doing in there?

What—

Oh, *no!*

She began to worry. Had she cleaned that room out yet? Queenie's shoebox—had she been careless and left it where someone would see? Had she put those letters in a safe place? She didn't want Carl snooping around and finding things that Queenie wanted kept private.

Then Susan Ann realized that she was not quite certain which Carl Jamie was talking about. Had he been for a walk with their son, or with his Uncle Carl who had gone to sea? She started to sit up—

Jamie's hand was pulling her back into the bed, touching her so gently—

But what if it was Uncle Carl downstairs, his namesake and their son's as well, what if—

Oh, Jamie, I—

"Shhhh—"

Long-lost Uncle Carl—what would he have told Jamie out on that walk?

"Shhhh now."

Which Carl? Which one? She was afraid to ask, because if Uncle Carl had talked to Jamie—

And if it was their own son snooping around in Queenie's room, he might find something he shouldn't. There were certain things down there that were nobody's business but Queenie's, things that she had kept hidden all her life.

"Did you miss me?"

Oh yes yes.

"I'm right here."

Oh, yes. Right here.

"And I want you to be right here with me, too."

Yes.

"Forget everything else for a while."

Yes, here she was with Jamie home, finally, and she needed to calm down, to relax and calm down. Because her mind wandered so sometimes, jumping from one worry to the next, from one unhappiness to the next—

His hand on her hip, his—

Oh.

When he touched her like that—

Oh.

When she was in bed with Jamie, those worries and feelings of unwantedness could stop shunting through her—

"Susiesusie Ann."

When he whispered like that, she could sometimes feel clear and sure of everything, because she was surrounded by Jamie, *Jamie, here, now.*

"Oh Sue." His voice was warm and soothing and his hand was

warm too, and insistent, his fingers working slow circles round and round the point of her hip. She felt as if he were smoothing the joint, wearing down that deposit of ache that made it so hard for her to get up and get moving.

Oh oh—

Then he was so close, so present, as if he were no longer outside of her, as if his fingers had slipped inside her skin somehow, and he could stroke her very bones.

Yet still, still, in the back of her mind, Queenie's room—

"Susan Ann, oh Susiesusie Ann."

We're not quite alone in the house, mister.

"Yeah? So?" She could hear him grin.

You better make sure no one can hear us.

His hand was nearly a part of her now, almost—

"Hear us what?"

You know as well as I do, Mister Man.

His hand opening, sliding, touching her belly, rubbing slowly, down and down to between her legs. How could she not think of skin gone pale and saggy, of hair that had once been dark and thick and soft gone coarse and thin and grey?

I'm sorry.

"Why?"

You used to say it was so pretty, but it's a sad-lookin' thing these days.

"It suits me just fine."

But she was glad for the dark in the room. He was whispering, "Here kitty kitty kitty," and she was thinking of how years ago, when they had called themselves nudelyweds, he had first rubbed his cheek down there, whispering, "My little pussy pillow," his baby talk making her giggle, making her giggle and laugh while her whole body was feeling for the first time that there was a place where it was supposed to be. She pushed up against him, her hands reaching down to brush against his.

And how's my Mister Man?

"Attenn-*shunn.*"

She giggled again. *Well, you just stay that way, mister.*

"No *At ease?*"

No sir, not while you're on duty for me.

They were both giggling now. His feet were warmer. He tickled her leg with his big toe and she shuddered, then he slid his foot up the back of her leg, wrapping himself around her. He wiggled his finger against her, gently moving it into her.

He had been gone for such a long time.

"No I wasn't. Just out to the Point and back, out to where the names are."

His whole clan had been chiselling their names out there, as far back as old Asa Roberts, well over a hundred years. Their kids' names were there, their grandkids' too, Uncle Carl's—

"Only thing I ever did that will last. Carved my initials on a rock when I was ten."

All downhill from there, was it?

"Pretty much. I did get to finger a pretty girl."

She snorted. *Ha, I'm hardly what you'd call pretty these days.*

"Still not too bad, I'd say." He was licking the tip of her nose. "Here, puss puss pusspusspuss."

Silly, silly Mister Man.

"Kitty kitty kitty."

She fell back on the bed and he followed her, covering her. He was both hard and soft, and she opened her whole body to him. She felt as if he were travelling down through his fingers, all of him travelling down, moving inside, as if he were flowing inside, filling every forgotten place. Her worry and upset began to flicker and then to disappear; Jamie was alive beneath her skin.

"Susan Ann, oh Susiesusie."

Outside, it had started to rain: a steady, strong rain that drenched the dry garden, that soaked the earth and raised the water in the well, that made the rocks on the shore slippery and dangerous. Inside of her, Jamie was swimming deeper and deeper, a little soothing flood coursing all around her bones, her whole body wrapped itself about him. She held onto him so tightly—he was everything.

"My Susiesusie Ann."

There's no one else in the whole world right now. Just us.

"Where'd they go?"

She giggled, she realized that she was playing a little trick on everybody. *They think I'm in the hospital.*

"You are."

No.

"Yes."

No, I can't be, I don't want to be!

"Yes, yes, you are," and then he was slipping away.

Don't go away, don't go!

"Oh Susiesusie Sue—"

Jamie? Jamie!

"Now, now—"

Jamie!

"Are you having a bad dream? Did you have a bad dream?"

Don't go, no!

"I'm not going anywhere. I'm right here. You must have had a bad dream."

What? Lorraine? What—

"Shhh, now—there there, it's all right now. There there, it's over. Mum, relax. You're awake now. It's over." Other hands were touching her forehead, smoothing her hair. Her daughter's hands. Lorraine.

"You pulled away the oxygen. Lie still, I'm just going to put it back."

Lorraine?

"Yes?"

But there was no way to tell Lorraine what was happening inside her. The ache that was replacing Jamie, an ache so heavy that it was pulling her down into the bed. Was he gone again, or hiding? Behind her bones, inside her bones—oh, Jamie, Jamie Jamie Jamie—

"Were you dreaming about Dad?"

No. Because she hadn't been dreaming. He had crawled into bed with her, he had woken her up. He'd been for a walk down through the salt marsh to the shore. He had seen a fox. His name was still carved on the rock and he had not gone walking alone— Carl had been with him. But which Carl, which one, and why hadn't she dared to ask?

"You must be dry, would you like some water?"

But her hands couldn't hold anything, it would slip out and spill and get lost.

"I'll use one of these sponge sticks, okay?" And there was something wet pushing against her lips, and she opened and let it in, a sponge on a stick, like a sucker, like a candy only it was water, and Lorraine was moving it over her gums and it was so wet and good. She sucked it dry.

Dry abba bone.

"More? Do you want some more?"

She nodded her head. Oh yes, it was so wet and good on her gums—

Where're my teeth?

Had Jamie caught her with her teeth out?

But the stick was in her mouth again, and the water made her so happy she sucked every drop. She had been parched, her whole body, and the water might bring him back—

Water—the water in the sponge, in the cup, the well filling up, the garden in bloom, and down through the salt marsh to tide pools and whitecaps, waves moving and moving, and then over the sea and through the waves—the water travelling like Jamie, soaking her, soaking. Lying back in the waves in September when the hurricanes brought the warm waters, Jamie and Lorraine riding the breakers, and Carl and Susan Ann jumping over them before they broke, and out there, out there, way out there, farther than anyone could see in the mighty ocean deep, the Emerald Bank, the restless wave and peril—

"Enough? Did you get enough? Do you want any more?"

What?

"Do you want more water?"

No no—

Bending down, coming closer to the pillow—

"Is that better?"

Rain, rain—

Lorraine.

She was awake again, she had been drifting off, looking for—

"I'm sorry, Mum, but you were calling out."

She had been back home, in bed with Jamie, and now she was stuck in this miserable hospital again.

"You woke me up."

I woke you up?

What was Lorraine doing here if she was so tired? Why didn't she just go home to bed? She could do that—she could stand up and walk right out of here. No one had tied *her* up and hidden her feet. Why hang around and gloat?

"Do you want me to sit up with you for a while?"

What? No, just—

She had been so happy dreaming about Jamie, it wasn't fair.

Did she dream about him very often? She didn't think so. It was a rare thing, and damn that Lorraine for ruining it, Lorraine and Peter, they—

Where was Peter? Where'd he go?

"What, Mum?"

Peter. Peter. Your husband.

"Peter? He's at home."

At home. She'd thought he was here. When had he gone?

"He was here, but he left a few hours ago."

A few hours ago.

"Yes, he went home after dinner."

Dinner? Was it past dinnertime?

"It's nighttime, Mum."

Nighttime? Was it very late? *What time is it?*

"What's the time? Is that what you said?"

Yes. What time is it?

"It's late. Now, you should go back to sleep."

Late? How late?

"After midnight. I'm here with you for the night, now, so—"

Here for the night? Why?

"Don't worry about it, just relax and go back to sleep."

But it didn't make any sense! If Lorraine wanted to sit up with her, why in the name of God wouldn't she do it at home? They would both be more comfortable back there.

"They've brought me a little cot—over there. Now you just go to sleep."

Lorraine was sitting down in the chair beside the bed; she put her hand on her mother's.

What in hell was going on? A cot? What was Lorraine doing?

Susan Ann was wide awake now. Awake in the hospital, in the middle of the night, with her daughter's hand touching her own, not holding it, exactly, but resting on top of it; the palm of Lorraine's hand cold and still; her fingers moving slowly up and down a few times, patting. Susan Ann thought that it was the way she would pet a cat, or a dog that wasn't her own. It was the touch of a minister who didn't know you.

"Go back to sleep, now." Her voice so quiet, almost a whisper, and her fingers were going *pat-pat pat-pat* on the back of her mother's hand.

Something felt unfinished and wrong, and Susan Ann wondered what it was—something back with Jamie that she needed to understand? Something back in that drowsy place where . . .

But she had lost her train of thought, could barely remember what he had told her, and it seemed that the drowsiness was a thing, a line, and somehow she had crossed over it and would soon even forget that he had come to her bed. Maybe if she relaxed, maybe she could slip back across it, into the warm comfort where Jamie. . . .

No, she had woken up too far, and now she was starting to get that terrible feeling, that—what was it called when you couldn't sleep? It had a name. *Im-something.*

Im-possible. No.

She never suffered from it, that was why she couldn't remember.

Only when she was so sick that time when she was a little girl. Those nights when those awful curtains kept her awake . . .

"Nobody loves you, nobody—"

No!

Im—Im—No, in-something.

In sar-nee-a.

Insarnia? No. That's a place, not a thing.

That lonely feeling in the night. Poor Queenie had it; Susan Ann would wake up in the middle of the night and hear her sometimes, roaming the downstairs, talking to herself. Even after she died, roaming around—

Wait now, what did Jamie tell her? Wasn't that it? Someone was down in Queenie's room, down there rummaging away, looking for something—

Who is it, who's down there?

Lorraine's hand pressed down upon her own. Had Susan Ann spoken out loud? She couldn't always tell what was inside and what was outside her head; things could get mixed up.

There was something she wanted to remember, had almost remembered, but it was gone again. She lay very still with her eyes closed, imagining her daughter watching so closely. After a moment, she felt the weight of the hand lifted from hers. She listened and listened. There was the hissing sound, and then there was a sigh. Exasperation? She couldn't tell. After another moment, she heard Lorraine stand up and whisper something to herself, *Psspsspsspss*, while she moved to the other side of the room.

There was a creaking sound—the cot, as her daughter lay down—and then another sigh.

She would probably go right to sleep. While her mother went on lying there with that *in-something*, Lorraine would just go to sleep. Although it was hard to tell with her sometimes. There were nights when Lorraine would pretend to be asleep when Susan Ann and Jamie looked in on her, long after bedtime.

What was that thing? *In—in—Insomnia!*

Ha! Thank God that was out of the way.

Insomnia, yes. Queenie roaming the downstairs half the night, "My insomnia's actin' up again," she'd say in the morning. Susan Ann had wondered at first if it really was insomnia or if she was just poking about, spying on everybody.

Insomnia, insomnia. She had remembered.

But wasn't there something else to remember? Queenie's room?

She remembered the insomnia, she could remember this. Jamie had come to her bed—

But which bed? Not this one, surely? Why weren't they at home?

Why in the name of God was Lorraine doing this?

When Queenie was dying, Susan Ann hadn't locked her away in a hospital, no sir! She had looked after her mother-in-law at home. Her mother-in-law! Queenie had died in the comfort of her own bed. But that Lorraine! Sticking her own mother off in a hospital. This wasn't the way Susan Ann had cared for her through all her growing-up years, through all those bouts of measles and mumps and flu, and it wasn't the way family should do things. Lorraine behaved as if she was doing her duty and no more, no more than that. Her duty. Susan Ann's own flesh and blood had locked her away in a strange place, far, far away from home. Why did children nowadays grow away from their parents? Something that had been so close—how could they grow apart the way they did?

How clearly she remembered that morning in the bedroom when she first felt the quickening inside her. She was standing at the dresser, combing her hair in the mirror, watching Jamie behind her, his long white back, when she felt that shiver of pleasure inside, as sweet as Jamie's fingers: quicken, quickening. It had been wonderful and terrifying both. She was going to have a baby, to be a mother.

Why did children grow up and grow away from their mothers?

One evening, Lorraine was waiting and watching up the lane. She had come in after school, and dumped her books without saying a word. Something was wrong, Susan Ann knew that, but when she asked, all she got was a snarly look. When Carl tried to tease his sister, she ignored him and went into the yard. Had something happened at school? Carl shrugged. He didn't know and couldn't care less. That was around the time that he and Jamie were always at each other, and Carl was either shut up in his room or off in the woods.

Why couldn't they get along, those two? Susan Ann had gotten along with Len and Boyd and Murd, but every time she said so to her own kids, they sighed in exasperation.

All the while she was getting supper, she kept her eye on the kitchen window, on Lorraine tossing a stick to the dog and watching up the lane. It was spring, the yard was muddy, and it was all she could do to keep herself from opening the door and calling out to be careful, to not let Scamp get all dirty, she didn't want a load of mud tracked through the house. Queenie came into the kitchen, and started watching out the window as well. "She wants to talk to her father," Queenie said, and immediately Susan Ann realized that this was the case. What could it be that she wanted to tell him, that she wouldn't tell her mother? When it was time for Jamie to come home from the plant, Lorraine hurried up the lane to meet him and he stood listening to her for a long while; then he walked back and forth with her, talking quietly while, from the kitchen window, his wife and mother looked on and wondered what was up. Supper was ready and on the table before they came inside.

"I promised her that I wouldn't tell a soul," he told Susan Ann that night when she asked him. "It's nothing for you to get all concerned about, I can tell you that." What could it have been? What was the secret that Lorraine didn't want her mother to know? "I gave her my word. Don't worry. She just wanted to talk something over."

But Susan Ann was certain that there were little secrets between the two of them, secrets and private conversations, all the time after that.

She didn't know what her husband and daughter talked about when they walked in the lane, and even though she realized that it couldn't have been all that earth-shattering—homework? teachers? boys?—how it bothered her! Why hadn't her daughter talked to her? Why instead was Lorraine working her way in between her parents? They would all be at the table eating supper, or in the living room watching the stupid old box, and Susan Ann would suddenly feel removed from everyone. Sometimes she would try to console herself by thinking, *Jamie has Lorraine and I have Carl*, but that wasn't the way things were, really. Carl was growing further away from everybody—if he was close to anybody, it was his Grammy Queenie. And then it seemed as if they were all alone together, the whole family, sharing very little. This wasn't the way she'd imagined having a family with Jamie. She had been determined that her own kids would feel wanted and loved.

Jamie had been the first person ever to love her more than anyone else; the first person to put her first. When she was little, she knew that Mum Wellman loved her deeply, but no more than she loved Dad or Boyd or Murd. They were all equal. She always hoped that Aunt Aggie loved her more than she loved Muriel, but then Muriel had gotten the farm. But she *had* been certain with Jamie. He had loved his mother the most, but then he had moved Queenie aside for Susan Ann. How Jamie had doted on his mother! Just look at the sacrifice he had made for his family! No one knew the depths of that sacrifice but Susan Ann.

"I love you, I love you, I love you," he said, while they giggled and kissed and downstairs Queenie was jealous as could be.

"Oh, Sue, she had a helluva life with my father."

He said this every time Queenie was mean to her, as a kind of excuse, "She had a helluva life with my father."

Susan Ann knew that Queenie's life with old Frank had been miserable; there wasn't a soul on earth who ever had a kind word to say about old Frank Roberts—and Jamie himself didn't even know the half of it, he didn't know about the things Queenie had hidden away her whole married life. Susan Ann kept that shoe-box a secret after Queenie died.

Jamie had moved his mother aside for his wife. If there was one thing in Susan Ann's life of which she was certain, it was that Jamie had loved her beyond all measure.

But he never did oppose his mother once, not once her whole life long; he never really stood up to Queenie, not until she was dead and things in the kitchen were going missing—the paring knife that turned up under the bathtub, the wooden spoon that reappeared on the top shelf behind the cereal, Queenie's blue china teacup that vanished forever. Then the toilet started flushing in the middle of the night, driving them both foolish. Every time they touched each other, it seemed, the flush would go, and then the water running and running until one of them went down to the bathroom to jiggle the handle. It went on for months, until Jamie stood in the centre of the house one night and shouted, "Mum, Jesus, for the love of God, will you please leave us the hell alone!"

And her ghost was silent then, for the rest of Jamie's life.

SALLY

How happy she and Sally were to see each other again! Susan Ann ran down the stairs, through the dining room and the kitchen, out the back door to the porch and down into the yard, where Sally was leaping into the air with joy!

Susan Ann went down the porch steps two at a time. "Sally Sally Sally!"

And her little yellow dog ran to her and jumped right up into her arms!

She found herself sitting on the second step up, laughing, and Sally licking her face, moaning and yipping with happiness.

"How's my girl, how's my girl, how's my girl?"

Holding her like a baby, a big, wild, squirmy baby. Then Sally wriggled out of her arms, flipped over in the air and jumped to the ground, where she ran back and forth at Susan Ann's feet, her tail wagging like a little dizzy propeller.

"The bestest-bestest doggie!"

Susan Ann could not remember the last time she had been so happy. She clapped her hands and shouted for the sheer pleasure of it, "Yes! Yes! Yes-yes!" while Sally jumped and bounced and licked and whined happily.

"Yesyesyesyesyes!"

Then they both calmed down for a minute; Sally came and nestled her face into Susan Ann's lap.

"Oh, my girl," and Susan Ann scratched Sally's big floppy ears and tickled her throat and petted her golden coat. "How've you been? How've you been, girl?" She pulled back and looked down, but as soon as she saw Sally's big dark, sad eyes looking up at her, she bent down and buried her face in Sally's warm coat, smelling the wonderful doggie smell. "What a beautiful dog. The most beautiful ears in all the world. Ears like a princess, yes, yes, a beautiful, golden doggie princess."

Sally moaned with pleasure, wiggling and wriggling against her, that tail of hers wagging away.

Then Sally ran out onto the lawn and got her ball, and came back and dropped it at Susan Ann's feet like a wonderful gift. Susan Ann reached down and picked it up. "Here you go! Go get the ball!" And she threw it back out into the yard. They were laughing and barking—Sally running back and forth, chasing the ball and bringing it back, while Susan Ann sat on the steps, tossing it over and over.

Then Sally came to her, holding the ball in her warm, soft mouth, and climbed up onto the step to lay her head down on Susan Ann's lap. They stayed together like that for quite a while.

What a funny little dog she was, with her wise, sad face and her droopy ears that made Susan Ann think of periwigs and pictures of kings and courtiers with ermine capes. She was such a bundle of fierce, fierce love and devotion. Uncle Hay had found her on the road outside Moncton, standing beside the bodies of three other pups from her litter, wailing and guarding them. Her uncle was on his way to meet Susan Ann and Mum at the train, and had put Sally up into the wagon and buried the others. No one ever found out where she had come from, or how she had arrived on that road. All that Susan Ann was told was that she was an orphan.

The winter that Aunt Aggie came and stayed in Ragged Islands, she told Susan Ann that the other puppies had been horribly beaten. "It upset your uncle a lot that someone would do something so miserable to poor, defenceless animals," she said.

"Did he say what they had done?"

"He said it looked like someone had gone at them with a hammer."

That was why they hadn't told her the circumstances when she was a girl. They didn't want to upset her.

"But you knew all along, didn't you?" she said to Sally. "You were there when that terrible thing happened."

Elsie Steeves lived a few houses up Inglis Street with her mother and sisters. She was a sour old thing, and she used to stick out her tongue at Mum Wellman and Susan Ann whenever there was no one else looking. "She's not simple, even though she acts like it," Mum had said. "She's not simple, she's *strange.*"

"Pay no attention," said Dad. "She's crazy as the birds."

When Elsie's husband became bedridden, she stuck him in a home and came back to live in her mother's house on Inglis Street. She went into Moncton every morning to see him, and came back to Shediac on the afternoon train. Twice a day she walked past Susan Ann's house, and twice a day she antagonized Sally, first by saying nasty things, then by throwing rocks and handfuls of dirt. On the days that Sally was tied to the clothespole by a rope, Elsie would come into the yard waving her cane and trying to hit the poor thing. When Mum heard the afternoon train whistle from the crossing on Riverside Drive, she would hurry out and try to get the dog into the house; but Sally was smart and she hated Elsie. Her favourite place to hide was under the veranda.

"She drove you crazy, didn't she, girl?"

Sally moaned in agreement.

"You saw her be mean to me, didn't you?"

And Sally lifted her head and nodded.

"She was an awful thing."

Susan Ann was sick with pleurisy when Elsie and her high and mighty friends, like Banker Chipman, went to the police; she was sick in bed and not able to save her dog. The policeman came to the house with a gun.

"Not this time, though," she said, tenderly stroking those gorgeous ears, that brave little head. "I won't let her get you this time. No nono."

But as soon as she said this, her heart was filled with dread. After all, she couldn't be sure of what might happen next. That damn ugly apartment wouldn't allow pets; there was a lady down the hall who got in trouble because she had a cat. Besides, Susan Ann wouldn't do that to a dog, she wouldn't dream of keeping her cooped up in that puny space. A dog needed to run the countryside—the city was no place for them at all.

Oh, but what if that miserable old Elsie Steeves stormed into the yard again with a policeman?

"I won't let anything bad happen to you," she said. "Ever."

Sally lifted her head and looked up into Susan Ann's eyes. She opened her mouth and let the ball fall gently into Susan Ann's lap. Then she leaned upwards and licked Susan Ann's cheek.

"I won't let old Elsie get you this time," Susan Ann said. "Or any old policeman either."

Despite her dread and worry, despite her fear of what might happen next, Susan Ann felt an enormous sense of contentment. How comfortable it was to sit on the back steps with Sally's warm body near to her. After Jamie had gone, there had been no one she could just hold close and hug tight. Her family's hugs lasted no time at all. These days no one wanted you to hold on and hug them—they thought you were clingy and desperate.

The old gardens were gone, the lilacs and fruit trees too, but it was beautiful to sit and look out at the grass, to see the familiar shape of the house next door silhouetted against the morning sky. It was wonderful to breathe such good air, to inhale such fresh-ness. This was where she had sat with her brother Murd and that Italian airman, where she had hulled peas and strawberries with Mum Wellman, where she had talked to Mum and Dad about Jamie's proposal—

Jamie had come to her in a dream that very morning! He had stood at her bedside and reached out to her. "I miss you terribly and I am counting the days." That was what he had said. It had felt more important than a simple dream: she knew it meant something. Old Pharaoh took his dreams to Joseph—where could she take hers?

Maybe she *should* go on to Ragged Islands; maybe that was where she was supposed to be. Could that be what the dream meant?

Sally was looking up at her, wagging her tail as if to say, "Let's go, let's go!"

"Wait," she thought. "Now just wait."

The people who had bought Jamie's house were summer peo-ple. By the time she got there, they would be gone. She knew where the spare key was hidden, in the mustard jar on the Flintstone rock down in the cellar. She could slip inside the cellar door on the side of the house. They would never even know.

Yes, that was what she would do.

She would walk back to Jamie's house, and be home. She closed her eyes and moved through that house: the painted woodwork, the doorways, the windows, the stairway up to their bedroom. She was thinking of all the times she had looked out her upstairs window down into the yard—Lorraine pushing little Carl on the tire swing, Meg and Tommy climbing over the round outcropping of rock, Queenie in the rhubarb patch nestled beside it, Jamie's garden in rows and rows, the spruce trees, Boyd and Joyce sitting outside their camper trailer parked up on the grass, and then, beyond the yard, the path out through the woods, down to the salt marsh and the small crescent beach nestled between the rocks, and Gull Island sitting there, just offshore.

But what about that thing that had been following her yesterday? She couldn't be on the road knowing something wild was on the loose and after her.

Sally moaned contentedly, and Susan Ann realized that she had her dog for protection. "That thing wouldn't dare come near my Sally," she thought.

Ragged Islands was far away. Due south as the crow flies, but the old crow could fly straight over Chignecto Bay and Minas Basin, and she would have to walk around them. She imagined a map of the Maritimes hanging in front of her, and traced her finger in the air: the route out of town, then down and eastwards into Nova Scotia, across the Isthmus of Chignecto, inland towards Truro, through the Wentworth Valley, past the village where Mumma Mac came from, then turning southwest to march through the province and down the shore: Lunenburg, Bridgewater, Liverpool, Ragged Islands. All those places she had known, and now missed so terribly—

"It'd be a darn long haul."

Sally startled her by jumping down to the ground, all excited again, as if to say, "I'm ready, let's go!"

"It's so far," she said. "If only we were a couple of crows, we could do it in no time. We could fly there lickety-split."

She tossed the ball and Sally leapt up into the air and caught it.

"Do you want to come with me? Do you want to come away with me?" she asked.

Woof!

She couldn't let Sally stay here, that was for certain, and with a dog beside her she was sure that thing would keep its distance, and leave them alone.

"You stay there, that's a good dog." And she went into the house.

The kitchen was exactly as it had been when she'd arrived yesterday: the clock on the shelf frozen at ten after three, the half-peeled potatoes and carrots beside the sink, Mum's favourite cup beside the teapot.

"Hello?" she called out. "Mum? Dad?" But her voice sounded so lonely in the empty house that she couldn't bear to stay there another moment.

When she went back outside, Sally dropped the ball at her feet. Instead of throwing it, she put it in her bag. "Well then," she said, "let's go."

As they went around the corner of the porch, Susan Ann looked up and down the street to make sure there was no one coming. Just up the way, Elsie's place stood dark and empty. It had been a handsome house at one time, but now it was unfriendly and cold, as if it had always been abandoned. The paint was peeling, and hanging on the front door was an old, dead wreath of rust-coloured fir branches. It was sad, really. Elsie had been the youngest of five daughters; the house had been lively and happy once. Kitty White's mother had told her that when she was young, the side garden had been a lovely thing, and that Elsie's mother had had tea parties there on Saturday afternoons in July.

They set off down the street, Sally trotting on ahead, exploring, running in and out of the front yards, sniffing the trees. Susan Ann hoped there was no trace left—no scent, no trails—of the creature that had been following her yesterday; she wanted Sally to steer clear of it.

They turned onto Main Street. The veranda on Kitty White's house was so large that her brother Willie used to ride his bicycle on it, pedalling slowly back and forth in a long oval, wearing a battered, tall silk hat that had belonged to their father. Susan Ann's need to be Kitty's friend used to make her very unhappy; there were times when she was so twisted around Kitty's little finger that she couldn't think straight.

Then they were walking past the houses of the high and mighties.

Right square in front of A.J. Chipman's, Sally abruptly stopped. She stood stock-still and sniffed the air suspiciously, her tail sticking straight up, motionless and stiff, and she growled low in her throat. She was glaring at the banker's house, her little body tensed as if ready to strike.

"Oh no," thought Susan Ann, afraid that if her dog went running and barking into that yard, something terrible might happen. Were people watching out the window?

She crouched down and whispered in Sally's ear, "Who's the bestest dog in the whole world?" Sally looked up, her eyes questioning. The tail began to wag again.

"That's right, that's good." She kissed Sally's ear. "That's my girl, yes, yes—" as she looked over Sally's head at Banker Chipman's house.

Who were those figures in the downstairs window? In the study at the front of the house, a man and a woman—oh God, was it Elsie herself in there talking to the old villain? Scheming and planning, up to their no-good tricks?

"Let's go, let's go girl." She stood up and started moving quickly down the sidewalk. "Come on! Come on!"

Sally was running behind her, then beside her, then ahead.

"Good, good girl!" The danger was past and Sally was sniffing the sidewalk, the roots of a tree, a fencepost. Then they could see the blue waters of the bay. At the edge of town, Sally went into the ditch and did her business.

"What a smart dog!"

And they crossed over the bridge and left Shediac behind.

Susan Ann kept looking all around, but she could not see anything watching them or following them. Ahead of her, her dog was chasing a chipmunk, barking and playing along the edge of the pavement. Had she ever seen her little dog so happy before?

"If only my family could care for me as much as you do," she said. "You'd never stick me in that old room, would you? You'd never leave me locked up all alone, and go off to whisper about me, no, you wouldn't."

"No, never," those big dark eyes said.

"'I miss you terribly and I am counting the days.' That's what Jamie came to tell me. Do you think we can make it to Ragged Islands? To meet him there? It's a long, long way."

She wasn't so sure she would make it. It was as far as her great-great-grandfather John MacDonald had walked, on his trek from Cape Breton to the Settlement. It was a helluva long way.

Great-great-grandfather John, Daddy Mac and Mum Wellman's father's father's father—he had walked through here from the other direction, a little over two hundred years ago. Next to his own father's name on the boat list, in the column that cited reasons for coming to the New World, the words read, "To seek a better life." That was why her great-great-great-grandfather had left Scotland in 1773, and that was all she knew about him—she didn't even know where in Scotland William MacDonald had come from. The only reason she knew about the boat list was because Meg did one of those charts—what was it? There was a name for it. She went off to the library and researched the family tree. It started with a G.

"G, G, G," she said, "G *something* ology. Not *geology*, no. And not *gynecology*, that's for sure. G, G, Gee—*genealogy!* That's the ticket, yes."

They walked and they walked, they walked all day. When they came to the far side of the woods, they were on a hillside looking out over the Tantramar Marshes, which marked the boundary between the two provinces where she had spent most of her life. It was here that the southeast corner of New Brunswick tapered down to form the Isthmus of Chignecto, which reached out between the great Bay of Fundy to the south and the Northumberland Strait to the north, and held Nova Scotia to the rest of the continent.

The marshes spread out before them, sprinkled with ponds and crossed with rivers, muddy-banked and tidal: the Tantramar, the Aulac, the Missaguash. The rivers and their squiggly creeks snaked through rich lands that the old Acadians had drained and turned into fields when they built their earthen dykes three hundred years before.

"That's not so long ago as it used to seem," she thought. Once, it had seemed an eternity. But that was before she had lived for eighty-six years.

At one time, she had been awed by the fact that her parents had lived in two centuries; now that she had done the same thing herself, she understood that time was both more and less impressive than she had once thought. She had lived through to the end of the Century of Progress—and that had been no mean feat.

"The Century of Progress. That's a hot one."

Dirt roads crossed and connected the fields, and hay barns dotted the countryside. From her vantage point on the hill, those fields were a hundred varieties of green: the marsh hay waving and pitching in the wind like water in the bay, wide undulating waves of dark and light that swept over the vast marshlands.

Buried in those greens, she knew, were hundreds of colours that could not be seen from a distance—the yellows of buttercups, the blues of bachelor buttons, the purples, pinks and oranges of a thousand wildflowers. She remembered a crazy bouquet from a long time ago, from a Sunday afternoon in the thirties with Boyd and Joyce in their new Ford V-8, driving along the High Marsh Road. They had trudged through fields to see the floating island—a forest of hackmatack growing on the wet, spongy moss—and they had seen the petrified stumps of an ancient forest beneath the waters of a creek. She had picked every flower she had come across, and all the way home, they had lain beside her, a fragrant heap in the back seat.

The Tantramar River was fed from the Jolicure Lakes on the borders of the marshes; her eyes followed its course as it wove southward through the land, appearing and disappearing in the waving countryside. Way to the south, where the river entered the Cumberland Basin, she could see a glimmer of big water on the horizon. "That's the head of the Fundy there," she said. The basin opened up into Chignecto Bay, which opened up into the Bay of Fundy, and twice a day the Atlantic Ocean heaved itself up, lifting the bay's mighty waters far into the wedge between New Brunswick and Nova Scotia, and sending tidal bores up the rivers. "The highest tides in the world," she said to Sally. "And Fundy's where they go to nowadays to see the whales."

Sally stood still and quiet, leaning against her leg, as they looked out over the land. Straight out from the hillside where they were standing, a marsh hawk was gliding, hunting; that meant there would be lots of things down there for a dog to chase: mice and voles, tiny skittery things. It would be better than the woods, where there was always the danger of animals that might want to hunt down a little yellow dog: a bear, maybe, or a lynx or wolves.

"Due south," Susan Ann was saying, "that building perched way off there? Up on the hill? That's Fort Beausejour. That goes back before the Expulsion."

When she was a young girl, she had been taught that the Acadians were a bunch of gripers who got what was coming to them because they wouldn't swear allegiance to the King. It had seemed like a reasonable request to her back in those days, when they had all sung, "In days of yore from Britain's shore, Wolfe the dauntless hero came." She was an adult before she realized that the poor buggers were just trying to be neutral and stay out of harm's way. These lands were French one year and English the next, back and forth time and again with each stupid war in Europe, and those poor people just wanted to be left alone to live their lives on the land they loved. The Expulsion was more about taking Acadian lands than about whether or not people had sworn an allegiance of any kind. It was like most things in politics—greed all gussied up with another name.

All her growing-up years, she had believed that the British could do no wrong, because that was the way things were taught. And stories like those of the Acadians, or the Black Loyalists down near Ragged Islands, well, they were either changed or forgotten.

It was easy to see why the Acadians had loved this land so much, and why so many of them had wanted to come back to it. "My God, Sally," she said, "isn't it just beautiful?"

Susan Ann had always wanted to show this part of the world to her grandchildren, but that had never really happened, and unless they were looking for her now, and caught up with her very soon, it never would. It would be their loss, too, because she knew things about this place that they would never be able to know without her. She knew where to find the samphire greens that were so salty and tasty, and she knew where there were fossils on the sandstone rocks beside the shore.

"Sackville's over that way," she said, pointing to her right. "Lorraine went to university there, and never learned a single thing about this place." That was true; she never went outside the town, never went out on the marsh once; she never went for a walk along the top of the dykes. "Too busy running around with that Elliot," Susan Ann told Sally. He'd always seemed a prissy thing to her, more interested in his old books than in people. When Lorraine brought him down to Ragged Islands the first time, Elliot had been quiet and polite but he had hidden out in his room reading, and hadn't seemed interested in getting to know anyone in the family. Queenie had decided he was sneaky, and Susan Ann found herself agreeing with her mother-in-law. She'd known from the start that the marriage would never last; she had said so herself, and had said it to Jamie. She'd tried to talk to Lorraine about it, but had gotten nowhere. When Elliot took off with one of his students, Susan Ann had to bite her tongue. It would have been mean to say, "I told you so."

"It lasted fifteen years," Lorraine said, which, in this day and age, was supposed to be an eternity.

However, without Elliot there would be no Meg and Tommy. Without him she would not have had the grandchildren who had for so long been such a joy to her. He had been unfriendly and standoffish, but he had never failed to support his kids, she had to give him that. He had always been a good provider.

Which was more than she could say for her own son, actually—Carl had taken off and left his daughter behind. Jamie had been so mad, had never forgiven him for leaving Bernice, and even though she had defended Carl, because she understood how trapped he had been in that marriage, she was bitterly disappointed when she realized that he had abandoned little Melody.

She had been a fool to think that her son would ever help her.

A few miles down the road, Sally came running to her with the handle of a broken hockey stick in her mouth. It was about four feet long—just the right length for her to use as a walking stick; the taped end was comfortable and easy to hold.

"What a smart, thoughtful dog," she said. "Thank you kindly."

Sally bounded on ahead. The sun was up; the day was fine. Jamie was ahead of her, the house on Inglis Street was behind her now.

A walking stick made her think of her grandchildren, made her fondly remember the summer they had each made one and gone hiking along the shore. They had carved their initials on them with Jamie's jackknife.

> *I love to go awandering along the mountain track*
> *I love to go awandering my knapsack on my back—*
> *Valereeee*
> *Valeraaaa*
> *Valereeee*

Her voice wasn't what it used to be. It was hard to believe that when she first went to the United Church in Ragged Islands, Noreen Whynott had called her an asset to the choir. She was a screechy old woman walking the roads with her little dog: her hair all wild, her clothes all mussed up, while she leaned on a broken hockey stick from the ditch.

"Do I look as bad as that sorry thing beside the liquor store?" she wondered. Back in Toronto there was an old doll with too much makeup and a ratty hat who always asked her for spare change. "Oh, surely to God I don't look as far gone as that!"

What would people make of her? Would they think she was crazy or would they think she was a poor soul, like a refugee, walking along by the side of the road?

"Well I am," she thought. "A refugee from that miserable apartment."

Valereeee

Valeraaaa

The first time she'd had one of her episodes and landed up in the hospital in Toronto—last year was it? Or was it two years ago? She couldn't quite remember—she had lain there all night with her headphones on.

"The long lines of refugees," the voice on the radio had said, time and again, "forced to flee from their homes."

She couldn't sleep, and had listened to the story of a Muslim woman who said that soldiers had come to her door and given her *five minutes* to take what she could and get out of her house forever—and it was the house she had lived in all her life! Her family's home. This had been shortly after Susan Ann was forced to sell Jamie's house and move into that damn apartment, and the woman's story had struck a chord. *Forced to flee from their homes.* The matter-of-factness of the announcer's voice was upsetting to her—he had obviously never had anything bad happen to him.

The soldiers wore masks but the refugee woman knew who they were, because she had grown up with them—they were her *neighbours.* They were Christians.

"The Balkans," Susan Ann thought, "must be a terrible place!" She imagined that they were always filled with turmoil and upset. Why should she think otherwise? Every time she heard about them, there was a war there.

When the Muslim lady on the radio had turned back to look at her house, turned back that last time even though she said she had told herself not to, it was because she had heard a loud *WHOOSH!* The *good* Christians had poured out gasoline and thrown down a match; she found herself looking at a house made of fire.

Sodom and Gomorrah all over again.

Sarajevo, the Balkans—those were names she hadn't heard in years; they were places she only heard tell of when men went overseas. When she was in the hospital and first heard the stories on the radio, she became quite muddled. "What war is this?" she had thought, all confused at first because they were place names from her childhood, from the past. Because, other than refugees and wartime, what did she know about the Balkans?

They ate yogurt, that was about it.

"A sorry, uncivilized place it must be over there," she said.

A noise beside the road made her jump.

"What's that?"

She turned towards the bushes and saw to her relief that her dog was in there, chasing after something.

"You stay close by. Hear me?"

Sarajevo.

That was where the shot was fired that was heard around the world. That was Archduke Ferdinand, who got himself a bullet when he went there to visit. Mum and Aunt Aggie had told her all about it, had made it sound like Archduke Ferdinand got exactly what he deserved for setting foot in a place like that. That was because Uncle Hay had heard that shot and gone to France, and when he came back to the farm he had spent one whole summer sitting on a kitchen chair in the yard, his heart breaking with misery, his life ruined.

During the Second World War, she had seen newsreels at the movies, black-and-white images of people moving along roadsides with their belongings: old men and women in sad clothes, mothers with their children, poor people, ordinary people dragging carts and lugging their bundles—*the long lines of refugees in the countryside.* They had seemed so removed from her, so very far away. They were the reason that boys like her brother and her uncle went overseas.

As she lay there at night in the hospital listening to the radio, she had wondered what she would have done if men like that had come to her door.

"You have five minutes," she imagined them saying, and she would try to figure out what she would do next. What things would she try to save? In her mind, she raced through the downstairs grabbing photographs and knick-knacks; what had she forgotten in the bedroom? The picture of Aunt Aggie that was on her dresser, the family ring that Jamie had given her on their thirtieth anniversary.

If you were a refugee, would you agonize over what you had left behind for the rest of your life? The refugee woman on the radio—what could she have thought when she turned around and saw a house of fire? Everything she had known, lost forever.

"Damn uncivilized foreign place," said Susan Ann, as she walked through the familiar countryside. Sally had emerged from the trees beside the road; whatever she had been chasing through the underbrush had gotten away.

The Balkans, Sarajevo—

What awful places they must be, real hornets' nests. "Thank God I didn't grow up in a crazy, foreign place with people like that."

Sally was running back to her.

"Aren't we lucky to live here?" she said. The whole idea that your neighbours could care so little about you that—

But as she looked at her lovely golden dog coming closer to her, she thought of Elsie Steeves, and of Banker Chipman. Wasn't he quite capable of putting on a mask like one of those Balkan Christians and telling Mum and Dad to get out of their house? And even if she couldn't quite imagine old Elsie with a mask and a gun, she sure could imagine her turning the other way, locking her doors, pulling her blinds down tight and closing the curtains when men with masks and guns came up the street to knock on her neighbour's front door.

She wondered what she would have done if she'd been looking out the window one day and had seen men with masks knocking on Elsie Steeves' front door. Would she have tried to help old Elsie, or would she have thought, "Good. Finally. That's what she deserves. She's just getting what's comin' to her."

HAD HIS MOTHER BEEN KEEPING Bernice's letters for him all these years, or had she written his name on the envelope so that she could identify them for herself? At some point, she must have sorted through all the years of junk she'd squirrelled away—would that have been here, or back in Ragged Islands when she was packing up the house? Would Lorraine have helped her?

When had she written TO BE SAVED, and why? Had she saved them for herself, or was the package something she wanted found?

The only reasons Carl could imagine for saving those things Bernice had written were petty and small.

Well, no one else would ever read them now.

Although the wastebasket was full and there was a growing pile of torn and crumpled papers on the floor, there was plenty more on top of the bed still, envelopes with designations like FURNACE, NEW ROOF, or CHURCH GROUP. There was also a small stack of manila ones marked for Lorraine and her family that Carl had set aside.

If his mother were to stand in the bedroom door right now, she would say, "What are you up to, ratching around in there?" It meant rummaging, looking, scrounging. When he was a boy and asked for a quarter or fifty cents so he could go to the movies, she would have to go ratching around in her purse to find it for him.

His legs were cramped from kneeling beside the bed, so he stood up and stretched; then he shuffled into the kitchenette and poured himself another drink. No ice this time. Leaning against the counter beside the sink, savouring the comforting warmth of bourbon, he looked back through the doorway to the drifts of papers on the bed and the floor around it. It was getting late. If he were smart he'd clear things off, make the bed and try to get some sleep. Tomorrow would be another long day.

Early on a Christmas morning, fifty or more years ago now, Carl had toddled downstairs and plugged in the lights of the tree. For the few days before, everything had been tense and snappy, and he'd felt pushed aside; his father barked at him constantly, his mother had little time for him, even Grammy Queenie was neglectful. All lit up in the quiet room, the tree was no longer the bare, empty thing that his father had brought into the house—his grandmother and mother had turned it into something so strange and wonderful that he wouldn't have been surprised if it had suddenly started to sing. He remembered a lovely feeling of quiet and aloneness—perhaps he had awoken into another, more beautiful world? Perhaps every morning from now on would be like this one?

The presents were arranged invitingly beneath the branches, so exotic in all their coloured paper and trimmings. Even though he knew it would be wrong, he realized that he could be the first to know what was inside each and every one of them, and the idea of having that knowledge made him ignore the consequences. He started opening packages.

By the time Lorraine came downstairs and started to scream, he'd opened them all.

And hadn't his Grammy Queenie laughed!

Back in the bedroom, he knelt down, setting his glass on the floor beside him. He knew that he had no business, really, opening the envelopes his mother had tagged for his sister and her family, but he couldn't help himself. He knew that he would go through them—and with no compunction whatsoever.

His nephew's was the slimmest, containing only a few thank-you cards, some old crayon drawings on lined scribbler paper and a single letter.

Tommy had been the focus of Lorraine's hysteria for most of the day. Carl knew that she was not being all that unreasonable, given the circumstances; but she had gone on and on in a way that, as far as he was concerned, was more about her own self than her son. Why did she always have to be such a centre of attention? Even an international crisis was all about her.

The letter had been sent to his mother from St. Lucia.

The Park
Downtown Castries
St. Lucia, WI
June 19 '96

Dear Gram,

I hope that you are having an excellent birthday.
HAPPY BIRTHDAY GRAM!

I want you to think about what you were doing on your birthday at 10 in the morning because that is right now and I am writing to you. I am imagining that you are in your lazyboy having a cup of coffee and one of your powerful Old Doshe Muffins.

I'm sorry I won't be able to phone you today. It will be the first birthday I've missed in a long time. I hope you aren't turning down a hot date and staying at home waiting for the phone to ring. I'm sorry that this will arrive so late. I know you think that it's always better to get a letter at birthday time anyway. (Even if its late like this one will be) I know that you feel that way because you are the only person now who still sends me a card any more, (Poor me). I remember all the cards you sent to Meg and to me when we were growing up. You always put "folding money" in them. They were the best! It meant that we could

buy whatever we wanted. Gramma Howe always gave us clothes
that we couldn't stand and had to wear whenever she was
around. Mom still teases me about a green shirt I really hated.
Can you remember that one? We called it "the leprechaun puke
shirt."

I'll be back in Canada very soon. The boat I'm working on
now is just fine. The owner is a very decent guy, and his wife is
nice. I know that it seems crazy to put everything on hold and
do this, but I am very happy being a beach bum / sailor boy for
a few months. (I know that I don't have to explain the attraction
of salt water to you!) I think of the stories that Grampy told
you about his grandfather sailing to the West Indies. The
whale's tooth with the picture of your house on it is my very
favourite thing in the whole world. We are working our way
through the Windward Islands and will be in St. Lucia all this
week. Today is my day off so I came into Castries (the big city)
by minibus this morning and am sitting in the square under a
huge samaan tree that they tell me is 400 years old. Just across
from me is a beautiful old cathedral with a handpainted
mahogany ceiling. I think you would like it here. The water is
so warm. Tomorrow we take the boss–man's family down the
coast to the Pitons, which are these old twin volcanos, and
maybe do some fishing. Yesterday we went to the ruins of a
British fort from 1778. It made me think of driving down east
to visit you, because Meg and I always made Mom stop at Fort
Beausejour when we were driving to Ragged Islands. We would
run around on the hills and stretch our legs and when we got
back in the car we'd all holler, "Next stop Nova Scotia!"

I hope that life in Toronto isn't too horrible for you. I know
it must still be very hard adjusting. Mom is so impressed that
you wanted to do it. She was really worried about you staying
in Ragged Islands on your own and was so happy when you

suggested moving near to her and Peter. When I talked to her the last time, she just kept saying how amazed she was that you are going out everyday to do your banking and getting groceries all on your own.

So tell me, are you going out to night clubs yet or turning into one of those ladies who lunch at the museum?

After I finish this I'm going to go back into the church and light a candle for you for your birthday. It's not a cake, but it will have to do. The church is really beautiful.

So happy birthday Gram and a great big kiss. And this folding money is for you! You can spend it when you have had enough of Toronto in the winter sometime and you want to come south.

Love
Tommy
P.S.
In RAIN. Afternoon

Now I'm sitting in a restaurant that's called "Rain" after the old Joan Crawford movie. Did you ever see it? It's the one where she says "All men are pigs!" after the preacher makes a pass at her. Walter Huston I think. It's a Somerset Maugham story. Gloria Swanson made it too, and Rita Hayworth. Sadie Thompson—that's her name in the movie. I had a nice lunch and am having a Pina Colada or two to celebrate and toast your birthday, after I lit the candle that is burning for you in the cathedral down the street.

This is a beautiful place. The whole trip. Everywhere we go. This has been a good time for me. You know how messed up I was after Chris died. It was so unreal, and his parents were just so creepy. I never liked them, not even when they used to be nice to me, back when we were taking sailing classes at RCYC—but I never thought they would be like that when he was sick. It still seems impossible that they would be like that. He was so important to me from the time that we were like twelve or something—he was so important to me. Like your friend Ellen Firth who you miss so much. I am down here without him and that seems weird because our big plan was to do this together someday, and he was the one who wanted to do it the most anyway—yet it was so important to bring some of his ashes here and I am glad I did that. So it has been a good thing to do and I think it will help me when I get back and do my last year at York. Mom is pushing for me to go to grad school but I'm not sure yet.

Chris thought you were so cool because you said you liked his crazy hair.

I'm going to mail this to you now. I'm toasting you one more time! HAPPY BIRTHDAY GRAM!

Love, Tom

Folded into the letter was an East Caribbean ten-dollar bill.

It doesn't surprise Carl that Tommy would write so frankly to his grandmother—the whole gay thing was right up her alley, all in keeping with the people and causes that she'd championed throughout his own growing-up years: Steven Truscott, and Dr. Morgentaler. She'd always fancied herself some sort of champion of the underdog—just look at the way she'd constantly supported and sided with his father. It had driven him crazy when he was a teenager and realized that she wanted to see him in that same way—as an unpopular cause that needed her support.

Carl hasn't seen Tommy since the summer Lorraine brought her kids to Vancouver and stayed with him, twenty or more years ago—the summer when she finally left Elliot. Meg had been a pain in the ass the whole time, and Tommy hadn't been a bad kid, really, but he was so faggy that Carl was uncomfortable with the way his son followed him about. Greg would have been four or five and suddenly he was saying, "Faabulous," in the same fruity way as his older cousin. But when he mentioned this to Bonnie, she put her hand to her mouth in a mock dramatic gesture and said, "Oh no! Suppose it's like the flu? Heavens to Betsy, we'll all catch it!"

"Very funny."

"Jesus, Carl, Tommy's not even a teenager. And so what if he turns out to be a fag? It's not like it's a crime any more, and he is your nephew."

She was right, of course, but why couldn't she understand that he was simply feeling protective of their son? Life was hard enough without being saddled with a problem like that one.

And that was before AIDS had even entered into the picture.

He hadn't realized how much he'd been dreading dealing with Tommy and his boyfriend until this morning's initial shock of confusion and horror had cleared long enough for him to experience a kind of relief that he might be spared that meeting. If the American airports were closed down for a while, maybe he wouldn't have to deal with them at all.

4—

MEG WAS HERE! Meg was holding her hand! She was bending down to kiss her old grammy's cheek!

"Hello, Grammy."

Hello hello hello! What a surprise!

"You just stay quiet now, just stay calm."

But had she been here long? Had she just gotten here? Where had she been?

"I got here a little while ago. Not very long. I didn't want to disturb your beauty sleep."

Ha. Beauty sleep, ha. She'd given up on that ages ago. Meg was holding her hand, and wasn't Susan Ann so happy to see her!

"Don't get excited, now."

Oh, but she must look like the wrath of God! She hadn't dragged a comb through her hair in weeks!

"Everything's fine."

But if someone had told her that Meg was coming, she'd have gotten ready. She must look somethin' awful! Were her store teeth even in?

"Don't now, just—"

And there wasn't a thing to eat, not a sweet in the house!

"That's right. Just lie down."

That mother of yours should have told me. She never tells me anything.

"Mum's gone home for a few hours. She said you were awake in the night."

Awake in the night? This was the morning, wasn't it? *What day?*

"What day is it? It's Monday."

Monday? And it's *summertime.*

"It's September."

Oh, that's right, she knew that, Lorraine told her.

"I brought you some ice tea in a can. It's still pretty cold."

She was a smart one, she knew just what her old Grammy loved.

"The sweet lemon kind that you like so much."

That was their drink, *sweet, sweet, sweet tea.*

"It's our drink, isn't it?"

Was Meg back home from her trip?

"Our drink from way back."

Those places were dangerous. She should stay put now! She and her brother running around all over the globe, from Dan to Beersheba. Tommy was back home, wasn't he?

"And here's some cranberry juice."

Good for the old kidneys, so they say.

"'Good for the old kidneys,' eh Gram? And I brought a fancy bottle of water, too."

She could just take that away with her. *Pah.* Meg knew what her grandmother thought of that! It was a sin to charge money for water. It was wrong.

"I know you think it's a real extravagance, but I know how much you hate Toronto water."

Blah.

"Maybe this'll taste something like the water back home."

Buying and selling water—what was the world coming to? There were some things the good Lord provided that shouldn't be tampered with at all. Selling water in stores, what a disgrace.

"Would you like some ice tea?"

Oh, yes, that would be lovely!

"Let me help you a bit."

Her hand behind Susan Ann's head was so comfortable, so warm, the tea in the straw so sweet.

"I talked to Tommy this morning."

Oh yes?

"He called me from New York."

New York? Why on earth would anyone want to go to a place like that?

"He's going to school there, remember? He and Louis."

Louis?

"His boyfriend. Louis. You've met him. They came to your apartment."

His boyfriend? Oh, yes, that nice coloured fellow. The one who said he was a professional student. He brought the ice cream that time.

"Yes, you remember him."

Susan Ann had thought he was an awfully nice person, but that Tommy sure wasn't making his life simple. She worried about the mean sort of things that people would say. Her own relatives, for example. Muriel and her bunch. And what would Jamie have thought? How he had loved that Tommy when he was a wee lad. Would that sort of thing upset him? That gay business?

Remember that crazy fellow with the crazy hair that Tommy was so close to?

"Grammy?"

Meg would remember his name, with the crazy hair, *the Bottle Blonde,* she called him, he had that AIDS and was so sick.

"I just talked to them. Tommy wants to come visit you. He and Louis are going to try and come up tomorrow."

Visit? Oh, but the place wasn't big enough. *There wasn't enough room!*

"Just relax now, Grammy."

But she had to get cracking! She wasn't ready for company. *Where would they all sleep?*

"No, no, no, no, no, Grammy, they won't stay with you. We'll all be at Mom's."

At your mother's?

"Yes."

Oh.

If she were still down in Ragged Islands, still living in Jamie's house, then there'd be room for everybody. Plenty of room. Tommy and his coloured fellow could have Queenie's old room. Wouldn't that shock her, ha!

"Tommy told me to tell you that they're going to Nova Scotia soon; they'll be down Ragged Islands way."

What? Ragged Islands? *Who?*

"Tommy and Louis, they'll be in Halifax for a week and then Shelburne."

Shelburne? Why on earth would they want to go to Shelburne?

"Louis is doing research on the Black Loyalists. So they'll be in Shelburne and Birchtown, I suppose."

The Black Loyalists? They lived in Birchtown. Now, there was a sad story. Queenie was the one who knew all about that. He should talk to her.

Oh, wait, when did Queenie go—a while ago, wasn't it? 1972. They thought she would go on the ides of March, but she hung on till Good Friday. And Tommy was born later than that, wasn't he? Meg was 1970 and he was *four years later.*

"Yes, Grammy?"

She was just trying to figure out how old people were. When was that foolish Y2K nonsense?

"I'm sorry?"

Queenie had been dead and gone for nearly thirty years. But she did know a thing or two about those Black Loyalists because she grew up next to a coloured family, down in Shelburne County. She was friends with them and they told her things. Most of those people had gone back to Africa first chance they had. Did Meg know that? They were given a raw deal, those poor people, the British broke every promise and treated them like dirt.

"Louis says most of the Black Loyalists didn't stay in Nova Scotia. They went to Sierra Leone."

Isn't that in Africa?

"In Africa."

That's what she just said.

"Some of the Loyalists, I mean the white ones, brought their slaves with them. So the Black Loyalists had a hard time making a living. Did you know that, Grammy?"

What?

"I'm sorry, you're so tired. I don't want to wear you out."

Oh, wear me out, wear me out! Don't go! *Don't!*

"No, now you just relax."

But don't go. Stay awhile now. Talk some more about Tommy's friend and the Black Loyalists. People were no good sometimes, the way they treated other people, people who were different, and it made her so mad! Like the way they treated that poor Truscott boy. *That was terrible.*

"Shh, now. Shh."

She was so tired again, all of a sudden, and a little confused, but she didn't want to be alone. She wanted Meg to stay close by. And she was getting frightened—why? What had brought that on?

"Just relax, lie still, I'm not going anywhere, just relax now."

Stay, yes, yes, stay awhile and she would relax, yes.

"I love you, Grammy, now just relax."

And Meg's voice was so soft, and she was holding her grand-mother's hand so lovingly, sitting in a chair beside her, leaning forwards, her head resting on her arm right next to her grand-mother's old head. Her other hand was touching her Grammy's shoulder, touching it so sweetly, she was talking so gently, and she was a woman now, Meg was, she was all grown up. Susan Ann turned her head so their faces were near together, just inches apart, their eyes so close, looking at each other, and her grand-daughter loved her. Meg had her mother's blue eyes, and they were Jamie's eyes, and Queenie's, too! How far back did those blue eyes go? Back across the ocean, overseas somewhere, hundreds and hundreds of years.

"—sleep?"

What was that? Meg was asking her something but she couldn't make it out. She was trying to listen to what she was say-ing but she was so tired, it was so hard to concentrate and . . .

Meg's blue eyes.

Tommy had blue eyes too, only they were her Mumma Mac's eyes, they made him so handsome, and those eyes would stop with him because he was like that, gay they called it now, and wouldn't have kids of his own.

From the very beginning, Meg and Tommy had cuddled with their Grammy. Toddled into the bedroom and crawled right in with Susan Ann and Jamie. Lorraine and Carl had done that too, when they were wee things. All of them in bed together, Susan Ann and Jamie lifting their knees under the covers, making hills and valleys for the kids to crawl over and tumble down into.

That Tommy was the one—he made up stories as he crawled about, stories about being a car in the mountains. He would go,

"*Brrum brrum brrooooom!* And he drives *fast-fast-fast up-and-up!*"

Susan Ann never imagined that she would have such a long life without Jamie. What would he think of Tommy and that fellow? But wouldn't he be so proud of Meg?

Jamie took them out in the rowboat, fishing in the back harbour. Or down off the town wharf. That summer Meg caught a fish that was almost as big as she was. That summer, yes, yes, there were so many of them at the house that the kids slept out in a tent with the dog. What dog was that? Was it Scamp? Or Tracy? She couldn't remember.

There'd always been a dog, and she'd loved them all, but not a one was special like her old Sally. Could Meg remember her? No, that was all mixed up. That was years and years before the time those kids and the dog slept out in the tent.

That summer, yes. The one and only time that Susan Ann's whole family was home, the only reunion that would ever be, and they all got along pretty well, even Carl and Jamie.

And the day they were supposed to leave, Meg and Tom hid down at the shore because they didn't want to go back. And Susan Ann and Carl knew right where to look. Down the hill and beside the salt marsh, along the shore to the ledge at the far end of the beach—Jamie and Carl had helped them chisel their initials there beside all the other Roberts on the rock face, and up under the bank, at the top of the lists of names and initials, there was a nook, a cranny, a space big enough for a kid to imagine it into a cave. If I were a kid, that's where I'd have gone, she thought, so she grabbed Carl and they went into the woods and down the hill and there they were.

"Grammy, we don't want to go home."

"Why can't we stay here?"

I know, I know, but you have to go. Even your Uncle Carl doesn't stay here any more.

They reminded her of Carl, Lorraine's kids did; they were like their uncle when he was young. He loved the poor old Maritimes back then. They ran about like wild things. They loved it: out in the rowboat, campfires at the beach, little Tommy under the Norway pines at nighttime, flashlight in his hands, waiting for flying squirrels. They played croquet in wool beanies to keep the bats from getting tangled in their hair. Crazy kids.

Bats! Ha!

"What, Gram? I can barely hear you."

Bats.

"Bah? Like humbug? Or baa, like a sheep?"

Bats. Bats bats.

"I'm sorry, Gram."

Could she make it any plainer? You crazy kids thought bats would get tangled in your hair so you wore those stupid hats. You made everybody wear them; it was a game. "You better put this on. You have to wear it, Grammy." Kids believed the craziest things. They wanted to catch squirrels and have a circus, and teach crows to talk.

"Grammy, if you catch a crow, you can teach it to talk, can't you? Isn't that right?"

Oh, yes. Mum Wellman had told her a story about Randall Leaman, who had a pet crow that could jump through a hoop and say *bye-bye*. Randall, Rebecca, Martha, too.

"The one time we were all together? In Nova Scotia one summer, remember? The year before Grampy died."

Your grandfather.

"Yes, Gram. We were there, Mom and Tommy and me. Dad stayed up here, remember? That was the start of the divorce, but we didn't know that then. And Uncle Carl and Aunt Bonnie came east that year. Before Greg was born. Remember?"

Yes?

"Mom and Uncle Carl and Aunt Bonnie, we were all back home with you and Grampy."

Carl and Bonnie. That's right. A prairie girl, came from a big family. She'd never seen the Maritimes before. There was a sweater she sent one Christmas. It was expensive, had to be dry cleaned, so Susan Ann never wore it. It was in the cedar chest. Wasn't that Bonnie? Oh, yes—she wrapped up her hair in a beach towel like a turban and paraded around like a movie star. She made the kids laugh. The sweater was turquoise and sequins, the damnedest thing.

"We made walking sticks, remember?"

Yes.

"Me and Tommy. And you'd go down to the shore with us singing, *Valderee, Valderaa.*"

You called it the Knapsack Song. Yes, that summer when Meg and Tommy went into hiding when it was time to go home.

"I can remember Grampy, but Tommy can't, really. You remember the summer Tommy tried to catch the squirrel? The little red squirrel that was getting into the kitchen? He sort of remembers that. But he can't remember Grampy."

Like yesterday. Jamie and little Tommy hiding behind the shed, holding the long string. Tied to a piece of kindling that propped up a wooden box beside a chink in the foundation. Peanut-butter cracker for bait.

"The Christmas we spent with you—Mom and Tommy and me. After Dad left. We came down to Ragged Islands that Christmas. And it snowed and snowed."

Yes. She remembered that Christmas. 1980. Her first Christmas on her own in the house.

"I was around ten. I don't think Tommy had even started school. Maybe he was in SK? I'm not sure. We flew to Halifax and rented a car."

That's right. Lorraine wouldn't let Susan Ann drive up to the airport. And long before she had any trouble with her eyes whatsoever.

"I can remember so much—where the tree was in the living room, and how I was seeing decorations that Mom had seen when she was a little girl. That seemed so special to me, somehow. Some of them you still have—the ones that came from your house in Shediac?"

Mum Wellman's decorations. They were German, those ones. She bought them when she was working at Eaton's.

"And those decorations that Mom made when she was little. Those silly clothespin angels she made with Great-Grammy Queenie."

Those were cute, Susan Ann had to admit that. Queenie was smart about some things, she was gifted in that way when she put her mind to it. Those Christmas cards with salt for sparkly snow.

"You played carols on the piano, and old songs like 'Roll Out the Barrel.' Everything seemed so much better than Christmas in Toronto. You know, at Dad's mother's. Up here, we had to wear our best clothes for dinner, and you couldn't touch anything, and Grammy Howe always had a fancy-schmantzy tree where the lights were all blue or the bulbs were all gold or something."

Blah. Susan Ann had never cared for Elliot's mother, she was all hoity-toity, "wouldn't say *shit* if her mouth was full of it," Jamie said after the first time he met her.

"It was the year Grampa died, and, well, that was one of the reasons we were there, so you wouldn't be alone at Christmas."

That's right. That's right.

But it was also Meg and Tom's first Christmas without their father. Lorraine came down with the kids because Elliot was off with some young girl. A student.

"That was the only time I was in Ragged Islands in the winter, wasn't it? The only time I was there in the snow?"

Susan Ann supposed that would be right. People only came to visit the Maritimes in the summer. Or the fall sometimes, to see the leaves.

"I have a memory from that Christmas that couldn't have happened."

What, what do you mean?

"There was a lot of snow. I'm positive that I was never there another time when there was snow. But I have this memory that's as clear as can be. Maybe I dreamed it, but it seems so strong and clear—as if it really happened."

"We were walking on the path out behind the house, going down to the shore. It had snowed in the night and the trees were just covered. All the evergreens, and the bushes all bent over under the weight. It wasn't sunny, I don't think, but it was clear. I don't think it was Christmas Day, exactly. Maybe Boxing Day. It doesn't matter."

Meg was caressing the back of her hand, and it felt so good. Her hand had been drifting off, she realized, and now it had an anchor. Meg's head was on the pillow beside her Grammy's. They were looking into each other's eyes. Was her granddaughter lying beside her? Oh, yes. Just like a little girl.

"It was so beautiful. And neither Tommy or I wanted to disturb anything. You know how kids usually are with snow like that, we want to kick the bushes and shake the trees, knock it all down. But we didn't. We just walked in single file on the snowy path.

"And there seemed to be tracks *everywhere*. Deer tracks, and a fox, and a bird like a partridge or something, you know, and rabbit tracks. It just seemed amazing. Everywhere we looked. Little ones and big ones. I remember you said, 'This is the way dogs know the world all the time, they know where all the animals tracks are. They smell what you can see in the snow.'"

That was true. Susan Ann had said something like that. It was something Dad Wellman had said to her one morning while they watched Sally race around in the snow. She had never forgotten it.

"But the strange thing, Gramma, is that in my memory Grampy was with us. With you and me and Tommy walking in the snow. Because I remember him going 'Look!' and pointing, and we all looked up and saw this huge thing, flying, against the snowy trees. We just saw it for a second. It was like a dream of a bird, a big brown owl. And I remember Grampy turning to Tommy and teasing him, saying, 'You be careful now. She's big enough to fly off with you.'"

An owl? Susan Ann couldn't remember this at all.

"I must have a couple of different times confused in my head. But that's what I remember."

An owl. They were a rare treat to see. They were smart, they said.

"Can you remember this, Grammy? Seeing the owl at wintertime?"

She was trying to picture it, but she couldn't quite. She wasn't sure if she had *ever* seen an owl, really. She must have at some time. A barn owl? Up at the farm, or maybe up in the woods with Dad Wellman? He had traps in the winter, he had snares for rabbits. There was something—

Meg was snuggled up to her, her arm around her grandmother's waist. They were so close together, so close—

She could *hear* owls at night, from the woods, sometimes, flying and hunting in the woods while she was safe in her bed. Hear them from her *bedroom window* . . .

"I'm sorry, Gram, it's just hard to understand you."

Meg was here! That's right. Susan Ann must have drifted off after Meg had come.

"Did you have a little nap? Are you feeling better?"

Oh, yes, much better, *much improved.* Now, just you wait. Let me get you a *little something—*

"Wait, Gram, now—"

Maybe there were some date squares. *It won't take a minute to—*

"Gram—"

What was—What? Oh no! *Dammit!* This damn old bed, this harness!

"You just snooze, Grammy, and I'll sit here and visit."

Get me out of here!

"Grammy—"

Get me out, take me home!

"Oh, now—"

Don't be like your mother!

"Just go back to sleep."

No! Look, look! They tied me up! Did Meg know that? *They tied me up!*

"Gram—"

I want to go home!

"Oh—"

Home! Home! I want to go home!

"Oh, I know, Grammy, I know—"

Then take me, Meg, Meggie, please, please!

"Oh, stop now, Grammy, don't cry, you have to stop now, *please!*"

HE COULDN'T GET OVER *the amount of mail that Meg had sent to her grandmother, and the fact that every single piece of it seemed to have been saved and annotated.*

Dear Grammy and Gramps Roberts,

It is raining and I miss you. Thank-you for the money tree card.
I bought berets with dimonds on them.
When you come visit we will visit Centre Island!
Love Meg XOX
Ps Not reel dimonds!
(1976 6 yrs)

Birthday cards, thank-you cards, Christmas and Easter cards, and letters and more letters—a letter written from his place in 1983:

Vancouver is spectacular. Uncle Carl and Aunt Bonnie have a nice house and lots of trees including bamboo! It is nice but I like going to Ragged Islands more and Tommy and Mom think so too. Next summer we will go and visit you like before. Last night they had a big party that was fun and we danced in the back yard. It was noisy though and a policeman came and said to turn down the music. There is a mean family next door who have been trying to get people mad at Aunt Bonnie for a long time. They have a yappy dog called Brandy like Dad's ex-girlfriend. Mom laughed and laughed when we heard them calling her. Greggie is hyperactive and is following Tommy everywhere.

Another one written before Lorraine remarried:

Dear Grammy,

I am glad you are coming to Mom's wedding. I think Peter is fine. I know I told you that he was dull but that doesn't mean he is boring or stupid. He is Mom's type, after all, not mine. He is thoughtful to her, and she is much happier than she has been for a while. They are both crazy about gardening and that seems to make them really happy. He and Tommy are both canoe crazy and like to go camping in Algonquin Park. I think that he and I will get along. He's not so much a know-it-all as he is obsessive about biology. I imagine that he is a really good professor.

I know how much you don't like coming to Toronto, but it will just be for a few days and you and I will have fun. Tommy says to tell you that he is looking forward to your visit. He was going to stay with Dad and Karen after the wedding but changed his mind when you said you would come here. I want you to teach me how to make the date pie that Grampy's mother used to make. Mom goes on and on about it. When they get back from their honeymoon we can have one waiting for her.

Dad and Karen are fine. He always asks about you. They may be at the wedding, too, but I don't think so really. I hope not really. I don't think that I'm ready for Mom and Dad to bury the hatchet and be all sophisticated about things. It's easier if they never see each other. I hope that does not sound selfish, but I do like keeping them separate now. It's funny isn't it, because when they were separating and divorcing and all that I couldn't bear the idea of it. Now I can't imagine them together and I don't understand why they ever were.

I'll talk to you before you come, but I do want to let you know that I will be the one meeting you at the airport. Maybe we'll just take the car and keep driving! Wouldn't that be fun!

There were postcards of dusty-looking scenes from Syria—The Village of Maaloula, An Arial View of Aleppo—from the time that Meg went off and did her archaeology thing for the university. When Carl asked her about it last night, Meg said she and her boyfriend would go back in a second if they could. She was studying cuneiform writing and translating divination texts from Mesopotamia. "They're wacky," she told him, "but they're a real attempt to understand the way the universe worked."

"For example?" Carl asked.

"For example, 'If a man pees against a wall and his urine flows to the south then the king will live.'"

"There's a very useful piece of information."

"Then, of course, 'If a man pees against a wall and the urine flows to the north, then the king will die.'"

"And west and east?"

"They're all in there as well. All very logical. It was the very beginning of the scientific method."

Dear Gram

I've been thinking of you all week and just wanted to send
you my love. I am fine here. I talked to Mom last Friday. She
said you were being an old worrywart over me so don't be.
Everything is going really well.

I am so sorry to hear that you will not be in your house in
Ragged Islands when I get home. I know it means that I will
probably see more of you in Toronto, but it won't be the same
will it? I love seeing you in Ragged Islands. By the time you get
this, you will be almost ready to move. It has happened so fast.
It will be strange for you to live in a city. I hope it all goes well
for you. I'm sorry I can't be there to help you move. It is very
strange for me too, realizing that I won't be going to your house
again. I have had so many happy summers there.

I am very fine. I am no further ahead in the "what am I
going to do with my life" department, but I am having a pretty
remarkable time. I don't feel like such a misfit here. (Maybe
everyone should spend time being a foreigner—then they
wouldn't be so closed-minded.)

Even though you have never done anything as foolish as
this, I think that I am doing it because of you. You always told
me to be different. It is one of the things that I remember
from my earliest visits with you and Grampy. I can remember
Tommy and I having a fight about something—what, I can't
remember—and afterwards Grampy took him out in the boat
and you and I went for a walk. I remember this so clearly. I
said something like "Everybody thinks I'm stupid" and you
said, "Are you living your life for you or for Everybody?" You
said Everybody like it was a bad idea, like watching TV all the
time. When I was a teenager, I wanted to be like everybody

else, but even at the worst of that I knew somehow that you were right.

It is weird to be in a place like this, a place that is on the news so often because of modern politics, but that is so old. I am working with the bones of people who lived thousands of years ago, before there were Christians and Muslims and probably even before Jews arrived with their one God. (You know the one, Mr. Jealous, the "no other gods before me" guy that we like to argue about.) Our religions seem ancient but are really pretty recent, and there was a whole long world before them.

We are working in the country, in a field. Some of us are digging at what was an ancient village. My team is working on the old cemetery. Just below the field there are around 100 or more tombs. Some of them seem to have as many as ten people in them and dozens of pots. Also animal bones, some with carving on them. Yesterday a ring turned up (copper) and a pot with wheels like a little toy car!

In one tomb there are five adults and two children. One of the children and one female adult are in very good shape. There has been a lot of damage in some of the tombs. Robbers, of course, but they're recent. They smash things sometimes and are looking for stuff to sell. (It's very weird to find cigarette butts mixed up with antiquity!) Their damage is stupid. (We'll never ever find out what they have stolen.) Most of the damage comes from the weight of dirt that accumulates over centuries as well as water damage—things like that. So skeletons are crushed, bones are missing or mixed up. Sometimes it looks like all the bones were just picked up and thrown in a corner. A part of what we have to try and figure out—and why we have to go so slowly—is whether a spring flood washed things over to one side, or whether they were moved to make way for other bodies— whatever. But that child and the adult seemed to be placed

together, and of course my first thought was of a mother and
daughter. That is total speculation on my part and bad science.
They could have been placed there two hundred years apart for
all I know at this point. But we uncovered them together, and they
had been there together for probably 5000 years. So even if they
were put in the tomb decades or centuries apart, they have been
together all this long time. It would seem wrong to separate them.

I know it may be bad science but a part of me wants to make
up stories about those bones. If they were a mother and
daughter—and I just realized I've never thought mother and
son: what does that tell you!—how did they die? Was it disease?
(Did you know that all our diseases like mumps and chicken
pox and so on were originally animal diseases and we have them
now because we started to domesticate animals way back
when?) Will we find anything on the bones that might indicate
a violent death? (I hope not.) More importantly, what will the
bones tell us about their lives? How strange to live for such a
short time and then have what's left of you be evidence for such
a long time afterwards.

A part of me wants to think about them the way I would
want someone to think about me, as someone who had a story
that was interesting.

I hope you don't think all this talk about old bones is mor-
bid. It's just the opposite for me. Jean Claude and I are going
into town for dinner tonight—my first tourist-like event!—so
I should go and clean up.

I love you so much.
Meg

*Carl folded the letter carefully and put it back in the envelope. He gath-
ered up all of Meg's cards and letters into a neat stack, but when he tried*

to secure them with the elastic band, it was so worn that it broke. He held the papers awkwardly, unsure of how to keep them together.

The ease with which both of Lorraine's kids had written to their grandmother didn't surprise him, and neither did their desire to tell her things, to have her know them in an intimate way; Carl had long known his mother's cravings for that intimacy. What had caught him off guard was a feeling that lay somewhere between resentment and jealousy, as if Meg and Tommy occupied a position that once upon a time had been his own; a position that he no longer wanted, and had relinquished long, long ago. Or maybe what he was feeling was more of a sense of loss on behalf of his son? His sister's kids had long had a place in his mother's life that Greg had never possessed. But Carl had always believed that his son was better off at a distance; it was too late now for him to know his grandmother.

Growing up, Carl had yearned so for that closeness with her, for all her hugs and secrets, but at a certain point they'd turned to clinging; her entreaties became desperate, then frightening, and in the end, annoying. For years and years, she'd gone back and forth between her husband and her son, like an emotional double agent; he'd loved the intrigue when he was a boy, loved it until he realized that, in the end, she would always choose his father.

On the plane yesterday, he'd hoped he would be able to overcome the resentment and annoyance that had built up over time; hoped he would be able to sit beside his mother's deathbed and reconnect with her in an uncomplicated way. He had imagined holding her hand, their feelings for each other coinciding, dovetailing.

"I love you, Mum."

"I love you, Carl."

A part of him had yearned for something shamelessly melodramatic. A scene of forgiveness and reconciliation.

"You haven't seen her for a while," Lorraine had said. "And she's had a fall. She's in pretty rough shape, so be prepared." And he thought he was.

LORRAINE AND MEG were whispering, they were out in the hall whispering with the nurse, talking about her, and she couldn't make out a word. She was straining her ears, trying so hard to understand what they were saying. She hated whispering; she hated secrets.

She'd woken up when the nurse came in. She was still stupid from sleep, but she said that she wanted to be untied, and she wanted to have a BM and she wanted to go home. But they'd left her all alone to go out whispering in the hall. She was sure they were giving her something to make her stupid. Medication of some kind.

She felt so damn uncomfortable! It had been days—no, *weeks*—she hadn't had a BM in weeks! If she were only able to sit down on the toilet she knew she would be fine. It was packed in there solid. She needed one of those things, what were they called? Where they stuck that thing up your bum? An igma.

No, that was wrong, that was something fancy. Igma. No, that was all one word, *enigma*. That was something else; that wasn't what she needed.

What was it called? Weren't they supposed to keep a record of these things? Wasn't there a chart of some kind? Weren't they supposed to be helping her? Why weren't the nurses doing their jobs?

She tried to listen to Lorraine and Meg, but everything they were saying sounded like *Pss-pss-psspsspss.*

All her life people had been whispering around her, and Lorraine had always been one of the worst, her own daughter, she even dragged Jamie into it, whispering out there in the lane. Poor Jamie, always getting dragged into things. The winter and spring when Queenie was sick, the house had been full of all that *psspsspss*, Jamie and his mother whispering in the bedroom, Jamie whispering to Susan Ann in the kitchen, even Queenie whispering to her at the end, giving her that shoebox behind Jamie's back, "Don't tell Jamie, but *pss-pss-psspsspss.*" There was no need for any of it, no need at all. Whisper whisper whisper, all her life, for as far back as she could remember—

Aunt Aggie whispering to Uncle Hay while Great-Aunt Doshe whispered to everybody else, Mum and Dad whispering about Sally, about poor Sally and that rotten Elsie Steeves. Or Daddy Mac and Mum Wellman that time, whispering in the living room in the house on Railway Avenue—brother and sister, what was that about? Mumma Mac was listening from the front hall. "I heard that!" she said.

What had she heard? Everybody was upset, and Mumma turned, looking up the stairs at Susan Ann sitting there with Dolly on her lap. That look on Mumma's face, suddenly so angry, as if everything in the whole world were Susan Ann's fault. "What're you lookin' at?"

She hadn't known what to say, because every time she tried to talk to her mother, Mumma would bark at her or say something sarcastic, so she sat on the stairs with her Dolly, trying not to cry.

"Don't go sneaking around here when you come to visit. Spying on me."

But she hadn't been spying, she hadn't—Muriel and Jane were upstairs hiding and she was counting to a hundred because she was It, and she hadn't understood a word from the living room. Her Daddy Mac and her Mum Wellman were in there talking about Mumma—she knew no more than that. Besides, wasn't Mumma Mac the one doing the spying?

What had they said that time? If she knew the answer, would she understand why she had been sent to live in the house on Inglis Street? There must be a record of those things somewhere. There wasn't a soul left living who knew or remembered, but shouldn't there be a place where the things she needed to know were written down? If she could sift through every scrap of paper that Aunt Aggie had squirrelled away up at the farm, say, or find something like a shoebox with a letter inside from her Mumma Mac—

She felt so uncomfortable, all blocked up in agony, if only she could—

Enema! That was it. That was what she needed!

What had she called it before? *Enigma.* Not like enema at all. An enigma was something strange that you couldn't figure out.

Like Mumma Mac. That was what she was, an enigma. What Susan Ann needed was an *enema*, and not one of those little Fleet enemas, either. She needed the real thing. If they would only take her home and let her park herself on her own toilet, then she could get things moving! Or if she could be in the bathroom back in Jamie's house. Oh yes, she'd have success in there, she knew she would!

When was the last time she'd had a pee?

As soon as she thought this, she realized that something was going on down there. Where were her hands? She wiggled them, found one of them lying on that hateful harness and moved it down. She was wearing the blue nightgown that Lorraine had given her for Christmas; her hand travelled down and down until it hit what felt like a lump wadded around her waist—

What was that under there? That lump couldn't be her, could it?

No, they had her wrapped up in something. Her hand moving back and forth, she thought of that line from Luke, *wrapped in swaddling clothes*—she was touching a diaper! How long ago had Lorraine put that on her? Why didn't they ask her if they could? Was it wet?

She reached farther down, to pull up her nightgown and see, and there, coming out of the bottom of the diaper, some sort of snaky thing—a tube. What in the name of God—?

A catheter. How long had that been there? How could that have happened without her knowing? How could it even *be* there without her realizing it until now? They must be giving her something to keep her confused and stupid. She was going to hide those pills and spit them out.

They were taking everything away, her body was no longer her own—her own feet had stopped communicating with her. She knew they were down there, but they seemed to have given up the ghost.

Maybe she had already had a BM and didn't realize it?

No, she was still so uncomfortable—she still needed to get to the toilet.

If only only *only* she had the energy to take a shit! If only she were sitting up on a toilet that she knew and loved! She didn't have the energy to do anything about it. All she could do was lie here and suffer while her family went out whispering in the halls.

"Pss-pss-psspsspss."

What?

"Psspsspss."

They were coming back in the room—

"I loved going down to Gramma's."

"She and Dad were wonderful to you and your brother when you went down in summers."

Listen . . .

"They spoiled you rotten. Didn't you, Mum?"

"Grammy?"

"Is she asleep again?"

Susan Ann kept her little eyes shut.

"I think so."

"Don't wake her."

"—a hard night."

She could only make out part of what they were saying; Lorraine had said something about a hard night. What did they expect? They had her tied up like an old dog.

Susan Ann decided that she would outfox them. She'd keep her eyes closed and her ears open and find out what sort of things they said about her when they thought she couldn't hear. She'd find out what sorts of secrets Lorraine had been hiding.

She didn't dare move. Stay very, very still, concentrate on everything—

They must be over by the window at the end of her bed—she couldn't make out what they were saying just yet—

"—Uncle Carl."

"As if he ever gave a *flying*—"

"*Sshhh!*"

Carl?

Wasn't he coming? Had Lorraine told her that or had she dreamed it?

"*Pss-pss-psspsspss.*"

Dammit—they were as sneaky as Mumma Mac.

What about Carl?

He'd listen to her. She'd get Carl to get her out of here. He was her little boy, after all, he was still.

Lorraine and Carl, the way they used to fight.

"Tell Carl to leave me alone."

Why can't you two try to get along?

"I hate him."

Lorraine—

"I hate him! I hate stupid Ragged Islands!"

Stop it, now.

"I wish I was dead. Then you'd all be happy."

"You're right on that one."

"Shut up, Carl!"

Will you two stop!

"You hate me!"

Try and count your blessings for a change, you're just making yourself and everybody else miserable.

"You hate me! You all hate me!"

"That's the first thing she's said all day that wasn't stupid."

Carl!

And Lorraine would start crying and slamming doors, and Carl would run behind and tease her, and Susan Ann would be terrified that Queenie or Jamie would be home before this mess was straightened out.

"You spoil them, what'd I tell you!" Queenie's litany, while all the time she was the one who spoiled them rotten. And every time Jamie walked in on a ruckus he blamed Carl, always always, and it wasn't fair.

I don't care if it is freezing outside—I'm going to throw the both of you outdoors. I'm throwing you both out into the snow until you can make up your minds to come back in and act like civilized human beings! *You're not so big I can't still give you the wooden spoon!*

"Grammy?"

"Leave her for a minute."

"—so restless."

"I know."

She was supposed to be listening to Meg and Lorraine but she had gotten lost, *stupid, stupid*. She kept her eyes screwed shut and listened.

"—talking in the night."

"To you?"

"Who knows? She was calling out for her brother and her mother."

What's this?

"Her Aunt Aggie."

Aunt Aggie? What was Lorraine talking about? What—

"—lived with you for a while, right?"

"Not really, just spent part of the winter. You know the story of Carl opening everybody's presents? She came that Christmas."

Was this Aunt Aggie?

What was Lorraine saying now?

"—to remember. Grammy Queenie couldn't stand her. I loved it at first 'cause they both tried to win me over with cookies and candy. They were baking all the time, the two of them."

"*Psspsspss.*"

Susan Ann could hear Lorraine, but Meg was whispering.

"One day in the kitchen, they were both at it like cats. Aunt Aggie was getting a spoon or something and Grammy Queenie slammed a drawer on her fingers."

"She slammed her fingers in the drawer? On purpose?"

What?

"*Shhh!*"

What was this?

"It was hardest on Dad, I think."

What was Lorraine saying? *Psspsspss.*

"All long gone now. Who's left to know any more?"

That winter Aunt Aggie came to stay? The winter when—

"Gram told me so many stories about her Mum Wellman."

"I always thought she probably lucked out with her Mum Wellman. Aunt Jane was all right, I guess, we didn't have much to do with her because she was in Florida. But the rest of that bunch, Aunt Muriel and her tribe, Jesus!"

Susan Ann was trying to keep up, she was—

"Of all her relatives, the Wellmans were the only ones who really liked my dad."

"Why didn't the others like him, Mom?"

"I don't know what they had against him. All of that stuff happened before I was born and no one talked about it. I do know that Dad was good friends with Mum's brother, Murd. They were in the army. She was talking about him half the night."

"In her sleep?"

"*Psspsspss*—"

They'd dropped their voices again. She couldn't make out what they were saying at all.

Murd.

The apple tree.

Mayflowers. Mayflowers, Murd in a white shirt, walking with Jamie before the war. Muriel and the McCallum boy and Murd and Jamie and Susan Ann back in Shediac, and all laughing like kids up in the woods—

Wait, what—

"What was she like, Mom? Your Grammy Wellman?"

"Haven't got a clue. I was born the day after she died."

What was this—

"Mum heard the news, she went right into labour. You know this."

"No, I don't."

"You did the family tree, for godsakes."

"Yeah, but . . ."

"I wasn't due to arrive for another two weeks. There was a telegram, I think, from the farm, and she went into labour."

"In the house in Ragged Islands?"

"Yes, in the front hall. Your Grammy Queenie delivered me at the foot of the stairs."

"Jesus!"

"Sshhh."

That wasn't right at all. Not at all!

No.

"Is she awake?"

Be careful, don't want them to know you're listening.

"She's so restless."

"*Psspsspss.*" Whispering again.

Queenie delivering Lorraine!

Queenie didn't deliver a blessed thing. She handed Susan Ann the telegram and went and hid in the kitchen, left her lying on the floor there all alone, all alone and scared to death.

The floor was so cold. She remembered that.

How awful everything was that day. All that pain and cramps and hurt.

Looking up the stairwell at the ceiling in the upstairs hall.

Only a few minutes before, she'd been up there reading Mum's letter from the farm, getting ready to write her a nice long answer. She was going to write about her crazy mother-in-law in a funny way. To try to make Mum laugh, because everything was so sad. Murd and the war—

If only she and Jamie had been able to live with Mum and Dad the way they had all planned. After the war was over, they were to get married and move into the house on Inglis Street. Murd and Jamie in business together—

If only Jamie's father hadn't died when he did—

If only Murd hadn't been killed, and Mum and Dad had stayed in Shediac—

If only that pisspot Elsie Steeves hadn't made everyone's life miserable—

If only, if only—

And the pain inside her was suddenly so heavy—

Everything went white and she could hear a fly buzzing against the windowpane. Everything just disappeared and the whole world went white. She could hear Queenie, but from miles and miles away. She couldn't see a thing. And the water felt like it was pouring out of her. When she turned to reach for something to hang onto, everything was slippery, and she fell—

Help me! I am going to have this baby right now!

Queenie was making a racket in the kitchen. Jamie was in the office at the fish plant, in a job he hated and was lucky to have. Dad was way out in Montreal visiting Boyd. The telegram said that Mum Wellman had died in her sleep up at the farm. *If only, if only—*

She was so scared and so angry—

Ragged Islands was so—

Queenie was so—

Jamie was—

Oh, on that day she had doubted everything! She really did love Jamie, didn't she? She wasn't just being a foolish kid. Had she made a mistake coming to Ragged Islands? *If only, if only—*

Was Muriel right, after all? Was she getting what she deserved for marrying a traitor? Had Susan Ann been one of the *if only* things that had killed Mum Wellman?

If only she hadn't married Jamie, Mum would still be alive. Mum was staying upcountry and hadn't gotten out of bed. Aunt Aggie knew something was wrong because Mum had always been first one up at the crack of dawn. "She was fine when she went to bed."

The doctor said it must have been her heart. She would have been just sixty that next year. And Dad, poor Dad, "I blame Elsie Steeves and that goddamn Banker Chipman," because they had hounded Mum for years and years, belittled her in front of people at the church, made it so hard for her to make friends in that town. They hounded and hounded her all the way back to Sally, poor Sally. If only Susan Ann had been living with her, had been able to be with her, to help her out—

When Dad came down to say goodbye after he sold the house in Shediac, after he decided to go to Montreal and live with Boyd—

When Dad came down to say goodbye, he told Susan Ann that he cared for Jamie like a son, that he thought the four of them could have all gotten along pretty well in the house on Inglis Street if things had worked out that way—

When Dad came down to say goodbye, he had barely arrived before he had to leave, because Queenie launched into the biggest episode of her career—

"Glory be," Dad said to Susan Ann out in the yard. "You've got your hands full with that one." And at first she thought he meant Lorraine, because she was holding the baby, who was making a fuss—

"Oh goodness no, not the little one. I mean *that one* in there."

When Dad came down to say goodbye, Queenie had headaches all of a sudden, she had backaches, she couldn't walk for the agony of it all, and dragged out those old canes of hers. Every little noise bothered her so they couldn't talk, they had to whisper, and still she cried, she wailed, she was the centre of attention because she was so jealous of Dad's feelings for Jamie, and as soon as Dad left she jumped out of bed and baked Jamie a batch of oatmeal cookies and date pie and his favourite pineapple upside-down cake.

When Dad came down to say goodbye, Susan Ann said to him, *I want to go back with you. Take me to Boyd's. I hate it here.* Because Queenie was so jealous of everything and everyone that she made Susan Ann doubt her own love for Jamie.

She had doubted her own love for Jamie!

But Dad was broken now. He couldn't help her. He would go to Montreal and be sweet to Boyd's children and be their grandfather, and not be Lorraine's or Carl's because he was so far away. He was all broken. He never came east again.

It took so long for Jamie to get there that morning.

She was lying at the foot of the stairs on the hard linoleum, and the pain inside was thick and horrible. Jamie, Jamie? Where was Jamie, where was he? Wasn't Hiram Firth supposed to be bringing him to her?

Wasn't Jamie supposed to be helping her get to the cot in the kitchen?

Wasn't he supposed to comfort her before he ran off to fetch the doctor?

She was lying there on the linoleum and the pain was so sharp inside her that she thought it would kill her.

Help me, help me please. Get me up off this old floor!

Queenie went on talking to herself in the kitchen, talking to herself and ignoring her.

Susan Ann wouldn't stand for it this time, it wasn't fair. Where was Jamie, where was he? It was no fair to leave her at a time like this, no fair, no fair at—*oh*—

"Hi there, stranger!"

Oh!

"How you feeling?"

Oh! Oh—

His face, his smile bending down over her!

Oh my Mister Man!

He was bending down over her, so warm and close after such a long time! Her body lurched upwards—*Oh!*—and she wrapped her arms about him, about his shoulders, she could smell the warmth of him, the soap and sweat, and now his arms were around her, holding her—"Are you glad to see me?"—holding her so tight.

"All right now, calm yourself, calm down—"

She was so happy, she would be saved now that he was finally here, and the pain inside her was so sharp. But here he was. And God sent Jamie to her. And her arms were about his neck and he felt so strong and warm and she was crying, crying—

Take me away away I hate it here she's so mean to me I'm sorry I'm sorry I ever doubted you!

"It's okay, there there—"

Her face buried in his shoulder, in his neck, the dampness the wet her tears his sweat, the warmth of him, the heat—

"Ssh now, ssh—"

Take me away with you!

"Ssh-ssh—"

But it was as if the floodgates in her had opened, she was so happy to see him she was *shaking*, she couldn't tell if she was laughing or crying—

I'm sorry I'm sorry I've never loved anybody else—

She didn't care what Queenie heard—

But then he was pulling back from her—

He was laying her down alone—

What—

He was moving away—

No no don't leave me down here, don't—

Looking frightened—

Frightened? What could be frightening him?

No don't be frightened don't leave me—

He was standing up beside her and she reached up to him—

Help me take me Jamie please! Jamie! Jamie!

"Mum—"

What—

"Mum?"

A hand on her shoulder from the other side. What? *Queenie!*

No, Lorraine standing on the other side of her, what the hell was she doing here?

"Mum."

Lorraine was bending down towards her—

Damn Lorraine, she was always pushy, it was all her fault—why she couldn't wait until the fifteenth of April to be born like she was supposed to—

No, wait—

Lorraine was bending down towards her, speaking in a firm voice. "Mum. It's *Carl.*"

What?

Lorraine's firm voice: "It's Carl here from Vancouver. He just came from the airport."

Carl? Where?

"Hi Mum."

What? She looked at Jamie, wasn't it Jamie? It was Jamie, wasn't it?

"Hi there." Bending down, one of them on each side of her—

Carl?

"Yes, Mum."

Carl? Carl all grown up?

And she was in bed, it wasn't the floor in the front hall. Because the house was lost—

Oh.

And this was bed, the hospital, she was an old woman, Jamie long dead, and she was making a fool of herself—

"How are you feeling?"

Carl? Taking me home?

"Sorry, what did you say?"

Take me home!

"I can't under—"

"She said she wants to go home." Meg. Meg's voice, that.

"Oh."

Sit up, show him that you can—

Oh—

Get up!

Trying to, but tied, tied to the bed like a dog to a pole—

Get me out!

"What should I do?"

"Just talk to her, Uncle Carl, for godsakes talk to her."

"Just visit with her."

"Mum? Mum, I . . ."

"For godsakes, Carl."

"I don't know what—"

Want to go home.

"Calm down now, Mum, just—"

Lorraine? Is that Lorraine?

"Bonnie's coming to see you soon. She sends her love."

Who?

"Bonnie. We were talking to Greg last night. He's working in Banff these days. He's got a girlfriend there. Pretty serious from the sounds of it. Well, as serious as you can be at that age. He sends his love, too. And I had a call from Melody, Mum. She and her husband are in Whitehorse now, working for the government. She came to see me last year—remember I told you?"

Who?

"Melody."

"He's talking about your granddaughter, Mum, Bernice's girl."

Bernice?

"It's okay, Gram." Meg's hand now, her granddaughter's hand—

"Bernice's girl." Lorraine's voice—

"I'm going to be a grandfather, Mum. She's going to have a baby."

Bernice? A baby? Did he find out that she helped Bernice?

"Too much information, Uncle Carl, give her some time to—"

"Mum, I—"

No sin there, it was her right, silly Baptists—

"Oh Jesus."

"Uncle Carl!"

Think now, calm yourself down, talk to Carl calm and he'll take you home.

"What?"

It wasn't Jamie's fault.

"What?"

"Uncle Carl, just try and listen."

He loves you, your father loves you, that's why—Try, try and understand, he loves you, he wanted you, he—

Carl was turning away from her, turning—

Your father loves you, Carl, he—

He was moving away—

Wait! Wait! Your father wants you to take me home!

But he was gone. Turned his back and left. Just ran away and left her—

Wait!

"It's okay, Mum, just relax."

Why oh—

"He'll be back soon. He—"

Stupid stupid stupid stupid stupid . . .

Talking about that trouble with his father—

But I didn't mean to!

"Sssh now, quiet...."
She hadn't meant to mention it....
She was just confused because she had been so *confused*....
Carl?
No, he was gone, run run away—left her, left her there.
Lying there all tied up on the floor.

THE COBEQUIDS

THEY WALKED and they walked; they walked all morning. Near the head of the Bay of Fundy, the Minas Basin cut a long wedge deep into the province, and they had to go all the way around it, which nearly doubled the distance. There'd been a ferry there ages ago, Jamie told her, but they'd taken it off in wartime and never put it back. It was rough going; Susan Ann's legs were sore, and she was constantly troubled with cramps. For the life of her, she couldn't remember the last time she'd had a successful bowel movement. Travelling in the wrong direction, east rather than south, only added to her frustration.

"If Jesus were on the road to Ragged Islands," she said, "would He bother with all this, or would He just go down to the shore and walk straight across that darn old basin? Just think of all the time and effort that would save you!"

But after a moment's wondering she decided that, no, He wouldn't walk across the water. It seemed like a cheap and easy way of doing things, little more than a trick.

"I'd make a lousy Saviour, Sally," she said. "As soon as Old Satan tempted me with something like that, I'd go right for it."

She was looking forward to getting beyond Truro, for it

marked the eastern edge of the basin. Then they would be able to swing around to the southwest. From that point on, she could be facing Ragged Islands while she walked. "The scenic route is all well and good," she thought. "But I *would* like to get home as soon as possible."

This was gorgeous countryside, though. They passed through the Wentworth Valley, and all around them the high, rolling hills of the Cobequid Mountains were covered in hardwoods. It would be fall soon, and the sugar maples above them would become scarlet, and the birches deep yellow. There were already traces of this in some of the leaves, and a little ways back they had seen a single maple that had turned a bright, brilliant red, like a tree burning high up on the green mountainside.

"The other side of the basin's not all that far, as the crow flies," she said. "But we're not crows, are we, girl?"

Sally had not been running around so much this morning; she was walking by Susan Ann's side and keeping pretty much the same pace.

"*If I had the wings of a swallow*," Susan Ann said, and Sally gave her a little *yip* of encouragement, so she sang through the verse:

> *If I had the wings of a swallow*
> *I would travel far over the sea*
> *And a rocky old road I would follow*
> *To a place that is heaven to me.*

Whenever Susan Ann and Jamie had gone on a trip outside the province, their first stop had always been here, in Wentworth, at a picnic site just off the highway, where they would have a pee break. Usually they stayed long enough for a doughnut and a cup of tea from the Thermos. It was a lovely place; the Wallace River curved through it, and there were tables scattered about under the trees.

When the sun goes to rest
Way down in the west
Then I'll build such a nest
In the place I love best

On hot days, Jamie would take off his shoes and wade in the shallow water of the Wallace. Sometimes he would pick up a pebble from the riverbed, and it would stay on the dashboard throughout the rest of their journey.

One time, she had driven up here with her friend Ellen Firth. They had packed a picnic and come up for the day. She had been telling Ellen how much she and Jamie enjoyed stopping in that little park, and Ellen had said, "Hiram and I drove by it dozens and dozens of times, you know, and we always meant to stop there, but we never did." After their husbands died, the two women had become close friends: The Old Girls, they called themselves, and more often than not they were giddy and foolish when they got together. Every couple of weeks in fine weather, they would hop in Ellen's car and go "running the roads," taking off for the day with a picnic lunch.

It had been on that particular trip to Wentworth that they realized they were related, "way back." Ellen's grandmother's maiden name had been Milford, which was Mumma Mac's maiden name; it turned out that Mumma's father and Ellen's grandmother had been cousins.

"So what does that make us?"

"Third cousins."

"It does? We're that close?"

"Well," said Ellen, "if our grandparents were cousins, then our parents were *second* cousins. That makes us *third* cousins."

It hadn't seemed possible at first that their relationship would be so direct. "Are you sure we're not something crazy like second cousins twice removed?"

"Don't confuse the issue."

"I never understood how any of that worked anyway," Susan Ann had confessed.

"Well I do, and it's real simple," Ellen had replied. "There's nothing *removed* about us, because we're in the same generation. Your mother's first cousin would be *your* first cousin once removed. See? It means one *generation* removed. Your grandmother's cousin is *your* cousin *twice* removed. Got that? We're third cousins. We share one set of great-great-grandparents."

They had discovered all this while they were sitting at a picnic table in the shade, having a gab about their families. Susan Ann had said that her Mumma Mac had come from a tiny place on the other side of Truro—somewhere in the Rawdon Hills, she thought. That was when Ellen had said, "My grandmother was a Milford from in there," and they had made the connection. It struck them both as miraculous, and deepened the final few years of their friendship.

Ellen had a photograph of her grandmother leaning back against an apple tree. The leaves cast such a strong shadow on her face that her features were nearly impossible to figure out. Did she look like Mumma Mac? Susan Ann couldn't tell.

"It's a terrible picture, I know, but it's the only one she ever had taken. It's the only thing that's left." In the background, however, the old Milford house could clearly be seen, a plain shingled farmhouse with a steeply pitched roof. "That house is long gone; I can just barely remember going there when I was a girl. But I know what road it was on," Ellen told her, "and I know that her cousins lived just down that road, so if we went there for a little drive, we could probably figure out where your mother was from, more or less."

Susan Ann's mother had never spoken much about her family. "Her lips were sealed, for some reason or other."

"Your great-grandfather had two sons," Ellen told her, "And he split his property up and gave them each a half of it. This caused some big ruckus, and *your* grandfather hated his brother and said he'd been given the better half. And apparently this was true, that a goodly portion of that original lot was fine land and the rest was all rock, and your old granddad, he got the rocks. Now, the bad feelings went way back to when they were boys, I think, but nobody knows anything about that any more."

"What were their names?"

"Billy, William, was your grandfather, and Jimmy, James, was the other. There were three sisters, Ellie, Nettie and Grace. They were my grandmother's cousins and Grace was her dearest friend."

Susan Ann had felt quite curious, almost dizzy. "I never knew my own grandfather's name till this moment," she said.

"Billy Milford, and his wife's name was Gladys, Billy and Gladys. Your grandparents. And that's all I know. Not a thing about your mother or her brothers and sisters."

"Mumma's name was Sarah, and I met her sister, my Aunt Lucille, who came up to visit once in a while. She would have been a year or two older than Mumma. But I never laid eyes on any of the others. Billy and Gladys," she said, "imagine that." She closed her eyes and tried to picture what they had looked like.

"Billy and Jimmy lived close to each other, less than a mile apart, but they never spoke. The story goes that on the day of his brother Jimmy's funeral, your grandfather hauled a load of manure right past the church, just as the pallbearers came out with the casket. Ha! I've heard that story a thousand times."

Susan Ann had never heard it before in her life.

They had always planned to drive up to the Rawdon Hills and find that road, but it had never happened. It wasn't too long afterwards that Ellen started to get confused. They made light of it, at first. "I'm turning into one of those dumb blondes from the TV," Ellen said, and they both laughed about her forgetfulness. She would put soap in the washing machine and then, not remembering doing it, add some more, and even more again, making a real mess, suds all over the kitchen floor. One time she found herself standing out in the middle of the driveway, holding a spatula in one hand and one of Hiram's old rubber boots in the other. "I didn't have a clue what I was doing out there," she said. When they went into Bridgewater for groceries one morning, she got lost in the dairy section at the Sobeys. "I could've been anywhere on earth," she said. "When I saw you come around the corner, I thought, thank goodness, I must be close to home." But there was no more joking when, after Ellen's bad fall, Susan Ann went to Surf Side Manor to visit her, and her dearest friend looked square into her eyes and said, "Do I know you?"

"Ellen, it's me. Susan Ann."

Ellen shook her head. "Who? Who's that? I don't know who that is."

"It was enough to break your heart," said Susan Ann.

Sally looked up at her.

"Every time I think of poor old Ellen, I start to feel sorry for myself. She was a good, good friend to me." She leaned down to give Sally's head a little rub, and suddenly felt an awful jab from inside her guts. "These cramps," she said, "are as mean and hateful as can be."

"You'd feel better if you had a nice big BM," Sally said.

"I know! But I *can't!* I've *tried* and *tried!*"

"'If at first you don't succeed,' the Bible says, 'try, try again.'"

"The Bible doesn't say that."

"The Bible doesn't say half the things that people say it does. Go over there right now, and squat down and try to poop."

So Susan Ann went off by herself, to hunker down in the ferns behind a maple tree by the side of the road. There was an old mossy stump, and she was able to keep her balance by leaning down and holding onto it while she hiked up her skirt and pulled down her pantyhose.

"Please," she thought, "please, God, help me get rid of some of this. I know I'd feel so much better."

Spreading her feet apart, she held onto the edge of the stump and squatted down. The ferns tickled her bum, and she held the stump with one hand and reached behind her to brush them aside with the other.

"There," she said. "All clear in the rear!"

But it was as if her body were all disconnected: she could feel the cramps but she couldn't do anything for relief. She tried to press down with her bum, but she couldn't really feel where her bum was any more. She tried again and again but it didn't seem to be any use. If only she could sit down on something comfortable, or eat something that might help, prunes or bran.

"I need a great big plate of Doshe's old bran muffins, that's what I need," she said.

"Keeps me right regular. Every morning, after my tea, just like a clock," Doshe would say.

"Old Tidy Bowels," Aunt Aggie whispered behind Aunt Doshe's back.

"Oh, if only my poor old bowels were tidy these days," thought Susan Ann.

Aunt Aggie, Aunt Bea and Mum Wellman would each try to get to the outhouse first thing in the morning, before Doshe was out of bed. "She lectures you, she sits there like a queen and lectures you while she has her shit! It drives me foolish!" said Aunt Bea.

"Meddlesome old pisspot!" said Aunt Aggie.

Mum said, "I thank the Lord that I am always the first to rise in this house."

They were young women then, Susan Ann thought, full of beans, and Great-Aunt Doshe was—well, she was *old*.

"Wait now, stupid, she was a lot younger than you are. Doshe was only seventy when the cancer took her."

And she tried to push down again.

"Oh, but what bit of difference does any of it make now?" she thought. "The farm's torn down, thanks to Muriel. Outhouse's probably gone by now, too. The only place any of it exists at all is inside my own stupid head."

She gave a little grunt as she pushed and she tried, but to no avail.

"Dammit," she said, "I am going to be dragging this load of shit to my grave!"

And then suddenly she was giggling, because she had thought of that day up at the farm when old Aunt Doshe made her and Muriel carry a bucket of water to the men out haying in the far field. Doshe filled the pail right to the brim, told them not to dare spill any, so they had to carry it together, one on either side, walking slowly and carefully. They were just small girls, it seemed to weigh a ton, and all on such a hot, hot, sultry day; they were both so mad that as soon as they were out of sight they put the bucket down and dropped an old dried cowpie into it. "This'll keep'm regular," said Muriel, and they left it in there until the men were just ahead, then Susan Ann took it out and threw it away into the grass. The men drank the water clear down to the bottom and Uncle Hay said, "Gosh, boys, that's the best water I ever tasted."

She and Muriel *had* gotten along for a while, back then. Things weren't so bad if there were just the two of them, but if anyone else was around, especially Daddy or Mumma Mac, then things could get mean.

The ferns were thick all around her, and she thought that maybe they were what Jamie used to call Banana Bread, because if you pulled them out of the ground you could eat the little white root, and it tasted just like that, just like banana bread. Her left hand was holding tight to the edge of the stump, which was covered with moss, a light green colour, very bright; as she grunted and pushed, she saw a little pair of round black eyes watching her from the moss. She jumped a bit, startled, but then she realized that it was a salamander, about two inches long and a very pretty red. It was very still.

"Hello, little fellow," she said.

The creature didn't move. They were such delicate things. She knew this because sometimes, when the kids tried to pick one up, its wee tail could break right off. They grew new ones, of course.

"I wish I was smart like you," she said. "Wouldn't I love it if my sorry old tail could break off right about now and I could grow me a nice new one!"

The salamander ran away, and as soon as it did, she could see something else move under the ferns, beyond the stump; she couldn't tell what it was at first, but then she saw it was a little brown rabbit, crouched down on the forest floor.

"Hello," she whispered. It didn't move. It looked terrified. "Don't be afraid."

She heard a noise beside the tree and looked over. Sally was peeking out at her from behind the ferns.

"No luck, old girl, I'm afraid. It's still packed in there like cement."

Sally came over and licked her face; the warm tongue tickled her. "Maybe next time."

"I have the terrible feeling I won't be able to have a decent BM till we get there. Oh well." She started to get up. "Sally," she whispered, "look there, at that cute little thing watching us."

But Sally no sooner saw the rabbit than she growled low in her throat and lunged behind the stump. Susan Ann was so startled she nearly lost her balance. "Stop that!" she called out.

But Sally had her nose in the ferns and she paid no attention to Susan Ann at all.

"*Sally!*"

When Sally lifted her head, Susan Ann could see the rabbit hanging out of her mouth, its body squirming and back legs kicking helplessly; it let out the most godawful screech.

"You let her go! You put her down! Right now!"

But her dog tossed her head back and forth, chomped down and broke the poor thing's neck.

"*No!*"

Then Sally set it down and started to eat it.

"*You bad girl!*" And Susan Ann reached out to slap at her dog—

"*Rrrough!*" Sally growled, baring her yellow teeth. "*Rrrough!*" She grabbed the rabbit in her mouth and turned and ran towards the road.

"*No!*"

When Susan Ann stood up and tugged at her pantyhose, she was so upset that she wasn't careful; she caught her nail, making a big run up the side of her left leg. "Dammit," she said. "Dammit all to hell."

When she got back to the road, she saw that Sally had disappeared. Susan Ann started walking, and it was half an hour or more before her dog returned. They walked in silence for the next few hours. There was a tension between them that had never been there before. Sally rarely came close to her; she trotted on ahead and was constantly making excursions off by herself into the woods. More than once, Susan Ann lost sight of her for such a long time that she worried she had been deserted and abandoned. But then, just as she was beginning to panic and despair,

Sally would reappear ahead of her, or come crashing through the bushes behind.

They walked and they walked; they walked all day. They crossed over Folly Mountain, walking on the edge of Folly Lake, high up in the hills where the air was cooler, even a bit nippy, and more than a few leaves had started to turn. The lake was such a deep blue it was almost purple; it looked as cold as could be. From every hillside she could hear the sound of water, of brooks and freshets running down into the lake. She had been through here once in wintertime, in 1960, when she and Jamie drove up to Moncton for Daddy Mac's funeral; all those streams and falls were frozen, the hillsides and the road were covered with ice and the driving was treacherous. It had been a terrifying beginning to a miserable stay with Muriel and Jack. After the service, those two had started into the rye and ginger, and Jack, who had never gotten along with Daddy Mac, had commemorated his father-in-law's passing by loudly singing "Ten Green Bottles a-Hanging on the Wall" and "Lili Marlene" over and over. Then Muriel had started in again on how brave Jack had been when he was overseas, and how wartime made a man show his true colours. Poor Jamie.

Today, it was a relief to arrive at the lake; the grade in the road was steep, the walking felt more like a climb, and she found herself stopping a lot to catch her breath.

At times the road seemed to dwindle to little more than a wide path through the woods. It became very dark then, as dark as a wet grey day, the walking was difficult, and Susan Ann had to watch her every step. When the road widened up again, there was more light and it was easier to manoeuvre.

Often Sally would lift her nose and sniff the air; she would look about in all directions, and then lead them on. Even though every place they walked through seemed familiar to Susan Ann, she still worried that they might become lost. "Is this right?" she kept thinking. "Are we going the right way?" She thought of Martha wandering alone, roaming the countryside, not really understanding what had happened to her people; how awful to spend eternity like that, going around and around in circles forever. She hoped her own journey wasn't a wild goose chase; when she got to Ragged Islands, she wanted to be home. She wanted to be home for good.

6—

SO DARK. It must be the dark after dark. And she was all wet, soaked cold, cold to the bone—

Was she inside or out?

Wait wait wait now. *Jamie?*

Go look see—Careful, ready set—

My feet!

Where, where—?

My hands! Where're they?

Was she dead? In the dark, buried? Earth coffin funeral *Jamie!*

"Just lie still now."

Jamie? No, that was wrong, not Jamie. *Carl.*

"It's Meg, Grammy. Carl will be back later."

What?

"Just lie still and get some sleep."

Hospital. She wasn't dead, she was in the hospital.

"Uncle Carl will come back."

He's left?

"Sssh. He'll be back to see you."

Carl. Yes. Yes. He ran away.

"Sssh now, go back to sleep. . . ."

They hate the hospital!

"Grammy?"

Men. S'the truth. Carl, every man, every man on earth. *He's no different!* They hate the hospital. Females are tougher, made of tougher stuff.

"Okay okay, there there. . . ."

Hospitals turn men into little boys. *S'the truth!*

"Sssh now." And a warm hand was touching her. Meg. Meg's hand. "Sssh . . ."

Men thought they were hot stuff, but women had the patience. Beat their chests and rule the roost, kill each other and blow things up, but they were the weaker sex, men.

Meg's hand was so warm.

Lookit Jamie.

"Sssh . . ."

Meg's warm hand was touching her. *No, lookit.* So, so warm. *Listen.* Carl was just like his father, he'd never admit it but that was the truth. Hated the hospital. He'd never've gone to that Surf Side Manor, he'd've hated going. And Queenie his own mother. Wouldn't have been right to put her in there. *Nosir.*

Queenie was grateful. She gave Susan Ann the shoebox. *She gave it to me.*

"Put this somewheres safe and don't tell Jamie."

She trusted it with me. Yes.

Didn't know who she was half the time, or talking to her brother Gordie, who'd died in the Great War. Poor old thing. She trusted Susan Ann to keep the truth. To hide it.

Wasn't I right? Wasn't keeping it tucked away the right thing to do? *Did I do right?*

But Jamie went to his grave without knowing.

But Queenie didn't want him to know!

Did she say that, though, did she ever say that?

But Jamie—
"Grammy, now—"
Oh no.
"Grammy, just—"
Maybe I was wrong?
"What's wrong? What is it?"
Should I've told him?
"Grammy, now sssh . . ."
Meg's hand. Holding her, holding her—
"Don't get all excited now. Just relax."
But Jamie, but—
"Relax now."
Oh. Yes. Because Jamie was dead, wasn't he? The hospital, Bridgewater, nothing but skin and bones—

Jamie was up in heaven with Mum and Murd and everybody. He was long gone.

And me? Am I?

No, because Meg's warm hand was holding her.

Meg!

"You need to get your rest, 'cause this is a big day for you."

It is?

"Uncle Carl'll be back. And Tommy and Louis are coming up from New York."

No.

"Yes. And Aunt Bonnie's coming, too. It will be nice to see them all, won't it?"

All this company.

"Tommy and Louis should be here by lunchtime."

Had she made enough sweets? Which ones did that Tommy like? His crazy friend with the crazy hair, the one that was so sick, five pieces of pie he ate that time! *Five!* Boys liked their sweets, and—

Wait now, *just wait.* She was a wee bit confused.

"Yes, Gram?"

Didn't he come *already?*

"What?"

Didn't Tommy come yesterday?

"Yesterday? Tommy? No, you're just a little mixed up, I think. Uncle Carl came yesterday."

That's right, Carl, yes. She was confused. Carl ran away.

"Tommy should be here with Mom today. We'll all be here."

Everybody? All of you?

"Yes. Me and Mom and Peter, and Carl and Bonnie too, and Tommy and Louis."

Everybody!

"Yes, everybody."

A picnic! A family picnic on the shore. Down by the names on the rocks. Was it fine today? Family picnic on the shore—

No, *wait!* The *hospital!*

"Shhh now, Gram. Shhh . . ."

Wait! They might find Jamie here! She could go back somewhere in the hospital before he died and find him! Oh, but how, with no hands, no feet? Bridgewater hospital, that awful room. Find him and bring him back for the picnic.

Meg's hand so warm, touching her, holding her—

"Grammy—"

How could she go find Jamie without her hands and feet? Where in the hospital was he, where? Can't move, all tied up, *damn leash.*

"Grammy, I'm right here with you now. Just relax and rest."

Meg. The bestest girl.

Bridgewater hospital, that last room, death's door—

Oh, Meg, I did a bad thing.

"Just rest."

But she had, she'd pretended that Jamie wasn't going to die.

Too embarrassed to say it, because she didn't want to lose him. She didn't lie, just pretended he would keep on living because anything else seemed like such a mean, such a dirty thing to say or think. She knew he was going to die, but she couldn't bring it up. She convinced herself he couldn't go before she told him about everything Queenie had squirrelled away. God wouldn't let that happen, wouldn't let Jamie go to his grave without those things. She didn't want the truth to be true so she pretended it wasn't. She said, *Tomorrow I'll bring you a treat,* knowing full well that yesterday was the last time tomorrow would ever mean anything to him, knowing that it was the end, it was, it was right there, death's door, but she went on and on pretending it wasn't. On and on about bringing him some berries or a little treat. What a lie that was, a little *treat.*

But he went so fast, it just ate him up! He didn't want anyone to know so she hadn't told the kids that whole summer. She knew he was right there at death's door and she pretended he wasn't, she lied to him and she never even kissed him goodbye the way she should have.

And he just looked so, so—

Then he was gone, she turned her head and he was gone, his soul had flown away.

The body she loved so much was all empty.

And the moment he went, she didn't notice—*didn't even notice!* And she didn't even kiss him bye-bye. He suffered so, that body was all that was left, why should anyone suffer so? All empty, like some old cocoon thing left behind.

And me, now that's where I am.

And would she be with him after? Go through death's door to heaven? Where did your soul live before you died?

"Inside of you," said Mum Wellman, pointing her finger at Susan Ann's heart.

In a tiny room close by her heart, it must live in there. Her soul all safe and sound in a tiny room as pink as a conch shell.

A soul was a small thing, like a birdie so fine you could see right through it almost, trans . . . something, trans, trans, *parent.* No, not so much, not like that, the other one, like beach glass, trans, trans, *lucent!* Yes, *translucent,* and the moment you died, the door to that little room would open and it would fly away—

Where to?

"To Jesus in Heaven," said Mum Wellman. Death's door would open and her little soul would fly up.

And what would be there? Heaven? In the shade of the trees, all of them waiting with Jesus? Jamie, Aunt Aggie, Mum, Murd, even Queenie? A family picnic—yes, lovely, like that warmth she could feel touching her.

What would their souls be like? Gathered all around like birdies at the feeder, happy and flying and hopping about? But how would she know who was who? Wouldn't they look the same, all their souls? Jamie? Mum? She couldn't tell one bird from another, one robin looked like every other.

Because you're not a robin.

That was right, those birdies could tell one from the other, they all knew who was who. That old crow up at the farm—she'd know him anywhere. Mean thieving thing.

That warm touching her was so comfortable.

Pink room, the little door there would open and her soul would fly out. Out and up, through the doors and windows, away up there all the way to Kingdom Come. Our Father, which art in Heaven, hallowed be thy name, that's heaven, Kingdom Come. And she was coming there. She was—

But what if it wasn't there, what then? What if it was all nothing? What if the door opened and there was dark and everything stopped, the whole world. It would keep on for everyone else but not for her. And all those things that no one knew but Susan Ann would end forever. Queenie and her shoebox, everything.

No. The pink door would open and her soul would fly out and up past the clouds, the moon and outer space. Airplanes and rocket ships. That thing with the arm from Canada. All those planets you saw on the old box. Saturn with the rings. More rocks on Mars than on the beach at Ragged Islands. Past Venus morning star, evening star, she was always there even when she disappeared for days on end. Away out there way past the seasons, out and up and up until . . . what? God on his throne and Jesus beside him?

What does God look like?

No one knows but Jesus.

Who was God's mother?

And Mum Wellman laughed and said, "He doesn't have a mother."

Poor God. Was he an orphan?

Mum laughing and Aunt Aggie almost scandalized.

Then where did he come from?

"He didn't come from anywhere. God never began, he always was."

And Susan Ann would try to think of something with no beginning, a piece of ribbon that was so long it could wrap itself all round and round the world over and over and still go back and back and back forever as far as . . .

She couldn't imagine it. Couldn't imagine never beginning.

She could remember her own life back and back, but never as far as the beginning. No one could. No one ever remembered when they were born. Or before that.

But this would be a good time to ask, to come right out and ask Mum—

What was this? This nice warm—

A hand. Touching her, a warm hand.

"Oh, Grammy . . ."

What? Who was that?

"Gram . . ."

Was it Meg? That warm, comfortable—

"Who are you talking to?"

Me?

"And where are you?"

Where am I? She had to think and remember. The pink door—

"Grammy."

Meg, yes, but Meg was—she wasn't here, really, couldn't be, could she? No, Meg was still back with Susan Ann in that hospital, because the pink door had opened and her little soul had flown away and there was something she had to ask Mum and Aunt Aggie—

"Grammy? I'm going to take off this harness. Okay?"

What?

"I think you'll be more comfortable."

What? Oh, that miserable thing. Yes! Get rid of it!

Meg was unfastening it, untying it and sliding it away—

Oh, the relief, so good—

"What are you doing?"

"Making her more comfortable."

"Psspsspss!"

What? Who said that? There was someone big—

"What's the matter?"

Someone in the doorway, someone suddenly talking to Meg—

"Haven't you heard anything?"

Lorraine, was it Lorraine?

"What's the matter?"

"Hasn't anyone told you? *Oh Jesus!*"

"What?"

"Carl's found a TV down the hall, come see!"

Lorraine, yes, that was Lorraine in the door. And Carl—

"Told me what?"

What was she—

"—terrible terrible terrible!"

Where was she—

"When?"

"Just now, just before we left the house."

Lorraine, why was she standing inside the door, hissing and whispering—

The door, but that was the hospital door. Where was the little pink door? Where had it gone?

"What? Two planes? Like an accident?" said Meg.

"*Psspsspss.*"

"Where'd they come from?" Meg was saying. "Who were they?"

"No one *knows*, no one knows a *goddamn thing!*" Lorraine was so upset, crazy-sounding, "The whole country's scared to death!"

Then Meg stood up, and Susan Ann knew right then that one of her own hands had come back because Meg was holding it so tight. Her right hand, oh her right hand was back! Good, yes, and now she could—

But Meg was standing up and—

"What about Tommy? Where's Tommy?"

What was, what was—Things were all mixed up and all—

"I don't know, I *don't know!*"

Her hand was back but Meg—

"Oh Mom!"

Meg let go! She dropped her grandmother's hand, and Susan Ann fell, she was falling down and—

But her right hand was back, yes, her right hand, so try to grab—

But there was nothing near her, nothing, nowhere—

The deep dark never beginning always was—
Grab hold the pink door high above—
Gone.
The door! The wrong door, someone was—
"There's *another* one!"
"Jesus, Carl, what?"
"Another *plane!* A third plane!"
Carl? Carl?
"*Sssh!* Don't let her know!"
What? But she needed to know, she wanted to—
"Come see!"

And then they were gone, they took Meg with them and they were gone.

Planes? Airplanes? What was this?

They took Meg and ran away and shut the door. Shut the door and left her all alone in her little bed.

Wait for me! Wait!

But she was all alone. There was nobody else.

"*Nobody, nobody, nobody . . .*"

ORION

It was nearing dusk when they came to the crossroads.

"Thank heavens," she said, glad to be this far along, finally. Truro lay behind them. The road to the left, the eastern road, went through and beyond the Cobequids and on to the island of Cape Breton; it was the route that her great-great-grandfather John MacDonald must have walked two hundred years ago. The southern road, which stretched before her, ended in Halifax. Just a ways along it would be the western road through the Rawdon Hills to the Annapolis Valley, and on to Digby Neck. Beyond that western road, and before they reached the outskirts of the city, they would come to the road she would turn onto, the southwest road that travelled along the shore to Ragged Islands, *her* road to home.

"We've come a goodly piece," she said. "Now let's find ourselves a spot to spend the night."

And they did, just a little ways ahead. It was after dusk, and they'd had a long, exhausting day. By the roadside, at the edge of a small field, newly mown, Susan Ann sat down on a little stack of hay, and ratched around in her bag till she found a cracker to nibble on. All around her, crickets were singing. At this time of year, they seemed to be at it day and night. "The last hurrah before winter," she said.

She and Sally were on slightly better terms than they had been earlier in the day. It still upset Susan Ann that her dog would eat a defenceless little creature. "I know I do it all the time," she thought. "What could be more defenceless than a chicken or a haddock?—and I dearly love to munch on them both." But there had been something frightening about the way Sally had instinctively jumped on the little rabbit and gobbled it down. It had seemed as if she wanted to kill it as much as she wanted it for a snack, and this bothered Susan Ann a great deal.

In the west she could see Venus, the evening star, growing brighter in a sky that still had traces of pink. "Red sky at night," she said, "Sailors' delight." She was aware, suddenly, of the necklace, and she reached into the neck of her blouse and took it out; holding it out a bit, she looked down at the lady, who was milky white, the same lovely shade as the moon. "Hello," she said. "Hello." The cameo seemed to be glowing in the soft dark. She held it tenderly while she watched Venus in the darkening sky above the treetops. What a beautiful night it would be. The air was warm and still, and there were just a few wisps of cloud low in the west, catching the last colours of the sun.

"'When I consider thy heavens, the work of thy fingers, the moon and the stars, which thou hast ordained,'" she quoted, "'What is man, that thou art mindful of him?' Eh, Sally?"

Tonight, she felt she would be able to see every star in the firmament.

"Tomorrow, it won't be too long before we get through Shubenacadie, and that'll be good. That's a good distance." When the kids were young, they were always excited when they drove by Shubenacadie because it was exactly halfway between the equator and the North Pole, right on the forty-fifth parallel. Why wasn't there a proper name for it, a northern equivalent to something like the Tropic of Capricorn? Faraway places always puffed themselves up with fancy names and institutions. Like when people made a big show about crossing over the equator, and pretended to meet with old King Neptune, the Lord of the Sea. Her grandson Tommy had almost crossed the equator once. "We were only a few days shy of it," he had told her, "not too far from the mouth of the Amazon." She had imagined a frightening and dangerous place, even hotter than Toronto in the summer; the waters at the mouth of the Amazon River would be filled with fifty-foot snakes. "You were darn smart to turn that boat around and come back," she told him.

Sally had lifted her head and was sniffing at the air.

"What is it, girl?"

Was that someone walking towards them on the road? Out walking in the evening? She tucked the necklace back safely inside her blouse. Sally jumped up and was standing at attention, all braced and ready to strike. Susan Ann knew she was about to bark, and so she reached over to hold her—

"Calm now, be careful—"

But the sturdy little dog simply trotted over to the road, tail wagging happily as could be, as if she was greeting an old friend.

"Does this dog bite?" It was a young woman's voice, sounding more annoyed than frightened.

"Oh-oh," thought Susan Ann, and she called out, "She's never bitten me!" Then she thought of Elsie Steeves and the little rabbit, so she added, "But it always pays to be wary at first."

"Hello, dog? Hello?" Her voice was very cautious-sounding.

Sally sniffed about the stranger's legs, her tail still wagging.

"What's your name, hey?"

"Her name is Sally!"

"Hello, Sally? Hello?" The stranger bent down and patted Sally's head. She seemed to be fifteen or sixteen years of age, from the looks of her, around the same height as Susan Ann, five-six or -seven.

"She seems to like you!"

"It would appear so. Not all dogs do." As she came closer, Susan Ann could see that she was stocky, with large breasts and wide hips, and wore a dress with a delicate pattern of teeny blue flowers. Her brown hair was pulled back in a very severe way, and on her head was an old-fashioned straw hat. She was carrying a worn carpet bag. When she came even closer, Susan Ann could see that her eyes were a bright, bright blue.

"Yes, you're a nice dog," she said, and then lifted her head and wished Susan Ann a good evening.

Susan Ann stood up to greet the young woman, who asked, "Would you mind if I join you for a spell?"

"No, not at all. Sally and I could use some company. That would be very nice."

Once her hat had been taken off, Susan Ann could see that the young woman's face was quite plain—if her eyes hadn't been so pretty, she might even have been considered homely. But those eyes, they sparkled, they were so blue. "Like sapphires," thought Susan Ann, except they weren't cold in the way an old jewel could be cold. Something about them reminded Susan Ann of her grandson Tommy, who had the loveliest blue eyes; they made him look so very handsome.

Otherwise, the young woman's features were ordinary and undistinguished. They were pleasant, though, and she looked like someone who wasn't afraid of work. There was something hardy about her, and not just in her stout body: she possessed a kind of resolution; she looked strong-willed and determined. Susan Ann decided that she liked the look of her.

"I'm tuckered out," the girl said. "I hope I'm not bothering you."

"No, no bother at all."

"I didn't expect to see anyone tonight," she said.

"We haven't seen a soul all day," said Susan Ann, and then she introduced herself.

"I'm very glad to know you, Susan Ann. My name is Sadie. But my sisters call me Sade."

"A plain, old-fashioned country name," thought Susan Ann, as she went back to where she had been sitting.

The girl came and sat nearby. "It's good to take the load off my feet," she said.

Sally had followed her from the road and was lying down beside her, on the side farthest from Susan Ann; she nuzzled her nose against Sade's thigh.

"Well, she took to you right away," Susan Ann observed.

It was clear that Sade wasn't entirely comfortable with the situation. "Dogs is queer things," she said. A moment later, she added, "There's a dog back home that's made me nervous of all dogs in general. It was mean and ugly."

"I'm sorry to hear that. That's too bad. A dog can be real good company."

"Where are you coming from?" Sade asked, clearly changing the subject. "If you don't mind my asking."

"That's a good question," thought Susan Ann, and at first she wasn't sure what to answer. "I'm coming from Shediac," she said, because that was where she had been raised.

"Why, that's up near Moncton, isn't it? That's where I'm headed." And she settled down in the hay, leaning away from Sally, towards Susan Ann.

"Do you have people up that way?" Susan Ann was curious, but she didn't want to seem nosy.

"My aunt lives there, on Botsford Street, and she has recently lost her husband."

"Oh, I'm sorry to hear that."

Sade shrugged her shoulders, as if to say, *He wasn't much.*

Susan Ann thought, "Young girls today are not so respectful of their elders as they used to be." She said, "So you'll be looking after her?"

"For a while. Yes. I'll be staying with her."

"And where are you coming from? If you don't mind my asking."

"Oh, back a piece. Down near the Gore. Where they mine the antimony? Near there."

Susan Ann thought this was somewhere near the Rawdon Hills. "Now that's a place I've always wanted to know, but I never got around to it."

"I'm in no hurry to go back."

"It's beautiful country there, isn't it?"

"I suppose, if you like hills. I'm looking forward to city life for a change." After a moment she added, rather scornfully, "My father doesn't believe in electricity."

That was a surprising thing in this day and age. Maybe he was one of those odd fellows who still drove a buggy and didn't believe in anything modern, Amish or Mennonite or whatever they were; but Susan Ann hadn't thought there were any such people around these parts. "Is that for religious reasons?"

"Religious reasons? That's rich. His only reasons are stubbornness and irritability."

Sade had taken a penknife out of her bag, and an apple, which she began to peel in one long, clean ribbon. She was quite focused and didn't take her eyes from the task. "If the peel stays all together in one piece," she said, "and you toss it over your shoulder, they say it'll land in the shape of the initial of the man you're s'posed to marry."

"That's true," said Susan Ann, remembering an incident in the kitchen on Railway Avenue; she had been standing beside her sister Muriel and looking down at an apple peel lying on the pantry floor. It was stretched out in the shape of a J, for Jamie, as clearly a J as a J could be, and that was the first time Muriel said Jamie was a traitor. This was just after he'd been discharged and the boy Muriel was engaged to had been killed overseas, poor little Alex McCallum.

The girl's hands were sturdy and brown from the sun. The lengthening peel was a delicate thing, very fine and narrow, less than half an inch wide and over two feet long. She was skinning that apple with considerable skill. "There!" she said, standing up slowly, taking care not to tear or break the peel; she moved from the haystack, then, lifting the peel high above her head, spun it around, slowly at first and then faster—once, twice, three times—before letting it go. The peel sailed and twirled in the air, the white underside gleaming in the growing dark.

It landed a little ways away, and Sade walked over and looked down at it. She was studying it, turning her head this way and that. "Hm," she said.

"What does it spell?" Susan Ann asked.

"Just a minute now. Hold your horses."

Susan Ann got up and went over beside her. "It looks like a wave," she said. "It could be a V. What starts with a V? Valentine, *Val*." There had been a Val Leger in Shediac when she was a girl. "Or *Vernon*." She had an Uncle Vernon, a man she had never met.

"*No*," Sade said sharply, "it's no V!" And she walked around to look at it from the other side. "I think it's an R."

"How do you get an R out of that?" Susan Ann thought maybe she could tease her a bit, they could have a little fun.

"Well, you come over here and see." Sade sounded very serious. "R. Robert, Randall, Richard—" she started.

When Susan Ann came around and, standing beside her, looked down at the apple peel curved about on the ground, she couldn't stop herself from teasing a bit more, so she said, "I don't see how you can get an R out of that. It's an upside-down V. Vernon, Val—"

"It is *not* Vernon!" Sade shouted, suddenly kicking at the peel with a violence that made Susan Ann jump. The peel broke in two, Sade's foot sending half of it flying into the air.

They both stood awkwardly.

"Oh, *dammit!*" Sade hissed, and she turned away and—

Susan Ann was certain she heard the girl spit! Just a little *pta!*—an angry exclamation—but a spit sure enough. She watched her for a moment. "She's got quite the temper on her," she said to herself, and she went back to sit on her little haystack. "She can just cool herself down a bit," she thought. "There was no need of that!" Sally's ears had perked up and she was watching Sade closely, but she did not move from her spot.

Neither of them said anything for a little while. Sade stood very still, her face and body turned half away from Susan Ann, facing the road; she was looking back the way she had come. Susan Ann watched the stars come out. Where was the Dipper? Where was Cassiopeia? She couldn't get her bearings quite yet. Sade took out her penknife again and cut the apple in two pieces; then she turned and walked back and handed one of them to Susan Ann.

"My sister says I have to do something about my temper," she said. "And I suppose that she is right."

Susan Ann accepted the apple. "Think nothing of it," she said, and "Thank you kindly." But what she was thinking was "That wasn't much of an apology for jumping down my throat."

The fruit, however, was extremely sweet and juicy; the flesh was firm but not too hard, and when she bit into it, she was mindful of how fresh and fragrant it smelled. It was, in fact, one of the best apples she had ever tasted. She bit off tiny pieces and sucked the goodness out of them before chewing and swallowing. "Mmmm," she said, because it was so delicious.

After a few moments, Sade said, "Vernon is the name of my tormentor."

"I see," said Susan Ann, and then, "This is a really tasty apple. Where's it from?"

"The Valley."

"Mmmm, it's some good!" and Susan Ann smacked her lips.

A few more minutes passed before Sade said, "I'm speaking of my brother."

"Oh," Susan Ann responded.

"I have no intentions of going back home," said Sade. "I don't relish putting up with the kind of things that my mother has put up with all her married life."

After a moment, Susan Ann said, "I'm not quite sure I follow you."

"Well, for one, I have no interest in being taken for granted."

"Good for you," said Susan Ann. "That's a smart attitude."

"When I bake a pie, all I want is for someone to tell me that it tastes good before they swallow it whole. Is that too much to ask?"

"No, it certainly is not."

"I have no use for people who wolf down their food and grunt."

"And you shouldn't, either." Susan Ann could tell that this young Sade had something she needed to get off her chest. "Is your brother disrespectful?"

"Vernon is mean and hateful."

"Oh."

"I have no idea why my mother favours him, but she does. He can do no wrong in her eyes, none whatsoever."

"He's the apple of her eye," said Susan Ann.

"Pah! Some apple." Sade paused for a moment, as if deciding whether or not to continue; then she took a deep breath. "Let me tell you a little story," she said, and she came and sat back down beside Sally.

While Sade was making herself comfortable, squirming her ample bum into the hay to smooth out a cozy seat for herself, Susan Ann was studying her. Sade was so serious for one so young, and didn't seem to have much of a sense of humour. It dawned on Susan Ann that maybe the girl was running away from home; perhaps she had a good reason to be short-tempered?

Sally had started to wiggle her head towards Sade's lap, when a firm hand reached out and gently pushed against her.

"No," Sade said firmly. "I'll let you stay right there, right beside me, but I can't stand to have an animal of any kind on top of me. You can keep your old head to yourself."

"What a queer duck she is," thought Susan Ann. "I wouldn't fancy getting too tangled up with her!"

Sade had finished her piece of the apple; she wiped the flats of her hands along the side of her dress and then she held them together in her lap. "Every single time my mother and her sisters get together," she started, "every single time, they complain about *their* mother, my Grammy Brown, and how she kowtowed to their brother and their father. It's all they can talk about."

"I see," said Susan Ann.

"Yes. Oh, and he was a tyrant, too, I can tell you. I was scared to death of Grampy Brown. He always had a stick of hardwood in his hand about a foot long, and he'd smack anyone, man, woman or child, that annoyed him or got in his way. He had a mean mouth, and whenever he said mean things Grammy grinned like a goon, as if he were a real comical fellow."

"She was probably terrified of him," said Susan Ann.

"I don't know if my Grammy was terrified of him or if she adored him, or if she was smart enough to even know there was a difference between the two. Now, she was always sweet to me when I was little, I'll give her that. But she never stood up for her daughters, and she spoiled her sons rotten, and two of them turned out to be no better than their father before them. My Uncle Alexander? Well, doesn't he just think he's the King of Heaven, and a more selfish individual you could not meet. He wouldn't give a glass of water to a man dying of thirst. And my Uncle Ezra! He's good for nothing. He's drunk day and night and has his mother convinced that he's a teetotaller."

"I've known people like that too," Susan Ann said. "When they aren't going on and on about the evils of drink, they're out in the shed with a bottle."

"Then you know the kind of thing I'm talking about."

"Yes, and I suppose anyone with a family does," she said. "Hypocrisy can run as thick in families as it does in politics or at church."

Sade looked at her a little oddly. Surely she couldn't be shocked? "You're probably right about that," she said, after a moment.

"When it comes to hypocrisy, religion and families can give even politicians a run for their money."

"I imagine that's right."

"Right as rain," said Susan Ann.

"I do have another uncle, named Ronald, but he had a sweet disposition and he wasn't dim-witted, so he took off for the Yukon and never came back. They talk about him as if he were some kind of traitor for wanting more out of life."

"They begrudge him his happiness, I suppose."

"They begrudge him the fact that he had the gumption to want to make something of himself!" she exclaimed. "The things that my mother says about him, her own brother, it's something awful."

"Families can be cruel," said Susan Ann sadly. "And that's a fact." They sat quietly for a moment, thinking on this, the both of them. Despite the fact that Sade had jumped at her earlier, Susan Ann found herself warming up to the girl a bit. There was something old-fashioned about her that was appealing; maybe it was because she was a country girl, and Susan Ann had been dealing with big-city people for quite a while now. She knew there was something more to Sade's reasons for leaving home.

"But you haven't told me yet about your brother," she said, "the tormentor."

Sade had begun to stroke Sally's back, scratching gently behind the floppy ears. "I was just getting to him," she answered. "What a good dog she is."

Sally moaned, a deep, long sound that at once seemed happy and contented, and yet filled with yearning and sadness.

"Yes, I love my girl." It hardly seemed possible that such a sweet little thing could have an ounce of violence in her.

Sade looked up at the sky. "As I was saying," she started, "every time my mother and her sisters get together, they go on and on about their mother and how she kowtowed and how she did *this* wrong and how she did *that* wrong. Rarely, *rarely*, do they say a word against their father or Uncle Alexander or Uncle Ezra. And those three men have made their lives miserable. But what does my mother do?" Here she paused for dramatic effect, and turned to look squarely at Susan Ann. "She goes and marries my father, who is a big bully, let me tell you, and not so very different from her father! In the end, she is no different from her very own mother! She *herself* is guilty of doing the *selfsame things* that she hates her own mother for doing!"

"History repeats itself," said Susan Ann. "That's a sad historical fact."

"Now, my father doesn't carry Grampy Brown's stick around, but he'll cuff you in the side of the head nine times out of ten just as soon as look at you. He's just so, so, oh, it makes me so mad that I don't even know how to say it! He just pays her no mind! Never a word of thanks, never a moment of kindness. He's a big, darn bully. She married a bully, just like her mother before her. And she has *raised* a bully. My brother Vernon is a bully, and she allows him to tease and torment me and make my life miserable just because I'm a female!"

"That's a darn shame," said Susan Ann.

"It makes my blood boil, I can tell ya!"

"I had a sister who was always miserable to me," she said, thinking of the way Muriel would pick on her up at the farm or when she went to visit at the house on Railway Avenue. Then she thought of how cold her Mumma Mac had been to her, and of the unkind things she had said and done. "And my own mother could be mean too, she could be a real bully."

"Your mother?"

"Yes, yes she could."

"How is it," Sade wanted to know, "that my mother can see the fault in her mother's life, can see it clear as day, and yet she can't see the selfsame flaw in herself?"

"Well, that's the sixty-four-thousand-dollar question, isn't it?" said Susan Ann.

"I beg your pardon? The what?"

"The—Oh, you're too young, dear, you wouldn't even know that program. It was on the old box a long, long time ago."

"The box?"

"I just mean to say that it is so often the case—we can find fault in others and not see the very same thing in ourselves."

Above them, the stars were arriving and the constellations beginning to form and appear. All the time Susan Ann had lived in Toronto, she had been deprived of the world at night; how she had missed the great and simple pleasure of standing out in her backyard and watching the stars. "Just look at them all," she said. "Once you get to Moncton, they won't be so clear with all those streetlights and such."

"Fine by me," said Sade, barely giving the heavens a glance. "I'd rather be modern."

"Ah, youth," thought Susan Ann. "Your mother," she started, "now she must, what I mean to say is, she wants you to go and be with your aunt, so she must—"

"Oh, no, she doesn't!" Sade blurted out. "I'm sorry, but she doesn't. You should've seen the look on her face when I told her I'd be leaving."

"What did she say?"

"When I told her that I aimed to go to Moncton, and that I wanted something more than I could get down there on the wrong side of Gore, that I wanted a better life than that, she says, *'Ya'll never be happy no matter where y'are.'*" She mimicked her mother's voice with a sharp nasal twang. "And then she said, *'Ya don't know what ya want. Ya never did and ya never will.'*"

Hearing these last two sentences set Susan Ann right off.

"*Oh!*" she said, sitting up straight as could be. "Oh, if there is one thing I *hate* to hear more than *anything* else, *that is it!*"

"You know what I'm talking about, then."

"I surely do, because my Mumma Mac said that to me, I can't tell you how many times! Nothing gets my back up like that does! *'Ya don't know what ya want, ya never did.'* Oh, that just burns me somethin' awful! It's a miserable thing to say to someone, to put them down that way."

"Because I know what I want!" Sade exclaimed. "I want something different. I want a better life!" For the first time, her voice lost its hard, knowing edge and revealed a softness, a yearning.

In the moment that followed, they looked into each other's eyes and then away towards the field on the other side of the road. The Dipper was low in the northeast sky, and looked to be standing on the end of its handle; the first two stars—*Randall, Rebecca*—had not yet risen from behind the trees. Across from the pointers—*Harvey and Hugh*—the North Star could barely be seen.

I want a better life! Susan Ann was thinking of the time that Meg had worked on the family tree, and had shown her copies of boat lists and ancient census reports. "To seek a better life." That was what nearly all of them had written down beside their names.

"I wish I could understand the way my mother thinks sometimes," Sade said longingly. "I wish I knew how she feels, how she—"

She stopped and slammed her fists against her legs: *once! twice! three* times. "I wish I knew if she even cared about me!" she declared.

Susan Ann was quite taken aback. "What makes you say that?"

"She never asked me why, she never wanted to know if something was wrong, she never . . ."

Sade rubbed her fist against her nose and sniffed loudly.

It suddenly occurred to Susan Ann that the poor girl might have *had* to leave home. Perhaps Sade was pregnant.

But just as she was trying to figure out a way to broach such an awkward and embarrassing subject, she thought of something even worse, something monstrous. Perhaps that bully Vernon had done a disgusting and terrible thing to his sister. You heard of things like that nowadays, things you never even dreamed of happening in the past. Brothers and uncles and priests and God knows who else. If that was the case, she should get to a clinic. There was one in New Brunswick now, in Fredericton. There was no way that a girl as young as Sade should sacrifice her future; things like that were simply not fair.

But how could she say such things to a stranger?

"Sade," she said, "there is nothing worse than feeling unwanted."

"I imagine not," the girl replied. She was wiping her chin roughly with one hand and had set her mouth in a determined way, not quite a scowl.

"It's a terrible thing," she went on. "It can eat away at a person from before they are even born."

Sade was sitting up very straight, her chin stuck out; she began to suck on her upper lip.

"There's nothing sadder on earth than the fate of an unwanted child."

"I'm no child!" said the girl.

"I know that," said Susan Ann. "I want to give you the same piece of advice I gave to my first daughter-in-law and to my granddaughter. Maybe the situation doesn't fit at present, but then, you never know, someday it just might."

Sade looked a bit confused. "Yes?"

"I am no fan of Mother Teresa," declared Susan Ann.

"Who?"

"Mother Teresa, you know, she was over there in India with the little babies."

"What?"

"All that talk about giving her the Nobel Prize—if they want to give it to someone worthwhile they should give it to Henry Morgentaler."

"Who? I don't know what you're talking about."

"I'm talking about a woman's right to choose."

"Choose what?"

Susan Ann hesitated a moment before she asked, "You're not in trouble, are you, dear?"

Sade turned away from her.

"I know it's none of my business, and you don't have to answer." She could not see the girl's face, could not see her reaction. All around them was the warm darkness of the late summer evening. A bat flitted in the air over their heads, and Sally's snout jerked upwards. Susan Ann reached out her hand towards the girl's shoulder. "You can tell me, if you like, if you want to talk about it. My lips will be sealed."

Sade took a deep breath. "I may be in trouble," she said.

"Oh."

"I will certainly be in a great deal of trouble if my sister tells anyone what I've done." Sade got up suddenly. "I have to have a pee," she said, and she walked a distance away. Sally got up too and trotted out behind her; she seemed to have developed a real fondness for the girl, but a part of Susan Ann wondered if Sally was trying to make her feel a wee bit jealous. She watched the two of them go out into the centre of the field.

"That girl is what I'd call an enigma," thought Susan Ann. "She's a real odd duck."

The sky was so dark now and the stars so bright that she could see the countryside as clear as if it were bathed in moonlight. Sade had lifted her dress and had crouched down; a few feet away from her, Sally stood very still, on guard. The nearby crickets had quieted down as the two walked out, and Susan Ann could hear the trickle as Sade relieved herself. Embarrassed, feeling that she was spying, she looked up, at the stars above them.

From the woods on the far side of the field, she could hear the deep *whu-whuu-whuu-whuu* of an owl.

Orion was brilliant in the southern sky. The three stars of his belt were as radiant as Venus had been after sunset, and she could make out six of the stars in his great bow. There was Saturn, over his left shoulder, and Castor and Pollux just beyond it. Above his bow, the clusters were clearly visible, the Hyades and, farther right, the Pleiades. Most clear nights she could *sense* them more than see them; they had always seemed more distinct when she caught them out of the corner of her eye, but this night she was able to count five of the seven sisters. Mars was clear and red, and Venus still shone brightly; the whole of the heavens were falling into place. There, near the hunter's foot, was Sirius, the Dog Star—his companion, the brightest star of them all.

Susan Ann had not seen a sky like this for so very long, not since she'd left Nova Scotia. When all the lights in the house were off, she would stand in the bedroom window, the window facing south, and she would see Orion above the trees, exactly where he was placed tonight; she would watch Orion above the snow-covered spruce and the bare branches of the hackmatack—

"Wait, now, I must be all confused," she thought, and turned her head to check the Dipper, to see again the handle pointed down towards the horizon. "That's odd," she thought, and looked back at Orion. This was the January sky, the winter sky, but it was late summer still. Orion wouldn't appear until just before morning. Her stupid old head must be playing tricks on her—

Whu-whuu whuu-whuu.

The owl called from behind her now, so close it startled her, and she turned to look—

Whu-whu-whuu-whuu.

No, there were two—one behind her, the other still in the woods across the field. She listened as they called back and forth.

Whu-whuu whuu-whuu.

Whu-whu-whuu-whuu.

Sally pricked up her ears and stood at attention. Then she started to bark and, darting away from Sade, she streaked towards the woods.

"Sally!"

Sade was coming back, glancing over her shoulder. Both women watched Sally run across the dark field, barking wildly, and disappear in the trees.

"She smells something out there."

"Let's just hope she doesn't get herself in trouble with a skunk or a porcupine," Sade said.

"Oh, Sally's a smart dog, she knows better than to do that."

"She's a dog," said Sade. "Smart has nothing to do with it."

Neither of them spoke for two or three minutes. Susan Ann wondered what she should say, how she might ask Sade to talk about why she was on her way to Moncton.

Still looking out into the night, out where Sally's barks were farther and farther away, Sade began to tell a story. "Vernon had this old dog named Bud," she said. "Had him since he was twelve or so, eight or nine years or more. I can't remember when he wasn't around." She rubbed her nose with the back of her hand. "He treated him something awful," she continued. "Played mean tricks on him, like he'd tie tin cans to his legs and laugh when Bud dragged them around. If the dog got in his way, he'd kick him— and hard, too, it'd make you wince to see it—and he'd slam him on the head with his fist when he was angry. I've seen him tie Bud to a tree and then throw rocks at him for sport."

"Shameful," Susan Ann said. "Shameful things to do."

"Yes. But that fool dog followed him everywhere, thought the sun rose and set on his arse, and he'd bare his teeth and snarl if anyone so much as looked at Vernon the wrong way. They slept together, every single night, all cuddled up, snuggly tight; they were never apart. Vernon treated him like dirt, but he loved him, I suppose. That's what he'd call it, anyway. Most folks would call it selfishness. But if he ever loved anything, Vernon loved old Bud. Which is why, the week before last, when my father took Vernon off for yet another damn argument with *his* brother Jimmy over who owned Grampy Milford's good pasture land, I poisoned that dog's food and I killed him."

"Holy Moses," Susan Ann whispered, glad that Sally was off chasing something and wasn't hearing this story.

Sade had sat down next to her.

"Poor Bud, I can say that I ended his misery, but mostly I used him to get back at Vernon. And I am happy to say I did. He cried like a big, fat crybaby." She sounded smug and very satisfied with herself. "'Vengeance is mine, saith the Lord.' Yes, and it's Sadie Milford's too."

And it was at that moment that Susan Ann realized that the girl sitting beside her on the new-mown hay under the starry heavens was her very own Mumma Mac, before she *was* Mumma Mac, when she was yet Sadie Milford, young and determined and on her way to New Brunswick to seek her fortune. She didn't know what to say or do, she just stared at the girl, who had tightened her mouth and stuck out her jaw in that stubborn, determined way that was so Mumma Mac. How could she not have realized it before?

Here was Sadie Milford, who was yet to arrive in Moncton and look after her Aunt Jane, yet to care for her, to wait on her hand and foot and to bury her; yet to meet Robert MacDonald, yet to marry him and give birth to a girl she would name Jane, after the aunt who had freed her from home. Susan Ann's sister Jane, the oldest girl, who had buried two husbands and a daughter and had died down there in her trailer in Florida when she was eighty-five. Sadie Milford, yet to give birth to Susan Ann, her own self, who Sadie would give away for reasons that were never explained to anyone's satisfaction; to Muriel, who would never forgive her sister for marrying a man who wasn't killed overseas; to Fred, who would become a schoolteacher and live in California; to the triplets, who would die, one after another, the day after they were born, and be laid out on the dresser like three pale dollies; as well as to countless miscarriages and a stillborn child with long blonde curls to whom she would refuse to attach a name, saying, "I don't care what you call it, I don't have another name left in me."

"I suppose you think I'm an awful creature," she said, defiantly.

Susan Ann wasn't sure what she thought or how she felt, other than the fact that her stomach was beginning to go all queasy suddenly, and a faint buzzing sound was starting deep inside her head. She knew she should say something, but she didn't have a clue what that something might be, so she said, "No, I don't." She realized that there were so many questions she had wanted to ask Mumma Mac all her life, so many things she had wanted and needed to know, but that this young woman would not have the answers, would not be able to help her understand a thing. Sadie

Milford was looking out towards the woods, and the look on her face seemed the very same as the look on Mumma Mac's that afternoon in the hallway on Railway Avenue, that grim determined look as she leaned forwards to eavesdrop on Daddy Mac and Mum Wellman talking quietly together inside the living room.

"Hear that?" she said.

"What?" asked Susan Ann. She would not have been surprised if Sadie had turned to her, a little girl sitting on the stairs with Dolly on her lap, and hissed out, "What do you want?"

"Listen!" Sadie commanded.

And she could hear it off in the woods, a terrible sound, growing louder and louder: it was Sally, and she was yelping and screaming in pain.

SHE'D BEEN SO TINY *in that bed that she looked lost in it, her body a frail wisp of itself. The scab on her forehead from the fall made him wince; the bruises on her arms and the backs of her hands were huge and the dark colour of old blood. With her dentures out, her face was as shrunken as a corpse; even her hair looked unhealthy—matted and thin. On the day before yesterday, after he left her room, after Meg came and calmed him down, he was standing on the street outside the hospital talking to Bonnie on the phone. "Jesus Christ, she doesn't know where she is or what's going on. I think she thought I was Dad, then she thought he was on his way home from work—she's completely out of it, and she just looks like shit!"*

"I'll be there day after tomorrow, hon, just hang in there."

But nobody would be going anywhere any time soon; every airplane on the whole goddamn continent was grounded. Bonnie hadn't been able to fly out with him because of a stupid house inspection for Howard Young, the most incredibly time-consuming client in the entire world, a man so neurotic and rich that they called him Howard Hughes. And Carl had no one to blame but himself; he was the one who worried that if they handed Howard off to somebody else, there was the chance they would lose him.

After Peter dropped him off at his mother's apartment, Carl phoned her straightaway, and the first thing she said was "For some fucked-up reason, the universe is determined to keep us apart whenever something serious happens in your family." This because, twenty years ago, she hadn't been able to come to his father's funeral—little Greg had been terrifyingly sick.

"I'll be okay. You'll get here when you can."

"How's Lorraine doing?"

"She's been crazy most of the day because of Tommy."

"What a nightmare all around! And with these evangelical crackpots running everything, Christ only knows what'll happen next."

What he could tell no one—not even Bonnie—was that the terrible events of the day had given him an excuse to spend as little time as possible at his mother's bedside. It was easier to watch, over and over, that airplane slip into the side of the building under the blue skies of the morning, easier to watch the towers collapse into storm clouds of dust. Anything rather than be near her dying body.

The entire day had been so unreal that his sister's genuine worry and concern for Tommy and his boyfriend had seemed hysterical to him. He'd felt so detached from it all.

At first, the letters that Lorraine had written home had seemed fairly boring: letters sent from Mount A and from the early years in Toronto, when Elliot was in grad school and she was living with her in-laws, the "Horrible Howes." They were typed and, even though each one began with "Dear Folks," they all seemed to be written to their father.

And then there was one just for him, a "Dear Dad" letter sent the spring that Queenie died.

I've been thinking all this Easter about Grammy and about all those things I associate with her. Her date pies, of course, and how much she loved her lobster dipped in cream. One of my earliest memories is sitting with her on the beach. She would walk up and down the sand with me at low tide determined to find every sand dollar we could. One time Carl smashed my collection of sand dollars because we were having a fight, and he said that they weren't good for anything anyway because they weren't real money. Grammy said, "Smarten up, buster. They're better than real money." I can still see the look on his face. She usually doted on him so and he was shocked as he could be. I was thrilled. But then, she always stood up for me when she felt I had been wronged. I'm going to miss her. I'm so glad I spent time with her last summer.

Meg is a little angel. She's sleeping through the nights now, and is great company when Elliot is teaching. I miss the people at the library, and I would like to get back to work when she . . .

and more boring stuff about Elliot and his family.

Carl can't remember smashing her sand dollars, but he probably did. What a Little Miss Know-It-All she'd been growing up. And every single time they fought, their father would storm into the room. "Carl Murdoch Roberts! What are you up to now!"

The man who was always Mr. Meek the Pushover with everybody else in the world would holler at him "I'll tan your hide."

But his grandmother did stand up for him when his father was being unfair—although things tended to get very messy between her and his mother when one or the other of them intervened.

Carl found the letter that Lorraine had sent home after he stayed with her and Elliot on his way west:

We talked a lot about Bernice. He really is a mess about all that, and feels quite terrible, but I don't think he fully understands. When he talks about Melody he gets all mushy and sentimental, and drags out snapshots to show them around. He seems to think that getting married was the right thing because it saved Bernice's reputation, but that's all it was about. He can just walk away, leaving her with a three-year-old on her hands. I know that her crazy mother was over there day and night, finding fault with everything he did or said, not to mention that she's that insane sort of Baptist who seems to hate all life on earth and is so damn certain and smug about her upcoming pearly gates reward. Add to that the fact that poor Bernice would have driven a saint crazy, but Carl does have to accept some responsibility.

I wish that people could talk sensibly about things, I know I'm more radical than most about this sort of thing, and that Elliot's mother was scandalized when I went to Ottawa last summer with the Abortion Caravan, but if Carl and Bernice had thought about any of this there wouldn't be so much unhappiness . . .

and then she was up on her goddamn pro-choice soapbox for the rest of the letter.

His sister and his mother couldn't stop meddling around in things that were none of their damn business.

At a certain point, the letters started to thin out—probably around the time Lorraine called Carl to tell him, "It wouldn't kill you to phone her every couple of weeks." Lorraine, of course, was phoning home every Sunday night, whether she or her mother wanted to talk to each other or not.

The most recent letter that he could find was handwritten on thin sheets of blue airmail stationery.

Berlin, May 31/92

Dear Mum,

Peter is off for the weekend to a big German shindig with a pile of his father's relatives. Since hardly any of them speak English in a way that I can understand, and since my German is so lousy, I've decided to spend a couple of days on my own. We are having a terrific time, but I'm temporarily worn out (trains, museums, cathedrals, and family reunions) and needed a little downtime.

It has been a wonderful trip, and Peter has really enjoyed reconnecting with his relatives and showing me where his family comes from. It is an exciting time to be here. I don't think anyone thought the Wall would ever come down. Some things are quite exhilarating, and others have made me upset.

When poor old Marlene Dietrich was buried here last week, I almost got in an argument with Grandmother Stieff. Grandmother thinks she was a traitor and should not be buried in Berlin. When I asked where she should be buried, the answer was "With her own kind." I didn't push it, but I wanted to ask, "Who would that be?" I mean, after all, she is buried next to her mother! On the one hand, Grandmother S. talks about the Americans as if they were gods who saved Berlin, and on the other, she hates Dietrich for aligning herself with them during the War.

Next week we head out to the Netherlands and I'll be sure to visit the Canadian war cemetery in Groesbeek for you. I'll try and get you a picture of Uncle Murd's grave.

I've been thinking about Dad a lot this trip. I miss him so much. A big part of how I feel is regret that the kids didn't know him for very long. Tommy was only six. How much will he remember?

It meant so little to me growing up that Dad wasn't in the War. I never thought much about it. Now, when I am so thankful that he wasn't, I'm realizing how hard that all must have been for him. Especially with people like Lloyd Ringer or Uncle Jack constantly talking about it. ("Rubbing his nose in it," you used to say.) I didn't understand for the longest time why he was so upset with me about Vietnam. Stupidly, I assumed that he hadn't gone to war because he was a pacifist. So when we had our arguments about draft dodgers, I was surprised. I wish it were possible to talk to him about it now.

I still can't get over Grammy Queenie petitioning the government to have him discharged from the army. To think that she dragged herself there on canes, the "helpless widow" who needed her son at home! He knew that he would be vilified for leaving the army, but he couldn't say no to her. I know that he wanted to fight, and believed that he should, but he went back to Ragged Islands because of some strange combination of love and duty that wouldn't allow him to do what he believed was the right thing. Duty to family did mean everything to him, didn't it?

I don't know if Carl will ever understand why Dad was so angry at him for leaving Bernice and Melody. He doesn't understand that it was about reneging on his duties, he still thinks it's just about the divorce. He still thinks it's no fair that Dad wasn't angry at me when Elliot and I split up.

I hope you are well and that Ellen is over her bad cold. Say hello to her for me. Tell her I still laugh at her story about the day she got lost in the dairy aisle at Sobeys.

Love, Lorraine

THE SOUTH SHORE

Susan Ann was the first to wake up. It was before dawn, and the stars were still out; Orion was gone, and Scorpius was rising in the south, the curve of his tail just hidden in the trees; Jupiter was shining where Venus had appeared last night—the morning and evening stars. The Big Dipper had swung so far around the North Star that its handle was pointing upwards now. Something wasn't right with it, though; the pointer stars, Harvey and Hugh, seemed to have moved, to be just a bit wider apart.

"My old eyes are playing tricks on me," she thought.

Sally and Sade were fast asleep, and curled up together. Even in the dim light she could see that the poor dog's snout was raw and tender-looking. Sally had come running back to them last night with six porcupine quills around her mouth, yelping and crying.

"What'll we do? What'll we do? We need a pair of pliers," Susan Ann had said, half-sick with fear of what might happen, of bleeding and infection; but while she got upset, Sade held the dog's head firmly and assessed the damage.

"Well, we don't have any, so we'll have to make do with what we do have." Sade had a pair of scissors in her carpet bag. "You hold her head steady," she said.

Susan Ann held Sally in her lap while Sade set to work. Sally squirmed about at first, but after Sade cuffed the back of her head and barked at her, "Stay still! You got yourself into this mess!" she quieted down, and lay stoically in Susan Ann's lap while Sade worked away. First she snipped off the tip of each quill, "Because they're hollow," she said, "and that stops them from sucking themselves on tight." Then, holding each one firmly near its base between her thumb and the nearly closed points of the scissors, she slowly and painfully pulled the barbed needles out of Sally's muzzle, one after another. After each one, she said, "Good girl, that's right." She never paused, she was patient and firm and unhurried; she was very matter-of-fact.

It took twenty minutes, and Susan Ann could tell that all the while her poor little dog was in real pain. She was worried that the quills might break, leaving their sharp barbs behind, but Sade's strong hands were assured and skilful.

Afterwards Sally slunk away by herself, and the two women were so exhausted that, after saying no more to each other than "Thank you" and "You're welcome" and "Good night," they fell asleep.

The eastern sky was growing a bit lighter. Susan Ann reached for her hockey stick—she was a bit stiff from the walking and her night on the hay, and it was an effort pulling herself up. For a few moments she was uncertain on her feet, but she stretched her back and lifted her arms; after a while she went out to the road. She knew there was a ways to go yet, but she was in the home stretch.

"I miss you terribly and am counting the days."

Jamie lay ahead.

Behind her there was a rustling noise; she turned to see Sade moving in her sleep. As she watched, Sade stretched out her legs and, moaning, rolled away from Sally onto her back; then she gave out a loud snort of a snore before snuggling into the hay and lying quietly again.

It was awful to know what she knew about the path that lay ahead for Sadie Milford. When she looked back on what she knew of Mumma Mac's life, she realized that she could not remember a great deal of joy or happiness. Her marriage to Susan Ann's father had never felt like much of a love match—when Susan Ann tried to understand it, it made less and less sense. She never hugged her children or seemed to enjoy their company. Enjoyment always seemed to come to her at someone else's expense. Sarcasm was one of the few things that seemed to bring her any satisfaction. It was a hard thing to look over at this girl asleep on the hay, knowing that she would die of cancer in 1949, at the age of sixty, in the back bedroom on Railway Avenue. Daddy Mac would be at work in the CNR shops. Muriel, who was pregnant for the second time, would tell her husband, Jack, to take their four-year-old over to his mother's for the week; she would be sitting beside the bed trying to make her mother comfortable. Mumma Mac would turn her face to the wall. Her last words would be "Leave me alone. I don't want another thing."

People always thought it would be wonderful to know the future, but they were wrong. It was a burden.

It was hard, too, for Susan Ann to begin to understand that perhaps Mumma Mac's rejection of her, in those first weeks after she was born, had nothing to do with her at all, really, and had to do with so many other things—with brothers and dogs and family feuds that went back to before God made Father Adam.

When Sade shifted in her sleep and moved away from her, Sally lifted her head.

"Are you ready to hit the road, girl?" Susan Ann asked quietly.

Sally sat up and then ran out to the road, her tail wagging.

"How's your poor old snout?"

But Sally had gone on ahead, down the road that would take them to the ocean.

Something was scratching at Susan Ann's neck. She reached back and pulled away a piece of hay that had gotten stuck on her necklace. Then she felt for the cameo lady through the fabric of her blouse.

"Hello," she whispered, and pressed the palm of her hand flat against the necklace.

The sky was turning to pink; above her, only a few stars were still visible.

While her mother-to-be slept on into the morning, Susan Ann picked up her hockey walking stick and her purse and set out down the road after Sally. Before she knew it, she had gone past Shubenacadie and was halfway between the equator and the North Pole.

They walked and they walked; they walked all day.

At first it was difficult; although there were no hills as steep as the Cobequids, she found herself leaning on her stick, walking more and more slowly whenever she was forced to climb a sharp rise. "Quit dragging your arse," she told herself, but she knew her journey was taking its toll. She did not have the energy to sing out loud any more. She tried to play the Knapsack Song over in her head, but her concentration kept waning: she would sing the first line and then her mind would wander off, thinking about Mumma Mac on her way to Moncton, or Martha Leaman searching for her lost family. She didn't want to think about how angry her brother Murd had seemed, how bitter and lonely he seemed to be.

But as the morning went on, she began to lose her sense of being weary and sore. She found herself less mindful of the aches in her legs and feet. She realized that she had grown accustomed to the constant cramp in her bowel. For a while she felt a stitch in her side, but it faded after an hour or so. As the sun moved through the sky overhead, she thought more and more about where she was on the surface of the earth, of the distances she had walked already: from MacDonald's Settlement to Shediac, and over the Tantramar and through the mountains deep into Nova Scotia. She could feel the weight of great waters in the distances around her: the force of the Bay of Fundy on her right, and the hugeness of the Atlantic, which lay ahead. Although she was surrounded by deep woods, her sense of the waters was powerful and gave her strength. As the day progressed, the Fundy ebbed fainter behind her, while the pull of the Atlantic grew and grew.

When she had her first glimpse of the ocean, she could barely contain her happiness.

"Oh, Sally, look there!" she said, pointing at the bright, dark blue in the distance, but when she looked about, her dog was nowhere to be seen. Sally had been spending a lot of time running into the woods beside the road; Susan Ann could hear her nearby, tearing through the bushes, chasing after something. "Just as well," she thought. "If she's out hunting herself some lunch, I don't want to see it."

Soon she would be back home. She would be in Jamie's house.

"I miss you terribly and am counting the days."

She hoped that the house key was still tucked away inside the old mustard bottle sitting on the rock shelf down on the cellar wall.

What would she do if it wasn't?

"I'll worry about that when the time comes."

Not very long after Jamie had died, Susan Ann had gone down in the cellar. One morning she had gone and sat down there with Queenie's shoebox. The house above her was so quiet, and she just sat there looking at the dirt floor, the old foundation stones, the beams and floorboards over her head. She had been married to Jamie for thirty-six years and the house was now her own. It amazed her that she had come to own this place that was so far from her childhood, not in terms of distance—for it was only a short day's journey from Shediac by car, although it had taken two days by train when she'd first moved there—but in terms of the kind of life she had ended up living in this place.

How had she come to own a fisherman's house? It had been built by old Asa Roberts for Bessie when they were young. When he had proposed to her, way back in the 1860s, he'd given her a whale's tooth on which he'd carved a picture of the house he wanted to build for them both, carved it while he was off whaling on the other side of the world, the scrimshaw tooth that Susan Ann had given to her grandson Tommy when she was forced to sell the place a hundred and thirty years later.

She sat there in the cellar thinking that one of her children should want this house. Or one of her grandchildren. It wouldn't be right to let it out of Jamie's family.

The cellar was just a hole in the ground. It was not like Mum and Dad's on Inglis Street, with a concrete floor, a furnace, Dad's workbench, and Mum's clothesline for rainy days. It was tiny, it was grubby. The floor was dirt and most of the foundation was made from stones that had been unearthed when the cellar was dug. At one corner there was a rock that was a good four feet across, with an odd shape—there was a flat surface halfway up one side that had always been used as a shelf. Meg and Tommy had loved it when they discovered it: "Grammy's cellar is like the Flintstones!"

In the kitchen above her the phone started to ring, but she continued to sit there. She would call Ellen Firth later; she knew that was who it must be. The cellar had a strangeness to it, like an empty church. There was a dried starfish stuck on a beam between two nails—had one of her kids put it there? Or Jamie, had he done it years and years ago? Old Frank when he was a boy?

Or Frank's brother Carl, who drowned out on the Emerald Bank the year Jamie was born?

"Who's responsible for you?" she asked the starfish. "Someone brought you in here and I'll never know who."

It seemed, on that day, that there were so many things in this house, in the world, that she would never, ever know. She had gone down to the cellar to talk to Queenie. Jamie and Queenie were both dead and gone, and although there were times when she *felt* Jamie, felt the *absence* of him near her, a lonely ache, it was different with his mother. She believed that somehow Queenie's ghost was still in the house. Even though she'd stopped bothering them, stopped flushing the toilet in the middle of the night, and hiding things while they were renovating the kitchen, Susan Ann wasn't convinced that Queenie had left.

She hadn't wanted to talk to Queenie upstairs—she wanted to keep this sort of thing separate from her daily life—so she had gone out the back door into the yard and around to the side of the house and down the cellar steps to sit on an old stump that had once been a chopping block. Even though Queenie's bones were in the Ragged Islands Cemetery beside the ocean, she could feel her mother-in-law watching and listening to her in the cellar.

"I have it, Queenie, right here."

She took the cover from the shoebox and looked at the contents. There was a book as tiny as a doll's, *The International Bible Reading Association Daily Text Book 1915*; it was inscribed "From Mrs. Roberts to Queenie" with the note "Trust in your Maker, Pray for Forgiveness, and Count your Blessings." Inside it, next to the appropriate dates, Queenie had written all her pertinent family dates: births, marriages, deaths. The first entry was January 2: "James Carl Roberts born 1915 My Darling Son." There was a picture of her brother Gordie in his war uniform—he'd been the only relative she'd really talked about fondly. At one point Susan

Ann had thought that Queenie and Aunt Aggie would be able to get along because they had both had brothers in the Great War; but she had been so very wrong. There was a heart cut from birch-bark, the edges stitched with red thread trim; it was old and brittle and the colour of the thread was faded. There was the obituary for sixteen-year-old Carl Roberts, and a letter from him as well. After Jamie died, Susan Ann took it out and read it over so many times that she knew it by heart. She thought about it so much while she cleaned the house.

Yarmouth
May 21 1914

Dearest Queenie,

I am smart at present and hop you are to. I toll big brother Frank about us and when I get back there he will be best man at the wedding. They will get it all set up for us. Don't be fraid of my mother. Her bark is worse an her bite like they says. We can stay with her for awhiles till after the little surprise come then we can keep house on our own. I can find us a good place maybe on town like you want.

Id like to bild you a mansun. for our very oun with duzins of rooms. I want you to live like a Queen just like your name says. I want us to be happy with lots more kiddys.

I miss you somthing awfull. I wish I had a pitture to ware in my shirt close by my hart. Than youd be near me all the time day and nittime no matter where Im at.

Don't fret yerself. Well loader down with fish and be home in no time. Ill see you quick as a wink!

Forever your love,
Carl

The Ragged Islands Cemetery was on a steep hill beside the sea. Poor Jamie was buried there with his parents. Lorraine had promised Susan Ann that she would be buried with Jamie when she died, and beside him was where she wanted to be, but why did it have to be there with the rest of his family? Hadn't they already spent enough time with Queenie?

FRANKLIN JAMES ROBERTS

1871—1943

HIS WIFE

QUEENIE MARGARET BULMER

1903—1972

Poor Queenie, pregnant and married at fifteen. No wonder her nerves were bad; and now forever after, until the end of time itself, her bones were stuck in the ground beside old Frank. No wonder, as well, that she preferred to stay back and hang around the house.

"She went through hell when I was growing up," Jamie had said, and he just couldn't say no to his mother. "The only peace we ever had was when he was out fishing or sleeping it off."

Queenie had stood up to Frank when he was sober, though. She fought with him to keep Jamie in school. She sent him off to business college. Under the circumstances, she was a good mother. And he was a damn good son to her.

Old Frank had gone on such a rampage one night that Queenie had grabbed Jamie and run out of the house. They hid out in the woods for a while, and then, when it started to rain, they snuck down through the outside door into the cellar, where they spent the night listening to him storming over their heads, terrified, the two of them, of what might happen if he discovered where they were hiding. It was years before Jamie told Susan Ann that story, and when he did, she began to understand why he was so caught between her and his mother, and why he had allowed Queenie to get him discharged from the army even though he wanted to go overseas and fight. Even though he knew that some people would consider him a coward for the rest of his life.

"Queenie?" She was holding the tiny book, rubbing the pale brown cover, which was as soft as skin. The pages had gilded edges, like a miniature Bible. "I have it right here in my hand."

When Queenie died, she had left less than a dozen books behind her. There was the big family Bible in the living room, and the hymn book that she used to carry to church. There was the Ragged Islands United Church Women's cookbook in the kitchen drawer, with her famous recipe for date pie on page 50— "For special occasions substitute cream for the milk." And there was a little stack of Harlequin paperbacks on the shelf in her closet. They were her favourites, the ones she kept because she might want to read them again. Just those few, and that wee one hidden away in the shoebox with her old letters.

"Queenie, I know you're still here. You stopped flushing the toilet half the night but that doesn't mean you're not still in this house."

She looked at the words that Queenie had written in the little book beside a date in March:

> 1943 Frank fell down stairs and died on the spot
> "Instead of the thorn shall come up the Fir tree and
> instead of the Briar shall come the Myrtle Tree" Isaiah
> Jesus do not hate this miserable sinner

When she was dying, she'd wet the bed one morning, and Susan Ann had washed her, and changed the sheets, gently moving her mother-in-law from one side of the bed to the other.

When she was done and had got a clean nightie on her and had her tucked in, she thought it might be nice to receive a word of thanks for once.

"There," she said, "you're all set."

Queenie looked right at her and said, "Bessie Roberts *hated* me."

"That's too bad." At the time, Susan Ann hadn't realized why Jamie's grandmother had hated her, had had no idea of what had happened when young Carl drowned on the Emerald Bank.

Then Queenie said, "You never let me know if I got your goat. I'll give you that."

That was no kind of thank you, but it was the only one she ever got from Queenie.

Down in the cellar that day, she held onto the little book with the birthdays in it and she said, "Whose idea was it for you to marry Frank?"

The house was silent, hushed and waiting.

"Queenie?" She wondered, if the ghost answered her, if they might be able to have the kind of conversation they had never had in life. "Did Frank propose to you, or did his mother make him do it?"

The first time she had read through the contents of the shoebox, she had imagined a grief-stricken, terrified Queenie, fifteen years old, being summoned to the house, her fate completely in the hands of others. Susan Ann had lived with Queenie for nearly thirty years, but that day, the day after Queenie's funeral, was the first time she had a clear image of her mother-in-law as a vulnerable human being. She had been alone in Queenie's downstairs bedroom while Jamie worked outside, repairing the bird feeder after a raccoon had torn it apart. What would have happened if her first impulse had been to tell him what she had just discovered?

"Queenie?" The air in the cellar was musty and there was a faint smell—most likely a mouse or a squirrel had a nest and had peed on something. "Or was it your idea? Did you come here with a plan for Bessie Roberts, a plan that would make her grandson legitimate?"

If she had told Jamie, if she had shown him the contents of the shoebox instead of hiding them away again, what story would he have imagined? Queenie forced to marry Frank? Frank forced to marry Queenie? Or Queenie herself doing the forcing? What would he have felt, knowing that Frank had never been his father, that his father had been a boy who was lost overboard on the Emerald Bank?

"Should I have told Jamie the truth? After I read your little book? After I read the letter from Carl? Should I have told him about his real father?"

She waited for an answer. There was only the dirt floor, the stones, the starfish, the musty damp.

"Oh, Queenie, *please!*"

What makes you so sure he didn't know?

"He never mentioned it to me."

But you never mentioned it to him.

"Yes, but—But we didn't keep things like that from each other."

Well, you did though, didn't you, missy?

The cellar was so damp and unfriendly.

"Did Jamie know? Was it a secret that he kept from me all those years?"

She waited and waited for Queenie to answer. She was getting a chill, so she hugged her arms about herself.

"Queenie?"

But there was no answer. Just the creaking of the old house above her, just the sound of wind in the spruce trees outside, just the beating of her own heart. She would never really know; Queenie had taken each and every secret to her grave.

She sighed and looked up at the little dusty starfish. Who had put it there, and why did it matter to her? Jamie, Frank, Carl? Or her own Carl, or Lorraine? Her grandchildren?

To the rest of the world, to her own children even, she was Susan Ann Roberts, a member of the Roberts family, but that wasn't how she felt; rather, she felt that she had been Jamie's link to a world outside his family. And her mother-in-law would always have thought of herself as Queenie Bulmer from Churchover—never Mrs. Frank Roberts from Ragged Islands, but Queenie Bulmer, who lived in a miserable marriage in this house for nearly thirty years, who bore everything for the sake of her son.

Without Jamie in the house, she realized, there would be no reason for Queenie's ghost to remain.

Queenie, Frank, Bessie and Jamie. Ghosts now, all of them.

Susan Ann too, almost.

"Queenie never wanted me there," she said aloud. "But she accepted the fact that Jamie loved me. Just as I had to accept the fact that he loved her." She tapped the hard dirt of the road with her hockey stick for emphasis. "And she worshipped her grandchildren."

And her kids had worshipped their grandmother, and Susan Ann had never interfered with that in any way. Her son had adored Queenie; Susan Ann had been the one to phone and tell Carl when Queenie died, and he had fallen apart, cried and cried so much that it shocked her. He was somewhere up in B.C., planting trees, and he had sobbed on the phone.

Queenie had named him. Susan Ann was in the hospital, her newborn in her arms, when Jamie said, rather sheepishly, "My mother thinks it might be nice if we named him after Dad's brother."

"Oh?" This was the first she'd heard of it.

"Yes. My uncle Carl." Susan Ann had wanted to name him Murdoch James, but he became Carl Murdoch.

Had Jamie known the truth about Uncle Carl all along?

When she packed up her things to move to Toronto, she'd left Queenie's letter from Uncle Carl behind her, folded it up and tucked it beneath a loose board at the back of the closet under the stairs. It would have been wrong to take it out of the house where it had always been hidden away.

The sky had grown overcast; the ocean in the distance was no longer blue but a pale and lonely grey. She had reached another rise in the road, and stopped to look at the view. She wasn't quite sure where she was; well beyond the turn to Halifax, she hoped; maybe even beyond Mahone Bay and all those other places with shops filled with tourists and tartans and English bone china. The pavement had ended a while back, and the telephone and hydro lines had veered off into the woods and not yet come back to the road; there hadn't been a pole for quite a while, this seemed to be an old dirt road. But it was smooth and wide and she knew she was headed the right way; when she sniffed the air, she thought there was salt in the breeze.

"Just a couple of days," she thought. "I might even be there late tomorrow."

"I miss you terribly and I am counting the days."

What would she find when she arrived in Ragged Islands?

Jamie was dead, she was perfectly aware of that, and at times she wondered if she was as well; she hadn't seen a living soul in ages.

Something was moving rapidly back and forth, in the ditch on the other side of the road.

"Sally?"

When she started across, she could see the telltale golden brown of Sally's coat, and when she was closer she could see that Sally was lying on her back, moaning and wriggling about happily.

"Ummmm."

"You're a happy-looking puppy," she said.

"*Ummmm*," said Sally, as she continued squirming her body and wagging her tail.

Susan Ann giggled at the dog's silly antics, and then she noticed that there was something in the grass on the side of the ditch that gave the illusion of wings stretched out on either side of Sally's head, something white in the long grass. "Oh, it's my little puppy angel," she said, and she laughed as she stopped and stood on the shoulder.

It was then that she smelled an awful smell, something rotten, strong and rank enough to make her gag.

"Pee-you," she said. "What's that?"

Then she could see clearly that wings did seem to be coming out of Sally's back: huge, pale grey wings with white spots on the black tips. The one on the left was stretched out beautifully, like an angel's in a painting, but the right was clearly broken at the wrist and badly mangled. As her dog's little body twisted again, Susan Ann could see what remained of a head lying beneath Sally's head. There was enough of it left for her to know that it was a herring gull.

"Get off! Get up! Get out of that!"

Sally continued to roll and rub herself against the dead bird.

"Sally, stop that!"

But Sally didn't stop, and when Susan Ann started to move into the ditch to haul her off the carcass, Sally bared her teeth and growled. Susan Ann could see that the gull's body was badly decomposed. "That poor thing is dirty and rotten. It stinks, and now you will too."

"Why're you so upset at the way something smells when it's dead? You'll stink yourself too, soon enough."

Susan Ann stepped forward, putting out her hand—"Stop that *right now!*"—but Sally's head jumped upwards and her teeth snapped viciously at Susan Ann's fingers, not a warning snap either; her dog had tried to bite her. She pulled her hand back so quickly that she nearly lost her balance. The sharp yellow teeth looked so cruel that Susan Ann stepped back, away from the ditch and onto the road.

"It was *you!*" she said suddenly. "It was *you* following me from Five Points the other day!"

Sally just lay very still, glaring at her and growling.

"You nearly scared me to death."

"I'm all that's keeping you *from* death right now."

"What do you mean?"

"I'm the only comfort you have." And with that, Sally began to bear herself down and wriggle even harder against the putrid bird.

Susan Ann couldn't bear the look in Sally's eyes, so she turned away and faced the road ahead. She was frightened and cold, and the fog had started to settle in. She struck the ground with the end of her hockey stick and began walking southwards.

A moment later it began to drizzle, and then to rain.

THE LAST TIME he'd had sex with Bernice, he'd been pretty drunk; but even so, he was fully aware of what he was doing and why. Her need for him had become overwhelming; at some point, he'd started to feel that it had very little to do with him—he was the object that her need had seized upon, and with a desperation that was frightening.

That last night they were ever in bed, he was allowing her to wrap her legs around him, allowing her to cry and cry out, "I love you, love you so much," because he was avoiding telling her that he was leaving. Afterwards, he went outside and threw up in the yard. When he came back into the house, he turned on the light and told her. By the time she realized that she was pregnant, he was in B.C., maybe he'd even started tree planting by then. She never called to tell him, never tried. Instead, she called his mother, because she knew her own would be vicious.

He'd found out all of this from Lorraine. Their mother had phoned her and she'd helped to make the arrangements in Montreal. His mother and father and sister had paid for everything: the plane ticket, the "procedure," the works. Bernice had stayed with his Uncle Boyd and Aunt Joyce, probably sleeping in the same bed that he'd slept in not that many weeks before, when he was hitchhiking west—Grandfather Wellman's old bed. Melody had stayed in Ragged Islands with her grandparents.

Lorraine told him about it a few months after everything was said and done. He was furious with all of them, and it wasn't the abortion that upset him so much as the idea that such a decision had been made without even bothering to talk to him, that he was somehow unworthy or incapable of being consulted—too juvenile, too immature to be considered. He'd gone to the bank and set up an account for Melody—his plan had been to put some money in it every month—but after Lorraine's phone call, the few hundred dollars that he'd deposited in it sat there. "If that's what they think of me, then fuck the lot of them," he said, even though he knew he was proving them right.

Night after night, for five years or more, he would dream that he was back in the house in Ragged Islands, living secretly in a room that no one else knew existed. Grammy Queenie would come through the door in a panic, whispering, "Your mother and father found out you're in here!" and he would try to run and hide.

The last time he'd seen his father, he'd gone home because Bonnie had insisted; Lorraine had called and suggested that they all go east for their parents' anniversary.

"I'm not up for some big reconciliation number."

"You you you—what makes you think it's about you? I want to meet them. Fair's fair—you've been to Drumheller, I get to see Ragged Islands."

He'd watched his father dote on Lorraine's children—taking them fishing, giving them toys, devoting himself to their every whim and desire. "He wasn't like that with me," he told Bonnie.

"Are you jealous, you big baby? He wasn't like that with you because he wasn't your grandfather."

When his father died, twenty years ago, he felt a kind of sadness but no overwhelming sense of loss. He cried, but not the way he'd cried when his Grammy Queenie died, not even the way he'd cried when he and Bonnie watched E.T. with Greg. He told himself that he'd lost his father already, long before. The morning of the funeral he got up before daylight and went for a walk, down through the salt marsh towards the point. The tide was low, and the sea was rough.

The rock face sloped up from the water at not quite a forty-five-degree angle; it was smooth and treacherous when it was wet, and huge rocks were scattered about on it, some of them the size of cars. It was incomprehensible that the sea could move and deposit anything so heavy. At the base were clusters of darker ones—some covered with barnacles, some with seaweed—and tide pools; at the top of the slope were scrabbly bushes and stunted spruce trees. He walked carefully out onto the slope and sat down, his knees tucked under his chin; the granite was cold beneath him, and he shivered. At Hemeon's Funeral Home, on town, his father was lying in a coffin. Carl imagined his mother back at the house, lying awake in her bed alone.

The night before, Bonnie had called to say that Greg's fever had broken and everything would be fine. "That's a piece of good news," his mother had said. A little while later, she had shown him the sympathy card that Bernice had sent to her.

As he sat there and the sun came up out of the ocean, fiery and blinding, the whole smooth slope surrounding him went golden, and the letters and numbers chiselled onto it were clearly visible, the slant of light outlining them with lush black shadows. His own name was on one side of him and Lorraine's on the other, both with the same date from the mid-sixties; just a short distance away, his father's, carved in the 1930s; five feet or so above that were his grandfather's, his Uncle Carl's and his great-grandfather Asa's, his name as elaborately carved as on a nineteenth-century headstone, with the date Carl still remembered, July 1864. "Before Confederation," his father had told him when he was a boy, and he had been awed. The newest names were from two summers before; Meg and Tommy had come down with their grandparents, and Carl's father had helped them to chisel their names on the date of his wedding anniversary.

Carl had brought Bernice here to show her where their infant daughter would one day carve her name. She had been eager to see the spot, but once they arrived she was too nervous to walk on the rocky slope. "I can see it all fine from here," she said, looking down from the top.

"I'll hold you, you won't fall."

"It's too GD steep! I'm fine just where I am, thank you very much."

When his parents came here with Meg and Tommy, it occurred to him that genetics had given them all the ability to be fairly nimble on their feet. His whole family could scamper about on the rocks like mountain goats.

In the fierce light of the sunrise, the names and dates of his family were so clear and seemed so permanent—he was sad because of the two names that would probably never be here: Melody, his lost daughter, and Greg, his infant son. The whole slope around him was gleaming. The moment lasted hardly any time at all; the sun rose up into a cloud bank, for an instant the eastern corner of the sky turned a livid peach, then all colour dispersed; the world was grey, and the names were dulled and ordinary.

On the walk back to the house to get ready for the funeral, he felt both regret and relief. He was so glad to be living in Vancouver.

In the envelope with Lorraine's letters, there was one that had been written by their father. It had been read and reread so many times that it had fallen apart and been pieced together with Scotch Tape that had grown brittle and yellow over time.

My Dearest Susan Ann,

How are you? I am well, and my mother is much better. She sends her regards.

We have both been hard at it the past two weeks, but there is still a fair amount of work to be done here before you and I can settle in. There are a few things of my father's to be dealt with, although we have given away the bulk of his clothing.

Mother has moved into the little bedroom downstairs and we shall have the upstairs more or less to ourselves. There are three bedrooms there, all of them a good size. We would share the front one, which is the biggest. The possibility of having kids of our own in the other two makes me very happy. "A girl for you a boy for me," like that song says. The room that my father shared with his brother growing up has been closed off for quite a while, and I am in the midst of repairing the plaster in there and building a clothes closet. It is a solid old house, built by my grandfather in the Eighteen Sixties. It is modelled after a house he saw down in Nantucket when he was a whaling man. We still have a drawing he made of the original, carved onto a sperm whale's tooth, which he gave to my grandmother when he was courting her. It has indoor plumbing now, one of the few good things that my father did in the last few years.

I know you will understand that Mother has had a rough time of it, being a delicate woman. He was not a bad man, really; his drinking made him so bad tempered. I do not think the meanness in him would have surfaced as readily if he had been sober. By all accounts, he was a changed man after my Uncle Carl was drowned. I cannot say, because these things happened before I was born.

Please understand that her inability to attend the wedding is due to her present frail health and not for any other reasons. I know that she would very much like to attend and to meet your family. I will hire a girl from on town to stay with her while I am away. She is so much stronger than she was when I first arrived. In all honesty, I did not think she would pull through some days. I imagine that the last few years with my father were hellish.

I am so thankful to you for reaffirming my proposal. For much of my life, I did not think it could be possible to feel this. Whenever I think of you coming to live here with me in this house, I realize that I am very happy. I miss you terribly and am counting the days.

Say hello to Mum and Dad Wellman for me. When you write to Murd, tell him that my thoughts and prayers are with him.

I am sorry that our honeymoon will be so short. "Short but sweet," like the saying goes. I could not ask for more than that one extra day. I am very lucky to have found work in the office at the fish plant. The job suits me just fine.

Fondest love,
Jamie

7—

HER NOSE WAS ITCHY. There was something tickling it—

Lorraine and Meg were watching at the window. Watching who for? Was supper ready yet? They were talking—

"—probably fine. He's probably trying to let us know he's fine."

"I *know* that but I want to—"

"Shhh."

Was it Jamie? Were they watching for Jamie? Was he late?

"And all the bridges closed, I just can't believe it!"

Lorraine and Meg were looking out the window, and was Jamie coming?

"*Pspspss.*"

"—and with the lines all down, that whole end of the island."

What island? Was it a snowstorm? What month was this? Dad Wellman skated to Shediac Island that time and was stuck in the lighthouse for two days, the snow came on so sudden—

But that was long, long ago.

"—the not knowing."

"Uncle Carl's right, though. It's just chaos—"

Carl, yes. Carl was coming, yes, right. Home for Christmas? Wait, where was he, wasn't he here now? Wasn't he—Oh, he was, and—

The *hospital*. Meg and Lorraine were at the hospital window.

Itch, itchy nose. She had her hands back now, both of them, so she could scratch it—

Oh no, don't let them see or they could take them away again, like her feet. Keep those old hands secret and safe.

"Try Peter again."

Under the covers, hide them there quick like a bunny—

"Look."

"Mum?"

No, slow, slow so they won't notice . . . yes. Slow . . .

"Is she awake, do you think?"

"Mum?"

Slowly . . . Yes. Slow.

The door there, someone coming in? She could just take a peep, they thought her eyes were closed.

The door, hadn't there been a door? Yes, it opened and—where had she just been? Somewhere . . . a pink door. Birdies and Kingdom Come? Or was that a long time ago? And secrets about airplanes.

"Is there anything new?"

Carl?

"Nothing yet. How's she been?"

"She was restless but she's quiet now, sleeping."

Like birdies at the feeder, they were all crowded round. Was everybody here? Meg, Lorraine, Carl—Oh yes, Christmas already? Oh dear, was the house ready? Cookies, cleaning. Jamie? Was he here? Where was, *Where is he?*

"She's awake."

"Hi Grammy."

Is he back?

"Sorry, Gram?"

Did he come yet?

"We hope Tommy'll be here soon, Grammy. The planes aren't flying—"

"*Shush!*"

"Why?"

"Because she doesn't need to know that!"

"Oh, Lorraine, you're crazy."

Don't argue, you two. Carl was here, she knew he'd come back. They liked their sweets!

And Tommy coming?

Go to the store and get me some dates—

"What is it?"

Dates and, what else? Dates, are we low on flour?

"What is she talking about now?"

"Carl, shut up!"

"She doesn't know what we're—"

"*Shut up!*"

Stop stop you two! Always at it again, stop it now, pay attention. Dates, flour, sugar. Mixing bowl. *Brown sugar.* And something, something. *What?*

Oh, Pledge. *Lemon Pledge.*

"Christ."

"Carl."

Just stop. Always have to argue and fight. Bad as your Aunt Muriel.

Jamie coming, and Tommy. His crazy friend, the poor sweet fella. But where was Jamie, where was—

"—and you're no help!"

What was Lorraine saying, what was—

"Shhhhh."

"You'll hear from him soon."

He was still late? Everything would be ruined. Turkey all dried out, not worth eating. Wasn't fair making him do this. Jamie hated the hospital so! If she was home everything would be fine. How could she cook a big meal in the hospital? Had everyone gone crazy?

"Lorraine, anything from Peter?"

Peter? Wasn't he here already?

"—not picking up, must be on-line."

I hate this bed. Take me *home* take me—

"Oh God!"

"It's okay Grammy, it's okay, just . . ."

Home!

Why won't they? Why?

"*Psspsspss.*"

So hard to hear what they were saying, to understand, and they were coming and going with their whispering and secrets, and—

Who's that, what's that now?—

"On the TV down the hall. Hurry and come see—"

Wait, I—

Hello?

Gone, all gone. Leaving her again? Home for Christmas and off to watch something on the old box? Leaving her behind for that. The same damn programs every year anyway. Wasn't there supposed to be something? A picnic? Christmas dinner? Left her behind, all of them. The hospital, Bridgewater, Toronto, no fair, leaving her all alone. *I hate this bed.*

Of all the beds she'd ever slept in, this was the very worst.

Jamie's bed was back in that damned old apartment. Yes, but oh, it was a nice familiar bed! The whole bedroom set ordered from Eaton's in Halifax. "We're livin' the life a Riley now," said Jamie.

And the bed on Inglis Street, there was a good old bed. Mum Wellman painted it yellow, the white chenille bedspread. Oh— those devil curtains—

Nobody loves you nobody—
No not that today, no—
Up at the farm! There, quick! The white spool bed, Mum Wellman's old bed, Aunt Aggie had promised her that along with Mum's cameo, but that damn Muriel—

White spool bed tucked under the ceiling like the upper berth on the train, the upper room, like Jesus for the Last Supper. Aunt Aggie used to say that, "Time to hit the hay in the upper room."

Itchy now, and she could scratch it finally, her hands were back. *Yes.*

She lifted them up, scratched the itch. Her hands close to her face, palms together like when she used to say her prayers. Lacing her fingers inside, and pointing her forefingers to heaven:

> *This is the church and this is the steeple,*
> *Open the doors and see all the people.*

A little story she used to tell her children with her hands. But her fingers were so old now, it was hard to do—*This is the church and this is the steeple—*

It made her think of the church at Five Points. Mum trying not to laugh when Reverend Trites got carried away, flapping his hands, spit flying, and how happy she was when they sang "Sweet Hour of Prayer," Aunt Aggie's favourite hymn. Susan Ann used to play it on the piano, Carl and Lorraine sitting on the bench beside her. They loved singing the last verse—

> *Till from Mount Pisgah's lofty height,*
> *I view my home and take my flight:*
> *This robe of flesh I'll drop, and rise*
> *To seize the everlasting prize;*

And shout, while passing through the air,
Farewell, farewell, sweet hour of prayer!

When they all came for Christmas, maybe they could sing?

Oh, but she couldn't play worth a damn with her old hands now. And they didn't want you to play anyway in that miserable place. They had rules about "noise."

Where was everyone? They'd rather watch the old box than be with her.

"It's a nice big apartment, Mum."

Pah! To hell with them.

You should get cracking.

Yes, there were things to do. Her hands were back, she was feeling much better. She felt like cleaning house.

She could remember everything. Up at the farm, the upper room, wee table with the cracked vase, lacy curtains, scallop shells on the dresser, the old rag rug with the sled on it, the chamber pot with brown flowers, the log-cabin quilt, painted stone doorstop. Move that aside so you can sweep behind the door.

Don't forget to dust-mop under the bed. Lemon Pledge.

When they moved her to the damn apartment, she was so lonesome for home that she didn't know what to do. Had to leave so many things behind. If she closed her eyes she could see them, clear as day. How she missed looking after that house! She closed her eyes and moved around all the living room: dusting the mouldings, the doorframes and windowsills, the moon-shaped knick-knack shelf that Boyd had made for her, the blue china dog that Carl had bought for Mother's Day, the whale's tooth and all those things she'd had to leave behind. She couldn't forget about them! Queenie's china shepherd girls. The cabinet stereo. Then on to the rest of the house, starting at the front door, working her way through, scrubbing the floors, cleaning the new cupboards, washing the stairs, the bit of carving on the newel post, paying close attention to the baluster on the second step, which had a crack from that night when old Frank raged and fell, split his head wide open and died right there—

What all *had* gone on that night? That wild, wild night, what words were said?

"Do you think Queenie pushed him?" Ellen Firth had asked her after Jamie died.

"Is that what people thought?"

"No one would've blamed her."

Slide the wet cloth up the banister and start to clean the rooms upstairs. The kids' bedrooms and her own. And after cleaning Jamie's house, then on to Mum and Dad Wellman's and then the farm. She kept herself from going crazy by cleaning those three houses she so loved, because that kept them nearby. There was no one else in all the world that knew inside those houses, she was their keeper now. Like a story that made her feel better, a story where she was back home. Her family didn't care about those old places, those old things. She was their keeper the same way she was the keeper of the last postcard that Aunt Aggie sent her, of all those things she had saved over the years. As soon as she was gone they'd end up in the trash. When Lorraine came over and read the letter that Elsie Steeves had sent Mum, she just rolled her eyes and said, "Why keep upsetting yourself with that? Why keep crap like that lying around?"

Crap like that.

Sally had been destroyed, Mum and Dad vilified, and all Lorraine could say was *crap like that.*

Was Susan Ann as bad as Queenie, stowing all her secrets away in that shoebox? Not wanting anyone to know, yet not being able to throw her secrets away?

"*Psspsspss.*"

What was that now?—Who was?—

They were back in the room, her family—

"What do you think, Carl?"

"Middle East crackpots."

"But that's what they said first about Oklahoma."

How long had they been back? Had she been asleep?

They were sitting and talking about something—Carl and Lorraine and—

"—not all that far from Damascus."

Meg, that was, Meg—

"You wouldn't go back there."

"Over my dead body."

"Oh Mom. I'd consider it. Jean Claude would for sure. If it sounded interesting and we could swing it."

They were talking about Meg's fella in Quebec—

"How is it with you two?"

"It's hard with him in Montreal."

"But *Syria?*"

"Will you talk about something else?"

"I suppose it's not as bleak over there as Ragged Islands—"

"All right now, Mr. Sarcasm. Don't start."

What was Carl saying about home? He—

"I miss the South Shore. And going back on vacation isn't the same as staying with Gram."

"Yeah, well, you never had to *live* there."

"All right, all right, Carl, stop. Don't start trashing home, not now."

"Then don't you start in on one of Mum's lectures about the *pore ole Maritimes.*"

"Oh, *pore you.*"

"She got it even worse than Dad. Every phone call. 'They took *this* away from us, they took *that* away from us,' Jesus. How many times have you heard about the Pan Am Clipper and that stupid Italian armada? What the hell do I care about a bunch of airplanes sixty years—"

"Keep your voice down."

"She's so out of it, she doesn't know what the hell's going on anyway—"

"Carl!"

Why was he being so mean, why—

"*Psspsspss*—"

Listen—

"Shhh you two."

"You couldn't pay me to go back east."

"But it's so beautiful."

"Meg, I don't care. Who cares? What's that got to do with anything? Jesus, I assume Serbia is beautiful but who the fuck wants to go there? Beautiful downtown Sarajevo, so what? The West Bank is probably beautiful—"

"Oh, shut up."

Lorraine was talking, but it was hard to understand—

She was whispering now—

"*Psspsspss.*"

Lorraine and Carl hissing at each other. So hard to hear what they were—

"—deathwatch."

"*Like* a deathwatch? That's rich."

"I'd feel better if there was something I could do!"

He could take her home, Carl could do that, and—

"You want something to do, Carl? You can start packing up that apartment."

"Right now?"

"She's not going back there."

"Lorraine—"

"Soon as Peter gets here, get him to take you over there. You can be the villain this time."

"Very funny."

"Maybe if you'd come to visit before things got to this stage—"

"Don't!"

"Shut up!"

"*Sshh!*"

"Look Meg, he does nothing for years and years and then—"

"*Mom, stop!*"

"The sun always rose and set on your arse! Mr. Prodigal Son. 'Home at last! Bring forth the fatted calf and—'"

"Oh stuff it, you sound just like them, for *chrissakes!*"

"And what the hell is wrong with that? Why shouldn't I sound like them? They're my parents!"

"Jesus!"

"Asshole!"

"*Mom!*"

"Well, you'd think they treated him like shit. She *doted* on you, she worshipped you. And Dad—"

"Don't go there, Lorraine, *don't!*"

"Not so loud, you two!"

"For chrissakes, she doesn't even know who she is any more! How many times did I have to listen to her make excuses for him?"

Susan Ann was as still as could be, listening.

"Every other fuckin' day she's whisperin' to me, 'Your father *really* wanted you. Your father *really* loves you. Your father *really* gives a *fuck*—'"

"All right, just—"

"If it was true, why'd she have to tell me all the friggin' time?"

"Don't start up on Dad."

"A dead-end office job in a crappy fish plant because—"

"Because he had a family to support!"

"No, because he didn't dare do anything else—"

"Like what? Like take off and abandon his pregnant wife and kid?"

"Don't drag that up again."

"Will you two stop it! You'll wake up Gram."

But she was awake. Wide awake.

"All hunky-dory now, the Prodigal Dad now too, but who got stuck with your mess back then? Who's the one who paid for Bernice to go to Montreal?"

"Mum had no right to interfere—"

"And it cost her her granddaughter! Bernice's mother made sure they never saw Melody again. You get the big reunion with her, but Mom hasn't seen Melody since she started to walk, and she never will!"

"It was none of their fucking business!"

"That's enough! *Stoppit*, the both of you!"

They were quiet now. Meg had made them be quiet.

Susan Ann was lying as still as the dead. So still, listening, but she felt as if the room were swirling all about her. How could Carl say those mean things? Had he never tried to understand who his father *was*? Not never ever? He was worse than Muriel had ever been, as mean as the devils with their bull faces in the curtains—

Nobody loves you nobody—

She was a stupid fool for thinking he was still and always the lovely little boy who had gone with his father to the Bridgewater five-and-dime to buy her an ornament for Mother's Day, the blue china dog on Boyd's moon.

What did he know, the things she tried to protect him from, that wedding day, and poor Bernice, it broke your heart. Jamie was so kind to her, and furious with Carl for getting her pregnant, and Susan Ann had been determined to help make that marriage work, and she had failed.

"Don't meddle," Jamie had said, but what could she do? Carl had left his wife and daughter and was hitchhiking halfways to China, out there to the West Coast, when Bernice turned up at eight in the morning looking like the wrath of God, throwing up and asking her if she had Henry Morgentaler's phone number— what else could she do?

"—just started!"

What, what was that?

"Hurry, come on!"

Who was—

"—TV just now when I came down the hall—"

Peter. It was Peter at the door—

"On TV—President Bush is about to speak."

Lorraine and Carl and Meg all standing—

"Hurry!"

They were all up and—

What was all—

Out the door.

Gone, the lot of them. Carl and Lorraine and Peter. Even Meg.

Gone to watch some old TV again?

President Bush?

Her family gone off to watch *that?*

Nobody, nobody—

Stop now, stop—

So quiet now.

She'd be better off like poor Ellen Firth, not knowing who she was or where, clueless in the TV room with half of Surf Side Manor yak-yakking away.

She'd lived too damn long.

Nobody, nobody—

Stop that!

Stop that, and to hell with them then, good riddance. That Carl, never wanted to understand his father, never wanted to know, never even trying. *Not like me,* she thought. *I'd give anything to understand.*

Itchy.

Go scratch it, you can now. Your hands are back.

She was so mad at Carl she could just haul off and—

What's that?

She felt so light, what was that, that feeling suddenly—something starting to float, to float up—what was it? Oh, it felt good. Down at the other end, at the foot of the bed it was—*oh, it was! Move, wiggle them, yes, my toes, oh, oh! My feet!* Her feet! They were back and she could wiggle her toes!

They felt like they were floating right up in the air!

Move them quick! Pull them down, keep them here and close by! Her good old feet. Her feet had come back to her! *Where have you been?* Her feet had come home.

Not home, the hospital. The middle of the night. Wiggled and waggled her feet. Where had they been?

Where were her kids? Off to the TV. President Bush? *They could give a damn about their poor old mother.*

She could go right now. She could. What did she have to stay for?

Next time the dark came, the deep dark that was like swimming out past the breakers, she wouldn't fight it. That door was out there, and she could sink right through it. There was no reason to go on, no kind of life, shoved away in some darn old hospital.

But what would happen to all those things after she died? The letters, the windowsills, the balusters?

I am their keeper.

You stay in this damn bed, you'll die in it. Yes, and all alone.

She could see the hospital room quite clearly. The windows on the side looking out on the city, the dreary walls, the curtain pulled halfway around the bed, just hanging there and ready to taunt her. Wide awake now, and not feeling so weak and woozy. Her feet were back. There was a bottle of water there beside the bed—she could reach out and get herself a drink.

Her hands were back, and her feet too.

Maybe she should go for a little walk, wouldn't that surprise them all! Off somewheres watching a damned old TV.

Wouldn't it surprise them if they came back and couldn't find her? That would show them. Like the time she went on the ferry by herself to see the swans and went somewheres else. But that young woman on the island was so nice. People could be like that when you travelled. Strangers could be nice like that.

There were things she knew and things she didn't know, and when she was dead none of it would matter any more to anyone, and that wasn't fair. Last year she had turned eighty-five and had thought, *I'll live till ninety*, but she won't live till Christmas, and eighty-six, that was no milestone anyway, just a number. And poor Jamie had only been sixty-five.

She thought maybe she should try to sit up, even though she—

But she could! She did! *She could sit up!*

Yes, because Meg had taken off that harness, and it felt so *good! Where are my teeth?*

She looked about and there was the pink plastic cup. She could reach right over and pick it up.

There were some crackers and a banana on the nightstand.

The bottle of fancy water.

That smart bag that Meg had given her on her birthday was hanging on the back of a chair.

She'd had enough of this damned foolish nonsense.

There were things she wanted to find out and know. The back of the shelf in Mum Wellman's old bedroom up at the farm. Was there a shoebox left there, like Queenie's? Or in Aunt Aggie's dresser drawer? Oh yes, perhaps. It would be good to see everything again. No one would take her there, not Lorraine, not Carl, she would have to do it herself. Just like in that old, old story she used to tell her kids.

"Very well, then," said the Little Red Hen, "I will do it myself."

And she did.

ON THAT NIGHT last year when the phone rang and Melody asked if he was the Carl Roberts she was looking for, her father, he had hesitated for a moment before he answered. Bonnie was in the kitchen loading the dishwasher, Greg was in his room getting ready to go out—he could say no, hang up and tell them that it had been a wrong number, and no one would be the wiser; their lives could continue along without disruption.

"Yeah, that's me," he said.

She would be in town the next week—maybe they could get together? Dinner?

"That suits me just fine," he said, and as those nearly forgotten familiar words came out of his mouth, he realized that he had rarely said them before, if ever. "'That suits me just fine'? Where in hell did that come from?" he thought—for it had been an expression of his father's.

His conversation with Melody had been polite, but he was worried that their meeting could turn into a series of recriminations: "Why did you abandon us? Where were you when I needed you?"

"Do you want me to come along?" Bonnie asked.

He did, but he knew it would be better if he went on his own.

"This is weird," Greg said. "It's really weird." As a kid he'd asked for a brother or sister the way some kids begged for a dog—"Please, please, pretty please?" When he was old enough to understand, Carl had told him that he did have a half-sister, living in Nova Scotia.

"Will I ever meet her?"

"I don't know," he'd answered.

Carl watched Melody come into the restaurant, an adult he had not seen since she was a baby, and she was so familiar—she had the same build as Bernice and, like her mother as well, her hair and eyes were a lovely dark brown.

But she looked like her great-grandmother, like Queenie, and like his own mother. How was it possible to see those two very different women in her face?

She'd turned thirty already, and had been living in Whitehorse, married to a man Bernice disapproved of because he had taken her away from their church. She was in Vancouver to visit a friend from university, from Acadia.

"How is your mother?"

"I think she's fine. Overworked. The twins are still at home, and my kid brother, Matt, is a handful. But she and Dad—my stepfather—are pretty happy, I think."

"They're church people."

"Oh God, yes." She said this as a simple statement of fact, without judgment.

After a moment he said, "Like your grandmother, Bernice's mother."

She shrugged. "I suppose. I barely remember her. She died when I was really young." Then he said, "I was close to my Gram and Gramps Nickerson." Her stepfather's parents.

Their talk during dinner wasn't as awkward as he had thought it might be, but they both skirted the same topics. He'd brought a photo of Bonnie and Greg to show her, but he never took it out of his shirt pocket. He waited for her to confront him with his leaving, his desertion, his abandonment of her, but she didn't. They talked about Whitehorse, her husband, Vince, her job with the government, the real-estate insanity of Vancouver. They became at ease with each other and the evening was pleasant. When *dinner was over, she said that "this was nice," and that she was glad to meet him, finally, and a part of him was relieved that he was getting off so easily; more difficult issues could be raised at another time, perhaps. The cheque came, and he handed the waiter a credit card.*

In the few moments afterwards, while they were waiting, there was something about the way she was sitting, something about the way she refolded her napkin, that took him back to an awkward moment with his father, to something buried and unsaid—it was something he could barely define, but it made his relief seem very wrong, almost indecent, and so he found himself saying, "I didn't love your mother. I'm sorry, but I was making us both very unhappy."

There was a long and awkward gap in the evening. She looked at him, nodded and turned away.

"I just, I can't ask you to forgive me for leaving. That's not what I . . . I just have to tell you. . . . Whole days would go by and we wouldn't even speak to each other. We just talked to you, talked this kind of baby talk, and . . . I just . . ."

He stopped because he didn't know how to say anything else.

His daughter was looking at him quizzically; she crinkled her eyes and said, "Mom told me that she left you because you drank."

How Bonnie had whooped when he came home and told her! "Bernice said that she left you!"

"It's not funny."

"I know!" she said, but she was laughing so hard that her face was turning bright red and her whole body had started to shake.

"All right, enough."

But she was gone. She started signalling with her hand to hang on, just give her a minute, she was trying to get a grip, but all she managed to do was slap the bed beside her repeatedly and howl.

"Thanks for nothing," he said, and got up and went into the kitchen.

A few moments later she joined him, grinning but penitent. "I am so sorry. I just couldn't help it."

He shrugged and put the ice-cube tray back in the freezer.

She came and put her arms around him. "My poor baby. So what did you tell her?"

"I think I got out of it okay. I stumbled around a bit and . . . Well, I do drink, as we all know."

"And thank God for that, or we'd never have met."

He kissed her and allowed her to hold him tightly. Then he stepped away and said, "I just, I think it's important that Bernice's version is the one that sticks." He'd thought about this on the drive home—thought about whether he should eventually tell Melody his version of events. Then he thought of all the other things Bernice had probably not told their daughter: things she never wanted anyone to find out.

"Why Bernice's version? Because she doesn't get dumped and you're still the asshole?"

"Partly. I think I do have to be the asshole no matter what."

Bonnie was taking a glass out of the cupboard. "Well, you are the male in the story." She put her glass beside his, and he poured them each a finger of bourbon.

"I'll drink to that," he said, and they clinked their glasses. "Cheers."

"Cheers."

After he'd taken a sip, he looked at her. "The really important thing is that in Bernice's version, Melody doesn't feel like she was dumped."

Bonnie thought this over and nodded. "That's right, that's good."

"Yes." Then he added, "In Bernice's story, Melody wasn't abandoned at all. She was saved by her mother."

They'd stood beside each other, leaning back against the counter, and he'd felt the warmth of her ample body next to him. Over the years they'd been together, this had become one of their favourite things—the nightcap in the dark kitchen, just the two of them, just before bedtime. It had become a nightly ritual, beginning when Greg was a toddler.

And now, thousands of miles from the safety of his house and the comfort of his wife, Carl was putting his sister's letters back into their envelope.

If their mother had included their father's letter in with Lorraine's because she thought Lorraine should possess it, she had been right.

For much of my life, I did not think it could be
possible to feel this. . . . I miss you terribly and am
counting the days.

Even though Carl felt these self same things, he had read the letter through without feeling any closer to the sad young man who had written it. But he knew that it would matter to his sister. It was a letter she would treasure.

It was so late, and he was very tired. It was finally time to make the bed and get some sleep. Tomorrow—today, rather, for it was long after midnight—would be another trial.

He started to gather up all of the papers, read and unread.

And that was when he found the old envelope that was labelled:

SALLY

RAGGED ISLANDS

She felt that she had been wet for days; the clothes she was lying in were damp and mildewed, and she was chilled to the bone. Beside her, the combination of wet fur and rotten bird had made Sally an unpleasant bedside companion. The dog was warm, however, and that was more important in the cold. Late yesterday they had reached a branch of the East Sable River, but she had not been able to find the road to the camp and had crawled under the wide, low branches of a huge spruce to sleep on the hard ground. Inside the darkness of the tree, they were curled around each other at the thick trunk.

They had been walking through fog everywhere, and it had not been the lovely soft fog that drifted through her yard in Ragged Islands, or that magical fog on a sunny day, bright and shining like a golden mist, but a thick, wet drizzle that made the whole world oppressive and dank. It was fog that would not lift because it was socked in tight, with nothing above it but layer after layer of heavy cloud.

She had hoped to reach the camp where she and Jamie had gone with the kids long ago. It hadn't been much more than a glorified shack, but there would have been a bed, an old blanket or two and an outhouse. It had been built by Ellen Firth's brother-in-law, Hiram's brother Sylvanis, who had been a bit of an oddball, living alone in the woods, making pets of the raccoons and squirrels. After he died, Hiram and his friends had used it as a fishing camp and, summers when they had very little money, Jamie and Susan Ann had rented it for next to nothing and brought the kids there. Even though it was only a short drive from the house, it felt far away from Queenie and Ragged Islands fog. One year, they had been there the whole summer, and even though Jamie had to work days at the plant and spend some weeknights back at the house with his mother, the family was together upriver every weekend. Carl and Lorraine had gotten along so well that summer—they would have been about eight and twelve.

On clear evenings they'd had campfires. Some nights while they were watching the pine branches above them, they would see movement high up: a family of flying squirrels. Every day at high tide, they went swimming in the river. While the kids played in the woods, Susan Ann read *David Copperfield* and decided that she would tackle all of Dickens, but she never did. They all knew there had been fights and tantrums and hysterics over wood ticks and skinned knees, but no one in the family remembered that summer as anything but idyllic and wonderful. In her memory, the flying squirrels had been a regular nightly occurrence. She remembered an evening sitting close to Jamie on the old bench, watching their kids run back and forth through the pine grove, laughing, chasing fireflies with empty jam jars.

Once the kids were teenagers, they were no longer interested in going there. Occasionally over the years, when they were out for a drive, she and Jamie would park the car by the side of the highway and walk up the short road to the camp; but after he died, Susan Ann had never wanted to set foot there again. Ellen had suggested it to her once; her daughter was taking her kids fishing.

"They'd like us to come up for the day and have supper. Kay'll pick us up an' drive us home so we can have a drink or two."

For a moment, the idea had excited her; how great it would be to see that old camp again. But then she thought that seeing another family enjoying the place might make her stupidly jealous; she knew for certain that it would make her sad. "I'll have to take a pass on that," she said, "but thank Kay very much."

It had been one of those rare times in her life when she had not been like Lot's wife: she had decided not to turn back.

Last night, when she couldn't find the road to the camp, when Sally was impatient with her while she paced about in the rain— knowing for certain that she *must* be in the right place, yet unable to find the way—she had wished that she had never left Toronto, that she was not journeying to look back on her old life. She was so miserable and lost-feeling; she felt she would have been much better off if she had stayed put where she was.

And Sally had been no great comfort. Sometime in the night, Susan Ann had woken up alone to the sound of some little animal nearby crying out in fear. Its voice was horrible and desperate, and when it stopped suddenly she didn't want to think about where Sally was and what she was up to. She was cold and couldn't stop shivering, couldn't stop thinking about the way Sally had pounced on that defenceless rabbit. What if Elsie Steeves had been right, and she really was a vicious dog?

"She has to eat," Susan Ann told herself, but Sally's behaviour had become upsetting and frightening. She knew that she had no control over the animal whatsoever; the dog would do as she pleased, and she would have no choice but to tolerate it.

All around her, the smell of spruce was pungent and thick; the branches were so low that she couldn't sit up. Although she wasn't comfortable, she didn't want to move. "I could just die here," she thought, and the idea was almost a relief; she was so achy and exhausted that she didn't want to do a thing; besides, she was starting to dread what she might find at the end of her journey. What if Jamie was nowhere to be found? What if he was mean to her?

Where could her children be now? Her grandchildren? Were they looking for her?

"You thought you were so smart," she said. "But you've gone and buggered everything and they probably don't want anything to do with you any more." The idea of Lorraine sitting up nights and worrying about her no longer gave her pleasure. How long ago was that night when Lorraine had slept on a cot at the foot of the bed? She had lost track of the days and nights, and didn't know how long her journey had taken. She was getting confused again, and that was worrisome; if she started to lose her marbles like poor Ellen, something really unpleasant could happen to her out in the woods, something far worse than the devil faces in the curtains had ever promised.

How many nights had she been away?

"The first night I was up at the farm," she thought.

Then, "No, wait, no. I wasn't at the farm an hour even. I walked to Shediac, the first night was in Murd's room."

Wait though, was that possible? Had she walked that far the first day?

How many days ago had that been?

Murd had been so cruel to her. And why, why, after all that time, would he be so mean?

After she died, would she be mean as well? Was that a part of being dead?

Was it meanness that had caused Queenie to stay behind in the house at Ragged Islands and flush the toilet, or was it simply a reluctance to lie forever in the rocky cemetery beside a husband she had never loved? Was it?—

"Wait, you've lost the thread, stupid," she said, because she had been trying to figure out how long she had been travelling. "The first night you were in Shediac. The second night you were with Sally and . . ."

She was not certain. How long ago had she arrived at the farm, and how had she gotten there? She couldn't remember. It must have been less than a week. Did that seem right? What day was it? What year? It was after the turn of the century, wasn't it? There had been all of the Y2K nonsense—how long ago was that?

"Now, Sadie looked to be about sixteen or so, and Mumma Mac was born about 1889, 1890—so . . ." She was about to add up the numbers when she realized how crazy and mixed up everything was. "I guess none of that matters any more anyway."

Early in the morning, Sally returned. "Let's get a move on," she said.

"I don't know if I have the energy, old girl."

Sally came over and licked her face. "Come on," she said firmly. Her tongue was warm and friendly, even though her breath was wild and rank. Susan Ann thought she saw a bit of blood on Sally's fur; she wished she hadn't seen it and didn't want to know where it came from. She slowly rolled over onto her belly, raised herself up on her knees; then, pushing her stick with one hand and dragging her little bag with the other, she crawled out from inside the spruce into the grey morning. It took her a couple of minutes to get to her feet and brush the dirt and needles from her clothes.

"I'm afraid to think what I must look like," she said.

Sally turned and headed towards the road. Just as Susan Ann was about to follow her, something bright moved in the branches just above her, just catching the corner of her eye.

Whoit whoit whoit.

That bird sounded familiar, but she couldn't place it and somehow it sounded all wrong for these woods.

Whoit whoit whoit.

"What is that?" she thought, looking up and searching the tree-tops, and then she saw a flash of red in the wisps of fog.

"If that's the Catholic bird, it's a darn long ways from Toronto."

And she thought about Meg and wished she was here to walk with her old grandmother. She ratched around inside the bag her granddaughter had given her and found the banana. It had turned so black and mushy that she couldn't peel it; she split the skin open and sucked out the inside. Even though it was sickly sweet, it did taste good, and gave her a bit of a boost.

The road down the peninsula to Ragged Islands was a rocky, lonely highway through scrubby evergreen forests that were broken up by acres of barren lands and fens, wild and raw, the whole place dotted with huge rocks that had been dragged there during the ice age. The fog was lifting, but the sky was grey. Although it was late in the season, the mosquitoes soon descended; the buzzing noise when they went for her ears made her frantic, and she slapped at the sides of her head and shook her stick at every moving dot. "Well, at least they don't hurt like a deer fly does when it takes a chomp out of you," she said; moments later the first of the deer flies arrived, buzzing about and snapping at her flesh. Each time one of them took a piece out of her, she slapped at the spot and cursed. "Well, they're easier to kill than mosquitoes. Slow and stupid, thank God for that."

Sally marched on, seemingly oblivious of every insect; when Susan Ann stopped to swat at them, she would glance back with a look of exasperation and annoyance.

"I can't help it, they drive me crazy."

But after a while, either their numbers decreased or she grew used to them; she stopped swatting and settled into the last leg of the journey.

The first time she had set eyes on this countryside, two days after her wedding, she had wondered who on earth would have ever thought to first come down this godforsaken way; it was like travelling to the end of the world. Of course, no one ever really *had* come down there first; Ragged Islands had been settled from the other end, from the sea. "The old Micmacs were the smart ones," she thought. "They would've travelled back and forth on the rivers, a much more pleasant experience than walking through an old bog." Over the years, however, she had driven this road so many times, and she had come to accept and love its wildness; it had become *her* road, the road to home.

It was late in the afternoon, with the promise of home and the sea closer and closer, when she noticed the first dragonfly. She heard it before she saw it; the frosts had buckled parts of the road, causing wide cracks and holes in the pavement, and she was moving forwards carefully, looking at where she placed her feet instead of looking ahead. There was a whirring sound just over her, a whirring and a clicking: a dragonfly, and then another, and then a half-dozen or more in a little flock flitting about in front of her.

When she looked about her, she realized that there were more of them, and more, flying all along the roadside.

"Look at all the devil's darning needles!" she said.

Once she started to look, she could see them everywhere, flocking together, thousands and thousands of them. When she was a child, they had terrified her; like all other children, she had believed they could dart at you and sew your lips together. Even though the logistics of this had baffled her, the thought of it made her shiver with disgust. It was Aunt Aggie who said, "They won't touch you, silly girl. Just be grateful they're around, 'cause they're eating the mosquitoes for you."

She and Sally were on a rise, looking down on barren lands on either side of the road ahead, lands that were dotted with dozens of dark-watered ponds; everywhere she looked, she could see dragonflies, hundreds of thousands of them, assembling and rising up in great swarms. Her son-in-law, Peter, would know what they were up to—he knew all about bugs and birds and why they did what they did.

"But what are they doing?"

"Winter's on its way," said Sally.

Susan Ann considered this. "You mean they're going south? How do you know that?"

"I know what an animal knows. And so should you." Sally trotted on ahead, ignoring the insects, as if they were of no more consequence than the gravel on the roadside. Were those hundreds of thousands of little beings aware of Sally's presence? Were the dog and the dragonflies moving through the same world, or through their own separate ones? What was that word Peter had told her, that German word, the name for the way birdies in cages acted when it was time for them to fly south? It started with a Z. Zoo-something, maybe. He had written it down for her on the back of a grocery list and she had put it with all the things she didn't want to forget.

"Hurry up."

Susan Ann followed behind Sally, walking queasily through the whirring, ascending clouds and trying, all the while, not to think about the hordes of locusts that God had sent down as a plague on old Egypt.

A resentment had settled in between her and her dog, and she did not know how to deal with it, how to make it go away. "If only she hadn't killed that rabbit, or rubbed herself in that old dead gull," she thought, even though she knew this was like saying, "If only she wasn't a dog." When they reached the house, she wondered if she should let Sally stay with her or send her off to live in the wild. "As if I had any say in it," she thought. "No doubt she'll do whatever the hell she wants anyway. She's as bad as my kids."

Before too long, the woods began to close in around them. First the ditches dried up and started to fill with stretches of touch-me-nots and asters, then the weeds grew thicker and higher, before giving way to scrubby alders and weedy poplars; suddenly it seemed the bushes were all gone and there were full-grown trees pushing onto the roadway. They hadn't turned off the road—she was sure of it—the road itself was vanishing as the forest walls pressed in tighter, until they were walking on little more than a path, and then the path was becoming so overgrown with grass that it was nearly as high as Sally's head.

When she looked around her, there was something familiar about it all: the placement of the trees on the gentle slope of the forest floor; the rocks the size of sheds that were scattered about where the glaciers had dropped them; and the lines of stones covered in moss of such a bright, vivid green. Nearly sixty years ago, Jamie had taken her into the woods just a few miles from their house; there had been old moss-covered stone fences running everywhere. "Who would ever fence off the woods?" she'd asked.

"This was all cleared once upon a time," he had told her. His Grammy Roberts remembered when it had been pasture land. He showed her the ruin of an old homestead, foundation stones lining a rectangular hole in the ground. Nearby, surrounded on all sides by young softwoods, was a tiny apple orchard, a dozen or so ancient trees; and a few hundred feet beyond that, on an overgrown hilltop with a view of the sea, three brown gravestones lurched out of the ground at crazy angles, tree roots wrapped around them like long snaky fingers. Apart from the letters OON on the front of one fractured stone, all names and dates were worn away, lost.

"Calhoon, Grammy said. One of the first families here." Jamie told her there was no longer anyone with that name on the whole shore. He and Susan Ann had been so young and crazy over each other that it hadn't occurred to them that the lost homestead could be anything other than a romantic place for them to visit. It was years later, when she was there with her granddaughter, that she thought of the Leaman house and the fire.

She had been amazed at how quickly the woods could take over; it was as if the land had never been cleared.

"Is that what's happened here?" she thought fearfully, as she and Sally ploughed on through the overgrown pathway. She had a vision of Jamie's house in ruins, of walking up the driveway and finding it abandoned and falling apart. "But I haven't been away for that long. We must've gotten ourselves onto some path that I never knew before."

But what if it had been torn down the way the farm had been? What would she do then?

Then, as if to calm her fears a bit, there was a break in the trees; the ocean was grey in the distance, with Gull Island just offshore. She breathed a sigh of relief because she knew she was very close to the house. Somehow they must have turned off into the woods; they had bypassed the garage and the old schoolhouse at the Junction, and gone right past the road out to the Point.

There was something warm on her back suddenly, a comfortable feeling; when she turned around to see, the sun had broken through the western clouds and all of the forest around her was dappled with light. There was a blue patch of sky, plenty big enough for the Dutchman to make himself a pair of pants; by the time they reached the house, the white shingles would be shining in the light.

Jamie's house.

"I miss you terribly and am counting the days."

Her nearness to home made her heart quicken—what *would* she do if the house was gone, or if the summer people were still there? Where would she go? "What kind of a mess have I got myself into?"

She wanted to tell Jamie all about her travels, about Murd and Mumma Mac, and about the other things too; she would tell him what was hidden away in Queenie's shoebox, and apologize for not saying goodbye the day he died, for pretending he would get better. She would tell him that their kids had been mean to her; that when you got old people thought you were a nuisance and they didn't want you around any more.

What would she do if Jamie wasn't there, if she had travelled all this way and he wasn't there and she was alone?

Or what if he was there and it was like one of the bad times? She preferred not to think about that, but there it was. Every couple on earth had tension and upset between them at one time or another. Like that winter when Aunt Aggie came to stay with them and Jamie was so frustrated that he took it out on poor Carl, finding fault with everything the kid said and did; or that year when they hardly spoke to each other, the year that Lorraine and Jamie had all their secrets. Or all the bad feelings when Carl left Bernice and everything was so mixed up, and Jamie got annoyed and said she was interfering. Those times had been hard: they could be alone in the house and not acknowledge the fact that they were avoiding each other.

The winter that Aggie was there, the year before she died, Jamie had been queer-acting: he had withdrawn from her and always seemed to be off whispering with his mother. And poor Aunt Aggie, who couldn't look after the farm any more and was so distraught about Uncle Hay drinking the antifreeze and dying so horribly—Susan Ann had wanted to help her, to pay her back for all those summers, but Jamie and Queenie hadn't allowed that to happen. When March came, Jamie told her that her aunt had to go, and he knew he was wrong because he couldn't look her in the eye.

"There just isn't room," he said. "You have to tell her she can't stay any longer."

They both knew that Aunt Aggie would never be able to stay at the farm by herself. Jamie was forcing her to send her aunt to live with Muriel.

"I lived with that mother of his for the better part of thirty years, and he wouldn't let my poor aunt stay in that house more than three months."

What if she got back to the house and Jamie was there and it was a time like that?

When those bad times had happened, when she felt as unwanted as when she was a little girl who realized that Daddy and Mumma Mac had given her away, she could make herself so miserable and unhappy. Sometimes she would watch him while he was working in the yard or while he was fixing something for Queenie, and she would be overwhelmed by his ordinariness; she would try to remember what it was about him that had made her crazy with love, and she could not, she could not begin to understand why she was living with him in Ragged Islands. What would have happened if she had listened to Muriel and turned down his proposal? Was he aware of how separate and distant she felt? How selfish and miserable? When they made love, her mind would wander and unwanted images would shunt through her head that had nothing to do with the present moment. Did he realize that she felt so far away from him?

But then he might turn to her for no important reason at all, just turn in her direction, or he might open the cupboard door to get a mug, and she would see him as perfectly as she had that first weekend when Murd brought him home to visit, and her heart would quicken and she would hate herself for forgetting that he was the best thing in her whole life. She would understand with her whole self that, no matter what else, they had saved each other.

She and Sally had emerged from the woods and were crossing

a scruffy clearing; beyond it, trees sloped down a hillside towards salt marsh and ocean. Sally was ahead of her, sniffing the ground. In the centre of the clearing, surrounded by scratchy low bushes—wild roses and blueberries, she thought—was a large lichen-covered rock. Susan Ann's feet were so wet and sore, she was so tired of walking, that she decided she would sit down for a moment and rest her weary bones. "Everything aches," she said. The rock was nearly as high as her shoulders; one side of it had a slight ledge at just the right height for her bum, so she went over to sit and take a load off her feet. "Poor feet, you're probably sorry you ever came back to me," she said, looking down at them. "I've sure put you through your paces." The rock was cold and raspy with lichens; stretching her legs out, she leaned back against it and looked all around her.

Even though the details in the land seemed a little askew, when she looked back the way she had just come, every bump and curve in the horizon was familiar—she had seen this view, pretty much, from her living-room window. In the opposite direction, through the trees, she saw the salt marsh and, beyond it, Ragged Islands' back harbour, with all its little islands. Through the trees, she could see one end of Gull Island. She was surrounded by the land she had looked at for fifty years.

"The house must be just over that way," she thought, looking towards the trees. "How things have changed." How long had this lonely little spot been near her house? She couldn't recall seeing it before, and there was nothing to indicate that any human being had been there before her. Yet someone must have started clearing this space in the woods, yes, clearing it and then abandoning it, leaving it to grow over. The prospect of moving rocks like the one she was sitting on must have been too daunting.

"Just through there," she thought. She would be home in no time now.

She was thirsty, so she reached inside her bag for the bottle of fancy water that Meg had brought her, but her hand grabbed something else, something round.

Sally's ball.

When she took it out of the bag and held it up, Sally barked playfully and ran over, tail wagging.

"Do you want this? You want the ball?" She was surprised that the dog would want to play.

Woof.

Standing up, she made a feint toss to the left. Sally started off in that direction and then ran back abruptly, happy with the trick, her whole body wagging and dancing. Susan Ann pretended to throw it to the right but Sally was too smart, she stood and waited. "Here you go, girl," and she wound up her arm and threw the ball towards the woods. Her dog turned and took off like a shot. A moment later she came trotting back with the ball in her mouth, dropped it at Susan Ann's feet and sat there, waiting for it to be thrown again. "Good girl!" All of the tension and bad feelings between them seemed to vanish with playing; as if Sally's animal wildness was gone and she existed to be a pet again.

"Dogs is queer things," Susan Ann whispered.

The second throw didn't go very far, no more than ten feet, so the dog was back in less than a moment and had to wait for Susan Ann to have a drink of water. "How smart Sally looks," she thought, "sitting there so straight and fine, her little tail thumping the ground." She bent down and ruffled the golden fur. When the response was a low, happy moan, she said, "First thing tomorrow we're gonna give you a bath."

Sally seemed agreeable.

She threw number three as hard and high as she could, away across to the other side of the clearing. Before it landed, she quickly sat back down on the flat shelf.

The ball bounced off an outcropping of rock; the dog jumped high up into the air but missed the rebound and scurried into the bushes. The outcropping caught Susan Ann's eye. It was about five feet long and gently rounded, as if a huge stone moon had been buried with only its last quarter sticking out of the ground; it looked exactly like an outcropping near Queenie's rhubarb patch, the rhubarb that old Bessie Roberts had planted there way back in—

But that was what it was: the rock near the rhubarb, her kids had played on it, climbed up it and jumped—

She sprang to her feet, exhaustion suddenly forgotten, and spun round to examine where she had been sitting. She knew that rock too, she'd seen it before, and she knew right where: in the cellar, ten feet below the earth, where it had been part of the very foundation of the house. "The Flintstones," her grandchildren had said. She'd been sitting on the shelf where the house key was kept hidden in a mustard bottle. She stared at it, dumbfounded.

How could it be above the ground? She'd always thought that when they dug out the cellar, they'd found it down there and started to build the foundation around it.

She looked all about her, she took a few wobbly steps towards the slope of the hill. "This is *exactly* what I saw when I was standing at the side of the house." She could see precisely where the backyard had once been, even though it was overgrown and the trees beyond it were all slightly different. The memory of her old property fell into place on top of this wild land. There was no lane; there was no house. She'd reached the right plot of land, the place where it had once stood, and there was nothing there, not a trace.

"I must be wrong."

She walked across the uneven ground.

"This looks like right where my kitchen was. Just about here." She was looking at one of the islands in the distance, moving her head back and forth, left, right, left. "This would be just about where the window was, over the sink." She knew this was so; she had seen this view a thousand times while she did the dishes. But there was no indication that any house had ever stood on this spot.

Sally had returned with the ball and was sitting on the ground beside the boulder, watching her closely, waiting to play some more.

"If this was the kitchen, then the old well should be over here," and she paced the twenty or so feet towards where the road had been.

Nothing, there was nothing in that direction at all, and that had been a fine, deep well.

"Oh, then, um—" and she was starting to look about her in desperation. How could the house have vanished without a trace? She had come such a long way; it was so mean. There was no sense of Jamie's presence, or anyone else's. She looked towards the ocean; if she went down to the shore, she knew in her bones that there would be no names on the rocks.

"Jamie's house hasn't been built yet," she said, and this frightened her so much that she started to tremble. That house had been built in the 1860s. "How could I have gone and come back here before the house was even built! What in the name of God am I going to do now?"

She stood there hopelessly for a long, long time. The sun would soon be setting. There was nowhere left to go.

Was this what death was going to be? This constant disappointment and confusion?

"This is the place I came to love more than anywhere else on earth. I first came here nearly sixty years ago. But what does *sixty years ago* mean to me now? God only knows when *now* even is."

She slowly turned and went back to sit on the rock. She didn't know what to do next.

Everything all around seemed the loneliest place she had ever been. Lonelier than the house on Railway Avenue where she was never wanted, lonelier than the hospital bed in the middle of the night. There was not a thing to indicate that there was another human being anywhere—without her own kind, the world was too empty to bear. "I wish I was back in that miserable apartment," she said, knowing that it was impossible and she would never ever see it again. When was the last time she'd talked to someone? Mumma Mac. Queenie. Martha Leaman. Murd. She had been travelling all this time with ghosts.

Was she a ghost herself?

There was a coldness touching her, a draft on her neck. Mum's necklace.

When she looked at the cameo lady, she thought of so many things—hymns, genealogies, Mum's kindness to her, pickles and rolls, whole summers up at the farm. Without those things, without her memory of them, it was a simple trinket, worth a few dollars perhaps, but of no great value.

Once you were dead and the people who knew you were dead, you were as meaningless.

Sally was sitting quietly at her feet, looking up at her; the ball fell softly from her mouth and rolled away. She lifted her head and put her nose on Susan Ann's knee.

"And you, Sally. I've longed for you all these years, and you've been dead and gone nearly—"

She was about to say "eighty years" but stopped when she realized it sounded pointless and silly. Her fingers gently scratched behind the big floppy ears.

"The best," she said sadly. "Just the bestest bestest . . ."

Where could she go to, what was there for her now? All that was keeping her from falling into uncontrollable despair was the nearness of Sally, her warmth; without that comfort, there would be nothing but fear. She shivered. There was a coldness growing in the air, it was getting chilly; night was coming soon, with its threat of devil faces. So many times throughout her life she had longed to do just this: go back in time and sit quietly with her favourite dog. "Be careful what you wish for," Mum Wellman used to say, because so few things turned out the way you wanted.

"I'm sorry, Sally," she said.

Sally's big doggie eyes stared into hers.

"I don't know what's going to happen to us."

What a strange little animal she was; right now, the dark eyes that looked up at her seemed filled with nothing but devotion and trust. How was it possible that something so sweet could be so savage?

"What will happen? What do you think will happen?"

Sally's nose was warm against her knee. She moaned low and sad, deep in her throat.

"The bestest, bestest dog."

Then Sally lifted her head. "Let me tell you a story," she said.

Susan Ann kept her hand on the back of Sally's head, her palm gently rubbing the soft fur.

"It was after supper. I was falling asleep under the kitchen table when the policeman came to the back door. I could smell how scared he was before he came inside. And rum. I could smell that, too."

Susan Ann did not want to hear this story, but she said nothing.

"I was lying there, watching. Dad Wellman went to get Mum; she was upstairs with you, in the bed where I couldn't go any more because you were sick. They begged him; he said there was nothing he could do. I knew I would be going somewhere else. Like before, when Uncle Hay found me on the road after the boys had taken us away from our mother.

"When the man came over to put a rope on me, I tried to bite him. So Mum bounced my ball, and I ran out from under the table. She tossed it in the air. I caught it and stood there happily while she put the rope on me. She led me out into the yard and tied me to the clothespole. She knelt down and kissed me. I dropped the ball and I licked her face. Then she went back to the house."

Sally's head was so warm and comfortable under her fingers. "Did Mum say anything?"

"No. There was nothing to say. When the man came near me I growled and he said, 'Good dog,' and pointed and then there was the noise and the loud sting, then another, and everything was stormy and black."

Susan Ann's fingers involuntarily clutched at Sally's fur. She had heard the gunshots from her bedroom. The policeman was drunk, Dad had said, that was why the first shot wasn't clean.

"It was all warm and wet. Then everything was so slow for a long, long while. Then, then I don't know, I could see you walking, and I was following you along the road."

After a moment, Susan Ann leaned down and kissed the top of her dog's head, smelling the musky richness. *"Everything was so slow for a long, long while,"* she thought. "That's like me sitting in that damned apartment." She felt the warm tongue licking her neck.

"Oh Sally, I don't know where to go from here."

"Climb up on my back."

"What?"

"Climb up on my back!"

"I can't."

Sally growled deep in her throat. "Now!" she said.

Even though she didn't think it was possible, she leaned down and held onto the fur on Sally's back.

"Lie on my back and put your arms around me."

She dropped the hockey stick, pushed the straps on her bag up to her shoulder and wrapped her arms about Sally's neck.

"Now hang on tight!"

She grabbed the thick fur in her hands, felt the warm, strong back support her.

"Here we go!"

And Sally leapt up and ran through the yard that used to be but wasn't yet, carrying Susan Ann across the clearing and down the hillside through the tangle of underbrush and trees, and all along the edge of the salt marsh.

*THE LETTER was written in fountain pen, the writing elaborately scrolled,
every word clearly legible. Many words and phrases were underlined in a
manner that could only be described as* furious.

Shediac.
October 14th

Mrs. Wellman,

   Mrs.has invited me to her home for supper.
I shall be returning after dark, and if your yellow dog is <u>loose</u>
and <u>runs out at me</u>, I shall see Mr. E. R. MacWilliams in the
morning and <u>he tells me</u> I shall have no further trouble with
your dog if I put the case in his hands. He says the costs will be
all yours. Mr. MacWilliams is a first-class lawyer and his
charges will not be <u>light</u>. He tells me no person has a right to
keep a dog that runs out on the street and attacks a person on
the street. I have had this worry for <u>eight months</u> and my
patience is exhausted.
   I greatly regret having to write this letter to a <u>neighbour</u>—a
<u>member of</u> <u>my own church</u>—the superintendent of <u>the Mission</u>

Band. I do not believe a <u>heathen</u> would treat his neighbour as you have treated me. During those awful heart-breaking weeks when I was going over to Moncton to visit my dying husband, you knew your sneaky pup was worrying me, and yet when my saintly husband was lying dead, you had the <u>boldness to come to my home</u>. From henceforth I shall not speak to yourself, your husband, sons or daughter. Our friendship is at an end. I shall expect you to keep your dog in the house this evening and <u>all other evenings</u>. In the daytime I can more easily see it coming and shall <u>use my heavy cane</u> if it comes close enough.

"A word to the wise is sufficient."

I have informed Rev. and Mrs. Rand and the Chipmans of my troubles with you. Some of the clerks in Mr. Chipman's bank saw your nasty dog fly at me one day.

Mrs. E. B. (Elsie) Steeves

It was undated—how long ago would it have been written? In October of what year? His mother had been a young girl, so seventy-some or eighty years ago, he supposed; a very long time to carry around the remnant of a grudge. He remembered Sally now—that is, he remembered that she was the dog his mother used to tell him about when he was a boy, the sweet little dog that had been tormented by a heartless neighbour. The story had made him sad—how could anyone be so mean to his mother and her family?

But it was such ancient history now, and for decades his mother had been the only person on earth who cared about it one way or the other. This silly letter was all that had survived, the only record of the dog she'd lost.

He thought that everything on top of the bed, every scrap of culch, was like that, an attempt to keep what had been lost close at hand—houses, childhoods, grandchildren, love—an attempt to stay nearby those things so that they might endure.

Carl couldn't remember a single detail of the story, or what, in the end, had happened to the dog—was she taken away? driven mad? destroyed?—for the story, he realized, was only part of a larger one: his mother's story about being hard done by, being treated unfairly, being unwanted. "Our friendship is at an end." His father's life had been part of that story too. "No one will ever know how much it hurt your father to leave the army," or "No one will ever know the unhappiness your father felt growing up in this house."

In some way, perhaps, this had been his parents' strongest bond, their sense of being set apart unjustly from the rest of the world. Despite the fact that they were loved—his mother had been loved by the Wellmans, and Grammy Queenie had certainly loved his father—despite that, a deep sense of unwantedness had been bred into their bones.

And into his own as well.

And his own children—Greg and Melody, the siblings who had yet to meet—did they possess it too? Was it possible to be human and not feel unwanted?

He could hear a siren far off, growing louder as it moved along St. Clair. It was very late, and it had been a long, long and terrible day. He could call Greg, he could even wake Bonnie, just to hear their voices; he could do that now, but he knew he would not.

The siren passed loudly on the street outside—an ambulance or a police car? He couldn't tell—and he was suddenly thinking of people in bedrooms and kitchens awake on this night, people he would never know who were suddenly lost and fixed on some object—an old shirt, a necklace on top of a dressing table, a grocery list—something left behind in the morning by someone who would probably never return. Ordinary objects unexpectedly filled with both despair and hope.

What was he to do with something as inconsequential as this letter from Mrs. E. B. (Elsie) Steeves?

He stacked the papers and envelopes and put them on top of his father's dresser, beside the package that said TO BE SAVED . There were clean sheets and pillowcases in the top dresser drawer. Making the bed was awkward because the room was so small and crowded.

He realized that he had left his toothbrush at Lorraine and Peter's; in his mother's bathroom he found a bottle of mouthwash. After he rinsed and gargled, as he lifted his head, his face in the mirror was grey in the awful fluorescent tubing, unhealthy-looking. As he moved deeper into middle age, there was no mistaking that he was his father's son. He snapped off the light.

He undressed, dropping his clothes on the floor as he crossed the few feet of bedroom carpet; then he slid into his parent's bed and, pulling the clean-smelling, fresh sheets and blankets over him, curled up to sleep.

When he was little, his mother had made up stories about a boy named Carl who lived beside the ocean, inside a big rock with his name carved on the side of it. And once upon a time, as well, there was a little girl named Lorraine who lived with a blue jay on top of the clothespole in the backyard.

Long, long ago.

When he'd first gone into the hospital room, his mother had been so lost and confused that it terrified him. "A lot of the time, she thinks she's somewhere else," Lorraine had said. "Back in Ragged Islands maybe, or talking to someone."

"Where is my mother now?" he thinks. "Where is she?"

And will she be living still when he goes to her bedside in the morning?

ATLANTIC

The tide was out, so Sally ran across a wet meadow of flattened marsh hay, darting around all the holes filled with soft mud, jumping over the dark folds of dried eelgrass that the high tide had abandoned, and plunging into a wall of high, dark rushes that swished against their heads.

Susan Ann bounced about on the little dog's sturdy back, even though her hands held fast to the golden fur and her knees pressed hard against Sally's sides. They were moving along at such a clip that she knew she would break something if she fell off.

Was this the dream Susan Ann had had about Jamie? When he came to her bed and told her that he had been for a walk along the shore and seen a fox? They were moving so swiftly, and she hung on for dear life, fearful and excited. If Jamie was walking and saw them streaking through the tall, reedy marsh grass, mightn't he think they were a fox?

The necklace had slipped out from the top of her dress, the cameo flopping and bouncing in the air. She couldn't let go her grip to hold it. "Don't break," she thought. "Don't fall and get lost."

When they came out of the green, there were patches of sea heather, and she could smell bay leaves; then they reached the little crescent-shaped beach where Susan Ann had walked with Jamie countless, countless times. The wind whistled in their ears as they flew over it, and Sally leapt up onto the rocks at the far end, jumping like a mountain goat from rock to rock and then up and over the bank. The ground was littered with wings, dozens and dozens of them lying there in pairs, poor sea pigeons that had been gobbled up by foxes. Sally ran and she ran, and before too long she came to a stop on a verdant field.

Susan Ann climbed from Sally's back and stood on shaky legs; she tucked the cameo back inside her dress. All around them was an overgrown tangle of flowers. Bachelor buttons, yarrow, black-eyed Susans, purple vetch, red clover so fragrant the air smelled like a honey jar, white clover as high as berry bushes, buttercups, Queen Anne's lace, asters, tansy—all the wildflowers she had picked for her mothers and her aunts when she was a girl, all the flowers her children and grandchildren had picked for her. They grew dense and tall, spreading out towards the woods on one side and the edge of the bank on the other.

Above the flowers she could see the ocean, the four islands in the distance.

There was a spot of blood on Sally's forehead. "You've cut yourself on something."

But her dog turned away from her. "Follow me."

With Sally leading the way, they waded deeper into the green. Susan Ann tried to stay close at her heels, but it was hard to keep up. They were in a thicket of flowers, and the stalks and leaves tugged at her. Blue, yellow, pink—the colours swayed about her, the white clover waved high above her head. She couldn't always see Sally, so she followed the sound of her in the underbrush, followed the trail of moving flowers. The sun was sinking down towards the treetops in the woods behind them; it sent long slanting shadows across the field in front of them.

Hmmmm.

What was that sound? It was surrounding her.

Hmmmm.

Honeybees. She could hear them at work. But wasn't this late in the day for them to be so busy? What time did bees go back to the hive to sleep?

Off in the distance, a crow cawed. He would be getting ready to sleep soon too. Then it would be time for the night birds and animals to come out: the owls and hawks, the porcupines and raccoons and foxes.

"This way!"

"I'm coming."

The flowers slapped against her as she walked; she missed having her hockey walking stick. Yellow pollen was dusting her arms, it was streaked across the front of her clothes. She had to be careful; there were burdocks that scraped and clung to her.

Her dog was getting way ahead. The plants were becoming so thick they were woven together, and Susan Ann was pushing through, parting the tendrils like a swimmer in a seaweed garden. Lorraine and Tommy had taken her swimming with goggles that time, and it had been a whole new world around them. The sunlight had shone down through the water and onto the swaying kelp. She had thought the seaweed touching her body would make her feel squeamish, but it was just the opposite. It had been wonderful—soft, wet caresses. How long ago had that been? Why hadn't Jamie been there? Where was the beach where they had done that? Over on what shore?

Susan Ann waded on through the field. Soon her hands became entangled in the leaves around her, so she lifted her arms above her head. Deep in the thicket, the flowers gave way to clumps of touch-me-nots and thistles. The thistles scratched at her and she had to be very careful; the touch-me-not seedpods burst against her like tiny fireworks, startling her time and again as she struggled through. Green stems snapped, oozing sap that stuck to her, making her feel dirty and uncomfortable.

There were wild cucumber vines climbing up and over everything, covering all else with a smothering layer of leaves and soft, prickly fruit. She had to lift and tear at them to keep going. The curly tendrils grabbed at her hands, her arms. The vines were like a green sheet spread out over everything else. She lifted it up and ducked her head. She went beneath it; she went inside. It was like going into a tent filled with green light, like the make-pretend kitchen in the lilacs in the backyard on Railway Avenue where Jane and Muriel had made their mud pies.

Sally was tunnelling ahead through the underbrush. It was growing darker below the vines, and the plants there were starting to wither and turn brown.

"Where is she taking me?" Susan Ann stopped for a second to catch her breath. "Where can we be going?" She could hear Sally moving farther and farther away.

"Sally?"

"Hurry up!"

"Where are we going? I'm moving as fast as—"

But Sally was suddenly beside her, startling her. The wound on her head was larger, and blood was trickling from it.

"What's the matter, girl? Let me see—"

But when Susan Ann bent down to touch her, Sally snapped her head away and growled.

"You're frightening me again, Sally."

The two of them stood there looking at each other. Susan Ann could see Sally's bared teeth, and blood flowing from the wound was dripping from her snout. The dog growled again.

"Where are we?"

But her dog didn't say another word. She turned and bounded on ahead.

She was gone.

Susan Ann looked all around her in the fading light. She heard the crow cawing in the distance again, far, far off and lonesome-sounding. The bees were gone now. She strained to hear them but there was nothing.

"Sally?"

She was so alone. She could be so easily frightened in the dark sometimes: the devils in the pattern of her bedroom curtains, their twisted faces in the roses—what if they turned up after the sun went down? They might come out then. A ribbon of seaweed began to wrap itself about her ankle. It might trip her, so she started to bend down to untangle—

No, wait, this couldn't be seaweed.

That was the time she was swimming with Lorraine and Tommy, with the goggles, in the seaweed. This was—

When was this?

What was curling around her ankle, wrapping around her leg?

She looked down and saw nothing at first, and then—

"Oh dear!"

A snake! It was cool and slithery and wrapping around her.

She panicked for a second, lost her balance and fell backwards onto her bum; she began shaking her foot frantically. "Get off there! *Get off!*" She pushed herself up on her elbows as quickly as she could and looked at her foot. In the dim light she could see the snake curling round and round her ankle. Her whole body shuddered. "Get out! *Scat! Go way!*" She shook her foot as hard as she could, but the snake only wrapped itself tighter and began to glide slowly up her leg.

"Sally!"

The snake kept moving up her leg, making her shiver and tremble.

"You get out of here before my Sally finds you. She'll bite you." But she knew this was a lie; Sally was gone and would never come back.

The snake was wriggling up her leg, just above her knee. It was green and slender, more than a foot long, its head swaying gently from side to side and its wee tongue flicking in and out; all the while, its eyes were on Susan Ann's.

"Go on! Sally will bite you. She'll bite you right in *two!* Go on now. *Scat!*"

But the smooth green snake kept moving towards her thigh, and she thought she might lose control and get hysterical, like that time Carl had brought a snake into the kitchen and it had gotten loose. Queenie had slammed it to a pulp with the rolling pin.

"Get away, get!"

She reached down to grab it. The snake stopped for a moment, as if it was sniffing at her fingers. Susan Ann slowly turned her hand over on its back and the snake's head brushed against the side of her palm. Was that its tongue she felt? So light, almost a tickle, barely touching her skin?

When it slid over her palm, she closed her fingers around it and held it. For a second it stayed very still, then it wriggled inside her fist. She lifted her hand into the air and the snake tickled her as it squeezed out from her fist and curled about her wrist like a bracelet.

Psspss.

What? Was it saying something? She was holding the snake close to her face when it darted its head forwards and whispered her name:

Susan Ann.

The snake had a tiny voice; if it were louder it would have been a squeak, but it was a whisper and she could barely hear it.

"What?"

Suesuesue.

Did the snake have something to tell her? She was about to hold it close to her ear so she wouldn't miss a word, but it moved so fast, suddenly. Twirling around her wrist, wiggling down her arm, slipping off into the undergrowth—

"No, stay!"

She began to dig into the plants after it, pulling them aside, reaching, pulling, scratching like Sally digging up old Elsie Steeves' flower bed. What had the snake started to tell her?

"Come back! Come!"

But it was gone. The little snake was gone.

Her hand scratched something hard below the tangle of flowers, hard and smooth and flat, a stone. What was it?

A stone like the little Leamans' stones, all flush with the ground. She slid her fingers across its surface. The snake was long gone, but her finger was tracing one of its curves in the stone. It was a letter—was it a J? J for Jamie, like the apple peel on the pantry floor? She got up on her knees, trying to uncover all of the stone.

No, it wasn't a J because it curved again. An s, it felt like. Yes.

She pulled away the leaves, the crisp brown flowers. She pushed the dry grass back to the edges of the stone, she smoothed away all the bits and pieces, but the other letters were faded and worn; she couldn't quite make out another one.

Was it the s in J A M E S?

J A M E S C A R L R O B E R T S

The s in R O B E R T S?

It almost felt as if there was another s beside it.

s s

If she were at Five Points she would have thought it was Mum Wellman:

TESS

And then she thought, "It's me."

SUSAN ANN

She brushed aside the old leaves, swept the flat surface with the side of her hand. There. She was squinting to read in the growing dark, but the letters and dates were indecipherable. "There's only one way to find out," she thought, and she started sliding her fingers along one edge of the stone, back and forth, moving them down between the stone and the earth until she could feel the bottom edge.

Then she wiggled her fingertips beneath the stone and tried to pull it up. At first it was solidly in place, but she was methodical, patient, and soon the stone was wiggling like a loose tooth, and she worked and worked it until there was a sound like air escaping—*Hsssssssss*—and it was freed from the earth. She lifted it up, opened it like a cupboard door.

The hole beneath was dark; she dipped her head inside to see rich soil, pebbles, and she could smell such freshness: the garden in the morning. When she leaned forward to get a better look, the cameo fell out of the top of her dress; she felt it brush against her chin and her nose, it dangled for a moment, then the necklace suddenly slid up over the back of her head and fell into the hole. Her hand flew down to grab it but missed; she could see the pretty lady falling and falling, a pale grey light in the deep. "Oh, no," she thought, reaching her right hand into the dark, leaning forwards and stretching her hand down—

But the earth at the edge of the hole gave way under her left hand, and she couldn't pull herself back fast enough—

She plunged downwards.

Darkness, darkness and deep—

She fell, struggling to catch her breath, trying to call out, but her mouth was sealed shut, she couldn't make a sound.

It was dark all around her, and tight, the darkness pressing down on her chest. The earth pushed down, the little stones: the entire weight of the field above her, all the grasses and flowers pushing down, making her panic. Claustrophobia, pleurisy, the leash, all that weight, she couldn't breathe, and there was an awful noise, like a huge fly buzzing and bumping against a window-pane—

Falling—

And something else, inside her, deep in her body, hauling her down, dragging her deeper—

Stop falling, stop falling, she had to stop falling—

She was very scared, the earth swallowing her up—

To stop the falling, to stop the falling—

She turned, rolled over like a wave within the earth, then again—

Rolling over and again, moving away from the fall, from the pushing and pulling—

Rolling, and the feeling inside abated a bit, the pulling down, it was slow, slower, slow. . . .

And then it was letting go.

There was a little space; she had come there. The earth was damp all round her. Roots brushed against her face like fine hairs. Almost like floating, weightless and floating beneath all that earth. So dark she had to see with her fingers. She moved them about, searching. Reaching out—

Something was glowing. Like a little shaft of moonlight in front of her. Mum's cameo necklace, shining a soft light all around inside the dark earth.

Susan Ann turned over onto her side and there was something—

She bumped against something hard, right there beside her. Reaching out both her hands to touch it, and running her fingers along a smooth, flat surface as if she were polishing it—

"Is it a wall?" she thought. "A door?"

What place could be on the other side? Was it where Sally and the little snake had been leading her?

It was made of wood, but she couldn't reach far enough to find an edge.

Then her hand brushed against something cold that was attached to it, made of metal and—

A handle, like a drawer only much bigger. And farther along, another—

Could she pull them? Would they open or—

Wait. In the dim light from the necklace, her fingers could see—

She was certain now, she knew these handles, what they were, for she had picked them out herself.

This was the side of Jamie's coffin. She'd know it anywhere; she'd stood close by it all through the visitation, knelt down beside it, held onto it. When Lorraine and Carl had taken her to Hemeon's to pick it out, she had thought that even though it was crazy to pay good money for something you were just going to stick in the ground, and even though Jamie had made it clear that he wanted nothing fancy, she wanted something fine for his body, and she'd have mortgaged the house for it if she'd had to; she'd wished she could afford a coffin of gold all lined with fine silk and sweet-smelling cedar to put him in. Not for show, as some had been, no, not at all, but because Jamie was precious and deserved to be laid to rest in a precious thing. Nothing else was truly fit to hold his body until the end of time.

The handles were silver-coloured, and for some reason they'd made her think about going into Halifax with Jamie after Queenie died, when they went shopping for the new kitchen and bought hardware for the new cupboards. That was why she'd picked the silver ones, and the only person she'd told that to was Ellen Firth, because she thought her kids would think she was crazy.

Jamie must be on the other side of the wood; she could scrape away the dirt, burrow through the varnish, reach in through the grain. How she longed to see him, to hold him—even if his bones were all that was there. She could curl up around them and go to sleep.

She ran her hand along the side of the coffin. How remarkable that she had found it. Sally had known right where to take her. Jamie was closer now than he had been for such a long while, but he was still so far away. There was dirt stuck to the side—she had to clean it off. She was brushing at it, using her fingernails to get at the parts that were stuck fast. In places, the wood seemed spongy as mossy ground, soft as a pillow.

She pressed herself against the length of it, and thought of all the things she wanted to tell him. How she ached for his fingers, the sound of his voice. How the days had been so long. How she had travelled so far but the house was lost. How the kids had lives of their own without her. How it wasn't fair. She wanted to tell him that she was sorry. How, after he died, the rest of the world hadn't changed. The sun had come up every morning, and the moon still went through its phases; after he died, nothing had stopped in the world, not even her.

"Let me in."

Could he hear her? Could she shove her hands through the soft wood?

"Let me *in!*"

The rocks and dirt were thick and heavy around her, and it was hard to move her hands, but she started to dig at the wood, calling, "Jamie, Jamie, *let me in!*"

There was no answer. She was clawing and pushing into the soft wood, making a hole, widening it—

"Jamie! Jamie!"

Like an animal digging at something—

"Jamie! *Please!*"

Then, then—

Then the whole side of the coffin seemed to melt, to yield itself up to her. When she pushed again, she rolled gently into it, sliding through, moving away from the dampness of the earth into the dryness and stale air inside. For a moment she lay very still. Her breathing was raspy and dry, like a rattle. She could hear her heart beating far, far away, steady and slow, like a rocking chair, backwards and forwards, back and forth.

Inside, the coffin was bigger than she had expected, like an upper berth on the train. Then, in the glowing, she could see that it was higher and wider than that; it was a little room. "An upper room," she thought, looking at the sloped walls that peaked above her. "Like up at the farm." In the middle, there was almost enough height for her to stand.

She lay there, waiting for her eyes to grow more accustomed to the dim light.

"Jamie?" she whispered.

She waited, but there was no answer. There were shadows on the sloped walls above her, but she couldn't tell what they were, where they were from. Although she knew that the light was coming from the cameo lady, she couldn't tell where the necklace was. It must be nearby, but she couldn't see it; hidden behind something, more than likely, but what?

And Jamie, where could he be?

What she longed for was to have him turn to her in their old bed, slip his hand over her side, fingers stroking first her belly, then down, snuggling together like spoons in a drawer and whispering, "My Susiesusie Ann."

There was something, a sound. . . .

A soft, quiet sound.

"Jamie?" she whispered again, and waited a long minute.

Was there—

Was someone else in here with her? She could hear something—

Wasn't it—

She held her breath and listened.

Maybe it was breathing, a breathing sound, but it didn't sound like Jamie.

"Jamie?"

She waited again, but there was no answer. Just breathing and—

"*Oh* . . ."

"Jamie?"

Nothing.

"Oh, *please*," she thought, and listened again, concentrated so hard—

"*Ohh* . . ."

But it wasn't Jamie, she knew it wasn't. He had slept next to her for nearly forty years, she knew the sound of his breathing, the comfort of it, and she knew in her heart that this sound was not him.

Where could he be?

"Maybe he's not here yet," she thought. "Maybe if I wait, he'll come along."

Yes, she could imagine that: one evening, there he would be, just like a story.

When Jamie crawled back into bed with her, she had no idea what time it was. Late, she knew that, but he hadn't tried not to wake her. . . .

She might have to wait for a long while, though, like what Sally had said, "Everything was so slow for a long, long while."

Like that.

Yes, she could wait patiently for Jamie to come and finish her story.

She had waited in that apartment for so long, now she could wait here.

"*Ohhh . . .*"

What?

But what was that sound, the sound like breathing?

Was it someone?

She could see more clearly now, there seemed to be a little table across the room, and lying between it and her—

There was a shape there, huddled up in the middle.

"Oh," she thought, "what could it be?" What if she was trapped inside the earth with something terrible? A wild animal of some kind? She thought of the queen of the ants in her Mum Wellman's grave at Five Points, and she shuddered.

It didn't move, though, it was still, so she eased a bit closer.

It wasn't a breathing sound, exactly, but what was it?

Almost like crying.

She could make out someone's back lying close by, big hips and wide bum—

Not Jamie, no, not a man at all—

A woman—"What the hell is *she* doing here?" thought Susan Ann.

It was her daughter, it was Lorraine.

"She always, always, *always* has to come between me and her father."

How had Lorraine gotten down in here? How long ago? Susan Ann had come such a long way, and nothing had gone the way she'd planned. How was it possible that Lorraine had gotten here first? Was she lying in wait for her? She was as bad as the crafty old wolf who knew the shortcut to Grandmother's house.

Except there was no house.

She wanted to say, "This is all your fault. You made me sell our house and now everything's gone, every last trace." Instead, she lay very still and listened.

"Oh . . ."

There was Lorraine and something else, another sound from far away. She thought of Sally lying in the field up above them, of the red blood gathering on her fur, of the whole world up there, how it was nighttime now.

Was Lorraine crying?

Was it a trick?

"Lorraine?"

Her daughter turned towards her. "Mum?"

She was surprised that they were so close to each other.

"Mum? Can you hear me?"

Certainly she could hear her, they were lying right next to each other. "Yes," she said. "Of course."

"How you feeling?"

"Tired." She was so exhausted, it was good to lie down after all her travels; she closed her eyes.

"Me too," Lorraine said, and sniffled. She *had* been crying.

Was it like the times she had waited for Jamie after school? Was that why she was here, she was upset and she had come to talk to her father?

But there was no Jamie for either one of them.

Susan Ann's hands were folded together and tucked under her chin; Lorraine reached over and held them in her own. "You don't feel cold," she said.

"I'm not dead yet," replied her mother.

And Lorraine laughed and sniffed again. "No, no you're not."

A long time went by, when it seemed that they both were hesitant to say things. Susan Ann was wondering why Lorraine was here, why she wanted to talk to Jamie. "Your father," she said, then wasn't sure what to say next.

"Yes, Mum?"

She still wasn't sure what to say.

"We both still miss him," Lorraine said. She was holding her mother's hands in the same way that Susan Ann had once held Lorraine's, years and years ago, when Lorraine was a little girl, Sunday mornings in the bedroom. When Susan Ann opened her eyes, she was looking into eyes that looked just like Jamie's, and Queenie's too.

"Not here yet," she said.

Lorraine nodded and sniffed.

They lay staring into each other's eyes. Susan Ann could feel the weight of exhaustion in her body, the relief of lying so still in this warm, dry place.

"This is all so hard," Lorraine said, "isn't it?"

Susan Ann nodded. She was thinking of her Sally again, up there under the night sky. She wanted to imagine her jumping to her feet, shaking the wet blood from her fur like water; shaking herself well, and running off through the wild world towards morning.

"I still miss Dad so much."

"Me too." No matter what differences she might have had with her daughter after the house was gone, she knew that Lorraine had loved her father.

"It just seems wrong to me that he didn't see my kids grow up. Tommy never even knew him."

Susan Ann watched the water in Lorraine's eye swell and spill over. "Meg remembers him," she said. "She told me not too long ago."

"Yes, I know. But Peter never met him. I hope they would have been friends. I really hope Dad would have liked him." And she took one of her hands away and wiped her face with her fingers. "I'm sorry."

After a moment, Susan Ann asked, "Why are you here?"

"Why? Because I want to be with you."

"Oh." But Susan Ann wondered how Lorraine had known where to find her.

"I'm sorry everything's been so confusing."

"How long have you been here?"

"I don't know, a few hours. I've lost all track of time."

"Time's all buggered up." Susan Ann wasn't sure what year it was, or how long ago she had travelled. Everything was topsy-turvy.

Lorraine nodded. "The whole world's buggered up, it feels like."

"Yes."

"I was really worried about Tommy and . . ." She had to wipe her face again. "Oh Mum, I *am* sorry, just a sec."

Susan Ann reached out instinctively and touched her daughter's shoulder. "There," she whispered, "there now."

Lorraine sighed and laughed. "That's bass ackwards," she said.

"What is?"

"You here, comforting *me*," and she giggled. Then she said, "There was a terrible thing when Tommy was supposed to leave the airport in New York to come see you, these planes crashed, and we weren't sure which planes they were or where he was and, well, he's all right and . . . Louis too, but they can't get back home just yet, they're staying with friends."

"Why, that's terrible," and for some reason she thought about the Italian fellow who had stayed in her house. His friend's plane had crashed on the way to Shediac. Wasn't it in Holland? That was where Murd was buried.

"They still hope they'll be able to come see you."

"What?" She had lost track for a second.

"Tommy and Louis, they'll try to come see you."

"Good," said Susan Ann. "Good." She remembered now. She would like to see them both. The house was gone, though. "It's too bad your grandmother isn't around. She knew a thing or two about those Black Loyalists."

"The Black Loyalists? Oh, you mean Louis and his thesis?"

"Yes." The world up above them was acting so strangely now that time was all mixed up, so she said, "If they were to go a little ways downshore, I'll bet they even might be able to find a couple of them."

"Of what?"

"The Black Loyalists."

"Oh, I see."

And she was thinking that maybe Jamie would see them on his way, that he would be nice to that Louis fellow and try and understand about Tommy. She hoped he wouldn't be as mean as God had been to Sodom and Lot's wife. There was no need for that kind of behaviour.

A moment later she said, "Your father wasn't narrow-minded."

"I know, Mum."

"He made me very happy."

"I always knew he adored you."

For some reason, this took her by surprise. "You did?"

"Yes. I was talking to Peter the other day, remembering how much he doted on you, how it used to make Grammy Queenie so jealous she'd just be *green*."

"*Ha!*" said Susan Ann. Then, "*Good!*" She liked the idea that Queenie's jealousy had been so apparent. "Am I wicked?" she wondered. "No, not wicked. But selfish. No less selfish than poor old Queenie." On her deathbed, her mother-in-law had told her, "You never let me know if I got your goat. I'll give you that."

"Queenie and I . . . ," she started to say.

"Yes, Mum?"

How could she put it? "Way deep down," she said, "we kind of admired each other."

"Yes."

A little while went by, during which they both seemed to be waiting. Then Lorraine said, "Can I ask you something?"

"What?"

"You know when Grammy Queenie petitioned the government to get him out of the army, you know, during the war? So he could come home and look after her?"

She nodded.

"Was that when he proposed to you?"

"No, before that. When he came home with Murd the last time, when they were on leave." They had been walking up Inglis Street into the woods.

"Wasn't that how you met him? Because he was in the army with your brother?"

"No no no. He and Murd were friends in business college." Then in wartime, they signed up the same day. Inseparable, those two.

Murd's ghost had been unkind. She hoped that wouldn't happen to her after she died. He had always been so sweet.

But then, hadn't she dragged his poor ghost all the way from Holland? Maybe once you were dead, you wanted to stay that way.

Martha too.

Was that what Sally had just told her?

"—friends."

"What?"

"I said, Dad didn't have a lot of close friends."

"He and Hiram Firth went fishing once in a while."

But Lorraine was right. Murd had been Jamie's first real friend. Susan Ann had been the second.

"So you fell in love before the war."

"Pretty much. We planned to marry afterwards, then live in Shediac with Mum and Dad."

When he was on his way back home to Queenie that time, she and Mum had gone into the Moncton train station. The train was stopped for no time at all, not even an hour. Mum had kissed Jamie, given him a box with his supper in it and a war cake for his mother, then gone off and left the two of them together on the platform so they could talk. It had been awful. Susan Ann hadn't been sure how she felt any more, and she had hated herself for being so disappointed in the look of him; he was such a forlorn-looking thing standing there, pathetic almost, and the question he had asked had really frightened her, because she had realized that it gave her a terrible power over him.

"Do you still want me now?" he'd said, unable to look in her eyes.

She'd known that if she said no he would be devastated, that she would be sending him home in ruins.

"If I say yes," she'd thought, "will it be for him or for me?"

"Mum?"

Lorraine, had she said something?

"Yes?"

"Do you know what I think about the most?" She said this as if it were a secret.

"What?"

"How much Dad trusted me. I took it for granted, but it's such a hard thing to do. Trust your kids. I'm really bad at it sometimes."

That was the truth, it was a hard thing. "Your father worshipped you."

"Yes."

"And Carl too."

Lorraine smiled. "But they disappointed each other somehow."

Susan Ann didn't know what to say to that.

Lorraine squeezed her hands again. "We're the lucky ones, though, you and me, we never disappointed him."

Was that true? Was that really true? She supposed that, in the long run, maybe it was.

But Carl—

It was so sad that Carl and his father had stopped getting along.

Her son had come to see her, she thought, but she'd been asleep. Hadn't that happened? "Where's your brother now?"

"Where's Carl? He's gone to your place."

Her place? "Is it still there?"

"What? Yes. It's not going anywhere."

She realized then that Lorraine meant the apartment back in Toronto. "Are you two getting along?"

Lorraine's eyes rolled upwards. "No. We never get along. Doesn't mean I don't love him, he's my brother." A moment later she added, "Jesus, he makes me angry."

Susan Ann said, "I guess I don't understand him."

"Understanding is hard, sometimes." Lorraine was holding her mother's hands again.

"Maybe I wasn't a very good mother."

"You were fine, stop fishing for compliments." She squeezed her mother's hands. "I'm sorry," she said. "I wish you'd never had to leave your house. I know it was like losing Dad all over again. But there was nothing else we could do."

Susan Ann didn't like the fact that this was true, and she realized that Lorraine had come here to be with her, not Jamie. Would she stay with her and wait for him? Then the time wouldn't be so lonely.

Oh, but it could take a long while. It would be like what Sally had said, "Everything was so slow for a long, long while."

And then she shivered, because she was certain that all that waiting would be unfair to Lorraine, that it could be in vain. She didn't need to linger on here with her mother.

But Jamie? "Where is his poor ghost?" she wondered.

He *had* come to her, he had told her when she was asleep on Murd's bed—

But that was a dream, wasn't it? A dream she'd had in the house on Inglis Street.

Yes, but it had been a dream like Joseph and old Pharaoh! A prophecy.

And then she understood that it was wishful thinking, not prophecy. She'd journeyed all the way to Ragged Islands, and there was no evidence of the house where he had been born, where they had raised their family. Here she was with Lorraine, hidden away underground in this place that was *all* his, but he would never be back here in the way she had known him. Jamie was gone now, lost to them both and nowhere to be found, not even in his coffin. Ashes to ashes, dust to dust.

She knew this was the truth: Jamie was no longer a human thing. What once had been flesh had now become a tiny part of the earth.

"I miss you terribly and am counting the days," she said, knowing, finally, that there weren't enough days in all of creation for her to set eyes on him ever again. The only place his body lived was in their memories, in stories.

"What's that, Mum?"

"What? Oh. I . . ." She didn't know quite what to say. She thought of Jamie in the Bridgewater hospital, how she had pretended to him that things would go back to the way they had been. She didn't want that sort of thing to happen again so she said, "I'm going to die soon."

After a moment, Lorraine said, "Yes, I know."

"That's why you're here, to be with me."

"Yes, Mum."

Lorraine had come to this place to be with her when she died; now they were together, under the earth and waiting. And being right here at the end wasn't as awful as she'd feared it might be. She wasn't like poor Murd in Holland, or all the Leamans perishing in that fire; she was a lucky one because her life hadn't been incomplete. She was old and worn out, and finished with living.

But being here was too much to ask of anyone, worse even than the demands of Queenie on her deathbed—it wasn't fair. For her daughter's sake, they should go back; she wanted Lorraine to be back in Toronto with her family, safe and sound. "Can you get us out?"

"I'm sorry?"

"I'm ready now."

"Mum?"

"I think it's time for me to go back to the hospital."

"Oh. Well. I see. Oh." Lorraine nodded her head. "We can do that, yes."

This made her relax. She looked into the eyes looking into her own, those blue Bulmer eyes: Lorraine's, Jamie's, Queenie's and Meg's too. "Just give me a minute," she said.

"Okay, Mum. Take your time."

They would have to make their way back to the surface, to the field, and then they would have to—

How would they travel to—

They would need—

It was overwhelming all of a sudden.

"Just take your time." Lorraine could be very patient.

"You know the way?"

"To the hospital?"

Susan Ann nodded.

"Yes, Mum. I know how to get us there."

Lorraine would know. She would just have to put herself in her daughter's capable hands. She would try to relax and—

"Before we go back," Susan Ann said, "if there's time . . ."

"What?"

"I'd like to try and have a BM."

"Oh well, I suppose we can make time for that."

"Good."

When she closed her eyes, she could see herself crossing the field and moving down to the shore, to the edge of the sea, squatting down there, the good salt air on her bare bum. Oh, wouldn't that be lovely!

Once they got to the surface—

Then down on that little beach near the rocks where all the names were carved—

Not her name, though, she had never carved it. Or Queenie either—

But down there at the shore—

The waves and—

Did she forget the cameo! Oh—

Never mind. Leave it be. Someone like Meg would come along and find it someday.

Down to the shore, on that little beach with Lorraine—yes.

Susan Ann tucked her knees up towards her belly. She remembered so many times on that shore over the years, so very many—

Playing with Lorraine when she was a little girl, swimming with Carl when hurricane season down south brought the warm water, singing the Knapsack Song with Meg and Tommy, walking with Jamie, tide pools—

There was *one* time—

"What, Mum?"

There was something down there she wanted to tell Lorraine—

Down on that little beach, right there, she wanted to tell her a story about this place—

"You were there, but you didn't know it," she said.

Lorraine nodded, she was listening.

Susan Ann was standing calf-deep in the freezing water, looking out to sea—

The sun was setting behind her, and she watched her shadow grow longer over the water—

It was wartime, she was pregnant and, inside her, Lorraine tickled, she moved. Every feeling was brand new, and yet she was remembering that this was how it should feel.

She so wanted to be happy, but she was not.

A ways out from the shore, the waves were moving towards her in long advancing lines, spray blowing back from their crests. When they pitched up, she could see right through them, like thick green glass. She saw seaweed churning in them. Maybe this was the time she saw the seal swimming inside a wave; it was both magic and funny, and despite her unhappiness it made her laugh out loud. Was it that evening?

Maybe not. But it was a better story that way, she thought, with the seal swimming in the wave while she stood on the shore with her baby swimming in her belly.

The waves pitched up in wide rows that collapsed in a thunder of foam, over and over, advancing, dissolving, advancing, dissolving, advancing. She paced back and forth watching her shadow stretching ahead of her, thinking that it was two shadows now because of the baby inside her. She so wanted to have a baby girl. A girl first, then a boy. Her shoes and stockings were on a rock on the shore. She was holding up the hem of her dress in her hands. She kept moving forward as the waves drew back, and then stepped backwards as each new wave pushed against her. The water was so cold that her legs ached. Back and forth, back and forth, as if she and the waves were flirting with each other. Sometimes her shadow was clear and sometimes it disappeared within the moving water.

She was alone because she had walked out of the house and down through the salt marsh to the beach. She had stood up after dessert and said, "I'm going for a walk along the shore. I won't be long."

Back home, her husband and his mother were washing the supper dishes.

She wanted to be alone, to have this bit of time to herself. She also wanted to be taken away from a loneliness that she had felt since she'd been a girl.

"Did I make a big mistake?" she asked her shadow. "Do I really love him?"

She had moved far away from the people she had known all of her life, and everyday she had felt her mother-in-law try to pull her husband away from her. At supper tonight, she had felt like an intruder. While she was frying the haddock, she could hear them whispering to each other in the living room.

And now she was the one whispering. "This can't go on," she said. "It can't, it can't. Should I pack up and go home in disgrace?"

The waves told her nothing. They just continued on and on. Their story was a mystery to her. The names in it were the names of fish and whales, of lost boats, of storms and tides and the phases of the moon. Far away, across the ocean, her brother was fighting the Germans. She watched the waves, she watched her shadow that was two shadows now. She thought it was the loneliest thing she had ever known, because she was feeling so sorry for herself, and she was ready to give in to this feeling, to let it *be* her. She thought, "What would happen if I just started to swim? How far would I be able to get?" She wondered where she might be washed ashore; who might find her. Would the currents carry her far away, to some distant place? She wanted to be so far away from here.

But then, remarkably, there was another shadow stretching out beside hers in the water, and Jamie was walking behind her, with his pants rolled up to his knees. His socks and boots were on the shore beside her own. He would not say anything of importance. He would walk with her and show her a tide pool. Periwinkles grazing on ribbons of kelp or moving oh so slowly along the rock. He would fold back seaweed to show her, gently lifting out a rock crab, and there, clustered in the crevices, thousands of tiny mussels, the purple dark of midnight and as small as pearls.

And limpets, scattered about on the rocks under the water, their shells oval and beautiful, the most silent creatures she could ever imagine.

The pools, tiny, complete worlds, their colours as rich as heaven.

Anemones that she was timid to touch at first, the way she had been timid to touch him between his legs on their wedding night. "Go ahead, it won't bite," he had whispered, a joke that was so tender.

And she had known right then, known from the way he opened her hand and placed a sea urchin in it—the spines tickling her palm—known that even though she had never imagined this place before, and even though it was unlike any place she had loved, and even though her mother-in-law had bad nerves and was crazy as the birds, she had known right then and there that this could be home.

It was such a little story, hardly worth the telling, as small and ordinary as a pebble.

"You don't know what you want, you never did," her mother used to tell her.

"Oh, but I do know," she tells Lorraine. "I want to *be* a story."

A story like the rocks along the shore, like the Big Dipper in the night sky over the barn—
Robert, Rebecca, Martha too—
Like the sea, as it pulls out the sand from beneath her feet—
The water moving backwards and forwards, back and forth—
Lorraine is a distance behind her now, still on the shore.
Then, the story of the wave, as it advances—
"Oh," she thinks. "Oh. Well, it's only water."
The wave, soft and powerful, cresting, slamming down—
Then running up the sand towards her, covering her—
Chilling her to the bone.
It lifts her up—

ACKNOWLEDGMENTS

First and foremost, for his lifelong friendship and support, for his editorial and titular counsel, my love and thanks to the late Dayne Ogilvie of Railway Avenue, Jarvis Street and Pleasant Point: *You Send Me; Ich habe genug.*

I would like to acknowledge the generous assistance of the Canada Council, and the Woodcock Fund at the Writers Trust. I would also like to thank the MacDowell Colony and the Boorstein Foundation.

For their editorial advice and support, many thanks to Diane Martin, Angelika Glover, and Gena Gorrell. Thanks as well to my patient agent, Anne McDermid.

For providing lengthy stays in lovely places to live and work, I am forever grateful to Rita Howell and Gary Akenhead. Thanks as well to Jim Duke, Kathy Fisher, Charles King, Margaret Mcpherson, Mark Selander, and Kathleen Weiss.

For their expert advice, my thanks to Candace Burley, Sue Cheesman, Janet Guildford and Colleen Murphy.

For their financial (and other) generosities, much thanks to David Arnold, Betty Lou Daye, Ken Garnhum, John and Marion Hannah, and Pat Wilson. Special thanks to Mr. Garnhum for an encouraging read.

For helping to make my writing time financially possible, I would like to thank Maureen LaBonté, Joan MacLeod, Kim McCaw, Andy McKim, Jenny Mundy, Jan Selman, and Kristen Van Alphen.

For their many kindnesses in Nova Scotia, Toronto, and Edmonton, my thanks to Paul Massie, Monique and Len Michalik, Alex Pierce and the Do, Janet Cornfield and David Tamblyn, Mary Bower and Martino Lea, Connie Golden, Ruth Vander Woude, and Salena Kitteringham.

And a very, very special thanks to Tom and Jean Guildford, and to all their kith and kin, for their affection, warmth and welcoming hearts.

DON HANNAH is the author of *The Wise and Foolish Virgins*, a novel, and *Shoreline*, a collection of his plays. In 2006 he was named the inaugural Lee Playwright in Residence at the University of Alberta. He was born and raised in New Brunswick and calls both Toronto and south shore Nova Scotia his home.

A NOTE ABOUT THE TYPE

The text of *Ragged Islands* has been set in Antique Jenson, a modern face which captures the essence of Nicolas Jenson's roman and Ludovico degli Arrighi's italic typeface designs. The combined strength and beauty of these two icons of Renaissance type result in an elegant typeface suited to a broad spectrum of applications.

BOOK DESIGN BY LEAH SPRINGATE